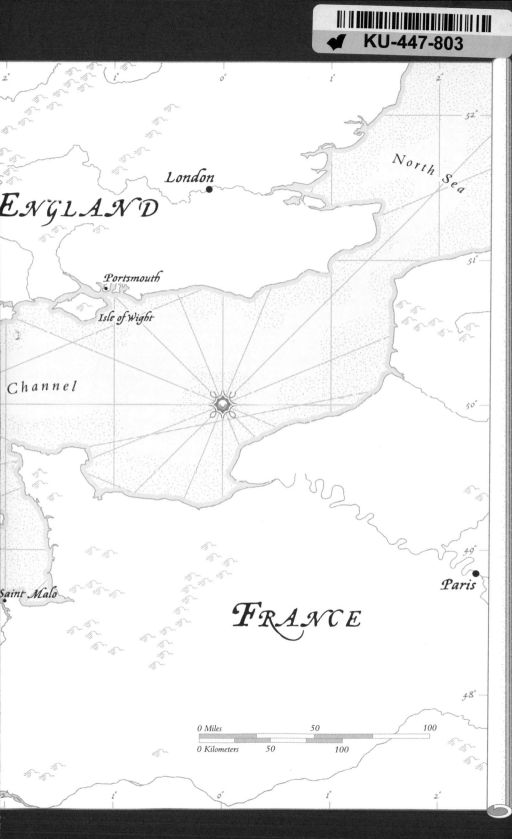

KU-447-803

ENGLAND

London

North Sea

Portsmouth

Isle of Wight

Channel

Saint Malo

Paris

FRANCE

| 0 Miles | | 50 | | 100 |
| 0 Kilometers | 50 | | 100 | |

UNDER
ENEMY
COLOURS

UNDER ENEMY COLOURS

Sean Thomas Russell

MICHAEL JOSEPH
an imprint of
PENGUIN BOOKS

MICHAEL JOSEPH

Published by the Penguin Group
Penguin Books Ltd, 80 Strand, London WC2R 0RL, England
Penguin Group (USA) Inc., 375 Hudson Street, New York, New York 10014, USA
Penguin Group (Canada), 90 Eglinton Avenue East, Suite 700, Toronto, Ontario, Canada M4P 2Y3
(a division of Pearson Penguin Canada Inc.)
Penguin Ireland, 25 St Stephen's Green, Dublin 2, Ireland
(a division of Penguin Books Ltd)
Penguin Group (Australia), 250 Camberwell Road,
Camberwell, Victoria 3124, Australia (a division of Pearson Australia Group Pty Ltd)
Penguin Books India Pvt Ltd, 11 Community Centre,
Panchsheel Park, New Delhi – 110 017, India
Penguin Group (NZ), 67 Apollo Drive, Rosedale, North Shore 0632, Albany,
Auckland 1310, New Zealand (a division of Pearson New Zealand Ltd)
Penguin Books (South Africa) (Pty) Ltd, 24 Sturdee Avenue,
Rosebank, Johannesburg 2196, South Africa

Penguin Books Ltd, Registered Offices: 80 Strand, London WC2R 0RL, England

www.penguin.com

First published in the United States of America by G. P. Putnam's Sons, a member of
the Penguin Group (USA) Inc. 2007
First published in Great Britain by Michael Joseph 2008
1

Copyright © Sean Thomas Russell, 2007

The moral right of the author has been asserted

Illustration of H.M.S. *Themis* on pp. vi–vii © John W. McKay

This is a work of fiction. Names, characters, places, and incidents either are the product of the author's imagination
or are used fictitiously, and any resemblance to actual persons, living or dead, businesses,
companies, events, or locales is entirely coincidental.

All rights reserved
Without limiting the rights under copyright
reserved above, no part of this publication may be
reproduced, stored in or introduced into a retrieval system,
or transmitted, in any form or by any means (electronic, mechanical,
photocopying, recording or otherwise), without the prior
written permission of both the copyright owner and
the above publisher of this book

Printed in Great Britain by Clays Ltd, St Ives plc

A CIP catalogue record for this book is available from the British Library

HARDBACK
ISBN: 978-0-718-15341-0

This book is dedicated to my son,

Brendan Thomas Russell,

with all my love.

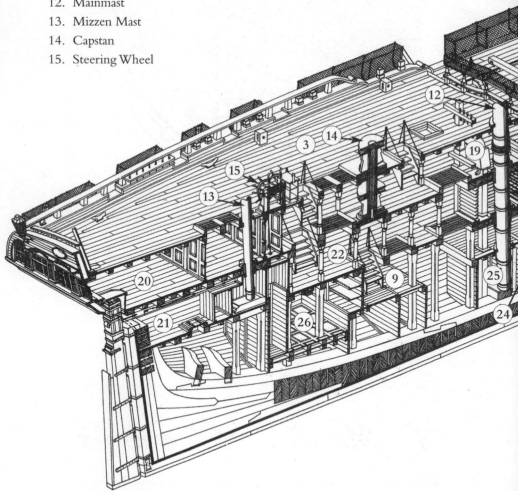

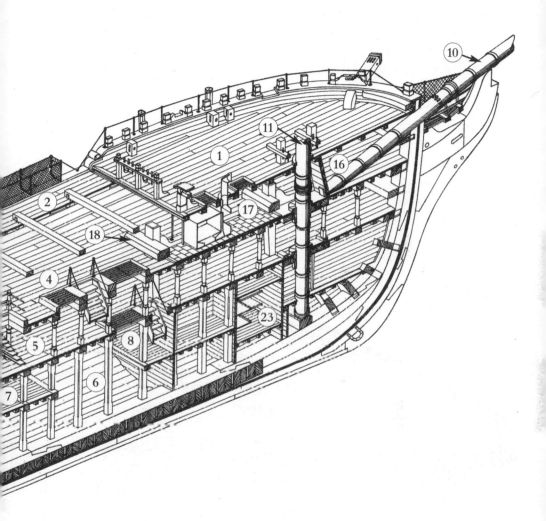

H.M.S. Themis

1793

One

Ahard gale blew in off the Atlantic at dusk, west by south, raising a
steep, breaking sea. All through the first watch pale crests surged
out of the darkness, lifted in ghostly rumblings, then boomed against the
forward quarter, staggering the ship.

Just before eight bells a thin, angular man emerged from the aft companionway, crouched precariously on the slippery planks, and looked
anxiously about. Perceiving a cascade of water break along the deck, he
made a reeling dash to the windward shrouds just as water spun about his
knees. The frigate, deeply laden and labouring, rolled heavily to leeward
and a blast of wind struck the man, Griffiths, wetly across the face.

"Is that you, Doctor?" a voice sounded over the wind.

A timely flash of lightning illuminated the sailing master, not two feet
before him, face pale and streaming, hat clamped down to his eyebrows
and bound tightly in place by a length of blue cotton.

"I must have more hands," the sailing master shouted almost into
Griffiths' ear.

"I have given you all who can walk, Mr Barthe," the surgeon responded in like manner. "Those remaining are too ill to stand."

"Is it the yellow jack, then? That is what men are saying."

"It is not, Mr Barthe. It is acute poisoning from some substance in-
gested—likely the pork served this very day. But I have never seen it so

severe. Men cannot stand, and have disgorged more fluids than their bodies can bear. It was my hope that you could spare men to aid *me . . .*"

"I cannot, Doctor. I have been reduced to sending boys and reefers aloft, where they should not be. I can spare no one."

The ship rolled again, and water sluiced across the deck, slopping about them. The doctor felt Mr Barthe's hand grasp his shoulder to preserve him from harm. The master began to speak again, but a gust devoured all human sound.

In the distance, lightning branched down into the sea, illuminating, for an instant, the chaotic waters, the spider-work of rigging. Four men wrestled the wheel, their eyes sunken, faces faintly blue.

A boy struggled toward them, crabwise, hand over hand along the lifeline. In the flare of godly light, he slipped and fell, then dragged himself up on the taut line. He reached them, breathless, dismayed.

"Mr Barthe!" he shouted. "We have lost Penrith."

"What in hell do you mean, you've 'lost' him?"

"He went aloft with us, but no one saw him climb down. We do not know what became of him."

"Did you not number off the men as they reached the deck?"

A second of hesitation. "No, sir."

The master cursed. "Has he taken ill and repaired below?"

"Williams made a thorough search. We fear he's gone overboard, unseen."

"Damn this night! Have Mr Archer go down to Captain Hart!" The master began to struggle forward but turned back to the doctor. "Will you take yourself below, Doctor? There is naught you can do here, and I should be happier knowing you were below in such weather."

Griffiths agreed, and scrambled toward the companionway, his last view of the gale, Barthe, and some others in the waist, gazing up at the yards—stark, angular, gone. He backed down the companionway stair, which moved with the ship, describing a long, irregular arc. Finding the deck, he stepped aside and let the few men ascend who could stand watch. As the last man went cursing up into the moaning night, the off-watch came slipping and thumping down, throwing spray about them, glistening in the smudge of light from a stained lamp.

Down again they went, to the berth-deck, and as they descended there ensued some shoving at the bottom of the stair so that one man tumbled down the last steps. Voices were raised in anger.

"You men!" Griffiths shouted down. "Do I need to call Mr Landry?"

Several *No, sir*s came floating back up and the shoving and cursing stopped. The hands went muttering forward as Griffiths descended.

"They've done for Penrith," the surgeon thought he heard one man say. "The fucking blackguards. Penrith!"

Two

Philip Stephens had been First Secretary of the Admiralty for thirty years. Previous to that, he had been Second Secretary. Through his delicate hands passed the correspondence of admirals and captains, First Lords, ministers, and spies. Lieutenant Charles Hayden was well aware that no one in the offices of the Admiralty was more intimate with the details of the Navy and her distant fleets than the little man who sat, mostly hidden by a writing-table, before him. That he should be aware of the existence of one Lieutenant Charles Saunders Hayden, however, was still something of a surprise.

The First Secretary bent over a letter, his spectacles refracting the dull London sunlight from the nearby window into a faint prism on his cheek. The most prominent features of the man's face were inflamed arteries that spread, crimson, over his bulbous nose. They meandered onto his cheeks and branched into deltas beneath the rainbows from his spectacles. It was not so much a face, Hayden thought, as a landscape.

"Captain Bourne holds you in high regard," Stephens rasped, his voice throaty and thick.

"An honour I strive to deserve."

Stephens seemed not to hear this, but put the letter down upon his tidy table, removed his spectacles, and rather directly took Hayden's measure. Too easily trespassed against, the lieutenant felt heat flush into his face. It was, however, not the moment to take offence; that anyone in the Admiralty building had noticed him was an opportunity not to be squandered.

Hayden had come to think of the Admiralty as a court. The First Lord was sovereign, the Lords Commissioners his ministers, all men of rank. Below him, the courtiers in their tiers, admirals, vice admirals, rear admirals, captains both high and low on the list. Far below these influential personages waited the lowly lieutenants, all desperately hoping to be appointed governor of that tiny outpost of empire known as a ship of war. Those possessing family interest and the skills of a courtier tended to rise. Certainly, the Admiralty would always need a few gifted functionaries, like Philip Stephens, to keep things running smoothly; a handful of stouthearted, fighting captains; an admiral or two who could manage a fleet action; but for the most part the courtiers succeeded and everyone else bowed their heads, smiled charmingly when noticed, and hoped to find a patron who might advance their cause. Hayden was not, by nature, a courtier, but he did his best to appear receptive and amiable, all the same.

Stephens did not seem to notice. "I have a position for you, Lieutenant."

Hayden took a long breath and released it slowly into the small room. "I should be forever in your de—"

The First Secretary did not allow him to finish. "It is not the sort of position that puts you forever in another's debt. Captain Josiah Hart has need of a first lieutenant." A grim, little smile flickered across the pale lips. "I see by your face that you had hoped for a command . . ."

Hayden considered a tactful response, but then gave in to exasperation and perhaps disappointment. "I had hoped, by this time, to have earned greater consideration than a first lieutenant's position . . . But I will not refuse it," he added quickly.

The little man made a humming sound, produced a pocket handkerchief, and began to clean the lenses of his spectacles. "Captain Hart has at his command a new-built frigate, the *Themis*, in which he has been cruising the French coast . . . to damned little effect."

Hayden feared his eyes widened at this utterance.

"Five weeks ago he lost a seaman in a gale," Stephens continued, the linen being worked back and forth by the quick cocking of a wrist. "Man fell from the mainsail yard by night. Never found. Not an entirely uncommon occurrence, one must say. But on the morning next, when the course was set, this dropped from the bunt." The Secretary reached down behind his table and produced a glass jar, stoppered and sealed with wax. In murky, amber fluid, a thick worm lay suspended, washing slowly forth and back. And then Hayden saw the nail.

"It is a finger!" the lieutenant blurted.

"Severed, cleanly, by a blade—or so the ship's surgeon concluded. He saw it freshly fallen from aloft, so I must give way to his opinion. As everyone aboard had their full complement of digits, except for three men who were known to have parted with theirs sometime earlier, it was assumed that the lost man had left his second finger behind." Stephens returned his gaze to Hayden, as though expecting a response.

"But severed by a blade, sir . . ."

"Yes—hardly misadventure. The unlucky man was seen that very day in dispute with a landsman known to be of evil disposition. A knife in a bloody sheath was found rolled up in the landsman's hammock. He denies all, of course. Says he butchered some poultry—unfortunate bugger. He sits in Plymouth awaiting his date with the courts-martial."

"Surely he will not be convicted on such evidences as that?"

Stephens shrugged. Apparently the man's fate did not affect him overly.

"And what was a landsman doing aloft, if I may ask?"

"Half the crew were down with some malady—rancid pork, the surgeon posits. They sent boys and midshipmen aloft that same night." Stephens waved his hand, as though brushing aside this line of conversation. "Do you know Captain Hart at all?"

"I have not had the honour."

The First Secretary bobbed his head. "He is, how shall I say . . . ? A man of some influence through Mrs Hart's family."

It was the lieutenant's turn to nod. *Interest* was something he understood well—due to his utter lack of it. In the court of the Admiralty, having a wife related to a "minister" counted for any number of successful actions at sea.

"There is some concern about this affair on the *Themis*. Her first lieutenant invalided out at the end of the cruise. He claims to know nothing of the matter, and we pray that is so."

Hayden felt himself straighten a little in his chair. "If there are malcontents aboard Hart's ship, why not exchange them elsewhere?"

Stephens meticulously adjusted the position of a tidy stack of papers on his desk. "And suggest that Captain Hart cannot manage his own crew? I don't think that would answer in this case." He glanced up at Hayden. "But then you have dealt with a discontented crew before—most ably, I am given to understand."

Apparently the First Secretary knew Hayden's service record intimately. "When I was job-captain aboard the *Wren* . . ."

Stephens nodded once, but then a crease appeared between his meagre eyebrows. "Are you certain, Lieutenant, that you know nothing of Captain Hart? You are not being disingenuous?"

"I had not heard his name before entering this room."

Stephens gazed at him a moment, as though gauging the truth of this statement. "Hart's connexions within the Admiralty are of the highest order . . . It is, therefore, perhaps not surprising that I have received a request to place a lieutenant with . . . *bottom* aboard Captain Hart's ship—after all, even the most skilled captain has need of such an officer from time to time. Do you not agree?"

"What captain would argue against competent officers?"

The First Secretary indulged another grim little smile. "What captain, indeed. It was my intention to find such an officer to serve aboard the *Themis* . . . but I am looking for something more. I tell you this in the strictest confidence, Mr Hayden. Is that understood?"

Hayden nodded, liking this conversation less by the moment.

"I require a man who will keep a most accurate record of Hart's exploits. I'm sure the good captain's modesty is such that an honest account of his endeavours has never been made known within these walls."

Hayden sat forward a little. "I will not take this position, Mr Stephens," he said firmly, but then added, "though I am not ungrateful of the offer."

"But you have already accepted. Did I not hear correctly?"

Hayden tried to keep the anger from his voice, with only partial success. "That was before I knew you wished to turn me into an informant. Under such a circumstance I do not feel honour-bound."

Neither man spoke for a moment, but Hayden feared his voice had betrayed him. Philip Stephens' face changed ever so slightly; drawn in but a little more, it would have formed a scowl.

"Allow me to be uncharacteristically forthright, Lieutenant Hayden." The First Secretary sat back in his chair and steepled his fingers before him. "You have little future in the King's Navy."

Hayden could not hide his complete and utter surprise at this statement—not because it was in the least untrue, but due to its audacity.

"Your friend . . ." Stephens shuffled through some papers, "the Honourable Robert Hertle, is about to make his post, as would you have, had you half his interest. Despite your manifest abilities—and I am certain Captain Bourne is too shrewd to have misjudged them—you are lodged in your present circumstances with little hope of forward movement. It does not help your cause that we are at war with France and that you are half a Frenchman."

"I am an Englishman, sir. My mother is French."

Stephens held up his hands. "Be at peace, Lieutenant. I have recently made the argument that your parentage weighs in your favour, for I am given to understand that you have lived in that country a good many years and speak the language as a native . . ."

Hayden nodded.

"You must understand, Mr Hayden, that I am your advocate, but the prejudice of others is not easily overcome. That is why I am able to offer you only this first lieutenant's position . . . at this time. It is true that

I am asking you to write an account of your cruise, but certainly you would keep a journal, as a matter of course. Would you not?"

"It is not quite the same thing, Mr Stephens, as you well know."

"It certainly isn't if you choose to believe it is not. And I do admire your loyalty to the captain under whom I have proposed you serve, but sometimes loyalty to one's own cause is not such a terrible evil. Captain Hart, you should know, has a very good understanding of this distinction." He spread a little rectangle of paper on the table. "This is the address of one Thomas F. Banks, Esquire. My name should never appear on your letters in any way, but I will receive them all the same."

Hayden eyed the scrap of paper disdainfully but made no move to pick it up.

"That is not just an address resting on my table, Lieutenant. It might be better to think of it as representing your future in the Navy. You may take it up . . . or you may leave it lie. I will allow you the evening to consider, but I shall require an answer by tomorrow, noon. At such time the position will be offered elsewhere." He leaned forward and slid the paper closer to Hayden. "In case you decide in favour of a career in the Navy."

Hayden rose without taking the offered paper, but then found himself hesitating, hovering, as it were, over the table, eyeing the little rectangle of white overwritten in a spare hand. He knew if he left that room without it he would remove his uniform that day for the final time. His career in the Navy would be over—a decision not to be hastily made. His left hand reached out and took up the paper, slipping it quickly into a pocket. Philip Stephens had returned to his papers and appeared not to notice.

Three

Lieutenant Hayden stood with his back to the hearth, his sodden hose steaming like kettles. The little withdrawing room—Mrs Hertle's "Chinese Room"—seemed a bastion of warmth and good cheer that night. Outside, a summer rain battered at the pane. A gust rattled the sash. Mindful of the ancient vase, Hayden rested a damp elbow on the mantle, where a small puddle immediately formed.

"This will set you up, Charles." Robert Hertle passed his friend a steaming glass, the perfume of hot brandy filling the air. "Let me find you some dry hose."

"No, no, Robert—don't trouble yourself. The fire will dry me presently."

Robert appeared unconvinced by this argument, Hayden could see, but kept his peace. The two had known each other while still in the nursery, for their fathers had been close friends. It was, in this case, not an exaggeration to say they were like brothers, though they could hardly have been less alike despite identical years—four and twenty. Hayden was as dark as Hertle was fair.

Hayden raised his glass. "We must have a toast. To Post Captain Robert Hertle."

Hertle smiled modestly, pleased by his friend's kindness, and by the gratifying warmth the words seemed to spread through his entire being. "It is undeserved, as you well know."

"It is richly deserved. Think of all the deadwood that made their post before you—though the Lords Commissioners set them upon the quarterdeck instead of beneath the stern, where deadwood belongs."

Robert laughed. "What I was trying to say was that I am not as deserving as you."

"Well, I won't hear any of that talk," Hayden enjoined, trying, for his friend's sake, to mask his bitterness and disappointment.

"You shall hear it, I fear, and not just from me." Robert gestured to a chair. "Please, Charles, be at ease."

"As soon as I am dry."

Robert rang a little silver bell and a maid hurried in. She curtsied to the gentlemen. "Anne, can you find a blanket to lay over the chair? Lieutenant Hayden was caught by a squall with all his canvas up." He set his snifter on the mantle and peeled off his friend's coat. "It must be dried," he admonished. "I'll find you a frock-coat for supper."

The dripping coat went out with Anne, and a thick blanket came quickly back to be draped over a chair. Charles settled himself, suppressing a shiver.

"You must tell me all the particulars," Charles said. "What ship have they given you?"

"Just a little brig until a frigate comes off the stocks. My commission will be granted then." He was trying not to sound too pleased with his situation, Charles could tell; no doubt out of consideration for him.

"Now," Robert said, taking the seat opposite, "tell me about your visit to the Admiralty."

"How in this world did you know of that?"

Robert smiled, enjoying this small triumph. "You were observed, sir. Observed ascending to the First Lord's chambers. I have not been still all afternoon in anticipation of good news." Robert waited a moment. "Well, don't keep me in uncertainty," he said when Hayden offered nothing. "Did they give you a ship?"

"No. Nothing like it. A first lieutenant's position only—aboard a frigate."

Robert closed his eyes a moment and his face went pale with anger. "How can they treat you so? You've had command of a brig-sloop."

Hayden rose and paced back and forth before the fire. "Yes, well, apparently job-captains are abundant and command little respect in Whitehall Street."

"Even so, it is unjust. You should have been made Master and Commander—long ago. Tell me what the First Lord said."

"First Lord? It was the First Secretary with whom I spoke."

"Stephens?"

"None other."

This apparently surprised Robert, who leaned forward in his chair, a crease appearing between his eyebrows. "Pray, what did he say you?"

Hayden took a sip of his brandy by way of buying himself a moment to consider. Anger and resentment surfaced again, and he pressed them down. Hayden wanted his friend's council, but the truth was he felt ashamed of what had transpired, of what Stephens had asked of him—and the shame fuelled a long, simmering resentment.

"Are you familiar with a thirty-two-gun frigate named the *Themis*?" he asked, exerting all his energies to compose himself.

Robert sat back in his chair as though pushed. "Not Hart's ship?"

"The very one." Hayden gazed at his friend, unsettled by his reaction. "I am to be Captain Hart's first. Do you know the man?"

Robert let his gaze flow once around the room, as though it were suddenly unfamiliar. "I have met him once or twice, but his reputation precedes him. I am astonished you have not heard. Among his detractors he is known as 'Faint Hart.' The good captain has his command courtesy of Mrs Hart, whose family tree has more than one branch extending into the Admiralty. It would be very charitable to say that he is not held in high regard among his peers in the service."

Hayden cursed silently. "You are deeper into the Admiralty court than I, Robert. Have you ever heard of any cause for antipathy between Mr Stephens and Captain Hart?"

"I have not, but Hart gave me the distinct impression that he had little charm to spare for those he does not consider useful to his own particular cause. Stephens is a man of immense ability, so it is easily imagined that an officer known as 'Faint Hart' might earn his disdain. Men like Stephens have little time for fumblers. Did the First Secretary give you some indication that he harboured a dislike of Captain Hart?"

"I was left with the impression that someone within the Admiralty was no friend to Hart."

A small roll of the eyes by Robert. "You've not accepted this position, surely?"

Hayden drew in a breath and released it in exasperation. "And what other choice have I, Robert?" he asked, the edge of his anger making itself known. "Mr Stephens was at pains to point out my French parentage and made it clear that within the walls of the Admiralty building no one but he knew my name."

Robert looked positively alarmed at this intelligence. "Is he aware of your . . . affairs in France, do you think?"

"If so, he was too discreet to mention them."

Robert did not appear to be reassured by this, but also rose and went restively across the room to the window. "You've never told anyone what you told me?"

"No one, though any number of people know I was in France that year, even in Paris. That was never a secret."

Robert smiled bitterly. "Then your revolutionary past is likely still buried."

Hayden bridled at his friend's attempted jest. "It was but a few days, caught up in the moment . . . like everyone there. Once I had witnessed a mob set loose, I was soon back in my right senses. You cannot know, Robert, how much I have come to regret my actions of those days, and I was all but blameless in that place—an innocent."

"I have noted that you've come no nearer forgiving yourself, even so."

Hayden felt the usual distress wash over him when this subject surfaced. "There are times when it is important *not* to forgive oneself," he said quietly.

A look of distress crossed his friend's face. An awkward moment, and then Robert said, "I don't suppose Stephens mentioned if Hart had requested some other to be his first lieutenant?"

"He said nothing of it." Hayden was happy to turn away from the subject of his sojourn in Paris.

"Then let us hope Hart did not. Imagine your position if so? I do not like this situation one bit, Charles. I'm not convinced you wouldn't be better to refuse it."

"Then you will not need to return my jacket when dried. I will have no further need of a uniform."

Robert leaned back against the sill, his look pained. "Did Stephens promise you anything if you took this position? a ship, advancement?"

"Nothing. He seemed to suggest that he might be inclined to secure me a better situation in the future . . . but it was clear that success in the offered commission would first be required."

Robert cursed softly. "It is unforgivable that he should offer you a situation—so beneath your gifts—and promise nothing in return."

"That is not the worst of it. There is apparently some discontent among Hart's crew and Mr Stephens seems to believe I will remedy it."

"Blast the man to hell! If Hart has an understanding that you are being sent as his nursemaid you will be made most unwelcome."

"Let us hope he does not comprehend that." Hayden shrugged and placed an elbow on the mantle, finding the small puddle he had left earlier. "Such is the state of my career, Robert, that a refusal will see it ended. So I am for the *Themis*. I see no other course. Perhaps a few successful actions will place me in better circumstances."

But Robert did not even make an effort to agree with this.

"She never retires to her chamber, no matter the hour, but wanders about the house with a pack of dogs in train, and sleeps for two hours, now and again, upon a sofa or ottoman; any place it might please her. The consternation of the servants, who come to clean the rooms in the small hours, cannot be hidden. When they find the countess asleep amid her pack, they must tiptoe out and leave the room ashamble." Miss Henrietta Carthew laughed; a charming tinkling, Hayden thought, like water in a raceway. "I have come upon her myself, at two of a morning, amid a swarm of candles, her face buried in a book, her feet propped up on a sleeping hound she has christened Boswell." They all laughed at this.

Mrs Hertle glanced Hayden's way and he hastily withdrew his gaze from the fair speaker. They were seated around the table in the Hertles' dining room, the sound of horses' hooves, like dripping water, passing by on the comparatively quiet street outside. The bustle of London was a distant hum, not even remarked by anyone at table—as unnoticed as one's own heartbeat.

Hayden had heard many stories about the charms of Miss Henrietta Carthew, but had never expected to respond to her presence as he did. She should not be called beautiful, if the truth were to be admitted. Or perhaps it would be more true to say he had never met a woman in whom the line between "beautiful" and "peculiar-looking" was so fine. Considered individually, the features of her face were all beyond criticism, but taken as a whole there was something amiss, as though the elements were disparate, dissonant. Her nose, though straight and finely formed, appeared to have been made for a different face. The eyes, brown, bottomless, and flecked with amber, were just slightly too wide apart. But then she would smile, and all that appeared disharmonious would be swept away and he would understand why she was thought so handsome. The overall effect was utterly unknown to Hayden—he struggled not to stare.

"I don't know why you visit that madhouse," Robert observed, breaking into Hayden's reverie.

Henrietta appeared surprised. "There is no place like it. The beauty of the countryside is unrivalled, and you are left to your own devices from morning until dinner, Lady Endsmere arranging no amusements during the day. It is near to Heaven in that alone . . ."

Her voice drew Hayden's eyes back again: pearl-smooth skin, hair the colour of new-sawn mahogany: auburn, chestnut, copper, bronze.

". . . at night, the same disregard for convention is apparent. The conversation around the dinner table is of politics and art, natural philosophy and poetry. All the ladies take their cue from Lady Endsmere and freely offer their opinions upon any subject. There is no other house like it in all of England, I think. Only the most substantive gentlemen and ladies visit. The table is not decorated with those frivolous 'wits' so valued in London—"

"There is very little wit at our table," Mrs Hertle interrupted. "Are we fashionable?"

"You are quite the thing, my dear," Henrietta assured her, a smile like a cresting wave on a sunny day.

Another glance Hayden's way from Mrs Hertle, making him wonder if she realized how Henrietta's voice pierced right to his core. But how could it not? musical, nuanced, assured, able to subtly colour the meaning of words, reveal shades of feeling, or hide them utterly.

In her presence he felt as though he stood upon a cliff edge. The height stole his breath away, his head spun. But even so, he could not will himself to step away from the edge. Some unseen force drew him nearer.

Henrietta lifted a fork to her lovely mouth. "This is exquisite. Have you a new cook?"

"Did I not tell you? Charles found us a French cook who had served a noble family before all the troubles began in that country."

"I approve of your taste, Lieutenant Hayden," Henrietta pronounced.

"Charles has many such areas of specialized knowledge," Robert interjected. "Tell me what you think of the claret, Charles? From Spain, I was assured . . ."

"It is not from Spain, as you well know," Hayden stated, seeing his friend suppress a smile.

"Where is it from, pray?" Robert asked innocently.

"It is a finely smuggled wine from the French Pyrenees," Hayden said. He turned to the other guest. "Do your family keep a house in London, Miss Henrietta?"

"No longer, though my father did for many years. We are so close to town, it is hardly worth all the trouble and expense. Forgive me for changing the subject, Mr Hayden, but how do you know this claret is from the French Pyrenees and not Spain? Surely the two nations are but a border apart in that region."

Robert's partly suppressed smile blossomed fully. He took a malicious pleasure in making his friend perform.

Hayden took up his glass in resignation. "The style, largely; the French and the Spanish have different ideas about wine. And then each variety of grape has its own distinctive palette." Hayden tasted the wine. "This is a skilful blend of Carignane . . . Teret noir, with perhaps a hint of the Picpoule. But I am no authority. My uncles could tell you who made the wine and precisely where the grapes were grown. They would go on at length regarding the *terrier*, then shake their heads at the backward methods of the rustic wine-makers." He held the glass up to the light. "Where this wine is made the soil is often so thin over the rock that the vineyard owner must use a dibble, an iron bar, to break a depression in the stone into which the vine is planted. Then the vine is allowed to grow over the ground, wherever it will, rather than upon *echalas*—properly constructed wooden frames. They persist in crushing by foot, and refuse to use the press. Scientific methods have not reached them."

Henrietta glanced at her cousin, the look impenetrable to Hayden.

"When this foolish war is over," Mrs Hertle said, "Charles has promised to take us on a tour of France. Until then, I suppose, we must be content with seeing the parts of England we do not know, though I can't imagine when we will manage even that, with Dame Duty always knocking at our door."

"You must come to visit Lady Endsmere with me this summer, Eliza," Henrietta urged, returning to their earlier subject. "Captain Hertle shall be upon his ship, and you will not be disappointed in the countryside."

"Yes," Robert said, "you must not miss this chance. I want to hear the stories."

"You see," Henrietta said, "you will join 'the menagerie,' as everyone names it, for there are monkeys and exotic birds and who knows what all around the grounds. Lord Uffington said the only difference between the animals and the humans was that the animals only dressed for supper if they were of a mind to . . . because a monkey once spent most of a meal sitting in Lady Endsmere's lap, like a favoured child, eating whatever it fancied from her plate."

"Now we know you are exaggerating, Henri!" Mrs Hertle laughed.

"You will come with me this summer and see for yourself. Enough stories can be gathered in a fortnight to dine out on the rest of the year."

The smile suddenly disappeared from Mrs Hertle's face. "But I shall worry so for Captain Hertle," she responded softly.

Henrietta reached out and patted her cousin's hand. "We will pray the war will be over, the radicals all suffering the fate they so readily prescribe others."

"What do you think, Charles?" Mrs Hertle asked, lines appearing at the corners of her eyes. "You know more of France than anyone in our circle. Certainly this war cannot be as long as the last?"

Charles took a sip of claret. As his glass returned to the table the footman leaned silently forward and recharged it. "So we might hope, but it is my experience that wars often defy predictions of their brevity."

"But so many of the officers of both the French Army and Navy have resigned their commissions," Mrs Hertle said. "How will they fight without officers?"

"Recent evidence would indicate quite well," Hayden said, "in the case of the Army, at least. The Navy has yet to be tested."

Robert waved a hand. "Charles, you let your sympathies blind you, I think. Surely an entire officer corps cannot be replaced by ill-trained tailors and farm boys and success then expected."

Charles felt suddenly defensive. "But imagine a navy where promotion was by merit rather than interest. Would not our own service be the better for it?"

"Certainly it would, but if we destroyed the officer class and promoted from the foremast hands, what kind of navy would we have?"

Hayden did not have an answer for that, and when he did not speak, Mrs Hertle said softly, "Then it *will* be a short war . . ."

"Certainly it must be," Hayden offered, trying to sound reassuring.

"I should be allowed nothing but milk or water," Hayden said passionately. "Wine makes me too forthright. I do apologize, Robert, I didn't mean to frighten Mrs Hertle."

Robert poured two glasses from a decanter. They had retired to the library for after-supper port and conversation. A brief interlude of male association before joining the ladies in the drawing room.

"Don't apologize. Mrs Hertle is accustomed to hearing the truth, however distasteful. And you know I should rather have a harsh truth than a sweet lie." Robert pressed a glass into his friend's hand. Taking up a poker, he crouched and thrust it into the embers, tumbling a small hill of coal in a clatter. "You don't believe that this conflict will be brief, I collect?"

"I have no special knowledge of the future, Robert, but such pronouncements have often proved frightfully optimistic in the past."

Robert raked out the coals, then, satisfied with the effect, he stood, leaning a shoulder against the mantle. "What do you think of the situation across the Channel, now?"

Charles walked three paces, and turned, regarding his friend, propped against the mantle, a soft sadness come over him. "It grows more frightening by the day. That is what I think. The Girondins were the voice of moderation, and with them gone . . . I fear what might occur next. You read reports of the prison massacres last autumn. The resentments of the Paris mob are too easily inflamed; they have not done their worst yet, even without Marat to provoke them. I will own this, Robert: thank God for my English common sense or I might be among the mob even now."

"I am thankful for your English half, too," Robert said. "I cannot imagine having grown up without your friendship."

The two men raised glasses in a silent toast to that bond.

"Perhaps we should both take oaths of temperance," Robert said. "A bit of wine and you become uncomfortably candid, and I am overwhelmed by sentiment."

Charles smiled. He knew what was in his friend's mind, though neither would speak of it. Men went off to war and did not always return. Charles' own father had been lost at sea when his son was only a boy.

As if his thoughts had run in the same path, Robert asked, "How fares your mother, pray?"

"Very well, when last she wrote; life in Boston seems agreeable, her husband adores her. One might think America had been created just for her, so happily does it appear to suit her temperament."

"I am glad to hear it. She deserves happiness. God knows she has had sorrows enough."

Charles did not answer. Truth seemed to be in the air that night. Not the most common thing in London that summer.

"*And* a French mother," Henrietta observed. "That explains much."

Mrs Hertle could not help but note that her cousin had rather adroitly worked the conversation around to her husband's childhood friend, Charles Hayden.

"There is something in his face . . ." a crease appeared between Henrietta's lovely eyebrows—her thoughtful pose.

"Charles always says he inherited his grandfather's Gallic nose," Mrs Hertle responded. "His 'unfortunate nose,' he calls it."

"Though he seems entirely English in his manner," Henrietta offered.

"Indeed he does, but I have come to believe that he is more French beneath the surface than one would guess. One must be wary of these

Navy men, Henri, they are not always what they seem. Both Robert and Charles have been at sea much of their lives—since they were but thirteen—beginning together as midshipmen. Since that early date they have been trained to be very decisive—indeed, irresolution at an inopportune moment might cost many lives aboard a ship. Some Navy men bring this decisiveness ashore with them, where often their understanding is not so great as at sea. I have watched the ill effects of this many times. It is fortunate that Robert does not suffer this defect of character, or from its opposite disability—a chronic indecisiveness upon the land where they are so out of their element. These Navy men take some little study, I have found."

Henrietta nodded, her attention apparently focussed on smoothing a crease in the skirt of her gown. They perched on chairs in the drawing room, speaking quietly.

Mrs Hertle had noted before that women were almost never neutral in their response to Charles Hayden: they either found his overly serious mind an impediment, or they could not stop speaking of him. She could hardly remember how she herself had felt when first introduced, some four years past. Certainly, she had thought him well made, though thick of thigh, "just shy of a fathom in height" as he said himself. A strong, appealing face, surely—though rather full-featured—inky hair drawn back in a queue. Nose, aquiline—not unhandsome but neither was it modest in proportions; mouth full and pleasant, very used to smiling. His brow, however, could only be termed "heavy," imparting a certain intensity to eyes that would have been perfectly fine if one had not been blue and the other shading to green.

"The Lords of the Admiralty must be sensible of his parentage?" Henrietta ventured.

Mrs Hertle nodded.

"It is a wonder he has a commission at all."

"I fear you are right, Henrietta. Robert refuses to see it. In his mind Charles can do no wrong. Though I am sure he is a fine seaman and officer; Robert is not so blind as that."

"I wonder what will become of him?" Henrietta asked, now examining a fingernail with great attention.

"I believe his future is in America. His stepfather is a very prosperous Boston merchant and has offered Charles command of one of his ships. A few more disappointments and I think poor Charles will finally perceive this proposal differently."

"But it would be so demeaning—from officer in the King's Navy to master of a merchantman—an *American* merchantman."

"Indeed, but in America he would find acceptance, I think. His stepfather is a man of some influence."

"I should not want to live in Boston. Should you?"

"Whoever asked you to live in Boston, dear Henrietta?" Mrs Hertle said quickly.

"Well, of course, no one did," Henrietta protested. "And I did not mean *that*, as you well know!"

Mrs Hertle laughed gently at her cousin's response. "Let us call the gentlemen for tea. The hour grows late."

She was all long limbs and slim torso, Hayden thought, yet she perched upon her chair with such easy elegance, a look of amused contentment upon her face, that Hayden could not help but think her as lovely as a naiad. Her carriage was erect and proper but not without a hint of sensuality. In truth, Hayden was beginning to think Henrietta's distinctive appearance perfectly matched her somewhat unconventional disposition.

The Carthews, he knew, were of good family, distantly related to the Russells. Her father was a gentleman of some means, had married well, and spent life riding his own particular hobby horse, which was the matter of education, and the education of women in particular. As he was a father of six daughters, Mr Carthew's preoccupation with this subject was clearly defensible, and his daughters had been the subject of much experimentation in regards to their own learning, though it had gained them a perhaps undeserved reputation as blue-stockings.

Mrs Hertle was gently chafing her cousin, teasing about this very subject, as Hayden raised his teacup.

"How many languages do you speak, dear Henri? Come now, don't be modest."

"Fluently?" Henrietta asked. Apparently they had played this game before.

"Let us begin with those you speak fluently and pass on to the others presently. Is it five or six?"

"You are evidently more familiar with this subject than I," Henrietta protested.

"English we shall not count," Mrs Hertle rejoined. "French, of course." Mrs Hertle pushed up a slim finger, a glance finding Charles, then returning. "Italian, Spanish, High German—or is it Low?"

"Both," Henrietta admitted.

"Greek and the Latin . . ."

"Not to be counted, as I read them only."

"Dutch," Mrs Hertle continued. "Does it come in High and Low?"

"Mmm . . ." her victim shrugged, pretending not to know.

Mrs Hertle counted off another finger. "Six, or is that seven? And then either Danish or Swedish, I can never remember."

"Danish, but I am by no means fluent." Henrietta's unblemished skin had begun to colour—the object of Mrs Hertle's cross-examination, Hayden guessed.

"We shall count Danish . . ." Mrs Hertle said, "for you are rather prone to modesty. I will make that eight, or seven if you insist, but we must not forget Russian."

"By no means, Russian. I am unable to carry a conversation beyond mere pleasantries."

Mrs Hertle laughed. "Seven, plus one half for Russian, and I'm certain I have missed a tongue or two. It is quite a little catalogue, don't you think, Lieutenant Hayden?"

"Very impressive. Apparently Mr Carthew's pedagogical methods were as successful as he claimed."

"I think, the truth is that dear Henrietta has a genius for language."

"Rather like me," Robert declared, to a roll of the eyes from his wife and laughter from the others. Robert's attempts at French and Spanish were the subject of much teasing within their circle.

"He did manage some striking results with his gifted daughters," Mrs Hertle said, gazing unselfconsciously at her cousin.

"Charles speaks a number of languages," Robert noted. "French he had at his mother's knee and speaks it like a native. Of course, he spent almost half his childhood there. He is also fluent in the argot of Cheapside. The other day he said to me, 'You've dropped your foggle, Robert,' and I had not a clue what he meant."

"Pray, what does it mean?" demanded Henrietta. "Or should a lady not inquire?"

"'Handkerchief,'" Robert told her. "But then many men of fashion speak the *cant* these days."

"I did not realize you were such a follower of fashion, Lieutenant," Miss Henrietta observed, her manner a little mocking, Hayden thought.

"In truth, I'm not. I had, for a time, a servant aboard one of my ships who had been an 'angler'—a thief who used a hooked stick to steal things through gratings and from shop windows. He and a few others aboard spoke what amounted to another language. I'm not sure why, but I found it more than a little fascinating. I even began to compile a lexicon. For instance, 'balderdash' is watered-down wine."

"Tell them what 'bachelor's fare' is . . ." Robert urged.

"Bread, cheese, and kisses."

The ladies pretended to be shocked, but then Henrietta became quite serious.

"Do you miss it, Lieutenant?" Henrietta asked, almost solicitously. "France, I mean."

Hayden was not quite sure how to answer. "At times I do, for I am a man terribly divided. An Englishman raised on French food, wine, and their particular variety of conversation. At the same time, I am a Frenchman who prefers English order, government, and rationality. The French are passionate, proud, and prone to letting emotions make their decisions—which makes me cherish my English side even more."

"But if all the ills of France were cured tomorrow and order restored, in which country would you choose to live?" Henrietta regarded him closely, as though the answer to this question were of particular importance.

Hayden was no more given to introspection than many a young man of active temperament, nor were his brief forays into self-awareness productive of great insight, so to be questioned so closely, while wishing so to impress, had the effect of banishing all thoughts. He threw up his hands. "The truth is, when I am in France I feel like an Englishman masquerading as French. When I am here I feel like a Frenchman pretending to be English."

"Then you are at home in neither country," Henrietta observed softly.

Hayden was about to answer when Robert interrupted.

"He is at home upon a ship—preferably in mid-Channel between his two nations."

But Henrietta did not smile at this. She merely regarded him gravely a moment, then looked quickly away.

"Henrietta is writing a novel, did you know?" Mrs Hertle said, as though whispering a secret.

"Now, Elizabeth, there really is such a thing as a confidence," Henrietta chastised her friend, but Hayden thought she was not really sorry this had been brought to light.

"It is about two women," Mrs Hertle went on mischievously, "one a woman of education—rather like Henrietta—the other of no education to speak of but much social advantage. How does it progress, Henri?"

"Despite my greatest efforts, anything one might term 'progress' has ceased."

"You must keep at it. Art is not made without adversity." Mrs Hertle turned to Hayden. "I have read a good number of pages, now, and can avouch for the author's skill, which is very high indeed." She smiled, including both men. "But there is a matter that cannot be decided by the authoress and I seem to have very little influence, much to my chagrin. Now, give us your most considered opinion: should not the woman of education have the happier ending? That is what we have been arguing for several months."

"These gentlemen are not interested in novels!" Henrietta argued.

"I happen to know that Lieutenant Hayden has read Rousseau's *Emile*," Mrs Hertle stage-whispered behind her hand, "and Captain Hertle once indulged in a volume of Mrs Richardson's."

"Who do you think should have the happier ending, Miss Henrietta?" Hayden asked.

She shook her head, looking genuinely distressed. "First I believe it should be the one, then the other."

"Certainly it must be the educated woman who achieves the happier life," Mrs Hertle insisted, "while to the other befalls the unhappy; though, perhaps, not of her making. Not a downfall so much as a stifled kind of complacency. Just what one would expect for a person who had not thought deeply about the time allotted her."

"But you place so much emphasis upon happiness," Henrietta replied. "I do realize that the Americans have recently enshrined it in their Declaration, but I am not certain it is mankind's highest calling. What think you, Captain Hertle?"

"Oh, do not ask *them*," Mrs Hertle interrupted. "Navy men must all answer that the highest calling is 'duty,' like a flock of bleating, blue-coated sheep."

Robert Hertle did not look perturbed by his wife's pronouncement. "I do not pretend to have an answer where greater minds than mine have strived and failed."

"Certainly *lesser* minds than yours have had much to say on the subject," Henrietta responded. "Come, you are not usually chary with your opinions . . ."

Robert laughed, as though embarrassed. "Happiness is certainly of great import to me, but I am putting my happiness at risk by leaving Mrs Hertle's side and going off to war, so I must be one of those Navy men who bleat 'duty' by day and night."

Henrietta Carthew considered this a moment, then turned to Hayden. "And do you agree, Lieutenant?"

"I fear a great deal has been accomplished in the world by people who make no claim to happiness or contentment of any form. I am much of two minds as regards this; like Mrs Hertle, I desire nothing more than to be contented and comfortable, and yet I wonder if I should accomplish little under such circumstances. I fear your woman of education may not have the happiest life but might make more of it."

For the briefest second Henrietta met his eye, her gaze quickly withdrawn. "And I fear you are right. Once one has eaten of the tree of knowledge it is out of the garden and into the harsh world for all Adams and Eves."

"You see," observed Mrs Hertle, "there is our thoughtful Lieutenant Hayden, who hides his true nature away. Do you know, Henri, Mr Hayden is a prodigious reader—" But at that moment Mrs Hertle was called away to deal with some domestic matter, and Robert excused himself also, though only for a moment, and Hayden found himself alone with Henrietta. They were, to begin, silent—perhaps awkwardly so—but before Hayden could speak Henrietta broke the silence.

"Who is your favoured author, Lieutenant? Are you a Rousseau man? Elizabeth mentioned you had read *Emile*."

"I suppose if I could take only one book to sea with me it would be Sterne," Hayden answered.

To this, Henrietta appeared surprised but rather approving, he thought.

"Which?" she asked. "*Shandy* or the *Sentimental Journey*?"

"It must be *Tristram Shandy*. Do you know it?"

"I do. It is one of my father's favourites, as well. He knew Sterne a little, but then everyone did. He was an inveterate dinner guest for many years."

"I should have liked to have met him myself. And you, Miss Henrietta, if you will permit me to ask: what is your favoured book?"

"Well, sir, now you are delving into my intimate secrets. I don't know if I shall permit you . . ." For a moment she did not continue, but the smile on her face assured him that she but teased. "*Don Quixote* is the great novel, I believe. Sadly, not written by an Englishman. Have you read it?"

"My Spanish is not up to it."

"Motteux has done a credible translation."

"So I am told, but in my limited knowledge, all translations are failures of one sort or another."

"That is true, but even second-rate Cervantes is better than no Cervantes at all, I think."

"Rather like ships," Hayden said, "a fifth rate is better than no ship at all."

"He has you talking ships!" Mrs Hertle said as she swept back into the room.

"Not at all. We were discussing the merits and demerits of Cervantes," answered Henrietta.

"Ah, the Carthew family patron." Mrs Hertle took a seat. "Did you know that Henrietta's family gave each other the names of the characters from *Don Quixote*? It was something of a parlour game, wasn't it, Henri? One had to find the name most befitting the persona of each sister and their father. What name would you choose for Lieutenant Hayden?"

"Don Quixote del Mar," Henrietta answered without hesitation.

A delighted laugh escaped Mrs Hertle. "Well, there you are, Mr Hayden; you have the principal role. A high honour."

He caught Henrietta smiling at him, amused, perhaps, at his expense.

Robert put his carriage at Hayden's disposal after supper, the rattle of wheels over paving stones interrupted, now and again, by a prolonged hiss as they passed through irregular pools, the carriage slowing with a gentle lurch like a boat running up on sand. Darkened streets, greasy with rain, inhabited by linkmen and beau traps.

As the driver checked his team at a corner, swaying torches, smudged by the door-pane, burned through the smoky fog. Candled faces down a narrow alley, hands aloft, a shadowy gathering below. Hayden pressed back into his seat as though to hide, and then the company erupted onto the street—guildsmen upon some progress, gin-ruddy and grinning vapidly.

"*Merde*," Hayden whispered, the sight too familiar and bearing with it feelings from another place—Paris, a few years earlier.

Visions of that wretched man, Doué, who, for all Hayden knew, had been innocent of all his alleged crimes. Had anyone possessed a crumb of proof that he speculated in the grain market, or that he had really joked the hungry should be fed hay? The mob did not much care for such particulars once they got hold of him.

Hayden had witnessed the man being dragged through the street to the nearest lamppost. A wreath of nettles had been clasped about his neck and a bouquet of thistles thrust into his hand by jeering *sans-culottes*. His mouth forced open and stuffed with hay until he gagged, and then they hanged him, kicking, from the lamppost.

Hayden pressed palms to his forehead. The terror upon the man's face could never be erased from memory. As he had been dragged past, Hayden imagined that he'd looked at him—*l'Anglais* in his French coat—appealed to him, even as Hayden had heard his own voice calling out to hang the man.

Doué's son-in-law, who had been some kind of official in Paris—an *Intendant*, perhaps—had been treated much the same, and then their heads had been severed and paraded through the streets on pikestaffs. Every now and then the slack faces had been thrust together and the crowd had called out, "*Kiss Papa. Kiss Papa,*" as though this were some terribly funny jest. Three days later Hayden had been back in England, ashamed of what he'd done, horrified to find out that even he could be drawn into a mob.

Four

Hayden could not remember so much bustle and noise in Plymouth Harbour. The coach delivering him to that city had been held up more than an hour by insolent drovers with a herd of bullocks for the Victualing Yard. And now that he was upon the quay, the commotion was beyond all, the great harbour awash with boats plying to and fro among the ships as His Majesty's Navy prepared for war.

Ships brought out of ordinary were having their protective shells removed, and the sheer hulk plied among them, raising spike-like masts for the riggers to practice their arts. A powder hoy upon its rounds called out for a ship's fires to be extinguished, and all the boatmen gave it the widest possible berth.

"Mr Hayden, sir . . ."

Hayden looked down to find the young lieutenant—not so far removed from the midshipmen's berth—waving a hand in his direction. He had disappeared a few moments before, promising to carry Hayden out to his new ship. In a moment several sailors had scrambled across a noisome lugger and up onto the quay to take his baggage in hand. Hayden followed them back across the narrow deck of the fishing boat and down into the stern-sheets of the cutter. Sweeps flashed out, and they set off into the fray, the coxswain straining to see over the heads of the oarsmen, ever alert in such a crush.

"It was a stroke of luck, to find you, Mr Janes," Hayden said to the boy, whose face had only just met the razor, Hayden was certain. "And my congratulations. Have you had your epaulettes long?"

"I passed my examination in March, Mr Hayden."

"Well, you've overhauled me, Lieutenant, and I remember when you first set foot aboard ship, I think."

Janes all but blushed. "I may have equalled you in rank, Mr Hayden, but not in skill."

"I would not be so sure of that," Hayden objected, and then cast his eye toward the opening of the Hamoaze. "You are sure the *Themis* is still there?"

"She won't have gone anywhere, sir. She had but one mast standing when I passed her this morning." Janes was silent a moment, a bit awkward in the presence of his former superior officer, now his equal, which caused them both a little embarrassment. "Have you been aboard her before, Mr Hayden?"

"I've never laid eyes on her. An eighteen-pounder, thirty-two, I'm told—certainly something of an anomaly."

"They have several more in frame, sir. One, I believe to be called the *Pallas*, in Woolwich, set to be launched before year's end. The *Themis* is a handsome little ship, sir, despite all. Some say a bit undersized to carry a full deck of eighteen-pounders, but I've heard she sails well and is not at all overburdened."

"She sounds like some Admiralty scheme to save half a crown. Surely a thirty-six- or thirty-eight-gun frigate will stand a better chance against the frigates the French are building."

"I should take a thirty-two–gun frigate manned by Englishmen over a thirty-eight manned by French . . ." the newly passed lieutenant clearly remembered Hayden's parentage at that moment and coloured terribly.

They came within view of the dockyards at that moment, and Hayden began to search among the moored vessels for his new ship.

Janes raised a hand and pointed. "There, Mr Hayden, before the seventy-four that is just crossing her yards."

And there, indeed, she lay; one hundred, thirty-five feet on her deck,

Hayden guessed. Bigger than a twenty-eight, but still a small fifth rate. Janes was right: she was a handsome little ship, even missing two of her limbs. For a ship only recently commissioned, however, she looked rather the worse for wear, and Hayden hoped it was the sign of hard service and a great deal more action than his friend Robert had hinted at.

"She looks as though she's seen a bit of fighting," Hayden observed.

Janes gave a stiff little nod and glanced over at the far shore so that his companion could not see his face.

Hayden was received aboard His Majesty's Ship *Themis* without ceremony, met as he came over the rail by a single officer.

"Second Lieutenant Herald Landry, sir, at your service." Lieutenant Landry was a man of small stature, perhaps five and twenty, of unremarkable appearance but for an abundance of freckles and a chin so small that one had to look twice to find it. He tipped a hat that, in contrast, appeared comically large. "You are the new first, I take it—Lieutenant Hayden?"

"Charles Hayden. Good to make your acquaintance, Mr Landry."

"I shall introduce you to the other officers, Mr Hayden, then show you to your cabin."

"I should like an audience with Captain Hart; as soon as is convenient to him, of course."

"Captain's ashore, sir. We don't expect him to return much before we sail."

"I see." Hayden stopped a moment and surveyed the deck, which was in the most ungodly disarray he had ever witnessed aboard a ship that had not recently been raked by enemy fire. The deck itself was squalid, tobacco-stained, and fouled by gulls. There was but one mast standing: the foremast. Two others, obviously new, lay upon the deck like fallen giants. Men lounged here and there, eying him with suspicion. From the gun-deck he could hear a fiddle playing, and the laughter of what might be called the "fairer sex," had he not met such women before.

"What orders did the captain leave you, Mr Landry?"

"To prepare the ship for sea."

"Well, then we have a great deal to do. Assemble the officers, young gentlemen, and warrant officers on the quarterdeck, and ask the lieutenant of the marines to muster his men."

"Aye, sir." Landry swept off, not hiding a look of alarm.

A corpulent man made his way through the clutter and sailors on deck.

"Able Barthe, Mr Hayden, sailing master. Welcome aboard the *Themis*, sir."

"Thank you, Mr Barthe."

The master, hatless, his colour high, stood catching his breath, as though he'd been running. A man of indeterminate years, Mr Barthe had hair the red of new brick, though mixed with grey—ashes among the flames.

"I apologize for the state of the ship, sir," the man went on, "with both captain and first lieutenant gone . . ." The sentence was never completed, and the man shrugged in embarrassment.

Men began appearing from out of the gangways, and emerging from the waist, where the merriment did not falter or even miss a note. Hayden followed the sailing master onto the quarterdeck. In a moment, Lieutenant Landry reappeared, accompanied by another man in a lieutenant's uniform. The young officer was clearly trying to shake himself awake.

"Third Lieutenant Benjamin Archer, Mr Hayden," Landry said, presenting the man, who was somewhat less than presentable. "Mr Barthe you have met, I see. And . . . Where is Mr Hawthorne?"

"Forward, sir. Mrs Barber had need of his attentions."

"Our goat," Barthe explained, seeing the look on Hayden's face. "Mr Hawthorne is quite an authority on animal husbandry. Mrs Barber has taken ill."

"Ah, Mr Hawthorne . . . our new first, Mr Hayden."

Dressed in dirty sailor's slops, Hawthorne looked anything but a senior officer of marines. Despite his dress, he made a graceful leg and swept off what was apparently a hat. "Your servant, sir. My company shall be ready for inspection at your pleasure, Mr Hayden." He did not appear the least embarrassed by his dress—one would think, by his attitude, that the man wore his scarlet marines' coat, the straps all pipeclayed an immaculate white.

"The midshipmen," Landry continued. "Lord Arthur Wickham, Mr Hayden." A dimpled youngster tipped his hat, appearing for all the world like a cheerful schoolboy. "James Hobson, and Freddy Madison. There are three other middies, sir, all given leave to go ashore and visit their families."

"Where are the bosun and the carpenter?" Hayden asked, making an effort to keep his voice even.

"Coming directly," the master offered.

A brawny, broken-nosed man led another onto the quarterdeck, and was subsequently introduced as the bosun. The carpenter was an ancient seaman who appeared to have been constructed of wood himself—all angles and heavily sparred. His clothes hung limp, like sails in a calm. Landry named them Franks and Chettle, respectively.

"What is the hour, Mr Landry?" Hayden asked.

"About half-two, I should think."

"Then the day is yet young. Send all women ashore. There will be no women aboard by day, and none aboard at night if I am not satisfied with the day's efforts."

The lieutenant hesitated. "That won't be popular with the men, Mr Hayden," he said quietly.

"It is not my custom to make decisions according to what is popular with the men. Did Captain Hart tell you when he is expected to return? When we are to go to sea? For what duty we are to prepare?"

There was an embarrassed silence. "Captain Hart doesn't commonly take us into his confidence, Mr Hayden," Landry confessed.

"He did tell you we're at war with France, did he not, Mr Landry?" Hayden said, his temper getting the better of him.

The little second reddened. "Sir, we're well aware of it."

"Good. How long have the masts been waiting upon your deck?"

"A week, sir."

"And what has become of the sheer-hulk?"

"The bosun of the sheer-hulk said he would get to us by and by."

"Very kind of him. Have you not materials necessary for the work?"

The two lieutenants glanced at the bosun, who hesitated.

"Everyone seems to be looking to you, Mr Franks," Hayden said, addressing the bosun.

The man appeared to grimace, revealing a dark gap in the row of yellowed teeth. "We have all blocks and cordage, Mr Hayden, but I'm not sure how the captain will want it done," the bosun admitted.

"In his absence, and without specific orders, to the common practices of the Navy, Mr Franks."

There was another awkward silence.

"What Mr Franks is trying to say, if I may be so bold," offered Lord Arthur, "is that no matter how the work is managed, Captain Hart will find much to criticize, Mr Hayden."

"Thank you for that, Wickham," Hayden said, "but I assume Mr Franks can speak for himself."

The bosun looked at the deck. "I've been . . . tarrying, Mr Hayden, for fear of the captain's displeasure."

"I would imagine that finding the masts on the deck when he returns will earn even greater displeasure. We shall begin with the mizzen. Have you spars we can use for sheers?"

"I do, sir."

"Then gather your mates and begin preparation. Mr Landry, a crew will be needed to raise the sheers."

Landry looked to the bosun, who grimaced as he spoke. "Most of the men are half seas over, Mr Hayden," he said apologetically.

"Drunk, I assume you mean? After the women have been put into boats, take the men who are insensible and pile them in the waist. The firemen can douse them, assuming we can find anyone sober enough to man the pump. Any able seamen who can walk a single deck plank unaided, send aft to assist Mr Franks. Everyone else will set to and clean ship." Hayden glanced around. "This deck is a disgrace, Mr Landry."

"Yes, sir, I'll have it scrubbed immediately."

"No, I want to keep the quarterdeck dry so we can work. Have it swept clean, and everything properly stowed. I would like to get the sheer legs up by nightfall." He turned to the third lieutenant. "Let us make a quick inspection of the mizzen step, Mr Archer."

The third lieutenant and two of the mids led Hayden below, down into the darkness. The step for the mizzen proved solid, as one would expect on a ship so recently commissioned, but still something of a surprise to Hayden, given the neglect apparent everywhere. The *Themis* clearly had been honestly built to begin. Blessedly, the mast partners were also free of rot.

An ugly scene awaited them when they returned to the deck. Drunken seamen struggled with the marines as the visiting women were pried bodily from their clutches. An hour's battle was engaged, by which time the women had been slung into the boats, and the foremast hands subdued, though not without many a hard beating. There was a moment when Hayden thought the entire thing would get out of hand, and had been on the verge of ordering the armourer to fetch pistols for the officers and warrant officers.

It took some time to subdue the mob, and then set them all to work, cleaning and stowing. The surgeon cleared his table, and the wounded were carried to him, many so drunk they did not feel their injuries and only wondered later that a seamstress appeared to have been at work upon their battered derma.

Hayden oversaw raising the sheers, and was soon aware that Mr Franks was a sad excuse for a bosun, and his hapless mates had learned their trade from him. It said much of Hart that he could not find good men to serve aboard his ship. What young Lord Arthur Wickham was doing there was a mystery, for he came from a good and influential family.

"You need a block for a girt line, Mr Franks," Hayden said, as the bosun stood gazing dumbly at the recumbent mizzen mast, a horny finger scraping a scab on his ear. "Tail-tackles must be rigged fore and aft at the foot of the sheers, and the feet should stand on stout planks that span at least three beams, and four would be preferred. Shore the beams from below. Then a leading block must be positioned so we can take a line forward to the capstan." He turned to find Landry, who stood looking on, unsure what to do. "We'll need hands to man the capstan in about four hours, Mr Landry. Will we have enough sober by then?"

"I'm sure we will."

"How goes the deck cleaning?"

"I'll see for myself, Mr Hayden." The lieutenant picked his way forward, careful to get in no one's way.

Hayden took the measure of each man as he worked. An able seaman named Aldrich was the only man who took any initiative. He clearly had been at sea long enough to have learned his trade thoroughly, and had raised a mast before. Young Wickham was everywhere, watching, studying the way tasks were managed, holding the fall of a rope, fetching a block.

The crews of his respective ships had long been Hayden's special province of study, partly out of fascination with mankind in general but also because the crew was the instrument through which an officer accomplished the tasks bestowed upon him by the Lords Commissioners. Hayden had seen both good crews and bad, and spent much time considering how any given collection of men could become either one or the other. He'd seen bad crews evolve into the most willing under the tutelage of good officers, and he had witnessed an apparently willing crew turn sour and froward by the introduction of a single foremast hand. He thought of a crew as being like gunpowder, a mixture of elements that, in the right proportion, produced the desired effect, but in the wrong proportions was of no use whatsoever. The greater the proportion of experienced seamen, especially those who had fought in several actions, the better, for these men would be looked up to by the younger and less experienced Jacks, and their manner and habits emulated. Hayden could see few if any such men among the crew of the *Themis*, and this was a cause of some concern.

"Damn your worthless hide, Manning," Hayden heard one of the hands mutter, "take up the strain on that line. Put your fat arse into it."

To Hayden's great surprise, some pushing ensued among the men, and Franks, the bosun, took up his rattan, which brought order, though the damning and muttering continued.

Stepping back, Hayden asked a servant for water, and stood observing the crew muddle through their work. It was not just the spirit of co-operation that was lacking; the men appeared to actively thwart one another, moving to impede another's efforts, tossing a marlin spike beyond the reach of the man who required it, watching men struggle with some task that clearly required more hands, yet not jumping to and aiding where a willing crew would. Hayden also observed men labouring at some chore too great for them but never asking help—knowing none would be forthcoming, he suspected. Dark looks and glares, mouthed curses and warnings, jostling a man precariously balanced. He had never seen the like. He wondered if Philip Stephens had any idea what went on aboard this unlucky ship.

Aldrich appeared to have his acolytes—men who deferred to him, who seemed to surround him almost protectively—yet it appeared he did not desire to be placed in such a position. Gently, he turned aside all attempts to raise him up or to distinguish him in any way—a curious phenomenon to the new first lieutenant, who was quite aware that he himself had always craved responsibility and recognition.

He reminded himself that among this gathering of men, there was at least one murderer, and, witnessing the animosity that existed between the hands, it no longer surprised him.

The officers' orders were heeded to the least degree possible—the smallest increase in disrespect and negligence would have seen the crewmen flogged, but they had found the greatest degree of insolence that the officers would tolerate and this was now their habitual manner.

Doffing his coat and hat, Hayden weighed into the fray, attempting to bring order to the confusion. Usually he enjoyed such a challenge, but among these men, and the palpable hostility, he felt like a stage actor pretending to be at ease, to relish the task at hand. In the past he had often found that his enthusiasm would spread to others, but these men did not seem to notice and treated him with suspicion if not hostility.

Hayden had detailed a large sailor to make up the lashing that bound the head of the sheers, but soon realized neither the man's skills nor his inclination were equal to the task.

"What is your name?" Hayden asked him.

The man raised a large, pock-marked face, all nose and brow. "Stuckey, sir. Bill Stuckey."

Hayden guessed Stuckey was fourteen and a half stone, or thereabout, and taller than he by a good three inches. Ill-fitting slops, sweat-soaked, clung to his torso, and out the end of his sleeves thrust big, turnip fists.

"I will make up the lashing with you, Stuckey, for it is, I think, a task new to you."

The man rose and stepped back. Around them the work stopped. "I'm a landsman," the big man drawled, "taken from my chosen profession and forced aboard this bloody ship." Stuckey eyed him insolently. "The sea is not my calling nor will I have it be . . . *sir*."

Hayden faced the man full-on, despite the disparity in size, aware that everyone watched. "I am pleased to hear it, Stuckey, for I am always on the lookout for a man to perform the myriad labours that are beneath the skills of seamen. You will begin by cleaning the heads."

Hayden turned back to the gathering of men, all of whom had stopped their work to stare silently. "Where is the bosun?" Hayden called out.

The broken-nosed bosun stood up from among the men crouched over their work.

"Mr Franks," Hayden said evenly, "have one of your mates follow Mr Stuckey with a knotted rope. If he is not about his work with a will, he should be started, sharply."

"For how long, sir?" the bosun asked, looking perplexed.

"As long as it takes, Mr Franks." Hayden turned back to the big landsman. "When you are ready to learn your new trade, Stuckey, come and speak to me. Now be about your duties." Hayden turned away as one of the bosun's mates approached, knotting a rope.

Hayden would assign the man the most back-breaking work on the ship as well as the most demeaning. Two days would either see him come to Hayden asking to learn his trade or he would become completely insubordinate and require flogging. But Hayden had run up his flag for the men to see. Now to convince them that he was both fair and reasonable, for it was not enough to be severe, not if one was to earn the crew's respect—and no officer could expect to govern for long without it.

The men applied themselves to their tasks with renewed energy after that, and by nightfall, the sheers were raised and guyed in place, like a great, inverted V standing on the quarterdeck. Block and tackle and brute strength saw the mast positioned, ready to be raised. Hayden was confident they would get it in before the next day was very old.

He dined that night with the gunroom mess and invited guests. Mr Franks was so fagged by his afternoon's effort that he perpetually nodded at the table, much to everyone's amusement.

"There was one among them that could take on any man aboard," laughed Hawthorne, the marine lieutenant. "Laid out Smithers with a single blow. I think we should have kept her. Could lead a boarding party, that one. The French would not stand against she!"

The assembled men laughed.

"Will you not take a little wine, Mr Barthe?" Hayden asked, noting that the sailing master's glass had not been filled.

The laughter dried up like paint in the sun, though a few half-suppressed smiles—smirks, in truth—remained.

"I hope you will forgive me if I do not, Mr Hayden," Mr Barthe replied evenly. "You see, I have taken a vow of temperance from which, for all my honour, I dare not deviate . . . though it causes much amusement to certain of my messmates." Smiles were further suppressed around the table. Barthe went on. "You need not be concerned, Mr Hayden; I will not be pressing temperance pamphlets upon you or recommending the works of Hannah More. It is entirely a personal matter. A defect in my character will not allow me to partake of strong drink, even wine or ale, without the most disastrous consequences. I hope you will forgive me, therefore, if I toast with plain water. No disrespect is meant."

"By all means, Mr Barthe, forgive me for even bringing up the subject."

"No need. I tell my fellows in the gunroom to make not the slightest allowance for my vow. Partake as usually you would and never for a moment worry about the effects of this upon me. To be always coddled and have our people drinking away from me would deprive me of much good company and in the end I would be only the weaker for it, for one must learn to resist temptation. One must drill just as men do at the guns. The longer I resist, the stronger I become."

The small clatter of cutlery on china, glasses raised and returning to the table.

"Did you see much action on your recent cruise?" Hayden asked, breaking the awkward silence.

It seemed for a moment that no one would answer—or that each waited for some other to speak.

"No, sir, Mr Hayden," Landry said quietly. "We had no luck at all."

"It goes that way sometimes," Hayden said. "You lost a man, all the same, I understand?"

Again, an uncomfortable moment.

"Penrith," Hawthorne said. "Rated able. A good seaman."

"I'm sorry to hear it. They found the man that did for him, though?"
The men glanced one to the other.

"It's a subject of some debate, Mr Hayden," Land Arthur answered.

"And what do you think, Wickham?"

The youthful nobleman's dimples disappeared as he weighed the evidence, as solemn as a magistrate. "I think the man hanged was innocent, Mr Hayden."

The other men shifted uncomfortably.

"And what say you, Mr Landry?"

"The captain believed McBride was guilty," Landry answered, "and I'd never gainsay Captain Hart."

"No," Hawthorne said, "I am sure you wouldn't."

The look Landry gave the marine was not friendly.

"If it was not this man McBride," Hayden said, bringing his gaze to bear on Hawthorne, "then, pray, who did for Penrith?"

"I have no proof, Mr Hayden, only my own suspicions, and it would not be fair to speak those in the event the man is innocent."

"Do be careful, Mr Hawthorne," the sailing master warned. "The captain would not take kindly to such criticism."

"Certainly no one here would report gunroom conversation to the captain . . ." Hayden said, but the silence this brought told him that, indeed, someone would.

After servants cleared the table, Hayden found himself briefly alone while the other officers all saw to one duty or another. He hoped that the dinner had done something to acquaint the officers with his methods and outlook. There was, invariably, a brief period of uneasiness when a new first officer came aboard, and especially so in this case, with the captain away. Both crew and officers would be anxious to comprehend the standards and expectations of the new lieutenant. Many men, he well knew, would rather maintain the most disastrous situation than have change, whereas some smaller number would welcome it. His job was doubly difficult because the standards of Captain Hart were unknown to him and it was the captain of a ship who set the height of the bar that men must jump, not the first lieutenant.

Griffiths emerged from his cabin and nodded to the new lieutenant. Thin-boned and narrow-faced, the doctor stood a hand taller than Hayden, but two or three stone lighter. Prematurely grey, for he could not have been much over thirty, he appeared almost always serious, his scholarly demeanour seldom altering, even when he made a jest, which he did not infrequently.

"I feel rather foolish," Hayden confessed, "pressing wine upon Mr Barthe when he is a temperance man."

"No need for concern. It was the duty of his messmates to advise you, but we were remiss. Mr Barthe is not thrown out by such small things. He has been sober now these seven years, and shows no signs of returning to his former life of dissipation. You will find him a thorough, responsible officer, I believe."

"I am certain of it."

Griffiths regarded him a moment. "Our sailing master's name is unknown to you?"

"Indeed, I had never heard it before stepping aboard."

The surgeon took a seat across the table, leaning forward on arrowhead elbows that he might speak quietly. "Mr Barthe's story is not a happy one, I fear. You see, he was once a young lieutenant of some promise in the King's Navy, but was court-martialled. His ship was wrecked and though there was some evidence of incompetence by the captain, because some few aboard claimed Mr Barthe drunk at the time, he was convicted for dereliction of duty. He claims it is untrue. Unfortunately, at least for his family, that was not the greatest mischief that resulted from Barthe's drinking. He had a tendency to gamble, though without a matching tendency to win. He was, at the time of his court-martial, much in debt. But not all his friends deserted him; Mrs Barthe, who must be a tower of saintly strength, did not abandon him to his dissipation but appealed to him again and again to change his ways, giving him opportunity after opportunity to redeem himself. And, surprisingly, given the history of many similar marriages, he did. A captain whom he had once served obtained him a master's warrant and he sailed for several years with this officer until the poor man died of yellow fever. Barthe's luck looked as though it had turned against him again, when Hart took him on, perhaps being unable to find another to fill the position.

"Mrs Barthe has a brother who has made a great success of himself in some branch of trade, and he eliminated all of Mr Barthe's debts, allowing the sum to be paid back slowly and at no interest, which our good sailing master has been diligently doing these many years, to the great impoverishment of his family, I fear. Did you know that Barthe has six daughters? They all, very happily, have taken after their mother where it comes to their looks, and are beauties from the eldest to the youngest.

Mr Barthe is at great pains to keep our good lieutenant of marines away from them." Griffiths laughed.

"Has Hawthorne a bad reputation, then?"

"It depends upon whom you ask. Among the crew he is much admired. Mr Hawthorne has the same weakness for women that Mr Barthe had for drink; he is constitutionally unable to resist. And, happily for him, the female of our species cannot more easily resist the dashing Hawthorne. Much trouble has come of it. Hawthorne has fought two duels, with great misfortune on the other side."

"Every ship must have at least one rake. It is good to know we have our quota . . ."

"Hawthorne is as far from villainy in his heart as a man can be, I am convinced, but he is no more in control of his actions regarding women than an opium-eater is where it comes to his pipe. I have seen him in great distress over his conduct and the heart-break it has caused, but it does not long check his actions. He was blessed with too pleasing a countenance, I fear, and in both manner and address he lacks nothing. He is the most agreeable man aboard, and a great favourite in the gun-room, but if there is a woman to whom you are particularly attached do not introduce her to Hawthorne. You have been given fair warning."

"I shall heed your words, Doctor; the fairer sex show no signs of being unable to resist my charms. In truth, they manage it with very little effort, I fear."

"In this you have many a brother, Mr Hayden." The doctor's mouth turned down slightly at the corners—as though he had tasted something bitter. "You will find this crew an odd collection of misfits and fumblers, I fear."

Hayden was not quite sure what to say to that, but knew full well it reflected badly upon the captain.

"The middies seem first-rate," Hayden observed.

"Indeed they are. Outside of the service Captain Hart has a different character, I am told, and through Mrs Hart, many an influential friend."

"Which explains the presence of Lord Arthur Wickham . . ."

The doctor nodded. "But not all of the ship's people have landed here because of incompetence. Some of us merely have no interest."

Hayden glanced quickly at Griffiths, wondering if the doctor referred to him, but then decided the comment was not meant so. "I am sure there is many a good man aboard ship, Doctor. I shall not tar the entire crew with one brush."

Griffiths made a small bow of acknowledgement, or perhaps of thanks. "I must see to my charges, if I may, Mr Hayden."

"By all means, Doctor, do not let me detain you."

Mr Landry had assigned him a servant, a boy of twelve who went by the name of Joshua. He'd served the previous lieutenant in the same capacity and seemed to know his duties tolerably well. A "writer" was also assigned to him: a young Irish boy with the unlikely name of Perseverance Gilhooly. He was known as Perse, and seemed too alert for his station in life.

As Hayden was arranging his cabin, a space about eight feet square, there came a knock at the open door.

"Ah, Mr Hawthorne," he said. "Is there some service you require?"

The marine lieutenant slouched under the low deckhead, at his hip a heavy book resting upon the crook of one hand.

"I just wanted to report that I have stationed reliable men by the boats. No one will get ashore this night except they swim."

There were no women aboard that night, and no doubt this was causing some men to reflect upon the relative proximity of the shore. From what the doctor had said, he might be led to suspect the marine of being one of them. "Thank you, Mr Hawthorne."

But the man continued to hover outside the door.

"What is it you read, Mr Hawthorne, if you will permit me to ask?"

"*A Course of Experimental Agriculture*, Mr Hayden, written by Mr Arthur Young."

"That would seem an interest greatly removed from the sea."

"It is my hope to have a farm one day, Mr Hayden, though it causes my fellows in the gunroom no end of amusement." He hesitated a second, colouring a little. "I published, a year ago, in the *Annals of Agriculture*, a brief treatise entitled 'Observations on the Practice of Keeping Productive Laying Hens at Sea.'"

Hayden could not help but smile at this surprising bit of information, delivered with rather poorly concealed pride.

Barthe entered the gunroom just then, appearing behind the marine, moving a chair as he made his way past the table. "Is he telling you about the great estate he will one day own, Mr Hayden? How he will apply principles of scientific farming to make a great success of it all."

Hawthorne did not appear the least offended but pretended to be put upon, rolling his eyes. "It is a terrible burden, Mr Hayden, the petty jealousy of the uninformed."

"It is the price of being ahead of one's time. My mother's family have extensive lands in grapes, so I have witnessed scientific agriculture up close, for good and ill."

Hawthorne gazed at Hayden closely, no doubt trying to see if it were true that he had differently coloured eyes. "Not in England, surely?"

Hayden knew the truth would come out eventually; the service was a paradise for gossips. "France, Mr Hawthorne."

"France . . ." the marine echoed, clearly caught aback.

"A large nation beyond the English Channel, Mr Hawthorne," Barthe observed as he stepped into his cabin. "Most recently they've had a revolution. Have you not heard?" The master's cabin door ticked closed, obscuring a wicked smile.

Hawthorne laughed to hide his embarrassment. "You're half-French, then, Mr Hayden?"

"That's right, but I am an Englishman at heart. My father was a post captain in the King's Navy."

"It was not my intention to question your loyalties, Mr Hayden. If it seemed so I do apologize."

"No need, Mr Hawthorne; it is me that feels an explanation is required."

Hawthorne made a small bow of acknowledgement and continued to stand outside Hayden's door, clearly uncertain of what to say. Or perhaps he had intended to tell Hayden something more than the title of his single piece of published wisdom.

"Is there something else, Mr Hawthorne?"

The marine opened his mouth to speak, hesitated, then smiled. "Nothing, sir."

The marine lieutenant slipped away to his own cabin, leaving Hayden bemused, wondering. Perhaps Hawthorne would say whatever it was he had meant to when he knew Hayden better—or so the new lieutenant could hope.

He rolled into his cot some time later, but lay awake, listening to the burble and cant of water, to a small breeze whispering among the shrouds.

Five

Hayden woke to a distant whisper.

"*Doctor? Doctor Griffiths?*" The urgency of the voice reached deep into his sleep and drew him to the surface, where he sat, twisting knuckles into eye-sockets and shaking his head.

From the other side of the gunroom he heard Griffiths, apparently none too happy with being wakened. "What is the matter?"

"It is Tawney, sir. A sentry found him in the cable-tier, bloody and not able to be roused. He appears to have been beaten, sir."

Hayden rolled out of his cot and began pulling on clothes.

"Jesus, Mary, and Joseph . . ." the doctor muttered, and Hayden heard feet strike the deck.

The first lieutenant emerged from his cabin at the same moment as Griffiths, and both set off at once for the orlop-deck, the marine who had called them scurrying before, lantern in one hand, musket in the other. They pummelled down the steps and made their way quickly forward.

They saw two shadowy figures, one bent beneath the low deckhead, a lantern clutched in his fist, the other crouched in the waist-deep darkness created by the thick rounds of anchor cable. Hayden scrambled over the hawser after the doctor, who pulled spectacles from his pocket.

A man lay crumpled on the dark planks, limp as a sleeping child, mouth slack and swollen.

"We've not moved him, Doctor," one of the men said. "Left him as he was, just as you always say."

Griffiths appeared not to hear, but felt at the man's throat for a pulse. A long moment as the others held their breath.

"He is not done for, at least. Bring the light closer."

The lanterns were lowered to cast their faint glow upon the sailor's bloodied face. The flesh appeared bloated to bursting, inky-dark and crimson. Eyes were swollen shut, jaw oddly displaced.

"Who did you say he was?" Hayden asked.

"Dick Tawney, sir. Foretop-man."

"Who would have done this to him?"

No one had anything to say in response. The doctor gently probed the skull, and then, with Hayden's help, turned him on his side.

"It is a wonder he has not drowned in his own blood," the doctor observed, a barely controlled anger creeping into his voice. "Jump aft, Davidson, and fetch a cot from the sick-berth, if you please."

Tawney moaned, stirring a little. Griffiths took hold of the man's shoulder and hip, bracing against a shift in the man's weight, keeping him on his side. Blood dripped from his shattered nose and mouth. A moment later Davidson and the surgeon's mate, Ariss, appeared bearing a cot. Under the doctor's direction they shifted the deadweight of the sailor onto the sailcloth-covered frame. Tawney muttered something un-intelligible, then his head lolled to one side.

Bent low beneath the beams, they raised the cot, sliding it over the coils of anchor cable, waiting while Hayden and one of the seamen scrambled over, then bearing up the weight again. Tawney's feet began a convulsive jig.

"Is it the death rattle, Doctor?" the marine asked, clearly unnerved by what he saw.

"No. It is like to a fit—from blows to his head. With luck it will not persist."

In the sick-berth, the cot was slung from rings set into the beams. Gently it swayed forth and back and forth. One of the patients woke to see what went on, the fevered whites of his eyes peering out from beneath a thick dressing that swaddled his skull.

"It's all right, Hale, go back to sleep."

"Wot 'appened to 'im?"

"Exactly," the doctor muttered. "Let us clean his wounds, Mr Ariss. Then cut open his shirt; there is blood, here, on his rib-cage."

Hayden stepped out of the way, watching as the surgeon and his mate went about their work with a practised, dispassionate air, fingers moving mysteriously in the smudged light. Twice Hayden was called to help re-strain poor Tawney as he was taken by another convulsive fit, but then the man would fall limp again, unmoving. The doctor checked his carotid pulse each time, as the man had gone so still.

Finally satisfied that he had done everything possible, Griffiths motioned to Hayden and the two stepped outside the sick-berth. Leaning, one against the bulkhead of thin deal-board, the other against the ladder, they pitched their voices low so as not to be overheard.

"Tawney looks to be a broad-chested, well-made fellow," Hayden said. "I should say that he was not so badly beaten by one man—unless there is a veritable giant aboard, with a cruel disposition."

"You are right, Mr Hayden. I should guess that such a beating would take four men or more. Tawney is nine and twenty, or perhaps eight, strong as the proverbial ox. I should have said he was well thought of among the crew."

"Did someone say he is a foretop-man?"

"I believe that is so."

"His mates won't be liking this, I should think." Hayden shook his head. The top-men were commonly the strongest, most experienced seamen—the cocks of the walk among the foremast hands. "I will have you inspect the crew after breakfast. A beating like that will leave some bruised hands, maybe a broken knuckle or two."

"If they employed their fists. By the damage I would say he was cudgelled."

Hayden shifted his weight against the stair. "One man murdered, another beaten half to death . . . As I worked today, raising the sheers, I sensed among the men such ill will. I have never witnessed so unobliging a spirit, so many little things done to impede another's efforts. It is imperative that a ship's crew pull together, for their own safety if for no other reason . . . Has this fractious mood arisen since Captain Hart departed? Certainly it cannot have been so when you were at sea?"

The doctor removed his spectacles and massaged each eye in turn with the heel of a hand. "It has, perhaps, become more pronounced since the captain quit the ship and the first lieutenant the service, but it is by no means new to the *Themis*."

Hayden waited for the doctor to say more and, when he did not, said: "I have never seen the like, Doctor. How an officer would take a ship from anchor and get under way with such a crew is a mystery to me. How do the officers tolerate it?"

The doctor shrugged. For a moment he remained silent, but then leaned closer to Hayden. "You were asking earlier about Penrith. I cannot tell you who was responsible for the man's death, but on the night he went missing I overheard one of the hands say to some others, 'They've done for Penrith,' or words to that effect. Before the finger was found the next morning members of the crew already seemed to know it was a murder, though it was initially thought by the officers to have been misadventure."

"Who said this, Doctor?"

"I know not. It was dark, most of the crew were too ill to stand, and we were caught in the most dreadful gale. I confess, my thoughts were elsewhere. I was frightened and not thinking clearly."

Ariss, his mate, rounded into view at the moment. "If you please, Doctor; Tawney has taken to convulsing again."

With a perfunctory nod, Griffiths disappeared back into his lair. For a moment Hayden stood dumbly, then climbed the stair and slipped silently into the gloom of the gunroom, where he found Barthe in the light of a single candle, alone at table, staring fixedly at a glass of wine set out before him.

Hayden was not sure what to say, or even if he should acknowledge what he saw. But the sailing master tore his gaze away from the glass and regarded Hayden, apparently unembarrassed.

"No doubt you are wondering what I am about . . . ?" Barthe whispered hoarsely.

In truth, Hayden was not—the master was apparently drinking.

"I am testing my will." He nodded to the full glass, the wine lead-dark in the dim light. "I must do this from time to time—face the temptation. Today I could hardly focus my thoughts for want of drink, and now I must make my penance. I know it must seem passing strange, but I have been sober these seven years and have my own way of remaining so. If I can manage this tonight, tomorrow I shall feel no want of it."

"Do pardon my intrusion, Mr Barthe," Hayden offered, and went immediately to his cabin, pulling the door to behind. Even as he did so, the image of Barthe appeared in the small opening, softly aglow in his nightshirt, eyes fixed upon the glass, hands laid gently on the table to either side, and on his face, a tormented resolve.

Six

Asullen and sickly crew appeared the next morning, and Hayden put them to work. A frigate named for the goddess of order should make a better showing, he thought. His subsequent inspection of the ship, however, was enough to dishearten the most stolid officer. The bosun's stores were in disarray. There was but one useable cable in the cable tier—the others having been allowed to rot. The quarterdeck leaked and required repitching, and there was everywhere a general want of cleanliness and order.

The captain of the hold seemed to know his business, and smartly reported the state of their stores, though the reclusive purser did not know it himself. Hayden's most disastrous find, however, was in the forward magazine. By the dim illumination, which came through a pane of glass in the light room, he examined the powder—but it was the smell of it that truly angered him.

"Who is the gunner, Mr Landry?" Hayden asked. He'd met the man but the name now escaped him.

"Mr Fitch is acting gunner, Mr Hayden." Landry, who the day previous had been most obliging, was now sullen and resentful of Hayden's presence, as though the first lieutenant interfered in the running of the frigate. Having been found with his ship in such disarray was perhaps at the root of it, but Hayden did not care for the man's manner.

"Would you call for him, Mr Landry?"

Landry hesitated by the door a moment, as though he might refuse, but when Hayden turned and faced him, he touched his hat. Before he could comply, however, Lord Arthur, who had become Hayden's shadow, interceded.

"I'll fetch him directly, Mr Hayden," the boy offered, and was off at a run.

Landry walked out onto the orlop, bent low, as though he would examine the cables.

Hayden watched him, with more detachment than he would have expected of himself. He had known his kind before. Landry was a sad little fellow, he had decided, awkward and ungracious in both manner and address—the boy whom everyone picked on at school.

A moment later the acting gunner, the bald and tattooed Mr Fitch, shuffled into the magazine, followed by the second lieutenant. He glanced nervously at Landry as he made his way down the three steps.

"Is it not your duty, Mr Fitch, to keep this storeroom aired and dry at all times?" Hayden asked.

The man did not answer but nodded dumbly.

"Then how do you explain this?" Hayden reached into the powder barrel and removed a handful of tacky powder, which he let fall in doughy dollops back into the barrel. The acting gunner winced.

"What became of the gunner whom you replaced?"

"He died, Mr Hayden," Landry offered. "The surgeon said his heart gave out. We slipped him over the side some weeks ago."

"You are relieved of your duties as gunner, Mr Fitch," Hayden stated. "I will leave it for the captain to decide your fate when he returns."

"It was Captain Hart who appointed Fitch, Mr Hayden," Landry said, eyeing him with poorly concealed hostility.

"So I assumed, Mr Landry, but I will put another man in his place until the captain returns. We cannot have our powder thus neglected. Can we?" He gestured to the door. "You may go, Mr Fitch. Mr Landry will find you other duties. Count yourself lucky that I am not captain, here, for I would have you flogged this very day for negligence such as this." The man made an awkward knuckle and then backed up the stairs, retreating into the dimness, the quick padding of bare feet marking his flight.

Hayden turned to Landry. "Although there is little point, let us test this powder before I write to the Ordnance Board for more. Have a few cartridges made up for the carronades, if you please, Mr Landry." Hayden went out and left the lieutenant to suffer his resentments alone. Wickham followed quickly behind.

A few moments later they were on the quarterdeck, the tompion removed from a thirty-two-pounder carronade. The first cartridge did not fire at all and had to be drawn out with a worm—a long, corkscrew-like rod—a task no one relished for obvious reasons. The second made a dull thump, though much debris was left in the barrel. They managed to fire a ball after two more misfires, but as Mr Barthe observed, he could "throw it further himself."

Lieutenant Hayden would now have the unenviable task of requesting powder to replace that which had been spoiled. The quantities of powder in the magazines, however, did beg another question.

"How often do you exercise the great guns, Mr Landry?" he asked after the final cartridge was drawn out, split, and its contents spilled over the side.

"Never, Mr Hayden. At least not since I've been aboard. Gun drills are done without powder or shot."

Hayden felt his eyes close, and it took some effort to keep his face impassive. He turned quickly away. "Ready to raise the mast, Mr Franks?"

Men placed at the capstan put their chests against the bars and pushed, drawing taut a line running through the leading block to the sheer pendant. It creaked like an old door as it stretched, and the mizzen lifted a few inches.

"Stand clear!" Hayden ordered.

When the mast was raised a little more, it slewed suddenly to one side, swinging heavily back and forth.

The men at the capstan bars continued to turn until the mizzen attained an angle perhaps fifteen degrees shy of vertical. The back line, reeved through a block made fast to one of the sheer heads, was then hauled. It had been attached to the mast under the bibbs, and this brought the spar almost to vertical. Hayden and some of the larger men put their shoulders against it, and with the help of a tackle, wrestled the heel of the mast over the aperture where it would step through the deck. Slowly the great spar was lowered. It did not want to pass cleanly through the lower deck, but was finally coaxed and cajoled upright enough that it passed, the heel tenon seating neatly in the step beneath.

" 'Tis home, Mr Hayden!" came a call from below.

"Well done!" Hayden said to the men around him, then the same to the men at the bars. "We shall make up the shrouds, Mr Franks," Hayden ordered. "Perhaps Aldrich can assist you." He was sure that Aldrich would soon have the job in hand, if Franks did not get too much in the way, but Franks surprised him. Despite the man's obvious lack of proficiency in his trade, he exhibited a great capacity to learn, and was not embarrassed to do so, though many in his position would have attempted to bluster their way through, hoping to hide their defects. It raised Mr Franks considerably in Hayden's opinion. A man willing to learn was never a cause lost.

He assigned Stuckey another day of demeaning work, and set the bosun's mate to chase him about. Such an act could backfire, Hayden well knew, if the crew sympathised with the offender, but it seemed that Stuckey had little sympathy from the others, though no one had the nerve to mock him either, a fact Hayden took note of.

The shrouds were made up and the tops got over the mast. Attending to some job of work, Hayden lifted his head to glimpse something large plunging from above. A tumbling man grasped at the shrouds, his fall checked, lost his grip, fell, then caught hold of the still-slack shrouds once more, burning his hands as he slid too quickly the last thirty feet to the deck, landing with an awkward thump. Somehow on his feet, the boy—for it was a boy, despite his massive size—leaned against the rail a moment, shaken. Wickham approached him.

"Are you injured, Giles?" the young nobleman asked.

The boy shook his head, unable to quite catch his breath. "No, sir," he whispered. "Begging your pardon. I'll be all right in a moment, sir."

Hayden crossed the deck and realized the lad, who still trembled, was a good half a foot taller than he, and much broader across the shoulders and chest. "Giles? Is that your name?" Hayden asked.

"Aye, sir," the lad answered. His face had turned pale as a fish belly.

"Sit down on the deck and put your head between your knees. Someone bring the boy some water."

Giles slid down the bulwark and hung his head, great forearms thrown over his neck, elbows on the knees, none of this structure too steady. "Sorry, sir," the boy whispered, his voice barely audible.

"Don't apologize," Hayden bid him. "You've had quite a fright."

"If I hadn't grabbed the shrouds . . ."

Hayden crouched down, trying to get a glimpse of the boy's face. The lad lolled to one side and would have slid limply to the deck, but Hayden and Wickham caught him and supported his ample weight. The doctor appeared then, fetched from his charges by Mr Archer.

Griffiths bent over the boy and felt for the carotid pulse. "What happened?" he asked.

"He fell from the mizzen top," Hayden reported, "but managed to catch hold of a shroud or he would have come to much harm."

"He didn't fall to the deck, then?" the doctor asked.

"No. He slid down the shroud," Wickham said, "but then turned ashen and light-headed."

"Got the vapours," one of the crew whispered and the men laughed.

"Well, he'll come round in a moment, I'll venture," Griffiths said, and the boy did move at that instant, one eye slitting open. "There you are, Giles. All of a piece, I see. Nothing broken, no severed arteries, not even a modest contusion. I think you'll live. No, don't try to sit up. Lay still a moment and let the blood find its natural level." Griffiths looked up at

Hayden and nodded. "He'll be perfectly hale in a moment. Saved the deck a nasty bashing, I should think."

Hayden retreated with Wickham in his wake, and a servant called them for the midday meal.

"That was a bit of luck that he saved himself that way," Hayden said, as they reached the top of the companionway. "You know him, do you?"

Wickham nodded. "I do, sir. We are the same age but for three days."

Hayden must have shown his surprise.

"He has great size for his years, doesn't he?" Wickham stated.

"For any tally of years, I would venture."

Wickham looked around rather furtively and then leaned closer to Hayden, pitching his voice low. "Did you hear the men whispering, sir? saying that Giles didn't fall?"

"What did they mean, he didn't fall? We saw him come tumbl—" But then he realized what was meant. "They believed it was not an accident?"

"That's what I assume, sir."

Hayden pressed a palm against his forehead, appalled. "Did anyone see what happened? Did they see someone push the boy?"

"I don't know, sir."

"Send young Giles down to me."

A moment later Giles descended the companionway stair and Hayden met him outside the gunroom. Not being captain, he did not have a cabin suitable for private interviews, so he led the boy down to the or-lop and ranged forward of the sick-berth—the nearest thing to privacy they would find at that time of day. Giles' big, simple face could not hide the apprehension he felt, and Hayden wondered how much of that was just being young and called by a superior officer.

"Feeling better, Giles? No harm done?"

"I'm perfectly hale, Mr Hayden."

Hayden fixed his gaze on the boy-man, trying to read his doughy, rather inexpressive face. "Tell me honestly, Giles, did you fall from the mizzen top, or were you pushed?"

A small flare of alarm, open to interpretation. "Pushed, sir?! Why, Mr

Hayden . . ." but his sentence devolved into incoherency. Finally, in a small voice, he managed, "I lost me balance and tumbled, sir. There's nothing more to it than that."

"You are certain?"

"Yes, sir."

Hayden eyed him a moment more, but the boy's gaze slid down to the deck. "Who was on the mizzen top with you? I did not notice."

"Why, I hardly remember . . . Cole, I think. And that Dutchman van De . . . They call him The Demon, sir, but I don't know his right name. Oh, and Smithers, though he'd shinnied up the mast a bit by then."

"And no one bumped you or collided with you in any way?"

"No, sir. Just born awkward, that's all."

"All right. You may go."

Hayden followed the boy up the stairs, where he encountered Wickham outside the midshipmen's berth, clearly waiting for him. His eyes followed Giles up to the gun-deck, his footsteps heard retreating across the planking.

"Giles assured me it was an accident," Hayden observed in response to the midshipman's raised eyebrow, "but I am not convinced he told me the truth. Do you know Cole, a Dutchman they call The Demon—"

"Van Damon, sir."

"—and Smithers?"

"Harry Smithers I know well enough, Mr Hayden. He is a bit slow-witted but of good character, I think. Van Damon and Cole came aboard from the *Hunter* when she was decommissioned. I've never had any cause to think ill of them. Cole is a good seaman."

"Thank you, Mr Wickham."

"Not at all, sir." The midshipman turned to go, but then stopped. "There are some good men in the crew, sir."

This brought Hayden up short and he paused with his hand on the gunroom door. "I have no doubt of it. But what made you say such a thing?"

Wickham appeared suddenly reticent. "I don't know, sir. I suppose it's because of the ship's reputation . . ."

"And what reputation is that?"

"Well, you know, Mr Hayden; that the crew are all shy and don't know their business."

"Is that the character we've been given? Well, we'll have to change it, won't we?"

Wickham nodded, suddenly animated. "I should like nothing better, sir." The boy touched his hat and turned to go into the midshipmen's berth, but then turned back a second time. "Oh. Stuckey asked me what he might do to get back into your good graces, Mr Hayden."

"Next time I give him an order, he can answer 'Aye, sir' and then get to it. And if he doesn't know how the job is to be done, he should speak up and I will find someone to show him. Tell him to come to me after I've eaten and we will begin his education as a seaman."

When he returned to the deck, much fortified, the landsman, Stuckey, approached, made a knuckle, and stood with his eyes cast down.

"So, I am told you'd like to become a sailor. Is that correct, Stuckey?"

"If you please, sir."

"I am pleased. I'll put you to work with Aldrich. But if I find you are not learning your duties or are not applying yourself with a will, Stuckey, you shall wish you had not wasted this opportunity."

"I shan't waste it, sir," he promised.

"Then be about your duties."

The man went quickly off, but Hayden was sure that there were many harder cases aboard this ship than Stuckey, and he did not think Stuckey had been born anew. The man would cause him trouble yet, unless Hayden's judgement had abandoned him.

Griffiths emerged, pale-faced, from his sick-berth, down in the depths of the ship.

"And how fares Tawney?" Hayden asked the doctor, who appeared to have no other purpose but to take in a little air and expose his chalky skin to the sunlight.

Griffiths looked a bit confused by the question, his mind clearly elsewhere, but then his focus returned. "He is in an odd state—conscious but not sensible, if you take my meaning. Not a word has he spoken, but he watches every move of my assistant and myself as though we might at any point turn and attack him. But, odd to say, this state is an improvement over last night's. I think he shall come around, by and by."

The day flew by, and so did the next. Hayden wrote to the Victualling Yard about stores, and to the Ordnance Board, begging powder. The lieutenant also wrote his first letter to Philip Stephens—or, rather, to Mr Thomas Banks Esq. at the address the First Secretary had provided. It was a task he dreaded and every word was set down with the ink of resentment. Hayden had agreed to send these reports to Stephens, so felt honour-bound to a dishonourable task. How to write anything resembling the truth without appearing to undermine Captain Hart, who after all was not aboard ship, was near to impossible—but then he expected Stephens would not much mind if Hart came off poorly.

My dear Mr Banks:

I am pleased to say that I arrived safely at Plymouth on the 23rd day of July, and am aboard my new ship, HMS Themis, *the frigate we spoke of when last we met. Captain Hart is not aboard, nor is he expected much before we sail. In his absence, the ship, I am dismayed to tell, was in a state of dreadful disarray. Two of her masts had been lifted out and new masts left lying on her deck, with no attempt being made to get them in. Preparations for sea were not under way, though Captain Hart had left orders that the ship was to be ready upon his return. The vessel was rather overrun with women of a certain type, and the officers seemed barely in control. In the captain's absence, I have assumed command and reinstituted order. We are presently refitting for sea.*

Perhaps the most distressing thing I have learned since coming aboard is that many of the officers and warrant officers believe a man named McBride was falsely convicted for the murder of another seaman and subsequently hanged for it. A terrible miscarriage of justice, if true.

I hope all is well with you, and that your endeavours proceed apace.

I remain, sir, your humble servant,
Lieutenant Charles Hayden

Seven

Tom Worth lay in the swaying darkness, hammock gently moving in a small harbour swell. The seeping stench of his fellows he seldom noticed, now—no more than the two dozen other foul odours that infected HMS *Themis*—so it hadn't been that that had wakened him. Then he heard the low, urgent whispering. They were at it again—the same damned arguments.

"You're all being led to a flogging . . ." the deep voice of Bill Stuckey intoned, "those that aren't hanged. You'd do well to remember McBride being hauled aloft by the neck . . . Signing that petition could be signing your own death warrants. That's the truth. I'll never sign, that's certain."

"You've changed your story, Bill," another whispered. "I've a memory of you cursing the captain with more passion than any."

"I haven't changed a word. I say Hart is a coward, a tyrant, and not fit to command, but no petition or even a refusal to sail will see him replaced; any who believe otherwise are deceived. The Lords Commissioners love their blue-eyed son too dearly. Being flogged or hanged will not rid us of that whoreson, but I do not hate him less."

"Nor England," one of the men muttered.

"I am as loyal an Englishman as any, Pierce, but the English way of governing is near its end. That's as sure as old age and a shrivelled cock. The Americans and the French are but a few years ahead of us in their pursuit of liberty."

"Aye, let us have government in the French manner—government by the mob . . . That'll suit us."

"A few necks might have to be severed to bring us the liberty we deserve."

"Severed? We've already had a man with a severed finger lost overboard, another hanged—and if there was ever a less likely murderer than Mick McBride I'd like to hear his name. Now Tawney's beaten bloody, and Giles takes a little tumble from the mizzen top. I think we've suffered enough and got no liberty for it."

"Liberty is not so easily bought, Mr Pierce. The Americans signed a Declaration of Independence, not a fucking petition."

"If we don't sign the petition or refuse to sail, than what is left us, Mr Stuckey? Will you tell us that? A daily serving of Hart's beatings while he flies from every transport that ships a six-pound gun?"

"*Sentry . . .*" the lookout hissed, and the men scurried into their hammocks.

The sheer-hulk finally appeared and lifted the main mast into place, more than doubling the riggers' work, though Hayden knew it would go more quickly as the men grew confident of their skills, especially the bosun, who appeared to have been just waiting to learn his trade but had never had the opportunity.

As they were in port, the mail arrived regularly, and Hayden was surprised to find one day a package, carefully wrapped, come from London. Upon opening the mysterious bundle, he discovered a copy of Motteux's translation of *Don Quixote*, accompanied by a short letter from Mrs Hertle.

My dear Lieutenant Hayden:

This rather substantial volume was sent me by Miss Henrietta Carthew with the request that it be passed on to you when next we met. As I have no way of knowing when such a meeting might occur, and fear it might be later rather than sooner, I am sending the book along to you in the post. With it come my fond wishes that such a gift will give you much pleasure, as much for the spirit in which it was given as from the many hours of delight that reading such a prodigious book must provide.

Mrs Robert Hertle

It was, admittedly, a somewhat aged volume. Hayden took it up, running his fingers over the cover. There was no inscription, to his disappointment, but a leather placemark stood proud, and he opened the book to it. Someone had tooled a small image of a mounted knight with a lance facing what might have been a windmill—it was difficult to be certain. For some reason, he began to read at the open page, and in a few lines found this:

That's the nature of women . . . not to love when we love them, and to love when we love them not.

Hayden shut the book with a dusty "clap," and stared at the faded cover. Had Henrietta meant him to read this, or was it merely coincidence? Perhaps there was a message here from the long-dead Cervantes— or from his hapless hero. "Don Quixote of the Sea" she had named him, but then he had the impression that she was fond of the Quixotic in men. He decided he would take the book as Mrs Hertle seemed to suggest he should—as a sign of favour. As encouragement. The fact that he was rather easily encouraged he would not give much credence this day.

Some weeks after Hayden found his way aboard the *Themis*, Lieutenant Landry received a letter from Captain Hart stating that he would arrive three weeks hence, and expected the ship to be ready for sea. To manage all that was to be done the workday was lengthened and Hayden oversaw the rigging crew, spending much time teaching the arts of the sailor to landsmen.

"How is it," he asked Landry as they took a meal in the gunroom, "that we have so few seamen aboard this ship? I've never seen the like."

Landry shrugged. "We take what the impress gangs turn up, Mr Hayden. Prime seamen are in short supply."

They were certainly in short supply aboard the *Themis*, Hayden was sure of that. After dinner, as Hayden was about to mount the stair to the quarterdeck, he heard young Wickham above. "I've learned more from Mr Hayden in a few weeks than I've learned the entire last year in the service. He's a thorough sea-going officer, our Mr Hayden. Don't you think, Mr Barthe?"

"The captain'll soon take that out of him," the master growled.

Weeks passed, carrying summer away, and Hayden was pleased to see improvement in some fraction of the crew. It was not, by any means, a majority, but there were some who appeared to be gaining a measure of pride from all that they accomplished and in the smartness of the ship. These men went to work with a will and strove always to deliver their best. No more "accidents" occurred nor were any men found beaten—at least none of whom Hayden was aware. Tawney had returned to duty, though Hayden thought him dull-eyed and hesitant. The seaman's claims that he remembered nothing of the night he was beaten were believed by the doctor, but Hayden thought the man appeared always cowed and fearful.

Topmasts and yards were swayed up and the rigging completed. The ship was scraped and painted, and sections of deck suspected of leaking were repitched (time would, no doubt, prove their notions wrong in this—deck leaks were devilishly tricky to track down). The ship was gradually put in order, victuals stored by the master and the holders, and the ship watered. September saw the days shrink, but summer appeared determined not to be banished that autumn and the days remained warm late into the month, the fall rains delayed.

As the sails were being bent one such afternoon, the powder hoy came alongside, her people calling for all fires to be extinguished. The unsettling business of loading and storing powder took longer than one would imagine, for all the care put into it. There was, aboard, a peevish disquiet readily discernable among the men until the barrels were all safely stowed in the plaster-lined magazines. Then the crew began to breathe again, smiles appeared, and all hands went back to their business in the usual way.

"All the powder is stowed, Mr Barthe?" The two officers and Wickham stood watching the crew of the powder hoy cast off their lines.

"That was the last barrel, Mr Hayden."

"Well, I am glad of it. I don't know why, given that we handle powder almost daily, but the loading of powder unsettles me. I never get past it."

"I feel much the same, and think it just as odd."

Hayden reached into a pocket for a handkerchief to wipe his sweating brow, but found, instead, a folded square of paper. Opening the sheet revealed a crude drawing—a caricature, really—of a sailor with a quill, signing the name "Jack Tar" to a long sheet of paper entitled "Petition," but at the same time, another, identified by the label "Lord Commissioner," was crossing out the word "Petition" and writing above, "Death Warrant."

Hayden stared at the sketch for a moment.

"Is something the matter, Mr Hayden?" the master asked.

"I have just found this in my jacket, though I am certain it was not there when I first donned my coat this morning, for I placed my handkerchief in this very pocket." He passed the drawing to Barthe, who became suddenly grave.

Wickham tried not to appear intrigued, but let his gaze stray toward the sketch. Barthe returned it to the lieutenant, who passed it to Wickham.

"What does it mean?" Wickham wondered. "I mean, that it was in your coat?"

"It means someone very sly slipped it in my pocket, but why? that is the question. Do either of you have any knowledge of a petition being circulated—either among our own people or among the fleet?"

Both shook their heads but Barthe appeared very out of sorts, his hands suddenly agitated, a blush creeping over his face.

"Gather the officers and young gentlemen in the gunroom, if you please, Mr Barthe."

The master touched his hat and hurried off, leaving the lieutenant and the midshipman alone at the rail. Hayden began to search his memory for any man who might have been close enough to him that morning to slip something into his pocket, though he could still hardly believe it might be done without his knowing.

"The men bending the fore-staysails, Mr Wickham—do you know them?" Hayden had not yet learned the name of every man aboard.

"There you have Starr, Worth, and Marshall, sir."

"And how were these men employed before they came aboard the *Themis*, I wonder?"

Wickham tugged at his ear. "Starr worked the cod and haddock fishery, Mr Hayden; he's been all his life afloat. Marshall laboured in a limestone quarry—he says that life in the Navy is like to a holiday for a quarryman. Worth apprenticed as an Adam Tiler."

"An Adam Tiler . . ."

"I believe so, Mr Hayden. I'm sure that is what he told me."

"And do you know what an Adam Tiler does?"

Wickham looked a bit embarrassed. "Is he employed in the repair of roofs, sir?"

Hayden forced himself not to smile. "An Adam Tiler is the associate of a *Fork*, better known as a pickpocket. When the Fork has relieved his victim of their valuables he immediately passes these goods to an Adam Tiler, who slips off with them." Hayden turned to regard the men bending sail forward. All three had been near him that morning as the powder was slung aboard. It was not difficult to guess which might have been able to slip a bit of paper into his pocket unnoticed.

"It would appear, Mr Wickham, that Worth completed his apprenticeship and moved on to a higher calling."

"Will you want to have a word with him?" Wickham asked quietly, clearly chagrined that Worth had practised upon him so successfully.

"No. You understand how the sailors feel about informers," Hayden said, feeling his face grow warm at these words. "I would rather have a man provide anonymous warnings than none at all—which is what will happen if I confront him with this. Say nothing to Worth about this matter, Mr Wickham, nor to any other. I should not like to have him suspect that we are in the least aware of his . . . *gifts*."

Those who resided in the gunroom took the chairs. The remaining warrant officers and the young gentlemen gathered at the table's end nearest the door. Hayden stood opposite them, the incriminating sketch folded into the fingers of one hand.

"Pass this along, if you please." Hayden handed the sketch to Barthe, who unfolded it, glanced at the contents, and passed it on. From one set of hands to the next it made its way down the length of the table to Mr Franks, standing at its end. The men around him leaned forward to catch a glimpse of this mysterious object, then it made its way up the table's starboard side and back into the waiting hands of Lieutenant Hayden. The men stared at him expectantly with only the occasional glance from one to another. A throat was cleared.

"Does any man among you," Hayden began, "know of a petition being circulated, either aboard the *Themis* or among other ships in the harbour?"

Perfunctory denials, general shaking of heads, but few present met the gaze of their first lieutenant as this went on. Hayden felt his frustration build. He had no doubt that some were not telling him the truth—the very men he hoped to win over, whose trust he must gain.

The two rows of faces gazed back at him now, looks of studied blankness frozen in place. An outburst was bubbling beneath Hayden's surface—but then understanding washed over him like a cool wave. If there were a petition, it was almost certainly to request Hart's removal— and none of these men but Landry would oppose such a scheme. They might even secretly be encouraging it. How would *that* be received within the Admiralty?

"I want you to consider carefully what goes on aboard our ship," Hayden said, struggling to keep his voice calm. "Penrith was murdered. Tawney beaten . . . brutally. I am not convinced that Giles did not have some help falling from the mizzen top. If there is a petition being circulated aboard the *Themis*, it has stirred up some rather notorious passions, and it would seem that the petitioners are determined to have it signed . . . no matter the cost. All of us should have learned by now that revolts can start with a list of apparently reasonable demands. Any officer who is cognisant of such a petition who does not speak up will certainly face a court-martial. If you have heard even a rumour, unsubstantiated though it may be, it is your duty to speak out, now."

Again the heads shook, though barely.

"None, sir."

"Not a word, Mr Hayden."

Hayden felt utterly betrayed, his frustration waxing into a blistering anger. "Return to your duties," he snapped, making no attempt to hide his feelings.

The men filed out rather hurriedly, leaving only the doctor, who sat at the table's opposite end. When the room was empty he fixed Hayden with his intelligent gaze.

"You realize, Mr Hayden, that if there were a petition to remove Captain Hart, most of those men would happily add their names, would it not mean the end of their careers."

Hayden sat down in a chair. "I do realize it."

"Do not take this matter personally, Mr Hayden. It does not mean these men do not respect you or hold you in high regard."

"I cannot imagine what else it could mean, Doctor."

"Their dislike, even hatred, of Hart outweighs their loyalty to you, whom they have known only a short time. Hart they have endured for many months or even years." The doctor swept some crumbs off the table with the flat of his hand. "Do not expend your energies defending Captain Hart, who would not do the same for you."

What was Hayden to say to that? The First Secretary had put him aboard to bear Hart up, not to allow him to be undermined, no matter how justifiable the men's cause.

"A man has died, Doctor. Another was beaten bloody. Whoever circulates this petition, and I assume such a document exists, deserves punishment. It does not matter how legitimate their grievances might be, their methods condemn them."

A brief memory of a man being hauled up into the Paris night, above a throng of enraptured faces.

Griffiths nodded. "Yes. Of course, you are right."

Hayden closed his eyes an instant to drive the image away. "You know nothing of this matter, I take it?"

"Nothing—and that is God's truth."

"I doubt it has come from such a high authority." Hayden gazed up at the white overhead. "I shall be obliged to bring this matter to the attention of Captain Hart."

This captured the doctor's attention. "You might consider the case of McBride before doing so," Griffiths cautioned. "Captain Hart's idea of justice resembles firing a musket ball into a mob—he does not much care whom he strikes, believing the lesson will be that much stronger for its randomness."

Hayden closed his eyes. For a brief moment he found himself feeling a black resentment toward Philip Stephens for placing him aboard this cursed ship.

"Then what am I to do, Doctor? If I choose not to bring this matter before Hart, hoping to protect the innocent, I will be protecting the guilty at the same time."

"You have described my years of service under Captain Hart most accurately. It is always thus—damned no matter what course is chosen. All

I might say to relieve your distress is that one grows used to it over time, even if one never learns to like it." The ship's bell tolled, and Griffiths nodded to Hayden. "I must look in upon my charges." He rose to his considerable stooped height, but did not take his leave immediately, regarding Hayden seriously. "Do not be so downcast; Hart deserves whatever comes to him."

"Perhaps," Hayden said quietly, "but do I deserve it?"

The muffled clatter of footsteps, a knock on the door. Hobson's round face appeared in the narrow opening.

"Mr Barthe has sent to tell you our wind is fair, Mr Hayden."

"Some good news, at least. I shall be on deck directly. Have Mr Barthe prepare to weigh." But Hayden stopped suddenly. If the men will sail, he thought.

Despite taking the deck with some trepidation, Hayden found his fears were groundless; the men went to their stations without complaint. No delegation approached him on the quarterdeck bearing a list of demands. Of course they were only moving a half mile, the fair wind allowing them to shift their berth, from the Hamoaze out into Plymouth Sound. Hayden longed to take the *Themis* out of the sound and stretch her shrouds and stays, to gauge their efforts, but that exceeded his authority, so they came to anchor in the mostly open sound and hoped the wind would not veer south.

Hayden walked slowly around the deck, inspecting the ship. He had been up the masts and over every inch of the rigging. With her new paint she all but gleamed in the sun.

The master, Mr Barthe, descended the main shrouds and stopped when he reached the rail to examine the deadeyes and lanyards critically. Noticing the first lieutenant standing nearby he tipped his hat, his manner most deferential, almost fawning. Hayden suspected it was from feelings of guilt—from refusing to admit he knew of the petition.

"She looks very well, Mr Hayden," the master ventured. "Your efforts have not been in vain."

Hayden pressed down the desire to confront the man with his duplicity, realizing it would do no good. The officers had made their decision and would not change it now.

"I think she's up to whatever chance might send, Mr Barthe. Are we up to it? that is what I wonder."

The master glanced quickly away. "She'll take all the weather Biscay can send us, I should think."

"On deck!" came a call from aloft. "Captain approaching."

Barthe called for his glass, and peering through the brass cylinder, he nodded. "Captain Hart," he said, lowering the glass, and then, beneath his breath, "Damn my eyes."

Eight

Captain Hart came over the rail, wheezing heavily from the effort. Corpulent, florid, choleric—these were Lieutenant Hayden's first impressions. Hart's small boots settled on the deck and he looked around angrily, as though searching for some offender. Hayden glanced at Landry, who stood frozen in place, pale as a cloud, his gaze fixed straight ahead. Realizing the second lieutenant would not introduce him, Hayden stepped forward.

"Lieutenant Charles Hayden, Captain Hart, at your service."

Hart stared at him as though he had offered some insult, the man's jowls quivering with barely suppressed anger.

"So you're the Admiralty's beached lieutenant," he spat out, "undeserving of even a brig-sloop. Well, you can hardly be worse than the last." Then, almost as an afterthought, "Damn his eyes . . ."

Hart turned away from the startled lieutenant and glanced up at the masts. "Landry?"

"Sir," the little lieutenant said, taking half a step forward.

"Who got the masts in? You?"

"Lieutenant Hayden, Captain Hart." Landry's gaze dropped to the deck like a fumbled twelve-pound ball.

Hart turned back to the still-shocked Hayden. "How is it, sir, that you passed for lieutenant without learning even the rudiments of rigging?"

"I can't imagine what you mean, sir," Hayden said through clenched jaw, all his considerable anger thrown against its restraints. "Perhaps the captain would be so kind as to explain . . ."

"I'm sure you don't, sir." Hart pointed at the shrouds. "Are they not cable-laid?"

"They are—"

"Did no one ever explain that the tails of the shrouds on the larboard side should lie forward?"

Hayden could not believe what he'd just heard. "I believe they should lie aft, Captain Hart . . . as they do on every ship in His Majesty's Navy."

"Damn your insolence, sir!" Hart thundered, spraying the deck with phlegm. "Bring me a glass," he ordered, and in a moment a running midshipman placed a glass in his hand. Hart thrust it at Hayden and pointed at a nearby frigate. "Do me the honour, sir, of inspecting that ship's rigging."

Hayden raised the glass to his eye, forcing his hands, which trembled with anger, to be still.

"Do you see? The tails of shrouds on her larboard side lie forward," Hart stated.

"You will pardon me, sir, but they lie aft. I can see it plainly—"

The glass was snatched from his hands. "Are you blind as well as simple?"

"Sir! I protest—"

Hart, who had begun to turn away, spun back toward him, his face now crimson, jowls ashiver. He waved the glass in the air as though he might strike Hayden with it. "You protest? You protest! Damn your insolence, sir! Aboard my ship you protest nothing! Aboard my ship you heed my orders. You do not protest. You do not offer your precious opinions unless they are asked." He glanced to his right. "Does this amuse you, Mr Landry?"

"No, sir."

"Then make ready to get under way. We sail with the tide."

Captain Hart stormed below, servants scrambling to bring up his effects. Left standing in his wake was a stunned first lieutenant. Hayden had not been treated thus since he was an ignorant midshipman.

Hawthorne caught his eye and raised an eyebrow. He was suppressing a smile. "Welcome to our brotherhood, Mr Hayden," the marine said softly. "We call ourselves 'The Blind in Heaven,' for our eyes have been damned to Hell with such passion and frequency that we shall certainly proceed to the Hereafter without them." He tipped his hat, smiled, and set off about his duties.

Hayden gathered the shreds of his dignity and secluded himself on the aft-most portion of the quarterdeck, where he struggled to control his rage and to soothe his much-wounded pride. He had challenged a man to a duel for a less significant offence than he had just received from Hart! If the man had not been his commanding officer . . .

Almost worse than the treatment he had just received from Hart were the eyes of the crew upon him. If he glanced along the deck, members of the crew would quickly fix their attention elsewhere.

"Mr Hayden, sir?" It was Wickham, standing a few paces off, looking somewhat embarrassed. "There is a lighter alongside and a civilian asking permission to come aboard . . . Shall I call the captain?"

"I will find out what the man wants."

Hayden went forward in time to meet a gentleman as he came over the rail.

"George Muhlhauser, from the Ordnance Board," the man offered, then extended a hand and Hayden took it. "Are you the first lieutenant?" the gentleman asked softly.

"So I thought . . ." Hayden responded, still incredulous at the treatment he had just received.

The man looked a bit confused at this response but then went on. "No doubt Captain Hart told you I'd be along . . . ?"

Hayden shook his head.

"I'm to sail with you to test a new gun of my own conception . . . Lieutenant . . . ?"

"Hayden. Charles Hayden." He tried to shake off the rage that still boiled inside him.

"I will require the aid of the carpenter and his mates, and likely the gunner, too. We'll have to unship one of your present guns and put the new in its place. Not a small job, I will admit, but easily done by capable men who set about their work with a will."

"Am I to understand, Mr Muhlhauser, that we will be testing a gun on our cruise? That that is our purpose?"

"You are to make no allowance for the new gun whatsoever, Lieutenant, but to go about your business; engage the enemy as you see fit. The benefits of the new design will very quickly become apparent. It can be traversed easily, for it sits upon a truck that has transverse wheels at its stern. It then pivots . . . but you will see, Mr Hayden. Let us bring the gun aboard."

Hayden went to the rail, where a number of men had gathered to stare down into the lighter. Around him he could feel the palpable tension. A few men made efforts to conceal smirks. The new lieutenant had just received his comeuppance, pleasing the indolent no end. Hayden tried to concentrate on his task and push his recent encounter with Hart out of his mind—with only very partial success.

"Mr Barthe, rig tackles, if you please," Hayden ordered.

A gun of novel design was hoisted aboard. It was followed by an iron carriage of a type wholly unfamiliar to Hayden. The men gathered around to stare at this oddity.

"It looks like a foreshortened eighteen-pounder Blomefield, Mr Muhlhauser," Hayden speculated. "Is it not somewhat compressed in the chase, almost a cousin to the carronade?"

"It is a special casting, keeping all the best features of the Blomefield gun but shorter, as you say. Even so, it has most of the range of a standard eighteen, and far more than a carronade." He patted the strange carriage. "But herein lies the real difference—like a carronade carriage but of iron and with many small advancements, as you will see."

The second lieutenant appeared, and the bosun sent the men to their stations.

"Mr Landry," Hayden said, "which gun would the captain have us replace with Mr Muhlhauser's invention?"

"I cannot say, Mr Hayden."

"Well, could you inquire of him?"

"I could, sir, but he would just damn my eyes for not being able to make a decision on my own. Though were you to make a decision without consulting him he would berate you for overstepping your authority. You will be damned either way."

"Then let us be damned for independence rather than being poltroons." Hayden turned away from Landry. "Mr Muhlhauser, it is common to mount carronades on the quarterdeck and the heavier long guns below. As your gun is neither of these I am unsure where it should be placed."

"On the gun-deck, if it is possible, Mr Hayden. It is meant to replace long guns, not carronades."

"Then we shall mount it on the gun-deck, sir."

The *Themis* did not sail on the tide that afternoon, for the wind dropped away to a sigh and then the tide turned against them. As the captain did not invite any of his officers to dine with him, even though one was new to the ship, Hayden messed in the gunroom. Had he dined with the captain, Hayden might have been tempted to mention the cartoon he had found in his pocket, but it was scant evidence. The captain would likely think it nothing more than a prank on a new officer, and certainly Hayden had no more evidence than that to show Hart, so resolved to say nothing.

Mr Muhlhauser was invited to join them, which he happily accepted. With the town of Plymouth almost within a pistol shot, they dined well that night, and would continue to do so until their fresh victuals were exhausted.

After their earlier gathering in this very cabin, when Hayden had presented the officers with the sketch discovered in his pocket, there was a general air of discomfiture, which the men did much to disguise with heightened spirits and false good-will. All were especially solicitous and respectful of the first lieutenant, perhaps to take the sting out of his up-braiding at the hands of the captain, or out of guilt at having lied to him earlier in the day, which Hayden remained convinced they had done. It mollified his doubly bruised feelings somewhat, though he wished they would not laugh so heartily at his attempts at wit, as it embarrassed him more than a little—the hilarity being far more than his small jests deserved. In truth, he was still out of harmony with his messmates and had not yet recovered from the great humiliation he had received at the hands of the notorious captain.

"Naval gunnery has shown little advancement over the years," their guest said. "The Army has made better progress in the use of artillery."

"It is uncommon for the Army," Hawthorne suggested, "to use their guns upon ground which is heeled, rolling, pitching, and occasionally yawing, all at once. Claret, Mr Hayden?"

"And they don't have to work their guns crouched like monkeys," Mr Barthe added, his eyes involuntarily following the progress of the decanter as the marine raised it toward the first lieutenant.

"What Mr Hawthorne says is true," Hayden said, holding out his glass so that it might be refilled, "but here I must agree with Mr Muhlhauser—thank you, Mr Hawthorne—our accuracy at a distance is poor. Most actions are fought at less than a cable-length—often considerably less—where rate of fire and weight of broadside are decisive."

"That is my thinking almost exactly, Mr Hayden!" Muhlhauser enjoined with considerable passion. "The carronade is a wonderful weapon, and magnificently effective at very short range, but the long gun . . . I believe, is a weapon whose day has passed. Actions fought at one hundred to two hundred yards—that is what my new design is meant to address. It is shorter, so it will be quicker to run out and altogether easier to load. It can be readily traversed, making it more effective—to some degree one can aim the gun rather than aim the ship, if you take my meaning. The gun is elevated, like a carronade, by a screw through the cascabel. The carriage of iron and wood, by careful arrangement of its constituent parts, is not as heavy as one might think, and the slide and pulley system I have devised dampens the recoil and allows the gun to be run out with alacrity. Because of the use of wood in the slide, there need be no fear of sparks, which, of course, would be disastrous. With its robust pivot below the gunport, the carriage can never topple, with the injuries that commonly ensue, nor should one ever have a loosed cannon. Small improvements, but we must begin somewhere." He leaned forward into the lamplight, his enthusiasm for his subject clear on his face. "What I imagine will happen one day is that the cascabel will open so that the gun can be loaded from the rear."

"And how would that be managed?" Landry asked.

Their guest shrugged. "As of yet, I cannot say. I have thought that the cascabel might screw out, allowing the wadding, shot, and cartridge to be pushed into the afterbarrel, but I wonder if the explosive effect of firing powder would seize the threads, making it difficult to open. It is the recoil of the gun that most engages my curiosity, though." He began to make descriptive gestures with his hands. "It has occurred to me that the recoil of one gun, through a lever arm and pivot, could be used to run out a second gun. Do you see? All guns would be mounted in pairs, each pair connected by an arm with a pivot at its centre point. The gun in the aft position would be loaded, and the firing of the forward gun would drive the other ahead and into the firing position. The great weight of one gun would dampen the recoil of the other, for there would be, if not quite an equal, at least an opposite reaction."

Hayden was about to comment on the genius of this suggestion, though he might have also wondered about some of the more practical problems that would have to be solved, when the surgeon came in. The doctor had been called up to the captain's cabin just as the meal commenced. Folding his tall but sparse frame onto a chair, his legs tucking under the table with some difficulty, he nodded to his gunroom companions.

"Dr Griffiths," Mr Barthe greeted the newcomer. "I've kept your dinner warm and defended it from the ravenous hordes as best I was able."

"Thank you, Mr Barthe. I shall ask the captain to mention your singular act of bravery in his next submission to the Admiralty."

This brought laughter from the others.

"And how is our patient this evening?" Hawthorne wondered. "Down for a few days, do you think?"

Everyone looked hopefully at the surgeon.

"Perhaps. Difficult to know."

"Well, I dare say Mr Hayden can command the ship, if need be."

The others nodded eagerly, agreeing too heartily. Muhlhauser glanced at him, but Hayden was in new waters himself.

"Is Captain Hart often unwell?" Hayden asked, fearing that he sounded dreadfully uninformed.

"Often enough," the surgeon answered, after it became apparent that no one else would. "He must pass a small stone. After that a day of rest will see him on his feet again. As you are new here, Mr Hayden, and do not know the signs, the captain is often at his most . . . bilious when he feels the onset of the pains that signal his body is about to pass a stone. One is best to do nothing to raise his ire during such times."

"Advice I shall do everything to heed." Hayden felt a small change in the ship's motion. "Is the wind making, Mr Barthe, but in the sou-sou'west?"

"I'm not sure, sir. Shall I have a look?"

"Don't interrupt your meal, Mr Barthe," Landry said. "I shall send a midshipman up to take stock of the weather."

"No need, Mr Landry." Hayden rose from his seat, certain now that the wind had come up and not from a favourable direction. "I will see for myself."

He excused himself, happy to be out of the atmosphere of forced good cheer, and made his way out of the musty warmth up to the deck. From the south, across the Channel, a breeze of wind bore landward the sea scent—the bitter iodine of salt and rot. A shadowy squall darkened the horizon, thin stalks of rain dangling down into the sea. Against this bruised sky, caught in a spike of light, the glittering wings of gulls scythed down the rain like so much blackened wheat.

The master appeared a moment later. "So it has come around, just when the tide has turned against us."

"Yes, the weather glass is falling and the air has cooled noticeably."

A vast acreage of woollen, grey cloud drew slowly over the blue and a pennant at the masthead began to flutter and snap.

"I believe we shall have a gale, Mr Barthe." Hayden stood looking out to sea. "Will the hands sail, do you think, Mr Barthe, or will they come forward with a petition to be passed to the port admiral?"

Barthe slapped his palm on the rail cap—once, then twice more. "I don't know, Mr Hayden."

"Well, we have no choice but to find out." Hayden hesitated only a second. "Call the hands to veer more cable. I fear this will soon become an uncomfortable berth, but the tide will be against us for some time yet and we have little choice but to sit here and take whatever the weather sends. The moment the tide turns slack we will call all hands to weigh and clear the sound. Then we will know what the crew plan, I assume." Hayden looked around the sound. "A dozen other ships are preparing to do the same, and it will be to our advantage to be ahead of them and weather the headlands by dark."

"And if the crew won't sail, Mr Hayden?" Barthe asked softly.

There were too many possible answers to such a question, so Hayden confined himself to the most practical. "Then we shall need another anchor. Prepare the small bower, Mr Barthe. I don't know if we will be able to row it out if this sea gets up, but we might be forced to try."

"Aye, Mr Hayden."

Landry appeared on deck then. "Captain Hart wishes us to weigh and make sail, Mr Hayden. He wants us clear of Plymouth Sound before the gale freshens." The little lieutenant appeared grey-faced in the failing light.

"But there is yet a strong flood against us, Mr Landry."

"I made the captain aware of the tide, Mr Hayden. He was most emphatic in his disregard for it."

"I'm sure he was," Barthe mumbled.

Hayden took a long, calming breath. "Rig the capstan bars, Mr Barthe," he ordered.

The master leaned over the rail to assess the tidal current. "With this wind and foul tide we'll be lucky to hold our own, Mr Hayden."

"You are remonstrating with the wrong man, I'm afraid. Are we coiled down? Chafing gear fitted?"

"We are, sir." Barthe glanced at him, his manner suddenly guarded, shoulders round, his commonly ruddy face grown pasty.

"Then make ready to loose sail as the anchor breaks free. Larboard tack, Mr Barthe. Mr Franks?" He looked about and found the bosun six paces off. "I can have no tardiness among the sail-handlers. I want to lose as little ground as possible when the anchor heaves."

Franks made a knuckle, then nodded to his mates, leading them forward, though his common swagger was not apparent this evening.

Hayden took stock of the situation in the sound, marking the positions of other ships, gauging the distances with a practised eye.

"Helmsman? Have you spun your wheel?"

"I have, Mr Hayden. She runs free, the rudder answers, and I inspected the tackles and tiller-rope meself." The man at the helm—a master's mate named Dryden—raised a knuckle to his brow, tipping the invisible hat. "If I'm not speaking out of place, sir, this wind freshens. The sea will get up before you can say Jack Ketch."

"It will be a wet beat, that is certain. Cawsand Bay is filling with ships. We must be ready to come about. Do you hear, Mr Barthe? We will have to tack smartly at Cawsand Bay. We must shift our yards and trim sail with all speed."

The wind continued to freshen until white horses streaked across the bay, breaking now and again against the bow, spray flying up into the rigging.

The gentleman from the Ordnance Board appeared on deck and took hold of the rail to steady himself. "Your gun is secure, Mr Muhlhauser?"

"It is, Mr Hayden." He looked a little pale, suddenly. "We are beginning to plunge about . . ."

"Hardly a ripple. We shall see much worse in an hour's time."

Hands were called. Some came at a run while others lagged behind, a look of resentment clear upon their faces. Hayden had found some followers among the crew—men who were deeply displeased with the way their ship was run and who took pride in both her handling and appearance. These men were not in the majority, however. Hayden could see them setting to work around the deck, everywhere thwarted in their efforts by the shiftless and embittered. It was almost a contest—those who worked with a will and those who strove against them. Some men stood openly engaged in no duty whatsoever. But no party came forward with a petition or even a list of grievances.

"Shall I muster the marines, Mr Hayden?" Hawthorne had appeared at his side, and he too was unsettled by the scene unfolding.

"That will be the captain's decision, not mine."

"Captain Hart is in his cabin. In his cot, in fact, too ill to take the deck, I should think."

"Nonetheless, it is the captain's decision, so let us wait and see what transpires. There appears to be no unity of purpose among the men."

"That might be so, Mr Hayden, but some are clearly choosing not to hear orders."

The other officers and a few young gentlemen appeared on the quarterdeck, having abandoned their suppers. Upon their pale faces both anxiety and hope mixed, though they said nothing, gathering in a silent, waiting knot of blue coats.

Hayden felt his one chance to return to sea, to prove himself, slipping away, for certainly if Hart were removed the First Secretary would recall him as well. But Hayden had been trained never to vacillate, and began to make his way purposefully forward. He could see that the men were not all of one mind at this moment, and Hayden knew he must exploit that before the insubordinate faction got the upper hand.

"Ship the capstan bars," he ordered, making eye contact with one man after another. "Starr. Freeman. Marsden." He made certain to call them by name so that they must refuse the orders of an officer directly before witnesses. If it came to a court-martial this would weigh heavily against them.

"You heard the lieutenant," a deep voice growled. "Ship the bars." It was Stuckey, and Hayden turned in time to see the landsman give an ungentle shove to a seaman named Green.

"Mr Barthe?" Hayden said loudly. "Whom else have you detailed to the capstan? Call their names."

The master began a roll of names. Hayden found each man as Barthe named him.

"Smyth. Marshall," Hayden repeated. "Take your places."

Slowly, the men fell into place. Hayden noted that there were a few among the crew who pressed men forward. Threats were muttered. Clearly the crew was divided. A man stumbled to his knees, certainly shoved from behind, but he rose and went to his place. The carpenter and his mates came forward, for they had their parts to play.

Wickham moved among the men, prompting them, warning that he would take down their names if they refused. Hayden glanced aft to find most of the other officers and young gentlemen gathered by the taffrail—officially off-watch unless called. Landry had come forward to offer his aid, but the hands often ignored his orders and waited until either Hayden or Wickham had called them instead.

Hawthorne gathered up all the marines on sentry duty and led this small company, under arms, onto the gangway—only half a dozen men, but the mustering of red coats did not go unnoticed.

Even when the capstan was completely manned, the hands stood passively, none putting their chests against the bars. Hayden approached them.

"I have called you all by name," Hayden said, keeping his voice calm but firm, "and will do so again if you refuse to follow orders."

Franks steered for them, brandishing his rattan, but Hayden raised a hand to stop him.

"Mr Franks, if you please." Hayden turned his attention back to the men at the capstan. "If it comes to a court-martial, and you have refused to answer orders, I will be forced to give your names to the president of the court. You have all been read the Articles of War. Be sure your cause is worth your lives, for that is the gamble you take."

It was a decisive moment. A completely united crew would likely have their demands met—the Admiralty had done it before, usually removing unpopular officers—but part of a crew in revolt almost certainly would be dealt with most harshly and the men were well aware of it. Hayden had to prey upon the men's fears, though it shamed him to be driven to such methods.

"Mr Franks, prepare a boat. I will send Mr Archer to the nearest ship. We must inform them that we approach a state of mutiny here."

"Aye, Mr Hayden."

This had the desired effect. The hands began glancing one to the other, Hayden's words finding their mark.

"Who wants to be hauled aloft like Mick McBride—kickin' and squirmin'?" Stuckey asked. "That's where you lot are headed. Shall I tell Mrs Starr and the wee ones that you died in a good cause, eh, Jimmy boy?"

Hayden could almost feel the collective will of the hands vacillating. The wind chose that moment to die completely and ominously away, leaving only a little breeze wafting this way and that across the deck. The hands looked only straight ahead—not at their mates—each man seeing himself flying aloft, rope about his neck. Stuckey nodded to Cole and the two pressed their chests against the bars, bracing themselves to push. For a moment no one followed, and then Starr joined them . . . and then another did the same, then another. The men stamped bare feet on the planks and began to press the bars forward—stamp and go. With an eerie creak the cable stretched, and the wind, redoubled, returned, a gust lifting a mist of spray over the rail.

Hayden heard himself exhale—a long-held breath. Around him the men went, one by one, to their places, looks of fear and frustration upon their faces. Wickham appeared at his side.

"You've done it, Mr Hayden," the boy said quietly.

"We are not out of the sound yet." Hayden caught the bosun's eye. "Mr Franks? Thrashings will not aid us at this moment; indeed, they might work against us. Order your mates to start no one. And tell Mr Archer there is no need to go off to another ship—at this time."

"Aye, sir." Franks hurried across the deck, waving at his mates.

Hayden gazed up toward the sail-handlers waiting above.

"They will have the common sense to loose sail when the anchor heaves, will they not?" Wickham asked.

"That is my hope, Mr Wickham. If they do not, we will be ashore in a moment."

The capstan turned and in due course the anchor broke free, streaming a dark trail of mud as it reached the surface. It was fished and catted by sullen hands, many an accusation and whispered threat among them. Under any other circumstances Hayden would have called for silence, but this situation was more volatile than gunpowder dust. He dared not inflame the men's already simmering anger.

To Hayden's lasting relief, sail was made, the ship fell off, then gathered way. Yards were braced sharply around, and they began the short board toward Cawsand Bay.

Hayden turned and made his way aft past Hawthorne's marines. "Thank you, Mr Hawthorne. I think you might return these men to their duties now."

Hawthorne touched his hat. He looked as relieved as anyone aboard, for he realized how close they had come to lowering muskets and taking aim at their own fellows.

Hayden approached the wheel as the off-duty officers retreated below, hardly glancing his way, involved in their own whispering and recriminations. Barthe, Hawthorne, Wickham, and Hayden collected by the larboard rail, gazing out to sea.

"That was a near-run thing," Wickham breathed.

"Too damned near," Hawthorne intoned. He gripped the rail with both hands, rocking back and forth twice. "And where was our brave captain during this affair? In his cot! Had you not stepped forward, Mr Hayden, I think it would have gone against us. I really do. Thank God Mr Franks and his mates did not shirk. They, and a few of the hands, made all the difference." The marine was suddenly very still, a look of dumb surprise on his face. "I never thought I should be the one trying to preserve the rule of Captain Josiah Hart." He shook his head. "Duty is a strange mistress."

Hayden glanced over at Mr Barthe. The man had done his duty and supported him as he should, but he now looked like a man who'd lost a child. Such misery spread over his face, Hayden thought he might weep.

Landry hurried onto the quarterdeck then, whipped off his hat, and combed fingers through his thinning hair. He was so agitated he could not stand still. "Well!" the little lieutenant said. "Well! That was as near a mutiny as I shall ever want to see."

"Yes, Landry," Hawthorne answered, eyeing the officer with dislike, "we preserved your hero from the consequences of his own folly."

"Mr Hawthorne," Hayden cautioned. "All our passions are running high. Let no one speak words he later will regret."

The anger and pent up frustration of the men around him was palpable, but they had not given in to their feelings and had instead chosen reason and duty.

"Mr Hawthorne speaks the truth," Barthe growled. "We have saved Captain Hart so that he might damn our eyes and abuse us at every turn. That is what loyalty to England will bring you." He spat over the side. "God save the King." The master turned away and crossed the deck to speak with the helmsmen.

"We all have duties to attend." Hayden watched the master go, a little shocked by his oath. "I will keep the deck until we are in the Channel. Stay alert, this matter is not behind us yet."

The *Themis* was a weatherly ship, but her new rigging stretched a little, and she did not hold her own against wind and sea. By the turn she had lost ground, and then she was among a dozen ships beating out of the bay in a small gale, white-maned seas streaming across the sound and breaking against Hawkers Point. Slowly, board by board, they gained against the rising wind. Penlee Point passed beneath their lee with the last dim light, and a hard rain began to batter them as they stood out into the Channel under reduced canvas.

Hayden felt the muscles of his back release. "Your watch, Mr Landry."

"Aye, Mr Hayden."

"Keep the lookout sharp. At least a dozen ships fled the sound as we did. Mr Hawthorne has stationed more of his men about the ship than is usual, but keep your wits about you this night. We have had enough 'accidents.' "

The little lieutenant touched his hat, a mechanical gesture. Even in the growing darkness Hayden could see the fear.

Below, Hayden found Muhlhauser in the gunroom with Hawthorne and Griffiths, the surgeon, who sharpened an amputating knife upon a small stone. The marine lieutenant raised a decanter. "I am no medical man, Mr Hayden, but I believe our doctor might prescribe a small restorative . . . ?"

"God, yes . . . if the doctor recommends it," Hayden answered, and Hawthorne filled a glass. Hayden shed his dripping coat, Perseverance taking it forward to hang by the ship's stove.

"A little perseverance goes a long way," Hawthorne said as the boy disappeared.

Hayden actually laughed as he sank down on a chair. "Well, with a little help from the ebbing tide, we weathered, and are in the Channel proper. Are your marines all with us, do you think, Mr Hawthorne? I fear there will be much recrimination and ballyragging among the hands. We don't want it to break out into a brawl."

"I believe my men are loyal, Mr Hayden."

"Even so, put those you trust most to watch over the arms chest and the magazines."

"I've already done so, sir."

Hayden nodded his thanks, then turned to the civilian guest, who sat looking out of sorts and ill.

"How are you feeling, Mr Muhlhauser?"

"Better, sir, thank you."

"He fed the fishes," Hawthorne offered, "and that set him up."

Finding the gunroom excessively warm after the gale on deck, Hayden excused himself and retreated to his cabin to shed his waistcoat. As he unbuttoned it, someone came into the gunroom, huffing and stamping—Barthe, Hayden assumed. The rustle of clothing being shed, and then the laboured complaint of a chair.

"Four boards we made against a flooding tide," he heard the master protest, "and lost ground on every one. You do not gain a crew's confidence by such seamanship."

This brought an awkward silence.

"Has Landry run to the captain to tell what transpired?" Barthe wondered aloud.

"Be wary, Mr Barthe," Hawthorne warned.

"The little snitch isn't here," Barthe responded. "Well, Doctor, what do you say now? Did I not warn you that we would have such capers before long?"

A whispered warning, uncertain in its source. Hayden emerged from his cabin and Barthe all but jumped in his chair at the sight of him.

"What do you mean, 'such capers,' Mr Barthe?" Hayden asked directly.

Barthe glanced around at the others as though appealing for help.

"Mr Barthe has a theory that our crew has, for some time, been on the edge of mutiny," the doctor said, scraping steel over stone, "just waiting their moment. Then they will murder all their officers and . . . and . . . Well, I'm not quite sure what they will do then, other than hang."

"And did we not just have a near-mutiny, Doctor?" Barthe demanded. Rising from his chair, the master began pacing back and forth along the length of the table opposite Hayden. The slow pitch and roll of the ship hardly seemed to matter to him, he had been so many years at sea.

"I was below seeing to my patients, Mr Barthe. I heard no sounds of fighting. Did I somehow miss those?"

"Mr Barthe," Hayden interrupted, "how is it that you did not speak out when I gathered all the officers in the gunroom this very day?"

Barthe continued his pacing, hands tucked behind his back like thin wings—his arms could not quite encircle his substantial girth. "The disaffection of the crew is no secret, Mr Hayden; you have spoken upon the subject yourself. It can be witnessed at almost any hour of the day by those who choose to see it. Perhaps I should have spoken up when you quizzed us, but I possess no more evidence than any observant man might gather himself in a few hours. It is true that for quite some time I have felt among our crew a resentment simmering, which I have at times opined might boil over into something more violent."

"At times . . . ?" Griffiths wondered.

"What do you mean, Doctor?" Hayden asked, unable to hide his annoyance that neither man had bothered to speak of this earlier. Only the fact that Barthe had supported him so strongly when they weighed in Plymouth Sound kept him from roasting the man—sailing master or not.

"I think Mr Barthe should explain," the doctor answered. "It is his hobby-horse."

Barthe stopped to take a drink of penitent water a servant had fetched him, then glanced at Hayden, clearly uneasy with his situation. "No doubt you have felt the same things as I, Mr Hayden. I cannot offer you names, but I believe there is an element among the foremast Jacks—not all of them, by any means, but a good number—who have the other men cowed, frightened of them. Penrith's murder was at their hands, I believe."

"Ah . . . Penrith's murder . . ." the doctor intoned theatrically.

"I have heard the whispering among the crew!" Barthe said passionately, turning on the doctor for an instant. "And seen how quickly they fell silent when an officer or even another crewman drew near. You were not upon the deck just now, Doctor, but if Mr Hayden had not acted so decisively we should have had a mutiny, I'm certain of it."

"Now, Mr Barthe—you overstate matters," Hawthorne cautioned. "The crew might have refused to sail—were on the verge of it, I think— but that is not quite a mutiny in the sense that you mean. I don't think it would have come to violence."

"But we have already had violence," Barthe sputtered. "Penrith murdered. Tawney beaten."

"Were the same men responsible for both, Mr Barthe?" Hayden asked.

Barthe shook his head. "I—I know not. As I say, I cannot offer you names, but that does not mean I am not right. You saw what happened this night."

"I did, though it was difficult to make out who took what side. Stuckey and Cole clearly pressed men forward and supported my efforts, for which I have not yet thanked them. A few men went to their stations as soon as they took the deck, but any number of them might have been merely waiting to see how events fell out. There appeared to be a great deal of indecision upon the part of many. But I must tell you, Mr Barthe, if it is your belief that this ship is in danger from mutineers it is your duty to report it to Captain Hart."

Barthe stopped walking and stared into the darkened stern, where the rudder swept squeakily back and forth. He then fixed his gaze on the first lieutenant. "Mutineers are executed, Mr Hayden. One doesn't want to go about accusing anyone without strong, one might say incontrovertible, evidence."

Hayden glanced at Hawthorne, whose face remained a mask of mildness and disinterest.

"That is true, Mr Barthe," the first lieutenant continued, "but one might express one's concerns to the captain in general terms without naming any particular man. It would then be upon the captain to find the truth of the matter."

Barthe glanced around at the others, as though looking for someone to rescue him. "After what happened to McBride, sir, I would be afraid to speak."

Hayden felt a shiver run through him. "Then you think McBride was innocent, as well?"

The master shrugged. "He swung on a very slim rope, Mr Hayden, if you take my meaning. I shouldn't like to see it happen again." Barthe reached up and steadied himself by grasping a beam. "And what of you, Mr Hayden? Will you report what happened this evening to the captain?"

Hayden was taken aback by this. "I have no choice but to inform the captain. It is my duty."

"Whereupon you will be asked to name the men who were insubordinate, or nearly so, and some or all of these men will be flogged." Barthe stopped and turned quickly toward Hayden, surprisingly agile for a man of such girth. "Do you believe that will lessen the resentment of Hart among the hands?"

"Are you suggesting I should say nothing, Mr Barthe?"

"Certainly it is not my place to tell you how to execute your commission, Mr Hayden." He glanced up at the low deckhead. "I wonder if we haven't carried the mainsail too long? If you'll excuse me. Gentlemen."

The door clicked shut, leaving the gunroom silent but for the distant sounds of the wind, the creaking of the ship as she worked in the seaway. The smell of smoke and burning candles overlayed the odours of too many men living too close together.

Hayden turned his gaze to the marine lieutenant. He was tempted to ask Hawthorne if he shared Barthe's opinions, but knew full well that he dared not offend his supporters, who were too few as it was. "It seems that there are several men who don't believe in McBride's guilt. Did no one speak up on the unfortunate man's behalf?"

"Wickham did," the doctor said, holding his amputating knife up to the light to examine its glittering edge.

"And no one else?" Hayden asked, shocked.

The doctor reapplied his blade to the whetstone. "Only Lord Arthur has been granted immunity from the captain's wrath. Where one man is accused for so little cause, can there not be two? Or three?"

Hayden could hardly stay in his seat, and pushed it back from the table, bracing himself against the roll of the ship. "These are very serious accusations, Dr Griffiths."

"They are not accusations, Mr Hayden. Merely observations. I did not speak out because I had no information either for or against Mr McBride, though I believed him a man of mild disposition and unlikely to commit murder. Certainly that is no defence, as others of similar temperament have been proven guilty beyond a doubt."

A knock on the gunroom door preceded the face of the captain's servant. "Captain wishes to see you, Dr Griffiths, if you please."

"Immediately," the doctor answered, without looking up from his task, and then, as the door closed, he added softly, *"Damn my eyes."*

Nine

Hayden lay in his cot, mulling over the events of the day—the near-mutiny or insurrection or whatever one was to call it. Even a refusal to sail until demands were met was, by definition, a mutinous act—though surely there had been many such cases and in most the crew's demands had been met.

He wondered now what the First Secretary had known about circumstances aboard the *Themis*. Did he realize how deep the crew's disaffection went? Was it Stephens' belief that Hayden could remedy it? Did the First Secretary not realize that a first lieutenant, no matter how competent, without the complete confidence and support of his captain was next to powerless? Lieutenants merely wielded the captain's power in his place—and possessed no more authority than their superior allowed them. Hart's upbraiding of his officers before the crew undermined what little authority they had, and made the performance of their duties doubly hard.

What a contrast was his present situation to his position aboard the *Tenacious* under the able Captain Bourne. There was an officer who had not forgotten what it was to be a lieutenant! He would never criticize his officers before the crew, but instead spoke privately with them regarding any matter he felt had not been handled as it should. He guided his officers, aided them—oh, he demanded a great deal of them, but no one complained. They knew what a great service he offered. To graduate from Bourne's school was to have a most thorough knowledge of one's trade. Hayden had never imagined that he would ever find himself so thwarted by his own captain.

For a long time sleep remained elusive, and Hayden fell into a reverie of Henrietta Carthew, recalling her eyes, the high colour of her face, the delicate curve of her neck. A dream swept up and enveloped him like a wave. The slow motion of the ship became the act of love—Henrietta beneath him, the soft cushion of her breasts against his chest as she rose to meet each cresting sea. All around them water, warm, infinite, breathing, breathless.

Ten

The south-west gale freshened throughout the night, veering to west-sou'west, which ended all progress on their desired course. At first light, Hart ordered the ship into the shelter of Torbay, where the captain remained below, still laid low by the stone that would not pass. All through the squalling night, the surgeon had been in and out of Hart's cabin, plying him with physic that appeared to do little but mollify the pain.

Through the doctor, Hayden requested an audience with the captain upon a matter of some urgency. After being left standing for three quarters of an hour outside the captain's cabin before an increasingly embarrassed marine sentry, he was admitted into the sick-room.

Despite the greyness of the day, the cabin was darkened by curtains and a tarp covering the skylight on deck. Hart lay in his cot, barely swaying in the calm. His face appeared swollen, eyes narrow and glazed.

Griffiths stood to one side and favoured Hayden with a slight nod.

"What is it, Mr Hayden, that is so urgent?" the captain snapped, his voice a rasping whisper.

"I felt it my duty to inform you, Captain Hart, that yesterday, when we took the ship from anchor, there was a moment when I feared the men would refuse to obey the officers' orders. It appeared that a significant faction of the crew had some half-formed plan to refuse to sail."

"Is that so?" Hart pressed a hand to his forehead and closed his eyes in apparent pain. "Well, I am not greatly surprised. No doubt, in my absence, and without experienced officers to govern them, the crew formed many strange notions. I must tell you, I am amazed, sir, that you would come in here to inform me of events that do nothing but reflect badly upon you. Let me assure you, Lieutenant, that had I been on the deck, the men would have gone about their business with a will. Do not disturb me with such trivialities again. I am ill and do not wish to be plagued by confessions of your incompetence. Now leave me in peace, sir."

With barely a glance at the doctor, Hayden swept out of the cabin in such a fury that the sentry stepped back from him in no small alarm. Unwilling to meet his messmates in such a rage, Hayden climbed up into the air, where he paced across the quarterdeck before the taffrail, trying to master his anger. He had almost certainly saved Hart from being relieved of his command. *And this was the thanks he received!*

A fine, misting drizzle formed a glistening haze upon his coat, and chilled his face and neck. His temper, however, was not so easily cooled. An hour he paced until a deluge forced him below, where he secluded himself in his cabin and tried to smother his feelings in a forced reading of *Don Quixote*.

The anchorage at Torbay was crowded with an Atlantic-bound convoy forming, along with its escort of three frigates and two brigs. There was also a seventy-four-gun ship at anchor, having sought refuge to repair some damage to her bowsprit and jib-boom. The *Themis* had found a berth among the crowd, and settled down to await a fair wind, or at least the cessation of the present gale.

Hayden sat writing at the tiny table in his cabin. Even on the berth-deck, the howl of wind in the rigging could not be ignored, and now and then a blast of wind would strike the ship on either bow and she would sheer ponderously to one side or the other before regaining her proper attitude, head to wind.

Hayden examined two lists that had been delivered to him: the first, the sick-and-disabled list for the night of Penrith's murder, delivered to him by the doctor; the second, an enumeration of the crew. He began by writing names of men who were not ill on the night of Penrith's murder. With a crew of two hundred six, this took a little time, but finally he had a list of men who had escaped illness on the night in question. This list he compared with the men who had appeared to be considering refusing to sail, though this was a rather uncertain roll.

After some time spent in contemplation, he decided there was no clear correlation between these lists that he could see. Stuckey, he noted, had not been ill the night of the murder, but nor had someone as noble of nature as Giles—the foremast giant. Smithers had been well, as had Smyth, Price, Starr . . .

"Mr Hayden, sir?"

Wickham stood in the doorway to his cabin, a number of books in hand. Were it not for the uniform, he would have looked like nothing so much as a cherubic schoolboy, curly flaxen hair and all.

"Mr Wickham."

"If I am not interrupting, sir. There is a matter upon which I would ask your counsel."

"As long as it isn't marriage, Wickham. I know nothing of women—who, despite men's observations about ships' feminine qualities, I have found to be rather unlike ships."

Wickham did not smile but looked instead rather troubled. "No, sir, it is about these . . ." From beneath one of the books he took two worn pamphlets, and looking around quickly at the empty gunroom, passed them to Hayden.

To his surprise, the lieutenant found himself holding copies of *Common Sense* and *The Rights of Man*, penned by Thomas Paine.

"I found these among some books that Mr Aldrich returned to me." The boy bit his lip. "I was not sure what to do with them, sir."

Hayden gazed at the stained paper, and took a long, deep breath. Would there be no end of this? Holding up *Common Sense*, he asked, "Do you know what this is?"

"A pamphlet, sir, that criticizes the King and the English form of government."

"Aye, it is that and more. This little tract was read by almost every literate person in America when it was published. It inflamed a great deal of resentment toward the crown."

Wickham nodded. "I think Mr Aldrich gave them to me by accident, sir."

"I dare say, you are an unlikely convert to revolutionary ideals. You read them . . . all the way through?"

Wickham nodded again. "Do you think Mr Barthe is right, Mr Hayden? That there are radicals among the crew, who are mutinous?"

"I don't know, Wickham. You witnessed what happened so recently in Plymouth. The captain is of the opinion that it was the result of the ship being left in command of incompetent officers. But mutiny . . ." He glanced down at the pamphlet in his hand. "It takes a great deal of disaffection to drive a crew along that road, for more often than not it ends badly for the seamen involved. I don't think a little pamphlet will lead a crew to mutiny."

"It led a colony to revolt, sir."

"Perhaps it helped that particular cause, but the Americans had a better chance of success—most mutinies end with the perpetrators hanging from the yard."

Wickham considered this. He had the rather emotionless affect of a child when he deliberated—it was impossible to tell what he was thinking or feeling from his too-innocent countenance. "Then we should let the matter be, Mr Hayden? Say nothing?"

Having recently gone to the captain to report the insubordination in Plymouth, he was reticent to take him these pamphlets. Hart was likely to berate him as anything else. He glanced at the midshipman, wondering why the boy had brought this matter to him.

Perhaps Wickham had not forgotten what befell McBride—he'd been the only one to speak up on the man's behalf—and was afraid of such a thing occurring again. Hayden, however, had responsibilities. It was not the first lieutenant's place to keep secrets from his captain, nor was it within his authority to be dealing with possible sedition. At the same time, he was afraid of what Hart might do. After all, Aldrich was the best of the able seamen—diligent in the performance of his duties. Hardly the stuff of a mutineer.

"I will speak with Aldrich," Hayden heard himself say. "It is only a pair of pamphlets, after all, even if the author has been charged with seditious libel."

Wickham nodded and gave him a tight-lipped smile that revealed some relief: the matter was out of his hands and he hadn't had to report it to the captain.

"Can we keep this between ourselves, Mr Wickham?"

"I shall never repeat a word of it, sir." But the boy still stood in the door, and Hayden had a sudden fear of what he might reveal next. "It is strange, is it not, Mr Hayden, that a few words should be perceived as such a threat to the King? That a little pamphlet such as that could stir up such a fever for revolution?"

"I am of the opinion that ideas are born that fit their age, and this is the age of republican ideas—liberty and the rights of men. We have only to look across the Channel to see what ideas can do."

"Though helped along by a great incompetence of governance," Wickham said thoughtfully. "I don't believe there can be revolution where there is a just government, Mr Hayden." He waved a hand at the pamphlet. "That is but a seed, sir. It must land on fertile ground to grow, don't you think?"

Hayden was reluctant to admit anything of his beliefs to this young nobleman whom he did not really know. "Many would agree, Lord Arthur. Many would agree."

"Have you been to America, sir?" the midshipman asked.

"I have. My mother lives there, in Boston."

"She's American, then—your mother?"

"She married an American . . . some years ago."

"Then your mother is English?"

"French, actually."

"Is that why you speak it so well?"

Hayden nodded.

"I speak it a little, as well," Wickham said in French. "I had a French nursemaid when I was a boy."

"Commendable accent, Wickham. Very commendable."

"Thank you, sir. You've been to France?"

"Many times."

"Then why have they turned so murderous, sir? Mr Aldrich says it is a thousand years of pent up resentment."

Hayden felt a sudden oppression settle over him. It was a question that often haunted him late at night. "With all due respect to Aldrich, it is more complex than that. Have you ever witnessed a mob in motion, Wickham?"

The boy shook his head. "I have not, sir."

"It is not a sight you soon forget." Hayden drew in a long breath. "Mobs are lawless by nature, almost by definition. It is impossible to know who the mob might turn against, for its mood is both violent and volatile. Fear is what drives the people, I have come to believe. Once you are swept up in the pack you are in danger. To prove that you belong, a person must win the approval of the others—at any cost—and to accomplish this one must stand out, be seen performing some act more violent than the last. If one man breaks a shop window, someone else must steal the goods, another sets the building afire. And thus it escalates, each actor claiming his place in the mob. The shop owner and his family are dragged into the street. Someone kicks the owner, another strikes him with a club. Bodies are disfigured, men and women murdered. It escalates from acts that are lawless to atrocities, even abominations—drinking your victims' blood, eating their organs. Nothing is taboo."

"I read about what was done to the prisoners . . . in Paris," Wickham whispered, his face terribly serious. He hesitated, went to speak, stopped, and then finally asked hoarsely: "Do you think the hands feel such resentment toward us, Mr Hayden?"

"Perhaps some do, at least aboard this ship. I have found that the foremast Jacks respect officers who are fair, though not lax, in the performance of their duties. A tyrant might be feared but he will never be respected. But you have nothing to fear, Mr Wickham. You are well thought of by the crew, it is quite clear."

"Why thank you, sir, but I know I have much to learn."

"As do we all, Mr Wickham. The sea is a harsh schoolmaster and we will never learn all that we must know. But you have made a very credible start."

Wickham tried to smile. "Good night to you, then, sir."

"And you, Wickham."

The little midshipman went out the door to the gunroom as one of the servant boys stole in. Hayden slipped the pamphlets under his crew list.

"Well, well," he muttered. Young Wickham was proving to be a more interesting charge than he had expected. Having spent his quota of years in the midshipmen's berth, Hayden had, more often than not, found his companions to be a heedless lot and not much concerned with scholarly pursuits. But these midshipmen, in company with Third Lieutenant Archer, had formed a debating club, and read and debated every book they could acquire. And most, if not all, of these books Wickham lent to Aldrich. A strange alliance: a foremast Jack and the son of a nobleman. Hayden thought it said much for both man and boy.

He noted that Wickham had timed his visit well—there was no one in the gunroom, only Archer, asleep in his cabin. He was no fool, young Wickham, and a good judge of character, too, it seemed—or so Hayden flattered himself. But could he live up to the boy's obvious esteem? In truth, Wickham had put him in an awkward situation. His duty was to tell Hart about the pamphlets, but he knew now what that would lead to. He would have to deal with Aldrich himself, though he was uncertain what his course of action should be.

The lieutenant called for Perseverance and sent him to search out Aldrich. The able seaman appeared a few moments later, pressing a knuckle to his brow. It occurred to Hayden, and not for the first time, that Aldrich had the best mannerisms of a gentleman, though dressed in a seaman's slops. He was modest in character, assured but never boastful. The men before the mast esteemed him greatly, for he was the best seaman aboard and was always helpful to those finding their way. What struck Hayden most was the keen look of intelligence in the man's eye, as he observed all that happened around him. The high, smooth forehead, indicative of intelligence, was crowned by lank, yellow hair.

"You sent for me, Mr Hayden?"

"I did, Aldrich." Hayden was not quite sure how to start this interview, and for a moment regarded the sailor, too tall for the low deckhead, stooped in the open cabin door. "You are a prodigious reader, I am told?"

"Aye, sir."

"Where did you learn it?"

"From the parson upon the *Russell*, sir. I was his servant boy and he taught me reading and proper speech."

"Is it true you have read all the doctor's medical books, for so he told me?"

"Yes, sir. They were hard sailing, Mr Hayden, but I doubled all the capes of anatomy and navigated the perils of physic and bleeding."

"Is that your desire, then, to be a surgeon's mate?"

Aldrich looked a bit surprised by the question. "No, sir. I once assisted Dr Griffiths with an amputation when his mate was ill . . . It was a sight I hope never to witness again." The man made a face.

Hayden almost smiled. "Yes, I don't think it would be my calling, either. But you could be a bosun's mate and no doubt a bosun in short order."

"With all respect, Mr Hayden, I should never want a position where I might have to beat or flog my fellows." He paused a second. "Nor is it my desire to have authority over others. Mr Barthe once offered to put my name forward for master's mate, but I told him I could not accept."

"All men are created equal?"

Aldrich nodded tentatively.

"Which brings me to these . . ." Hayden retrieved the pamphlets, which he had hidden a moment before. "Wickham was showing me some books he had from you, and these were lodged among them."

Aldrich looked suddenly apprehensive, his mouth forming a tight line and a crease appearing between his eyebrows.

"This man, Thomas Paine, has recently been convicted of seditious libel and outlawed from England. I do not want to know if these are your property, or even how they came to be among Wickham's books, which, I realize, have been read by numerous men aboard. I have only one question: are you party to any subversion of, or mutinous designs upon, this ship or her officers?"

Even in the warm lamplight Aldrich appeared ghostly pale, stooped in the doorway. For a moment he regarded the cabin sole, and then raised his head and met Hayden's eyes.

"I'm not a mutineer, sir."

Hayden felt a little wave of relief. There was something in Aldrich's tone, in the way he carried himself, that would not brook disbelief. "No, I don't expect you are . . ."

"I must, to be fair, tell you, Mr Hayden, that I do believe even a lowly sailor has the right to protest his treatment if it is manifestly unjust."

Hayden closed his eyes. "Please tell me that it is not you, Aldrich, circulating this petition."

Aldrich lifted his head a little until it made gentle contact with the deckhead.

"I withdraw that question," Hayden enjoined quickly. "Do not answer it. I hope, however, that this crisis has passed and there will be no trouble when next we weigh . . ."

"I doubt there will, sir. The men seem resigned to their situation, if no less resentful."

"There is no petition circulating presently?"

Aldrich hesitated, a struggle clear upon his face. "None presently," he said under his breath.

"Aldrich, I must caution you: the Jacks esteem you greatly, and if you go about promoting the ideas of Mr Paine or circulating petitions it could put you in grave danger. More than one of the officers believe that Penrith was murdered by subversive elements aboard the *Themis*. A pamphlet like this could get a man flogged—or worse."

"I do not preach mutiny, sir. But only common sense. Our own ship proves the point: you are the most capable officer aboard, yet you are not the captain. Where is the sense in that, sir?"

Hayden raised a hand. "Mr Aldrich, if you please, sir! There is talk that I cannot countenance as an officer of His Majesty's Navy."

Aldrich gave a quick bow of the head. "I'm sorry, sir. I misspoke myself."

For a moment Hayden was at a loss for what to say. "If you do not desire a master's warrant, then what is your wish?"

A look of almost happy contentment came over the man's face. "When this war is over, and I pray it will be soon, I would, upon my discharge, find a ship and work my passage to America, sir. There I might become a farmer, Mr Hayden, or a lawyer . . ." He shrugged, a little embarrassed at this fancy.

"Have you been to America, Aldrich?"

"Not upon the land, sir, but in the harbour of New York." The man's eyes shone a little, as though he spoke of a sweetheart.

Hayden hesitated. "Well, I hope you land there one day. Until then, I might caution you to show great prudence. I fear there might be trouble aboard the *Themis* yet, and I would regret it most profoundly if you in some way were caught up in it."

Aldrich nodded.

"You may return to your duties."

Aldrich put a knuckle to his brow. "Thank you, sir."

Hayden sat at his little writing-table, staring at the letter he had begun. What a ship I am on, he thought. The captain is a coward and tyrant. The midshipmen are all parliamentarians, and the most able seaman is a *philosophe*. And someone aboard is a murderer. He stoppered his ink bottle and cleaned his quill. He was not sure how to explain all that to the First Secretary. He was not sure how to explain it to himself.

A knock on the gunroom door, and a boy put his head in. "If you please, sir," he said, "I have been sent to remind you that you are to supper in the midshipmen's berth."

"Thank you. I shall be along directly."

Eleven

The gale did not show any signs of abating, and the ship rode uneasily to her cable, rain battering down upon the swelling planks, like a drummer beating to quarters. The midshipmen were hosting the three lieutenants and the doctor for supper, and putting on their best for it. A rather passable claret had been procured—from smugglers, Hayden expected—and the main course of mutton, pease (boiled), and boiled potatoes was wholesome if not inspiring. The claret was the highlight of the meal.

Hayden looked around the crowded table. Beside Wickham was seated Mr Archer, then an unusually pensive Dr Griffiths, Freddy Madison, James Hobson, Landry, and the two other mids who had rejoined the ship a few days before Hart's return. Their names were Tristram Stock and Albert Williams. Trist and Bert, they were called by their fellows, who were forever after finding nicknames for the crew—most of which they could not use to the men's faces. Hayden thought it would be better not to know what they had christened him.

He wondered how a captain such as Hart had come by such a fine crop of middies. Certainly he did not deserve them . . . nor did they deserve him. But then Hart's wife was so well-connected it was perhaps not to be wondered at.

Hayden was answering questions about his service, and was a little embarrassed by the way the midshipmen hung on his every word. "After I passed for lieutenant, I was Third aboard a sixty-four."

"I've never been aboard a sixty-four," Madison said. "Was she crack, did you think?"

Landry looked up from his food, a dab of gravy upon his tiny chin almost lost among the freckles. "Everyone knows the sixty-fours are all crank, Madison," he said sourly. "A seventy-four is the ship you want to serve aboard."

"Is that true, Mr Hayden?" Madison asked, earning him a foul look from the second lieutenant.

"What Mr Landry says is true of many of the old sixty-fours, which is why they have been given such a poor character. But the ships built to the draught of the *Ardent*—the *Agamemnon* is one—they are fine sailers. Almost as handy as a frigate, but with a greater weight of broadside, of course, for they have a full deck of twenty-fours as well as a deck of eighteens. They lie-to very close, do not pitch overly, and almost never gripe or yaw. I don't remember ever missing stays if there was even a breath of wind. All in all, fine ships."

"Why, then, does the Admiralty not order more of them to be built?" Landry asked, gazing at him darkly.

"Well, Mr Landry, that is a good question. I believe it is because they are not really heavy enough to stand in the line of battle, unlike the seventy-four, which makes them very high-priced frigates. I have been told that one can build two frigates for the cost of a sixty-four-gun ship, so that is your answer. I have often thought the natural employment for a sixty-four would be to carry a commodore's flag in a frigate squadron. Three or four frigates and a sixty-four would make a formidable little fleet—fast and deadly."

The midshipmen glanced at one another, all of them now persuaded of the admirable qualities of a sixty-four. Landry went sullenly back to his meal.

"If you please, Mr Hayden, tell them the story you told me," Archer said, a little smirk appearing. "About the man on the mizzen gaff . . ."

Hayden had to smile himself, for the thought always amused him. "I was a middy at the time," Hayden said. "On the North American station."

"During the American War?" Wickham asked.

"In 'eighty-two. I was on the quarterdeck, and we were about to get under way with other ships of our squadron. Aboard a twenty-eight named the *Albemarle*, we all saw a man climbing out to the end of the mizzen gaff, apparently to clear a flag pendant. A visitor on the quarterdeck asked what the man was about and a lieutenant proposed that he was preparing to protect the flag with his own life, to which a wit responded, 'It must be Nelson.' "

The middies laughed.

"Who is Nelson?" Stock asked, though he had joined in the mirth.

"Captain Horatio Nelson," Archer said, rolling his eyes. "It is all well and good to have your faces stuck in books, but you should pay attention to events within your own service!"

"He is a fine officer," Hayden said, "but known to be a little . . . *zealous* at times. *He* has a sixty-four now, I've been told."

"Who is the finest captain you ever served with?" Williams asked.

"Bourne, without question," and then Hayden quickly added, "not to disparage Captain Hart, whom I have only served for a day. We used to say that if the men aboard his ship had been allowed to elect their captain from among all the souls aboard, they would choose Bourne without a dissenting vote, he was that well-loved. You have never seen such a seaman, nor a braver man in action. I believe I learned the greater part of my trade from him, and one could not ask for a better master." Hayden thought it was time to turn the conversation away from himself. "And you, Mr Landry . . . what was your favourite ship?"

"My service has been small compared to many: I was a reefer aboard an ancient seventy-four to begin, but she was condemned after my first real voyage, and later broken up; then I was aboard the *Niger*, a thirty-two-gun frigate; a little brig named the *Charlotte*; a ship-sloop; and our present ship. The *Themis* is by far the best, though I much liked the little brig as she was so very handy, and she bore us through a frightful winter storm in the Atlantic. We all lavished great love and care on her after that."

No one seemed much interested in Landry's career, and fell silent a moment. Hayden had never known a man passed for lieutenant who had served aboard so few ships, and wondered at it.

"Tell me what you've been reading," Hayden said to the middies in general. "There seem to have been some lively debates in the midshipmen's mess these past weeks."

"Mr Burke, sir," Madison offered, with a look of some pride; *"Reflections on the French Revolution."*

"Have you read it, Mr Hayden?" Wickham wanted to know. The small midshipman peered at him intently in the lamplight.

"My friend Captain Hertle was kind enough to lend me his copy," Hayden said. "Did you think well of it?"

"Mr Archer liked it overly," the normally quiet Hobson answered.

Hayden turned to the young lieutenant, who concentrated upon his mutton. "Did you, Mr Archer? And what was your judgement?"

Archer patted his mouth with a napkin, taking a moment before answering. "I thought it contained more common sense than the writings of that man Paine, who is such a darling of the radicals—"

"Burke is a radical himself!" Landry interrupted. The second lieutenant drew himself up in his chair, glaring at Archer, who did not seem overly intimidated. "He supported the cause of the American colonists, and should have been expelled from England for his treason. Let him go live in America if he bears such love of the place, say I. If not for the success of the Americans the French would never have dared turn on their King. But now it is like a plague passing from one nation to the next, the French determined to spread it throughout the Low Countries, and even across the Channel. And the guillotine will travel with it, for the radicals are ever anxious to murder their betters. To murder anyone at all who dares speak out against their excesses."

"If you took the time to read *Reflections*, Mr Landry, I think you would soon see that Burke is very far from being a member of the Revolution Club," Archer offered in defence. "And I might remind you that there was no guillotine in America. Indeed, most of the loyalists were allowed to leave."

"Oh, America will not prosper," Landry predicted. "You will see. The colonies will turn on each other out of jealousy and greed. Without the English rule of law their precious solidarity will be cast aside at the first hint of imbalance of wealth or power and they will fall to warring among themselves."

"I think they will prosper very well," Wickham said. "And they will quickly rival the great powers of Europe."

Landry waved this suggestion away as though it were a few buzzing insects. "Radicalism is a disease," he pronounced firmly. "You all saw it yesterday aboard our own ship. Men do not jump to do their duties as once they did, but obey their orders in a desultory manner, a look of naked insolence upon their rum faces. We shall have mutinies aboard His Majesty's ships. Mark my words. Men will have to be hanged, for that is the physic that cures the disease. Men will have to be hanged."

There was a moment of silence, the lanterns overhead swaying, as a gust of wind shook the ship and moaned painfully in the rigging.

"You talk like a Frenchman," Archer said, "prescribing a good course of hanging to cure the ills of the Navy."

Landry did not much like the mirth that this caused.

"Paine has written a clear answer to Burke's *Reflections*," Madison offered into the silence.

"And was charged with sedition for it!" Landry said. "You have not been reading that tripe, I hope?"

Madison turned his attention to his dinner. "It was in the papers."

An awkward silence settled over the cabin, and Hayden found himself listening to the wind, hoping to hear it moderating a little—but in truth it moaned as loudly as ever.

"And what of you, Doctor?" Wickham asked. "What has been your recent reading?"

"Medical texts, Mr Wickham. I have given up on finding a book that will give me pleasure as earlier volumes did. I do not know why authors can but repeat what others have done before. Shall we forever make new books, as apothecaries make new mixtures, by pouring only out of one vessel and into another? Are we forever to be twisting and untwisting the same rope?"

"Perhaps the difference lies in nuance, Doctor," Archer answered. "A sonnet will always be a sonnet—the same metre, the same scheme of rhyme, perhaps much the same subjects—but in the hands of a man of genius each can be different from the other in subtle ways."

"As sheep are different one to another," Griffiths replied. "I prefer one book to be a sheep, the next a fish, then I should like to read a hawk."

"Perhaps, Doctor, you can invent a new species of book," Hayden suggested. "The authors of this world would like a new pattern to copy, I should think."

The others laughed, and toasts were offered to the fortunes of their cruise.

"Is it true that Admiral Lord Howe's officers will not drink his health in their own wardroom?" Wickham asked.

"That is the truth," Stock answered. "Pellin, a lieutenant aboard the seventy-four anchored off our larboard quarter, told me the same not two hours ago. They say Howe is shy and will not quit Spithead for fear of the French."

"Do you think the admiral is shy, Mr Hayden?" Williams asked. The thought seemed to disturb him a little.

"No," Hayden answered firmly. "I am uncertain of his tactics, but he is not shy."

"What do you mean, 'his tactics'?" Madison looked at him over the rim of his wine glass, the last few crimson drops disappearing down an indelicate chasm.

"He has chosen to keep the Channel Fleet at Spithead, trusting to frigates and smaller ships to watch the French fleet in the harbour of Brest. If the French put to sea, Howe will soon know and set out after them. But I believe these tactics will give way to a close blockade, such as has been arranged at foreign ports in times past."

"He will preserve both men and ships by this method," Landry said, "while keeping the sea is destructive of both, especially by winter. Men are ever too quick to call another 'shy' who have the good sense to apply a modicum of reason. *Shy . . . !*"

"That is true, Mr Landry," Hayden responded. "None can deny it, but if the French fleet slips away on a fair wind and the Channel Fleet is becalmed, as could well happen, the French might do terrible damage before they are found. But I do not mean to criticize Lord Howe, who I believe is a brave and able commander and should not be excoriated so by men who ought to know better."

"Then let us drink his health," Wickham said, raising his glass. "Lord Howe."

"Lord Howe!" the others echoed.

Glasses clattered back onto the table.

"We are to look into the harbour at Brest and assess the strength of the French fleet," Landry said, retrieving his fork.

Hayden clamped his jaw shut, trying to hide his anger. Hart should have told him of their orders before Landry.

"And then will we return to England or continue to cruise?" Williams asked.

"We are to trace the coast of France south," Landry said, "looking into every harbour large enough to warrant inspection, and to cause all annoyance to the enemy as we go."

"Let us hope we cause more 'annoyance' than last we managed," Madison said.

"We were unlucky, that is all," Landry pronounced too loudly.

This brought a troubled silence in which everyone became interested in their suppers, faces a bit flushed.

Landry seemed to take this as criticism. "You cannot go about firing upon neutrals or taking on enemy squadrons. We have only a deck of eighteen-pounders, I should remind you. It is all well and good to be a fire-breather when you are a midshipman, but a captain has to weigh each situation to a nicety and preserve his ship and crew . . . or face court-martial. Is that not so, Mr Hayden?"

"Indeed it is, Mr Landry," Hayden answered. "Indeed it is."

Twelve

My dear Mr Banks:

We are presently anchored in Torbay, awaiting a change in the weather. Plymouth Sound was left in our wake at nightfall yesterday, though not before an unsettling incident as we prepared to weigh anchor. Many of the crew would not, to begin, answer the orders of the officers. As Captain Hart was too ill to take the deck, I was forced to call each man to his station by name. With the assistance of some of the officers and crew we carried the day and the crew all went reluctantly to work. I reported this incident to the captain, but he seemed to think it was due to his recent absence from the ship and the resultant loss of discipline. I was not allowed the opportunity to assure him that discipline had not been lacking in his absence.

Second Lieutenant Landry informs me that our Orders are to cruise down the French coast assessing the strength of the enemy in various ports and to annoy the French wherever possible. Captain Hart remains laid up, waiting to pass a stone, the Doctor says. I am also told the poor man suffers from persistent migraines. I thank the Lord for my good health.

It seems that the recent endeavours of the Americans and the French have spread even to His Majesty's Navy. Two of Thomas Paine's pamphlets were discovered in the possession of one of the crew. The Midshipman who found them was reluctant to take this matter to the Captain, I think due to *the recent hanging of McBride, whom the Midshipman believed innocent. The crewman involved is without doubt the best of our able seamen, and the most diligent in the performance of his duties. I spoke with the man and he expressed a desire to one day live in America—the new promised land for seamen, apparently. I don't think he is in any way a danger to the ship or her officers. There is no doubt in my mind, however, that there is a great deal of disaffection among the crew, and if the situation were to be mishandled, the consequences could be severe.*

I remain as always, sir,
Your humble servant.

With a strong feeling of distaste, Hayden pressed his seal into the wax and gathered up the rest of his correspondence.

"You don't want the last letter copied, Mr Hayden?" Perseverance asked. The boy was standing by the door to his cabin, waiting to take the lieutenant's mail, his face serious, freckled, contemplative.

"Thank you, no, Perse. It is of a personal nature, and I copied it myself."

The boy nodded, apparently disappointed. It was one of his several qualities that Hayden had come to admire; he never shirked his work or complained of it. In this, he lived up to his name.

Hayden passed his letters to the boy, who hurried out to add them to the shore-going mail. For a brief moment Hayden almost went after him. What would Stephens do if Hayden refused to send in his hated reports? But Hayden let the boy go, fully aware of his promise to Stephens—his word was worth something, even if it was in such a disreputable cause.

Madison appeared at his door. "Captain requests your presence on the quarterdeck, Mr Hayden."

The lieutenant slipped on his coat and, out of respect for the low deckhead, tucked his cocked hat under an arm. In a moment he was on the quarterdeck, where Landry, Barthe, and Archer all stood awkwardly by the captain. Several of the midshipmen attended at three yards' distance.

"Ah, Mr Hayden," Hart said as his lieutenant appeared, "kind of you to join us."

"My apologies, sir," Hayden said quickly, tipping his hat. "I was unaware that I was wanted."

Glancing up at the sky, Hayden could see that the gale had almost blown itself out, great blue tears appearing in the woollen cloud. The wind remained in the south-east, but had moderated, and the rain stopped, though the decks were still dark from it. Beads of water hung from the mizzen boom, where they swelled until plucked by gravity. A cold drop struck Hayden on the neck as he tipped his hat.

Hart regarded his first lieutenant with a squinty gaze, eyes hazy-blue, almost hidden beneath a slightly bulging brow. The man's face was lined and waxy, and glistened with a thin film of sweat. Hunching a little, as though the pain had not entirely abandoned him, he reached out and took a spoke of the wheel in hand.

"This wind will fall away shortly," Hart said, pressing his words out. "And I anticipate it will veer to the north or nor'east. Let us quit this berth while there is yet light. Whose watch is it, Mr Hayden?"

"Dryden's, sir."

The captain glanced up at him, his face turning a little red. "Dryden? The master's mate?"

"Yes, sir," Hayden said.

"Who are the officers of the watch, then?" Hart demanded brusquely.

"Lieutenant Landry, Mr Archer, and Mr Dryden, sir."

"You do not stand out of watch on my ship!" Hart growled. "Where did you ever get such an idea?"

"It was so upon every frigate I served aboard, sir."

"Well, it is not so on my ship. You will stand watch like the other lieutenants. Get us under way, Mr Hayden. Shape our course for Brest." He released the wheel and motioned for Landry, who hurried to him so that the captain might put a hand on his shoulder. "Try not to foul another's anchor," Hart snapped at Hayden. "I shouldn't like the good name of my ship tarnished by your incompetence."

Griffiths, who had been hovering nearby, came to Landry's assistance, and the two of them helped the captain down the companionway.

"Well, Mr Barthe," Hayden said, fists clenching, thoughts of violence hovering about the edge of his consciousness. "Let us prepare to get under way."

"Aye, Mr Hayden," the master said, giving him what he thought was a look of sympathy, "and let us hope that the hands are more willing than when last we weighed."

"It is the officers I worry about, yourself and a few others excepted, Mr Barthe. Where is Mr Franks?" Hayden asked, looking around the deck for the broken-nosed bosun.

"He took the mail over to the *Captain*, sir. It was his intention to view our masts from forward as he returned."

Orders were called, and to Hayden's relief, men began to bustle about the deck, coiling down halyards and sheets, rigging bars to the capstan and readying the messenger line to weigh anchor. The hands did not appear happy in their work, but had returned, at least, to their former level of deficiency. Franks came over the side in the midst of this, ordering his boat taken in.

"How stand our masts, Mr Franks?" Hayden called out to him.

"Straight and true, Mr Hayden."

"Will you see to the paunch mat on the main-course yard? It all but chafed through in the gale, and I should not want it to do so again."

"It will not, sir!" Franks took one of his mates and Aldrich aloft to see to the paunch mats and hanging mats that protected various parts of the rigging from chafe.

The boats came over the side and were stowed on the reserve spars. A tackle was readied to cat the anchor, and men took their places at the capstan bars.

"It is a wonder to me that order can be brought to such goings-on," a voice opined, and Hayden turned to find Muhlhauser before the binnacle, regarding the spectacle with a mixture of awe and amusement.

"There is much to do at once," Hayden agreed, "but the men know their business tolerably well." In truth they were slow and badly organized, he thought, but he would soon put that to right, if Hart would let him. Hayden, too, observed the men, noting faces, dredging up names. Some worked with a will, several stood by, mystified, and still others bent to their appointed tasks only when Mr Franks or one of his mates came toward them brandishing a rattan or a rope end.

"Would one refer to this crew as 'motley'?" Muhlhauser asked, forcing Hayden to suppress a laugh. He glanced at the man's face to be sure he was not jesting, but the look of wonder and innocence told him he was not.

"I believe, Mr Muhlhauser, that the term would not miss the mark by a great deal."

Hawthorne stood on the deck a yard away, smiling. "It is perfectly correct, I think," the marine said. "You should see this crew wear ship, Mr Muhlhauser. They even wear motley."

This made Wickham and Madison both laugh, and in company with the marine lieutenant, they quit the quarterdeck rather hastily.

The look on Muhlhauser's face changed. "I believe I have been mocked," he said indignantly.

"Not at all, sir," Hayden assured him. "It was a play on words meant to amuse you, I'm sure."

"A play on words? How so?"

Hayden cleared his throat and pressed down his own laughter. "To 'wear ship' is to come about by bringing the wind across the stern. 'Motley,' beyond its common meaning, is a word for the costume of a fool or a jester. To 'wear motley' is to dress as a fool, or by extension, to be a fool. Mr Hawthorne only meant that the crew run about like fools when they wear ship. An insult to the hands, if to anyone."

Muhlhauser did not look either amused or mollified. "Well, if you are certain he did not intend insult . . ."

"I am quite certain he did not. Mr Hawthorne has not a mocking bone in his body."

This seemed to satisfy the inventor, and he tried to shake off his anger. "It was rather clever," he offered.

Hayden smiled. Too clever, apparently, he thought.

"What is it we do now?" Muhlhauser asked.

"We will back the fore-topsail as the anchor heaves. At the same time we will brace the yards around on the main and mizzen topsails. As the anchor heaves, the ship will begin to make sternway—travel aft—and by putting the helm over we will turn so that the wind will strike the ship upon the starboard bow. Do you see? Smartly, we will brace the fore-yards around, the sails will fill, and the ship will gather way and we will be off . . . if all goes as planned."

The men began to push their chests into the capstan bars then, and after a moment of straining, the capstan began to slowly turn. It was another long moment before the ship began to inch forward, the anchor cable stretching taut. Although there was a great deal of bustle both on deck and aloft, the ship moved only very slowly, its great displacement resisting the men's efforts at the bars. Due to the great girth of the anchor rode, it could not be made to turn around the small circumference of the capstan, so it was tethered by nippers to a much smaller messenger cable, and the nippers were removed as the cables neared the capstan. Slowly, so very slowly, the anchor cable was hauled in and arranged in the tier below.

"Aloft, sail loosers!" the master called into his speaking trumpet.

Finally, the anchor heaved, and sail was loosed, tumbling down like falls of water, Hayden thought. The fore-topsail backed, pressing against the mast.

Midshipman Williams stood by the rail, staring down into the water.

"Do we make sternway, Mr Williams?" Hayden asked.

The boy spat down into the water and watched the little cloud as it dissipated. "Not yet, Mr Hayden . . ." Then, after a moment, "Aye, sir."

"Put your helm over, if you please, Mr Dryden."

The wheel spun and the ship moved aft. Hayden looked around, gauging the distance to each vessel, assuring himself for the fifth or sixth time that they had room enough to manoeuvre.

A little brig had appeared at first light and anchored too close astern of them in an awkward arrangement. He could see her commander ordering men to veer more cable, but Hayden was confident they would stand clear of her.

The head of the ship appeared to fall off onto the starboard tack, and the headyards were braced around. Sails filled with a *thup*—a sound no sailor ever forgot. For a moment the ship made leeway, then her great mass began to slide forward, passing near the bow of the brig. Hayden nodded to her commander as the ship passed. The mizzen and jib were quickly set to balance the vessel.

"Stand by!" Barthe called up to the yardmen. "Let fall!" And the main and fore course cascaded down, bellying immediately to the small wind. The sand-glass was turned and the ship's bell rung. Staysails flew up their respective stays, and the ship heeled but a little, and then stiffened. The *Themis* passed among the convoy, her new paint rain-slick and shining dully in the fading light.

There was something a little forlorn in the scene: the gale-battered ships lying to their anchors in the quiet bay, like seabirds with heads tucked beneath their wings, the single frigate standing out into the channel as darkness threatened. Hayden felt both pride and sadness mix in his breast: pride that it was his ship setting out to carry war to the enemy, and sadness . . . he knew not why. There was a loneliness to the scene—all the ships with their crews hunkered below out of the weather, the lone frigate going forth.

The *Themis* stood out into the channel, and was not four miles from shore when the wind died away, leaving the ship rolling in the seas left behind by the gale. Hayden took hold of the mizzen shrouds.

"Look at this slop!" the master cursed. He cast his gaze around the horizon. "And where is our wind?"

"It will find us by and by," Hayden said, "and this will go flat at the turn of the tide."

Muhlhauser clung to the shrouds nearby, his face ashen and shiny. "And why should the tide turning flatten the seas?" he asked.

Barthe pivoted toward the poor man, his face kindly. "When you have wind blowing in one direction while the tidal current runs in the other it results in steep seas, but when the tide turns, the sea will flatten in a moment. I have seen it many times. Have you not, Mr Hayden?"

"Many times, as you say, Mr Barthe. And this sea is just left-overs from the gale. It will not last." The ship pitched and rolled terribly, and the sails began to slat fiercely. Hayden braced his feet and gazed up.

"I think we shall have to get the sails off her, Mr Barthe, or they will flog themselves to rags."

"Damn this sea to hell!" Barthe swore. "Mr Franks? Call the hands, if you please. We must have the sails off her."

The clouds tore to ribbons overhead, and the sun blazed through just as it set, going down into the sea in flames and glory. It was dark before the Jacks descended from the yards, muttering imprecations against the "fucking bloody sea." The work aloft had been hard with the ship rolling, not steadied by the wind in her sails. Men went to their much-delayed suppers then, and Hayden's servant brought him coffee, which he drank with his rump backed up against the rail and his feet spread like sheers.

After several hours of flailing about, the wind filled in from the north-west, and the crew made sail again. With the favourable wind, the *Themis* easily laid her course.

"The French coast by morning," Hayden said to Wickham, who was midshipman of the watch. "What is she making?"

"Just less than four knots, sir," Wickham reported.

"Well, perhaps by mid-afternoon."

The two stood by the rail, staring out at the last shreds of daylight. Around them, the familiar noises of a ship under way offered some comfort, though the forlorn cries of gulls pierced through.

"Does it feel strange to you, sir?" Wickham asked. "Going to war against your mother's people?"

The question took Hayden by surprise.

"I'm sorry, Mr Hayden," Wickham said quickly. "Have I been too familiar?"

"No, Wickham. It's just not a question I've ever been asked, though perhaps I have been anxious to answer it. I suppose, in a way, my left hand has gone to war against my right, given my parentage, but one can feel compassion for the French and none for their government, for I will own that I had some sympathy for the French people when they over-threw Louis, but the revolution has gone awry . . . the so-called leaders of the revolution have fallen upon each other. In Paris the Jacobins and the mob have ascendancy, and much evil must come of it, I believe. It is imperative that the French are beaten before they carry their bloody revolution across the breadth of Europe—even across the Channel. To the extent of my knowledge, none of my French relations serve in the Navy, so I am unlikely to ever have to stand against them directly, which I admit is a comfort." He patted the rail. "Despite the great disparity of the populations of the two nations, I have faith in Britain's wooden walls, Mr Wickham, and in those who man them."

Hayden could barely make out the boy's silhouette in the darkness, but did see him nod.

"How came you to be a midshipman on the *Themis*, Wickham?"

"My mother has known Mrs Hart all her life, I think. They are upon Christian names, and have been since girlhood. As I have three elder brothers, it was either a parsonage or the Navy for me. I feared the par-sonage might be a bit dull, so I begged Lord Westmoor to let me join the Navy. Captain and Mrs Hart came often to our home before the war, and I thought him quite the greatest man I had ever known. Far greater than my poor father, who was only an earl." The boy laughed; an infec-tious, child's laugh. "I know a little more now. If I pass for lieutenant I will seek a position aboard a flagship."

"You will pass. How long until you are nineteen?"

"Three years, sir."

"Not long, and you could almost certainly earn your commission at eighteen, as the examining board is not likely to be too diligent about establishing your age."

"Was your examination exacting, Mr Hayden?"

Hayden remembered the three captains seated before him in the deathly quiet room. How stern and intimidating they had seemed. "Yes, they posed me any number of perplexing questions. It seemed to me after a while that they wanted me to fail, but I did not, and in the end the senior captain on the examining board paid me a very fine compliment, saying that he had never known a midshipman to stand up to such a rigorous grilling. Then he corrected himself, and said, 'I mean a lieutenant.' "

"I have heard of midshipmen passing upon being given a good character by a captain on the examining board."

"Yes, and they are commonly the most deficient lieutenants in the fleet!" Hayden said with passion. "It takes a great store of knowledge to properly run a ship, Mr Wickham. Be certain that you have mastered your trade before you sit your exam, on the chance that they pass you without question. You don't want to be one of those blockheads who cannot take a ship from anchor without ruin trailing in his wake."

"No, sir," Wickham said. "It is my intent to know my trade most thoroughly, Mr Hayden, so if they tax me as they did you I shall answer up smartly and to everyone's satisfaction."

"Good for you, Wickham. Now trail the log, if you please, and tell me that we are still making just shy of four, then change the lookout aloft, for I do believe I hear him snoring."

"Aye, sir."

Hayden wakened to a knock on his cabin door, and the face of Madison, holding a lantern in his hand. The lieutenant swayed in his cot, a dense fog of sleep obscuring his thoughts.

"What is it, Madison?"

"Two sail due south, Mr Hayden," the boy said excitedly.

The lieutenant sat up. "What o'clock is it?"

"Sun's not quite up, sir."

Hayden rubbed a knuckle into his eye. "If you would be so kind as to light my candle, I shall be on deck directly."

"Aye, sir."

A moment later Hayden ran up the companionway ladder and a midshipman put a glass in his hand. Pale turquoise washed the eastern horizon, though overhead stars glittered. A few frayed clouds, dark as smoke, spattered the sky. Hayden could still sense the gale in the air—a desultory dampness, and hollow quiet, the sea cloudy and drab.

Far to the south he could just make out two grey irregularities on the horizon. He focussed his glass there, bracing against a carronade as the ship rolled.

"Well, it is impossible to say what they are, but we could hope they are French transports blown up-channel by the gale, and now desperate to make some westing. Certainly we should make a closer inspection." He quickly searched the horizon in all directions, then lowered his glass. Mr Barthe had been roused from his berth as well, and stood bleary-eyed before him.

"What does the weather-glass say, Mr Madison?" Hayden enquired.

"Rising, sir."

"Excellent." Hayden took a quick but careful look around the horizon, assessing the condition of the sea, the sky, the wind. "We will require more sail, Mr Barthe. And we must shape our course to intercept these ships: west-sou'west, I should think. We'll beat to quarters in one hour." He glanced up at the main-top. "But I want a close watch kept. It wouldn't do to be surprised by an escorting frigate catching up with its charges," he waved his glass at the horizon, "or by these two turning out to be frigates looking to prey on a lone English thirty-two."

The rest of the midshipmen tumbled up onto the deck then, pulling on jackets as they came, hats left behind in the rush.

"Are there ships, sir?" Wickham cried out. All their faces were flush with excitement.

"Have you never seen a ship before?" Barthe demanded, apparently offended by their high spirits.

"But this close to the French coast," Williams said, "they must be French."

"Or neutrals, or part of an English squadron, or any number of other explanations." The master turned around to look over his shoulder at the distant ships, only just visible in the frail light. "Go about your duties, now, and don't make a nuisance of yourselves. It will likely be a lot of bother over nothing."

The midshipmen retreated from the master, gravitating toward Madison, midshipman of the watch.

They all focussed their glasses on the distant sails. "What does Mr Hayden make of them?" Wickham asked Madison quietly.

"He's only said that we shall make a closer inspection . . ." the boy whispered, "but possibly transports."

This received a little buzz of excitement and approbation.

Landry appeared then, as did Dr Griffiths.

"Sail, Mr Hayden?" Landry asked.

The first lieutenant handed Landry his glass and pointed toward the horizon.

The little man gazed through the brass tube a moment, then lowered it. "I shall inform the captain."

"He has only just fallen asleep, Mr Landry," Griffiths asserted. "Could you not wait until you know what ships these might be? Likely there will be no reason to call him, as we well know."

Landry stood there, wavering on the deck, his narrow brow pressed into creases. "Captain Hart's orders are to call him whenever we see ships that might represent a threat to the *Themis.*"

Barthe stood nearby, and Hayden saw him roll his eyes. "These might or might not," the master said. "Why don't we draw a little nearer, and if we are at all uncertain as to their nationality, we can call the captain." But then his patience ebbed like a tide. "Good Lord, Mr Landry, is it necessary to call the captain every time we wipe our noses?"

"Mr Barthe!" the offended lieutenant rejoined. "I am only following orders! You, of all people, know the price of provoking Captain Hart's displeasure."

"And you think to gain his approval by waking him because sails have been sighted? This is the English Channel! It is a veritable highway of shipping!" Barthe turned to the doctor in exasperation. "Dr Griffiths, you say the captain is not fully recovered?"

"He passed his stone," the doctor said carefully, "but is in need of much rest now, or migraine will certainly result."

The master turned back to Landry. "There can be no harm in leaving him in peace for a little while. When we draw near the chase, we will call him if it is necessary. Will that satisfy you?"

"I will bear any blame," Hayden said, sensing Landry's anxiety.

"Oh, Captain Hart will choose whom to blame, Mr Hayden," Landry answered, "not you." He glanced back at the horizon. "In an hour it will be light and we shall have some sense of what ships these be. Then I will call the captain." The little lieutenant thrust the glass back at Hayden and quit the deck, his manner stiff with anger.

"You know Mr Landry is right, Mr Barthe," Hawthorne said. He stood a few feet away, his red jacket like a sunrise. "The captain will not be pleased."

"Nor would he be pleased if you woke him, nor if you woke him in one hour, or in two. Let the man have his rest. The ships will likely be neutrals or English cruisers, then we will simply carry on—without our poor eyes being damned, for once."

Barthe departed, calling hands to make sail. As the light grew it became apparent that the ships were closer than Hayden had first thought. A hoist of signals went up from the nearer ship, and they wore almost in unison, heading toward the French coast.

"Well, I think that answers one of our questions," Archer declared. "They are not English cruisers."

"Indeed they are not!" Hayden agreed. "I think we shall have to call the captain, Mr Archer. They are making for Le Havre, and with a little luck we might overhaul them. Let us beat to quarters. Ah, Doctor, your arrival is most propitious. May we wake Captain Hart? Our chases have turned tail and are running for the French coast."

"I shall inform him myself, Mr Hayden."

The drummer took his place and began the roll that caused every heart to pound. Men came streaming up the hatches, some rushing aloft with buckets on long painters to soak the sails, others freed the guns, while men and boys began moving eighteen-pound iron balls up to the shot racks on the gun-deck. It was the first time Hayden had seen all the men respond with a will. They were of one mind about prize money, apparently.

Hayden left Archer in charge of the quarterdeck, and made his way forward to have a better look at the fleeing ships. A few moments later, Hart arrived with Landry and the doctor in tow. The captain's colour was improved, but he looked like a man struggling to wake from a deep sleep, and with the temperament to match.

"What do you mean, Mr Hayden," he demanded, "beating to quarters without my express instructions?"

"Enemy ships are in sight, Captain Hart. I am only following naval custom."

Hart shook his head. "And where are these *'enemy ships'*?"

Hayden handed the captain his glass and pointed. The sterns of the ships were quite visible now. Through the glass, men could be made out, staring at the English frigate through their own glass eyes.

Hart raised the glass and regarded the ships briefly. "French frigates," he announced, lowering the cylinder. "Mr Barthe!"

The master stepped forward.

"Alter our course for Brest."

"But with all due respect, sir," Hayden responded, his jaw tight. "When seen abeam they appeared to be transports. It would seem prudent to take a closer look. Certainly frigates would not turn tail so quickly when they have the greater number."

Hart turned his hazy blue eyes on his first lieutenant. "They are frigates, sir, as any fool can see! Would you have us take on two French thirty-eights with more than double our weight of iron?"

Hayden could barely control his own rage. "Certainly I would chase them, in hopes of catching one while the other was distant."

"That is why you are still a lieutenant," Hart said cruelly. "You have not the common sense to command a ship."

Hart thrust the glass into Barthe's hand and spun on his heel. "We are for Brest, Mr Barthe," he announced loudly. "And for God's sake, leave off beating to quarters!" Hart stormed back along the gangway and in a moment he was below, leaving his stunned officers gathered on the foredeck.

So that is why they call him Faint Hart, Hayden thought. The lieutenant had never been aboard a ship where the captain had acted thus—with the enemy clearly in sight.

Landry turned on Hayden. "I warned you, Mr Hayden. The captain tolerates no defiance of his orders."

"But those are French transports, almost without doubt, not frigates, as any landsman can see."

"Not according to Captain Hart, who has been at sea longer than either of us." Landry turned and marched back along the deck in the wake of his captain. The midshipmen hesitated a moment, then, gazing down at the deck in disappointment, went off about their business, leaving Barthe and Hayden alone on the forecastle.

The same disappointment was upon the faces and in the carriage of every man aboard. Hardly a word was muttered, but words were not necessary. The sail trimmers slunk to their places without energy, and the men on the quarterdeck began housing their guns, shaking their heads as they did so.

"For shame," someone muttered. "For shame."

"Please tell me, Mr Barthe," Hayden intoned softly, "that this is not the common practice aboard Hart's ship."

The master took off his hat and slapped it against his thigh in frustration. "It is always thus," he said too loudly. "There is ever a reason not to engage the enemy." He tipped his head toward the escaping ships. "Every man aboard—even Landry—knows them to be transports. And yet we must all pretend they are powerful French frigates, though they flee like we are a ninety-eight-gun ship. I am sorry you found your way aboard this ship, Mr Hayden. You deserve better."

For a moment Hayden closed his eyes, the roiling anger he felt like a brewing gale. He had his duty to think of and, when he addressed the master, tried to speak in an even tone. "I must caution you, Mr Barthe," Hayden said so that no other might hear. "Though I admire your zeal to meet the enemy, speaking out thus will bring you into conflict with your captain."

The corpulent master drew himself up, face redder than his hair. "I have given in to his fancies for too long, Mr Hayden, until I have been unmanned by my own deference. I shall do it no more. Let him court-martial me, if he dares. If he dares have it be known how he has fled the enemy times too numerous to count over the past months. And the way he speaks to you, Mr Hayden, and before the crew! Conduct unbecoming of a gentleman, sir. Were you not his subordinate you would call the man out. I believe you would."

"Mr Barthe! You forget yourself!"

"No, sir. I do not forget myself. I have only just remembered who once I was." The master spun and began giving orders to shift the yards and trim sails to shape their course for Brest. Hayden looked once more at the fleeing ships. Every man aboard would have welcomed the prize money—he not least of all—but even more important, taking an enemy ship would do much to change the spirits of the crew; Hayden had seen it before.

What, he wondered, would Philip Stephens make of this? Clear dereliction of duty. Hart could be court-martialled. He *should* be. But unless his actions, or lack thereof, were witnessed by a fellow captain or senior officer it would likely never come to pass. It was more likely that Barthe or Hayden would be court-martialled for insubordination—for attempting to pursue the enemy!

And where was the common sense in that?

Hayden sat at the table in the empty gunroom. Try as he might, he could not turn his mind away from what had just occurred—Hart had refused to chase a pair of under-armed transports!—and his indignation and anger could not be mastered for more than a moment. To think that he had to serve under such a pusillanimous ass! Perhaps it would be better to have no career, and to repair to America in Aldrich's place. Better to be a street-sweeper!

He tried to calm himself and bring his attentions to bear upon the work before him. Opening a folder in which he kept the accounts and correspondence that required his attention, he found a note, in an unfamiliar hand, scribbled upon a scrap of paper. It was only a single line misspelt:

The leftenants servent hears yor privat conversasions.

Hayden stared at the note for a long moment. It did not say which "leftenant," but then it didn't need to.

"The Adam Tiler," Hayden muttered to no one. How in the world had Worth, a foremast hand, slipped into his cabin? It should not have been possible. He slid the scrap of paper in among his letters and took out the hated accounts, his head beginning to throb at the mere sight of them.

It was more than an hour later when the doctor came in and found Hayden and Perseverance hard at work at the gunroom table.

"Am I interrupting . . . ?" he asked gently.

"No, Doctor, I am done with this . . . *damnable* business for the day!" He slammed the account ledger closed. "Let us have a glass of wine!"

He quickly gathered up his papers and gave them all into the care of Perseverance. The boy had more organizational abilities, at least when it came to paper, than Hayden would ever possess, and the lieutenant had not hesitated to take advantage of this invaluable skill.

The doctor took a chair and one of the gunroom servants drew off a glass of wine for each of them from the little quarter keg that stood on a shelf beside the door. The doctor slumped back in his chair and raised his eyebrows, then his glass in turn. "Confusion to the enemy," he intoned, and shook his head.

Hayden lifted his glass in response.

Among the common sounds of a ship at sea came a familiar voice from above, much muffled, the words indistinguishable but the immoderate rage unmistakable.

"Who is the captain's victim this evening?" Hayden wondered, with a glance up to the ceiling, where stout beams and planks separated the gunroom from the captain's cabin.

"Mr Barthe, I believe," Griffiths answered, his gaze following Hayden's. "The captain will not have liked the master's description of the 'frigates' sighted today. It will not do to have the official account of the cruise differing notably from the captain's own journal. The governor and his deputy have come into conflict over this precise issue before. No doubt it will not be the last time, either."

They sat for a moment, discomforted by the row overhead, but then the captain fell silent. Griffiths waved the servant out, put his elbows on the table, and leaned closer. "Mr Hayden," he began, "let me ask you, if I may . . . you seem very confident of your facility to fight an action with the French, and Lord knows you have proven that your seamanship is beyond reproach, but would you have really gone after two French frigates?"

"They were not frigates, Dr Griffiths . . ." but Hayden stopped in mid-sentence. He rose and circled the table, taking care to walk quietly. Without knocking he jerked open the door to Landry's cabin and the second lieutenant's servant boy all but fell out into the gunroom.

The doctor rose from his seat, indignation and anger written upon his face. "Why, you young whelp!" he stormed. "You were eavesdropping upon our conversation!"

"I was not, sir! I swear to you—" Seeing the rage in the doctor's face, the boy leapt to his feet, but not before the surgeon administered a boot to the child's retreating rump.

"Now, Doctor . . ." Hayden said, placing himself squarely in the man's way as Landry's servant flew out the gunroom door. "I suspect the boy was not eavesdropping of his own inclination . . ."

The doctor, still a picture of perfect outrage and indignation, stood a moment before he took Hayden's meaning. "Why, I shall go to the captain!"—but then he calmed enough for his mind to catch up, and he slumped down into a chair, a look of some horror on his face.

"I rather doubt that will serve much purpose," Hayden said evenly.

The doctor cursed softly but with impressive eloquence.

Hayden called for Perse, whom he stationed at the gunroom door with orders to alert him if anyone ventured within hearing. The surgeon then opened the doors to all the other cabins surrounding the gunroom. There was no one else present.

The doctor took a drink of his wine, several long breaths, and mastered himself. "Do forgive my outburst," he said evenly. "This cursed ship and its people . . ." but he did not finish. A moment more, and then he turned to Hayden. "I—I have forgotten the subject upon which we spoke . . ."

Hayden sat down and leaned across the table so that no other might hear. "You asked if I would have chased two French frigates, and I believe my answer was that they were not frigates."

"Yes, of course." The doctor, too, leaned over the table. He appeared to compose his mind for a moment. "Let me speak more to the point, Lieutenant. Captain Hart is often out of sorts when first he sets to sea . . . Anxiety, and the strains of command, I believe. Gradually, his condition improves. I should expect him to regain his health in three or four days. After that his migraines and other disorders will see him laid up with less frequency. As the commander of this ship, who might be called upon at any time to use his judgement to preserve his crew, I attempt always to give Captain Hart the smallest measure of any physic that might impair that judgement. There might be times, however, when his afflictions require greater doses of physic, large enough that he might not be fit to command for several hours, perhaps the better part of a day. I just want to forewarn you, for you might have to assume command for that period of time, and make all decisions as to the preservation of the ship and her crew, including decisions to engage or not engage enemy vessels. Do I make myself perfectly clear?"

Hayden was afraid to answer. "If you were utterly certain that such physic was necessary to the captain's health, Dr Griffiths, I should be prepared to do my duty . . . to carry out the Admiralty's orders as best I comprehend them."

The doctor nodded. "We have an understanding, then?"

"I believe we do, and I thank you, Doctor, for making me aware of this possibility."

"I thought it my duty," Griffiths said, then leaned back and took up his wine glass. "Let us drink the captain's health."

Hayden raised his own glass. "Captain Hart," he said, and both men drank.

For a moment Hayden closed his eyes. Conspiracy to take command of the ship, even temporarily, would call down upon the conspirators a punishment too terrible to contemplate. He was placing entirely too much trust in a man he did not know well. But there was revolution in the air upon His Majesty's ship *Themis*. The Jacks whispered among themselves, and the officers were in all but open rebellion. Somehow, Hayden didn't think this was quite what Philip Stephens had in mind when he offered him the position aboard the *Themis*: his agent conspiring with others aboard to set Captain Hart aside—at least for a few hours. But what else could they do? Flee the enemy upon every meeting? Hayden would never live with himself if he did so.

The lieutenant had a nightmare image of the poor man, Penrith, who'd been murdered: a seaman swinging from the main yard out into the darkness, clinging to life with the tips of his fingers . . . before the knife fell. The image came to Hayden now, but it was he who clung to the yard. He who saw the blade falling.

Thirteen

The cliffs of Brittany, broken blocks, stacked and shattered, were almost aglow in the day's last light. The sight produced a tide of emotion in Lieutenant Charles Hayden. As a child, he had played upon these cliffs with his cousin Guillaume. Disobeying every edict of his aunt and uncle, they had explored the ledges and gullies to gather seabird eggs. He shuddered to think of it, the bravado they had shown—rather short of common sense, he now thought.

But his reaction was more perplexing than that—he felt a great distress to be so close to one of his two homelands and know that he could only set foot there if he carried war to the French, who had once been as much his people as were the English. At the same time, it was in France that he had been swept up in the mob . . . and he now felt an odd disquiet, almost an apprehension of the place and the people. He could not trust himself among them. He did not know what he might do or what passions might be drawn up through the thin surface of his English rationality.

"I will tell you honestly, Mr Hayden," Barthe stated, breaking into his thoughts, "in all my years in these waters, I have never chanced the Four Passage." He gazed at the surrounding waters, impressed, but then his face changed and his manner grew anxious. "Are you satisfied with our situation?"

"I should like it better if the wind had not gone around to the west, Mr Barthe, but as long as it does not die altogether we are in no danger." Hayden extended his glass toward the shore. "Point St Matthew. The Outer Water of Brest Harbour lies just beyond."

They had fallen in with the French coast some hours before, and carried a following breeze along the cliffs of Brittany, steep-to and littered with off-lying rocks and shoals, much to the master's discomfort. Hayden, however, had sailed these waters before and was confident, if wary. His vigilance had been compounded an hour before when the breeze had shifted to the west, though it showed no signs of rising.

The lieutenant gazed out toward the western horizon. "What do you think this weather will do?"

The sailing master's gaze followed Hayden's. The sun had set, and low in the west a thin band of broken cloud glowed like hot coals. A low, easy swell barely disturbed the ship, and shags and grebes swam and dove in her shadow. Fitful north-east winds had carried them slowly across the Channel, until they had raised the Brittany coast, four days after escaping Plymouth Sound.

"We might be in for a few more days of calm and light breezes from all points, Mr Hayden."

The first lieutenant glanced around, gauging the distance to shore and the nearby islands and shoals. "Yes, I'm afraid you're right. I'll be glad to get into more open water. If the wind dies, the tide could carry us into difficulties. You have our anchor readied?"

Barthe nodded, but his response was cut off.

"On deck," came a call from aloft. "Sail. Two points off the larboard bow."

As the *Themis* rounded the high point, the Outer Water opening before them, a ship did appear. Hayden and the sailing master crossed over the forecastle to have a better view.

"Mr Hayden, sir . . ." the lookout called. "There is a second ship."

"So there is!" Hayden said, glimpsing the sails, half-hidden, behind the first. Lieutenant Landry appeared at his elbow, fixing a glass on the two ships.

"Transports, by the look of them," Barthe offered.

"Yes, but well out of our reach," Landry pronounced.

Hayden did not lower his glass. "Do you think, Mr Barthe, that we could overhaul them before they pass through the Goulet?"

Barthe did not hesitate to answer. "We certainly can try, sir!" The master lowered his glass and looked expectantly at the first lieutenant.

"But this wind does not favour us," Landry objected. "We might be becalmed just outside the harbour itself, and easy prey for gunboats."

"Oh, I think we are more than a match for a few gunboats, Mr Landry," Hayden said, feeling a tightness in his chest and yet an accompanying elation as well.

"The captain will never allow it," Landry said.

"Let us not have this argument again!" Hayden said hotly. "We have orders to assess the strength of the French fleet anchored in Brest Roads. To do this properly we must sail up to the mouth of the Goulet—if there are transports there at the time, we would be remiss in our duty if we did not try to take them." Hayden faced the second lieutenant, trying to control his anger. "Would you do me the honour of going aloft, Mr Landry? I trust no one else to make an accurate count of the diverse ships."

Landry turned crimson. "Mr Hayden, someone must inform the captain. You exceed your authority, sir."

The surgeon arrived on the forecastle at that moment.

"Ah, Dr Griffiths," Hayden greeted him. "How is Captain Hart? able to take the deck, I hope?"

The surgeon shook his head, his manner very grave. "I have only just given him laudanum for his migraine. I don't think he can be wakened."

"Would it be your medical opinion, Doctor, that Captain Hart will not be fit to command the ship for some time?"

The doctor considered seriously before offering his judgement. "Likely four to six hours."

Hayden raised his glass to view the transports again. "As it is our duty to 'take, burn, or destroy' the enemy wherever we find them, then I'm sure Captain Hart would not disapprove of an attempt to seize one of these transports before it makes the harbour."

"The wind *is* going very light, sir," Barthe cautioned, his enthusiasm curdling. He gazed anxiously at the nearby cliffs, and the shoals and islands to starboard.

Hayden lowered his glass. "So it is, but I have spent some time in these waters, and I can tell you that a reliable breeze almost invariably sweeps down off the land just after sunset, and in but a few hours the tide will turn in our favour as well. With luck, we can snatch one of those ships, and be carried out to sea immediately thereafter." He glanced up at the sails, which the small zephyr barely kept full. "Royals and studding sails, Mr Barthe, if you please. And, Mr Landry, the Admiralty will want to know every ship and her rating, at the very least." He turned away, leaving Landry uncertain whether to be more angry or more frightened. "Mr Archer, we shall go to quarters with as little noise and fuss as possible. Do you understand?"

The third lieutenant, no doubt fresh from his cot, nodded. "No drum, sir. But it will be impossible to clear for action without some noise, Mr Hayden."

"Yes, I know. But leave the bulkhead to the captain's cabin standing. We will do without the aftermost guns, which I think will be unnecessary." Hayden turned back to view the ships. "Mr Landry, why are you standing there, sir? Why are you not aloft?"

Landry eyed him with rancour, and the doctor after him. "Captain Hart will have much to say of this when he wakes."

"Let us hope it is only to congratulate us on our prize, Mr Landry," Hayden replied.

The little lieutenant glowered at them, then spun on his heel and went to the shrouds to climb aloft.

The surgeon stood by Hayden a moment as the lieutenant once again raised his glass to quiz the enemy ships.

"Are you confident of this beneficent offshore breeze, Lieutenant?" Griffiths asked quietly.

"It is well known hereabout, and, unless the moon has stopped in its cycle, the tide will begin to ebb soon, for we are almost at high water. My fear is that wind and tide will turn against us before the enemy can be reached, for we will never work to weather in the light breeze that I expect—not against the tidal current that rushes out of the Goulet."

"I shall go prepare my instruments, then. I pray my skills will go begging."

"If we catch one of these ships, Doctor, I predict she will haul down her colours without a shot being fired, except perhaps one across her bow."

"If only all sea battles were so economically decided." The surgeon went back down the larboard gangway, dodging among the hurrying men. The drumming of hammers taking down the bulkheads below echoed hollowly through the ship, and Hayden glanced quickly aft, half-expecting to see Captain Hart appear to stop this small endeavour. He searched aloft and found Landry there, his glass fixed on the inner harbour.

Mr Barthe arrived back on the quarterdeck. "We shall have royals and stunsails directly, Mr Hayden."

"Thank you, Mr Barthe." Hayden felt a strong sense of elation at having the cowardly Hart out of the way, at having an opportunity to take an enemy ship, even if only a transport. He had known Hart less than a sennight and already he felt an almost violent disdain for the man. Tyrant captains were not unknown in the British Navy, but the few Hayden had encountered were superb seamen and knew how to fight a ship—one had to respect them for that. They would never shrink from a battle or try to put themselves out of harm's way in an action. Even their miserable misused crews had a grudging admiration for them. Hart did not inspire even that.

The master gazed off at the slowly fleeing quarry, trying to gauge their speed. "Do you think there is any chance we'll overhaul them?"

"It is in the hands of Neptune, Mr Barthe. They are becalmed for a moment, now and then, while we have the wind, then the reverse is true. They might try to work into the Rade de Camara—there under the batteries, but I can see there is no wind within the little bay. We might overtake them just beyond range of the long guns."

A flock of wailing gulls swarmed after a small fishing boat that pulled for the harbour entrance, the fishermen eying the British frigate that had suddenly appeared around the headland, but Hayden paid it no mind. His eye and thoughts were fixed upon larger quarry, with only a glance now and then toward the opening into Brest Harbour, sensible to the fact that the port admiral would send gunboats out as soon as he was alerted to the presence of the *Themis*. These little craft, with their heavy gun, were more of a threat than he would admit to Landry.

"Are there not batteries on the northern shore as well?" Barthe asked, sweeping his glass across the cliffs.

"Further into the neck, Mr Barthe—the Goulet, as it is called. We will not venture so far."

A jet of smoke erupted on the nearest chase, followed quickly by the thunder of the gun echoing off the nearby cliffs.

"Mr Hayden . . . !" Landry called down. "They're firing at us, sir."

"Just trying to gain the attention of the port authorities, Mr Landry," Hayden called. "No concern to us."

There was some muffled laughter among the crew, for it was clear to anyone watching that the gun had been fired toward the harbour, and therefore would not have contained shot. The men, formerly so sullen and fractious, now went about their duties with a quick, light step, aquiver with anticipation. An action was just the tonic they required, Hayden thought.

Hayden glanced to westward. The sun was well set now, and the dusk would soon be upon them, rising, as he thought, like a dark mist from the lightless depths of the sea. He looked back anxiously at the transports. Their sails waved languidly as the breeze fell away. The *Themis'* sails filled with a dull *thup*. Across the water's surface, little cats'-paws could be seen scurrying, but without pattern that the sailor could discern.

"Do you know," the master said, "I think we make better speed than they when the wind touches us. These transports must have very foul bottoms."

"Thank God for our copper, Mr Barthe," Hayden said, for the bottoms of British Navy ships were sheathed in thin copper plates, against worm and to keep them from fouling overly in their long months at sea. "Who is our cleverest helmsman?"

"Dryden, sir. He's at the wheel now."

"We'll have to catch every puff, every zephyr if we hope to overhaul those transports. Once the ship is cleared, have the sail trimmers at their stations. We will send them down to the guns at the last possible moment."

"It is a curse that we are so undermanned, Mr Hayden."

"We shall have to make the best of it." Their civilian guest arrived on the foredeck at that moment. "Ah, Mr Muhlhauser. I don't know if you will have a chance to exercise your gun."

The inventor appeared very nervous, rocking from foot to foot, his face a little pale and taut. "Well, it is an education just to see a ship ready for action, Mr Hayden. All my years in the Ordnance Board and I have never seen a gun fired in anger."

"We shall be lucky if we get to fire a chase-piece in warning, but I hope we will fulfill your desire in the near future."

"*On deck,*" came the cry from above. "Sail in the Roads, sir."

"Gunboats," Landry called down from his perch.

Hayden turned and found his second lieutenant in the fore-top, among red-coated marines bearing muskets.

"How many, Mr Landry?"

The little lieutenant gazed through his glass a moment, then lowered it and called down. "Three that I can see, sir, but there are other sail in the Inner Waters—I can't tell what they might be other than a Chase Mary."

"And what in this world would that be?" asked Muhlhauser.

"A *chasse-marée*; 'chase-tide' in English. Boats used for fishing, coastal trade, and a little privateering, when the opportunity presents itself. They're luggers, and quite fast when well sailed, which usually they are."

"The gunboats do not concern you, I take it?" Muhlhauser said, attempting to sound casual.

"It will be difficult for them to beat through the Goulet in this little breeze. When tide and wind turn, they will carry us as well as them."

"Where are the shoals in the Goulet?" Mr Barthe asked. "I cannot make them out."

Hayden pointed. "They are barely awash on this high a tide. I know them well, Mr Barthe. Do not fear. If the captains of our chases know their business they will try to put Les Fillettes, the black rocks, between their ships and ours. Try to draw us onto the rocks, but we are sensible of their design."

"Surely you will not go in so far?" Muhlhauser blurted.

"Just inside Les Fillettes, no further. I do not want to expose us overly to their batteries." Hayden looked around. "Oh, give us a wind! It is a race between snails! The wind is dying. The transports have distance and darkness on their side, and we must overcome both." He looked around for the gun captain. "Ready the starboard bow-chaser, Baldwin. We might hope to bring one of these transports to."

The breeze teased them, pushing them forward for a moment, then dying away. Filling the sails of the transports, then leaving them slatting in a calm.

The Goulet opened before them, and the masts of the distant French fleet stood out in the last light like strangely angular, barren trees.

"Mr Hayden, it is a very substantial fleet!" Wickham observed. He was crouched, steadying his glass on the barricade beside the bow-chaser. "A number of three-deckers, and a passel of seventy-fours, not to mention the frigates."

"It would seem the French fleet has returned, then. The word in Plymouth was that it had been discovered anchored in Quiberon Bay." Hayden fixed his glass on the enemy fleet and felt a little wave of apprehension—the great ships so near and only his little frigate to stand against them.

"Will they send frigates after us when the wind turns, Mr Hayden?" Wickham asked.

"It is unlikely. The darkness will be complete by then, and it would be too easy for us to slip away, or for them to be separated, which might leave one alone for us to prey upon. They don't like to fight when the odds are even, Mr Wickham."

"That is rather cowardly, sir."

Hayden found this offended him, to his surprise, and he tried not to let it show. "Well, the French have great armies, and we a superior navy." Hayden lowered his glass. "It makes for a strange war."

The wind left the transports then and Hayden could see that the area around the enemy ships was mirror-calm.

"They've fallen into a wind hole!" Mr Barthe said, his voice rising a little in excitement. He glanced up at the sails, then out to windward. "If we can just carry this breeze up to them."

Hayden was trying to estimate the distances. "What do you make them out to be, Mr Barthe? a league from the Goulet? Perhaps two miles from the protection of the batteries above Camara Bay?"

"I believe that is so, sir. And somewhat more than a mile from our present position."

"We might just overtake them, yet," Hayden muttered softly, almost afraid to say it aloud. He felt his heart pounding, and his breath was just a little short—excitement, not fear. He kept expecting to hear Hart take the deck and break off the engagement. What excuse would he make, Hayden wondered?

"Shall I whistle, sir?" Wickham asked, a little smile appearing on his youthful face.

"Never on a lee shore!" the master warned.

Deep in the Goulet, Hayden could see the gunboats tacking to the north. They still had wind, which, the lieutenant knew from experience, gained in strength as it funnelled between the high cliffs.

The gun captain unstopped his powder horn and primed the bow-chaser, anxious to fire the shot that might bring a prize. Hayden could almost see the greed shining in the men's eyes. He glanced back at the enemy transports and his heart sank a little. They appeared to be in shadow now, as though dusk had overtaken them as they lay becalmed.

"I think they're lowering boats, Mr Hayden," Wickham announced.

"They'll try to tow her into harbour," Hayden speculated, "or at least into some wind."

"That is a bit of desperation, isn't it?" the master said.

"It is, and we should be prepared to man our own boats. If we can get close enough to bring our guns to bear we will need boats to take our prize, in the event that we are becalmed. Mr Archer? I want enough men to handle sail and fight one side of the ship left aboard, but everyone we can spare should be armed and ready to go into the boats."

Archer tipped his hat and hurried aft, calling out orders as he went.

"Begging your pardon, Mr Hayden," the gun captain said, touching a knuckle to his brow. "Shall we fire a shot now? Put a scare into 'em, sir?" The man had a trunk with no waist, skinny arms and legs fastened in a haphazard fashion, like an ill-made child's doll.

Hayden suppressed a smile. "Patience, Baldwin. I think we'll scare 'em more if we're in range. Don't you?"

The man looked a little sheepish. "Aye, sir."

They continued to creep across the bay, barely leaving a ripple astern. The tension on the ship was palpable, men standing at their stations, peering off at the distant transports, which drew ever so slowly nearer. Hayden glanced seaward, as he had every so often over the last hour, making certain that they were not surprised from that quarter. A French seventy-four or frigate appearing around one of the headlands would turn his little enterprise into a debacle. He did not want to give Hart that satisfaction, or turn his chase into desperate flight.

He raised his glass again. Even in the failing light, Hayden could now make out the anxious faces of the officers and crew of the transport. They were watching the *Themis* with the same intensity that Hayden's shipmates watched them, though with differing emotions, the lieutenant was sure. Wind rustled the near transport's sails, and everyone's gaze went aloft, but the canvas only slatted a little and did not fill. Hayden could almost see the disappointment in the candle-pale faces.

"How many guns will they have?" Muhlhauser asked.

"A handful," Mr Barthe said. "Likely six-pounders. They're no match for us, and know it well."

"Mr Hayden!" Landry called. "Frigate preparing to heave her anchor and make sail."

Hayden turned his glass toward the anchorage. "I see it, Mr Landry. Thank you."

"Is that one of the French thirty-eights?" Muhlhauser asked, professional interest overcoming his nerves.

"Difficult to be sure from this angle," Barthe said, "but very likely."

"Eighteen-pounders, then?"

"Yes, but they will never reach us."

"On deck!" called the lookout. "Second frigate preparing to weigh, sir!"

A little buzz passed among the crew, as they all seemed to shift positions at once.

"Thank you, Sparrow," Hayden answered loudly. "They will not weigh with tide and wind against them, but keep me informed."

Barthe smiled, then said quietly to Muhlhauser: "That was for the benefit of the crew. Best to keep their mind on the prize and not on the frigates."

"Mr Hayden, sir?" A distressed-looking Madison hurried onto the forecastle. "There is trouble on the gun-deck, sir."

Hayden continued to peer through his glass, but a cold wave passed through him. "What is the nature of this trouble, Mr Madison?"

"The gun crews are . . . quarrelling among themselves." He paused as though unsure what to say. "And insubordinate, sir."

Hayden lowered his glass. "Call Mr Hawthorne and a dozen marines. Have the armourer issue all the officers pistols and cutlasses. Mr Hobson: there is a brace of pistols in my sea-chest. Would you have my writer fetch them out, load, and bring them me?" Hobson raced off. Handing his glass to Muhlhauser, Hayden followed. "Mr Barthe, overhaul those transports, if you can."

"Aye, sir."

Hayden was on the larboard gangway in a moment, noise from the gun-deck becoming louder. Men were arguing and petty officers shouting, but the situation was no longer under their control.

Hawthorne and the marines came pounding along the deck, and Hayden relieved a marine of his weapon. In the fading light he could just make out the gun crews below in open confrontation.

"Train your weapons down into the waist," Hayden ordered the marines, then, pulling back the cock, fired the gun out to sea.

The men all looked up and found the muzzles of a dozen muskets pointed at them. Hobson appeared with Hayden's pistols just then, and the first lieutenant seized one, turning it on the nearest man standing below in the gloom.

"You will return to your appointed stations." Hayden hardly raised his voice, but the tone of it left no one in doubt. "Any man who refuses to fire his gun when ordered or who does not work smartly to follow the officers' commands during this action will be deemed in open mutiny and shot where he stands." The men hesitated scarcely a second and then hastened to their guns. Only one or two men were slow to comply or glared up at the lieutenant as they went back to their places. In the gathering gloom Hayden could not be sure who they were, though he suspected one of being Bill Stuckey.

"Lieutenant Hawthorne, I will leave this situation to you. Cry out if you require more men."

The armourer and his mate stood aft of the gangways, about to arm the boat crews but hesitating. Hayden knew immediately what went on—the armourer was afraid to surrender weapons to men who might be insubordinate.

"Mr Hawthorne?" Hayden called out. "The rest of your marines will join the boat crews, if you please."

Hawthorne began calling out the names of men for the boats, and Hayden went to the armourer, a steady, sober man who he was sure knew the Jacks better than he. "Arm those you trust, Mr Martin," Hayden said quietly, "tell all the others they are wanted for the ship."

He heard Barthe calling orders to the sail-trimmers.

"Have you a pistol, Mr Hobson?" Hayden asked.

"I have, sir," the midshipman answered smartly, his voice a little thin.

"Yourself and Mr Madison will take charge of the forward guns on the gun-deck. If any man tries to take your pistol, you must shoot him. Can you do that?"

The boy looked a bit disturbed but not frightened—at least not overly. "I think so, sir."

"Don't think so. Your life will depend on it, as will the lives of many of your shipmates."

"I will do it, Mr Hayden." The boy gripped his pistol tightly.

"Good for you, Hobson."

The midshipman called to Madison, and the two of them descended the stair into the waist, and though they might have walked a bit too closely together, they were admirably resolute, given that the Jacks were almost, to a man, larger than they.

"Mr Landry!" Hayden called out as he returned to the forecastle. "I will require your presence on the deck, if you please."

Something caught Hayden's eye at that moment: there was a sail beyond Île de Beniguet!

"Where in deepest hell did that come from?" Hayden said, pointing. "Look sharp aloft! Is that not a sail in the offing?" The lieutenant's heart suddenly began to race.

"Frigate to the west!" the lookout sang out, but he was in trouble now, as the lookouts aloft always were if any man on deck discovered ships, land, or any other object of interest, before they did.

"Damn!" Barthe said under his breath, wheeling around to gaze out to sea. "We are for it, now."

"Aloft, there!" Hayden called, forcing his voice to sound calm for the sake of the crew. "Is she one of ours, can you see?"

Landry was standing in the tops, his glass trained out to sea.

Smoke bloomed from the distant frigate, and a hoist of flags floated aloft—the private signal. At the same time, British colours broke out at the mizzen.

Hayden closed his eyes for a second and uttered a silent thanks. If the frigate had belonged to the enemy, they might have been ending their day in a French gaol. "Well, I shall be happy to share our prize money, if there is any to be had, just to know that isn't a Frenchman to the west."

"We shall not let Landry forget that!" Barthe declared. "Even if he was detailed to count the fleet."

"Everyone had their eye on the prize money, I think," Wickham said.

"Who is midshipman of the watch?" Hayden asked.

"Williams, sir," one of the crew answered.

"Have him answer the private signal and hoist 'Chasing.' " He turned back to the transports. "Let the French frigates see that we have an ally." It was unlikely that the distant English ship could reach them in the failing wind, but Hayden still felt a strong sense of relief just knowing the ship was there. If nothing else, his crew would be unlikely to mutiny knowing a British frigate lay in the offing.

Landry appeared a moment later, looking both frightened and resentful, but Hayden had no time to be conciliatory.

"Here are our circumstances, Mr Landry. I believe Mr Hawthorne and the officers can keep the crew in their places aboard the *Themis*, especially now that there is a second British frigate within sight, but I am concerned about the prize crew. I feel I must go with the boats, if it comes to that, lest they turn against the marines and officers. That will leave you to command the ship. Are you prepared to see this action through? I know you were against it from the start."

Landry looked around sulkily. "I see little choice now. We cannot break it off and let the crew think we are afraid of them. It would never do."

"No, it wouldn't," Hayden agreed. He waited, but Landry offered no more. "Will you take command of the ship, then?"

Landry nodded unhappily.

"Mr Barthe?" Hayden called. He quickly drew a sketch of the narrows that led into the harbour of Brest, indicating where the rocks lay in the entrance. Hayden suspected that Landry did not have the mettle to see the thing through if anything at all went awry; he would turn the ship out to sea the first chance he got, perhaps even if it meant leaving the boats and their crews behind. Hayden would then be relying on Barthe to support them.

What a position he was in—and he felt a fool for it. Never for a moment had he thought that the men would shy from action or that they would turn on their officers in a crisis. This was a far cry from signing a petition or even refusing to sail.

Hayden directed his gaze to the transports. The far ship had moved ahead, almost certainly beyond their reach now, but the near ship lay becalmed on the dark sea. Hayden looked down into the inky water, trying to gauge his ship's speed. Hardly two knots, he thought. But the chase was almost within range.

"How distant is that transport, Mr Barthe?" he asked the sailing master.

"Five hundred yards, Mr Hayden. Perhaps five hundred fifty. It is difficult to be sure in this light."

"I think you're right. Closer to five and fifty, I should think. I don't imagine they'll deem us a threat at this distance, even if we could put a shot across their bow."

"I fear you're right. It will be a close-run thing, Mr Hayden. They are almost beyond our reach."

Hayden turned to find the third lieutenant. "If you please, Mr Archer, embark the boat crews. And hold a place for me in a cutter."

Overhead, the stars began to appear in the last dispersed light of the sun. Hayden could still make out the transports silhouettes against the dark cliffs. The nearest had her boats out before, men straining at the sweeps to pull the ship out of the calm that gripped them. The second transport had abandoned her sister and was making for the harbour entrance, perhaps catching the eddy that ran beneath the cliffs on the outgoing tide. Beyond her, the gunboats had tacked again, and still further into the bay the frigates awaited the change of wind and tide.

Perseverance appeared in the dim light with Hayden's night glass, taking his ordinary glass under an arm. "Thank you, Perse," Hayden said.

"Can you make out the rocks in the narrows with that?" Barthe asked.

Hayden lifted the instrument and gazed into the gathering dark, the world suddenly upside down, for the night glass inverted everything and took some familiarity of use. "Just." He pointed. "Our present course will see us pass to seaward of them."

For a few moments they carried on, the fitful breeze bearing them over the dark, glassy waters. Hayden turned and could still distinguish the marines standing over the men in the waist, muskets raised. Even in the near-dark he could discern the fear and tension by the attitude of their bodies. Lanterns were lit, and the ship's bell rung. Along the deck, one of the sail-trimmers whispered to another, and a bosun's mate smacked the offender with his rattan.

A powder monkey, an orphan of ten or eleven, carried a cartridge up onto the forecastle, but the gun captain, Baldwin, turned the lad around. "That is for the carronades, Lytton," he whispered, and sent the boy off with a pat on the shoulder, as though he were his own child.

They were good men, most of them, Hayden thought. But the rest were a mystery: secretive and cunning. Murderous, too, perhaps.

It was becoming increasingly difficult to judge the distance to the chase, which was still utterly becalmed and barely making headway with the boats hauling.

"Baldwin? Aim your gun, if you please. We will put a shot across her bow. Try not to kill the men rowing."

"Aye, sir."

A handspike was used to shift the chase-piece, and the gun captain elevated the barrel, sighting carefully along its length.

"Ready, sir."

"Wait a moment yet . . ." Hayden held up his hand. As if that were a sign, the wind died away completely.

"Damn!" Hayden swore.

Still, the great mass of the ship meant that she would carry her way for some distance.

"It is now or never, Mr Baldwin."

"Aye, sir." The gun captain took one more look along the length of the barrel, moved clear of the recoil, and pulled the firing lanyard. The report of the six-pounder broke the stillness, sending up a flock of seabirds. The smoke vomited out before the bow, and slowly the boat drifted into the cloud.

Wickham ran out to the end of the bowsprit, stood a moment in the cloud of smoke, and then pulled off his hat and cheered. "They've struck, sir! They're hauling down their colours."

Hayden felt himself sigh. "The ship is yours, Mr Landry. But you must support us until the prize is secured. Do you understand?"

The sour little lieutenant nodded; he glanced resentfully over his shoulder at the distant British frigate—witness to all that would occur.

"The tide will turn of a moment, and soon there will be a breeze from out of the bay. We must get the prize away before the frigates can reach us."

Again Landry nodded, and just as sourly.

Hayden returned the gesture, then hurried along the deck. "You have this in hand, Mr Hawthorne?" he asked as he passed.

"Not to worry, sir. Just secure our prize."

"That I will, Mr Hawthorne."

Hayden took his cutlass from his servant and scrambled over the side, finding a place in the bow of the cutter instead of in the stern-sheets by the coxswain. He would be at the back of the men at the sweeps, who could not see him unless they turned; an advantage, given the state of affairs.

"Away boats," he called. "Make for the prize, Mr Childers."

The boats pushed off and the sweeps flashed out. Hayden stared into the gloom a moment, the prize a dusky mass against the cliff.

"These Frenchmen might play us a trick yet," Hayden said to the men, "especially now that the *Themis* has lost her wind and might be unable to bring her guns to bear. We must be prepared for them to attempt to repel boarders."

"They would never—" but then Childers caught himself. "Would they, Mr Hayden?"

"If they were French Navy I would trust them to be honourable, Childers, but the masters of these ships could also be the owners, and they might be a little more desperate, and not think through what resistance might mean. But let us hope that is not the case."

Hayden looked up toward his own ship, almost still upon the calm sea. A voice broke the evening quiet.

"What the bloody hell is this? Landry, damn your eyes! Who fired that gun?" A second's silence. "Mr Hawthorne . . . what is it you do, sir?"

The marine's answer was too quiet to understand.

"I feel unwell . . ." came Hart's voice, travelling freely over the water. "Give me your arm, Doctor. Landry . . . ?"

"Sir," Landry answered, the quaver in his voice clear at two hundred feet.

"Steady on, lads," Hayden said quietly. "There is no turning back now. Our prize money is there for the taking."

Would Landry have the sense not to tell Hart the boats were away?

"Are these the cliffs of Brest?" Hart asked. His voice was heavy, the words slurred.

"Damnation!" Hayden whispered. *"Pull!"*

"We were reconnoitring the French fleet when the wind died, Captain," Hayden heard Barthe announce loudly.

Good man, Hayden thought. Draw the captain's attention away from the prize and the boats. It was now so dark that Hayden thought the boats might be all but invisible from the deck of the frigate.

He turned to see if the prize showed signs of resistance. The barge was to starboard of them and pulling hard—gaining on them, actually. The second cutter was just in their wake, but keeping station. With a little luck, the master of the transport would not know how many men came from the English ship, which might make any thought of resistance less appealing.

Hayden stood up in the bow, cupped his hands to his mouth, and called out with the greatest confidence he could muster: *"Préparez-vous à être abordés! Au moindre signe de résistance, notre navire ouvrira le feu."**

He waited, wondering if a musket ball would be the answer, but there was only hushed conversation in French.

"Mr Hayden!" came Landry's voice out of the dark. "Captain Hart requires that you return to the ship at once."

"Fucking poltroon!" one of the rowers muttered.

---

*"Prepare to receive boarders! Do not make any sign of resistance or our ship will open fire."

"Silence, there," Hayden snapped. He looked back at the *Themis*, barely visible in the gloom.

"What shall I do, sir?" the coxswain asked over the heads of the men.

Hayden hesitated only a second. "Row on. They can court-martial me if they wish. I will do my duty, even so."

One of the men at the oars spoke up. "I'm sure Lieutenant Landry said, 'Return *with* the ship at once.' He must mean the chase, sir. Return with the chase."

"Wickham . . . ?" Hayden said. "Is that you?"

"Yes, sir."

"How did you get aboard?"

"I thought you might need some help, sir."

Hayden almost laughed. "Are you sure Landry said 'with the ship'?"

"Quite certain, sir."

"Then I'm sure you're right. Row on!" he ordered, and was gratified to see the other boats did not hesitate but stayed their course.

"Mr Hayden . . . !" Landry called.

The steep topsides of the transport loomed out of the dark, and the sharp report of a musket and a tongue of flame greeted them. The ball struck the oarsman nearest Hayden, who grunted once then slid limply down.

Raising his pistol, Hayden fired at the dark form above, and a man toppled into the sea not a yard distant. The boat came alongside with a thump, and gunfire cracked all around as his own men brought their weapons to bear. Hayden threw a grappling hook at the shrouds and scrambled up the side of the ship. He fought a man off with his cutlass as he came over the rail, but a second man managed to run a bayonet through his jacket. Wickham shot the Frenchman as he pulled back for a second try, tumbling him to a deck turning rapidly bloody.

Gunfire quickly gave way to the clash of steel, the English sailors grunting and cursing as they went to work. It was all over in a moment, or so it seemed, the crew of the transport unwilling to give up their lives for their cargo. Many escaped in the boats, and the few who remained were herded together on the forecastle.

Wickham appeared out of the dark, flushed with excitement. "Are you hurt, sir?"

"A scratch. Mr Franks? Are we secure below?"

"Aye, Mr Hayden. Flushed a few Frenchies out of their hidey-holes."

"Well done." Hayden stared along the deck, barely visible in the cold starlight. A few men were down, tended by their fellows, and some others were being slid over the side—he hoped they were not his. "Wickham? Spin the wheel, if you please, and see if the helm answers."

The boy jumped to the helm.

Hayden knew if the French master had disabled the steering they would be in trouble. Walking quickly about the deck, Hayden assessed the situation. The sails were still set, though they wafted about with every roll of the ship, no wind to make them sleep. The brief altercation had done no damage to the ship that he could see. As he came onto the quarterdeck, Wickham spotted him.

"The helm answers, Mr Hayden."

"Then we have a chance of slipping away. I want a lookout aloft. Price—up you go." One of the crew jogged to the shrouds and ran lightly up. "Can you see the gunboats?"

There was a moment of silence. "Lanterns in the necks all, sir."

"That will be them, I think. The French frigates . . . can you see them?"

"No, sir, but there's a mass of lights in the anchorage, Mr Hayden."

"I'm sure there is," Hayden said to himself. "Can you make out the *Themis*?"

Silence from aloft.

"There she is, sir!"

Hayden suspected the man was pointing, but he could barely make him out in the dark.

"Where away?"

"Nor'west by north. A mile or more, sir."

"Tide's turning, Mr Hayden," Franks reported.

Hayden stood a moment, aligning the top of the nearby cliff with a distant star. "So it is, Mr Franks. Let it carry us out to sea."

Hayden took the wheel. "Mr Wickham, will you make a count of our wounded . . . and any we've lost."

"I will, sir." The boy went to the nearest gathering of men all crouched about a comrade, and Hayden heard him whispering. The boy had a good touch with the men. There was sincerity in his manner that could not be feigned. The men sensed his concern was genuine.

Hayden lined up another point on the cliff and a star, gauging their speed. A breeze rustled the sails. He felt it on his face—a warm, fragrant wind off the land. A fair breeze. Whether it would also carry gunboats, he didn't know. It blew a moment, then died away.

"Mr Franks? You are now sailing master and bosun together. Station the men as best you can to work the ship. Square the fore-topsail yard. As soon as we have sternway I shall put the helm over for the starboard tack. We must get clear of these cliffs and out to sea, if we can."

"Aye, sir."

Franks began calling out names, and much to Hayden's relief, the hands responded with a will, just as they had when boarding the ship. The disaffected aboard the *Themis* had not come off in the boats, apparently—either that or prize money had temporarily dulled their republican ideals.

The yards were shifted just as the breeze filled in. Hayden put the helm over, and in a moment the ship began to answer. As the bow fell off, the sails filled gently, and the fore-topsail yard was braced around quickly. Hayden could feel her motion check. Slowly the ship began to make way.

"Keep the wind on the quarter, Mr Franks. When we are able, we'll wear and stand out to sea on a south-westerly course. Aloft there! Can you see the *Themis* or the other frigate?"

"The *Themis* is on the other tack, Mr Hayden," came a voice from aloft. "The other frigate . . . I can't see, sir," the lookout called. "Wait, sir! I can see lanterns. Due west, Mr Hayden."

"That will be she," Hayden said. "Keep her in sight, if you can."

Wickham came quietly onto the deck, his manner very grave. "Two dead, sir: Green and Starr. Six wounded." He hesitated. "Though Smyth won't live out the hour, I don't think. We can't stop the bleeding."

"I am dismayed to hear it. We need Dr Griffiths, but we'll never catch the *Themis* in this bucket." Hayden had no illusions of his own medical abilities, but handed the helm to Wickham and went forward to see to Smyth.

The man lay on the foredeck, tended by his mates. They had made him as comfortable as they could, but a thick pillow of cloth pressed to his side was quickly turning sodden with blood.

"Are you in pain, Smyth?" Hayden asked the man, his face barely visible in the moonlight.

The wounded sailor did not speak but only shook his head—a silent lie, Hayden was sure. He stayed a moment longer, then took his leave, beseeching the men to do what they could for his comfort. In a moment he was aft, where he took the wheel from a sad-looking Wickham. The two stood in silence for five minutes.

Hayden gave the wheel a spoke. "So, that was your first action, Wickham?"

"Yes, sir. It was. I should have thought better of it had we not suffered men killed and wounded."

"Yes, damned French master. He hauled down his colours and then had a change of heart when the *Themis* could not bring her guns to bear. The villain!"

"He paid for it, sir. Franks cracked his pate."

"Is he still aboard?"

"No, sir. We put him over the side—dead."

Hayden had no answer for that. The man had paid dearly for his treachery, but so had Hayden's crew: two dead, likely three by morning. And then there was the wait to see whose wounds would develop putre-faction. The sailors feared that more than death in action.

"Did you hear about the cargo, sir?" the boy said, his mind turning away from the sad news.

"I did not."

"Grain, sir."

"Well, that is good news!"

"Aye, sir. My first prize."

"We have not got away yet, Wickham. There are frigates and gunboats and shoals and rocks, and nary a handkerchief of wind to carry us to safety."

"We will slip away. I have no doubt of it." The boy's confidence was heartening. "But what will happen when we find the *Themis*, sir?"

Hayden knew precisely what the boy meant. He wondered the same thing himself. Hart would no doubt be furious. They had disobeyed a direct order—and he was not sure their claim not to have heard it properly would hold much water. But they had taken a prize and reconnoitred the fleet in Brest Roads. Hart had been too ill to command the ship, and when he did come on deck and given orders his speech was slurred and he could not stand unaided. His competence could be brought into question.

"Sir?"

"Pardon me, Wickham," Hayden said quietly. "I don't know what will happen. I am not Captain Hart's protégé, that is certain. Prize money might not counterbalance disobeying orders and getting three of his crew killed."

"Oh, he shall not be troubled about the deaths, sir. I can assure you that. Disobeying his orders, though . . . The captain does not like to be defied in the least thing. Mr Arnold, our old first, used to say that if the captain ordered you to steer south and you deviated to avoid wrecking the ship he would have you court-martialled for insubordination."

Hayden wished the men would not speak to him so—as though they all conspired against the captain and so could say whatever they liked. Yet what was he to do? Defend Hart? He had just disobeyed the man's orders and conspired with the doctor to take command of the ship, however briefly.

Lurking beneath the surface was an awareness that he had done more than disobey Hart—he had proven to the crew that he was not in the least shy. Let Hart abuse him in public all he liked, the timid captain would now never be shut of the knowledge that Hayden could do what he could not—and that the crew were, to a man, sensible of it. All Hart's bullying would now be seen for what it was—malice inspired by envy.

"Divide the crew into two watches, Mr Wickham . . . I will stand the first watch and you the second. The off-watch may sleep on the deck. It will be a quiet night, I expect."

"Aye, sir." Wickham went off about his business, without question.

He posted lookouts, for there were frigates about and maybe gunboats, too. His disposition of the crew showed an admirable balance between the needs of the ship and the requirements of discipline, while still rewarding the men for their part in the action by easing the regulations a little.

Some spirits were found and the off-watch—and some of the men on watch, he feared—sat on the deck in the moonlight and got quietly drunk. Hayden cautioned them to make no noise as there might be enemy ships in the dark. He purposely carried no lanterns and trusted to sharp eyes and starlight to keep them safe. If his prize were run down by a British frigate he would look the fool, but they were no match for a French frigate and had to trust to darkness to keep them safe.

The shore breeze carried them a few miles out to sea, where Hayden hove-to for the night. Two hours after midnight the wind died away altogether, and the ship lay on a glassy sea. The waning moon rose at midnight, forming an almost unbroken silver path to the shore.

Hayden could not sleep. It was not worry about the morrow, though his mind did stray there, now and again. More he thought of his childhood visits to Brittany and his mother's people dwelling there. How different they had seemed to his parents' friends in England. The smells of the houses came back to him on the land breeze. The scent of gardens or baking bread, hay new-mown. He felt what he could only describe as a deep longing for his mother's homeland—a place where he had known great happiness as a child. How he regretted those few weeks in Paris now, for they had tainted his perception of his mother's people, and made him question his own understanding. If only he'd been at sea for that time, far from the mobs and inflammatory speeches, the calls to the barricades.

Until he had taken this commission, Hayden had always found matters clearer at sea. The enemy sailed under a known flag and one was never puzzled about their culpability—it was a simple matter of sinking or taking them before they did the same to you. The sea he had known since childhood, and he had managed a ship in almost every imaginable condition. He trusted himself at sea far more than upon the land. But clarity aboard ship had been surrendered the day he set foot on the *Themis*, where nothing was as it seemed. To find himself, now, but a few miles from his uncle's home, aboard a French prize, waiting to be castigated for doing his duty—it was a strange pass.

Hayden had been on voyages where the wind and the sea would not allow you to go where you wished. The forces of weather were too great to contend with, leaving the captain either to wait until the weather favoured him, or to adjourn to some place the weather would allow. He wondered why he persisted in His Majesty's Navy when the Navy itself was like a force of nature trying to turn him back. There was no indication that this weather would ever change.

But he had sided with the English in this improbable war, and there was a part of him that believed success in his career would mean acceptance among his father's people.

Hayden's self-awareness was certainly enough that he knew his father could not be forgotten in this matter. He had been a promising officer whose career had been cut short. There was a trust there. A task to be completed. A standard to be taken up. Foolish, perhaps. Sentimental, certainly. But he wished to finish what his father could not.

"You cannot make a dead man proud," he muttered to himself.

A throat quietly cleared not a yard away, making him spin around.

"I think it is my watch, sir," Wickham said. The moonlight threw a shadow net of rigging over the boy.

"Is it?"

The midshipman nodded. "Yes, sir."

"Then the deck is yours. You won't object if I sit here on the rail? The moonlight is very fair."

"So it is, sir." Wickham came and stood by the rail, looking out to sea. "It is a strange night, sir. Reflective, I suppose."

"Why is that?"

The boy shrugged. "Even a small action, like the one we fought today, makes a body philosophical. It is hard to grasp that a man can be alive one instant and dead the next. Like a candle being snuffed. I ran my cutlass through a Frenchman's breast—right through the heart, I'm sure. He fell, and I could see his face as I withdrew my blade. He knew in that instant that I had killed him. I shall never forget his expression, sir. What an appalling thing to have done—stolen away a man's life . . ." The boy fell silent.

"Yes, it is. There is nothing worse. Was that the man who tried to bayonet me?"

"Aye, sir."

"You killed him, but you saved my life, for which I have not thanked you."

"No need, sir. You might save my life someday. Shipmates," he said, as though it were all the explanation necessary.

"The Frenchmen we killed today," Hayden said suddenly. "I felt I knew them. The harbour at Brest was well known to me when I lived here, and the docks were thick with such men, all in their Breton sailors' caps, shirt-sleeves rolled." Hayden glanced at Wickham in the moonlight, only to find a look of desperate distress on the boy's face. "I wish I had some sage advice for you, Mr Wickham, but I think the best a man can say is: it is a war. Those men would have killed you without a moment's hesitation. It is a terrible thing, but the radicals must be stopped. Best we keep the guillotine on their side of the Channel." Hayden wondered if his own misgivings made his words sound as false as they felt.

The boy nodded, trying valiantly to regain his composure. "Yes, sir. It was just the first time . . . I'm sure I'll make my peace with it."

"I'm sure you will."

One of the crew walked by, keeping himself awake on watch by staying on his feet.

"It is rather like a holiday, isn't it, sir?" Wickham said, making Hayden laugh. "I mean, the men all sleeping about the deck, and no one turning the glass or striking the bell."

"Yes, exceedingly like a holiday," Hayden agreed.

"The men are all very pleased about the prize money, Mr Hayden."

"Tell them not to spend it before our claim has gone through the Prize Court."

"Is it true that the men aboard the other frigate will share in our prize?"

"It is, yes."

"That hardly seems fair."

"Well, a prize might not strike so quickly if there were not another ship nearby. So even if she does not fire a shot, a second ship can influence the action."

"But the other frigate could never have reached the transport on that wind, and we were forced to fight, despite her presence."

"All that is true, but one day it will be your ship in the offing and you receiving a share of the prize money for doing little or nothing, and then you'll see the justness of it, I'll wager."

Wickham laughed gently. "Perhaps you are right, Mr Hayden. I will leave you to your thoughts, sir."

Hayden was not sure that he wanted to be left to his thoughts. The many notions that found him in the dark of night—anxieties and doubts—come morning, often seemed not worth all the anguish. But these ideas visited him by night whether he made them welcome or not.

Fourteen

Hayden woke at first light, groggy and out of sorts. His sleep had been full of dreams, some dark, violent, and cruel—reliving the brief skirmish he'd just survived—but others had been so sweet they had made his heart ache. Dreams of a girl he'd adored as a boy spending the summer of his tenth year in France. In his dream she had told him his blue eye was "for the sea" and his green "for the earth," though in real life she had been much given to laughter and not to sounding like some gypsy fortune-teller.

"Good morning, sir." Midshipman Lord Arthur Wickham was standing at the taffrail, perusing the sea with a French glass. "I can see the *Themis*, sir. And the French coast is just visible to the east."

They were under way in a faint north-west breeze, making perhaps two knots due south. Hayden rose stiffly and turned a slow circle, examining the sea. The sky was opalescent, splashed across the eastern horizon with volcanic orange and red. High, irregular clouds dappled the vault, the moon in its last quarter pale among them. It was shaping up to be a fair day.

"Good morning to you, Mr Wickham. And how fare our sick and wounded this morning?" Hayden asked.

The boy made a face. "We lost Smyth, sir, though he clung to his life for a beastly long time."

"I'm sorry to hear it. May God rest his soul."

"Aye, sir. So said we all."

"If you please, Mr Hayden . . ."

Hayden turned to find the coxswain, Childers, bearing a tray.

"It's just boiled porridge and apples, sir. But that's the French master's own coffee. Mr Wickham said you might not mind eating on deck, sir."

"I would not. Thank you, Childers."

The coxswain made a knuckle and retreated back to his duties as steward, apparently. Hayden sat himself down upon a little bench-seat built up against the taffrail, and placed the tray on his knee. He was, to his surprise, famished.

"What of the prisoners, Mr Wickham?"

"Mr Franks is seeing to their needs, sir. He rousted out their own cook and put him to work. He said French victuals would be good enough for the prisoners, but wouldn't answer for Englishmen."

Hayden, who had grown up on French fare, hid his smile. A few bites into his breakfast, and the lookout called: "*On deck!* Sail sou'west by south."

"Is it the second frigate, Mr Lawrence?" called Wickham, who seemed if not his usual self, at least not overly subdued, which Hayden was happy to note.

"I think it is, Mr Wickham. It's making to intercept our course about where we'll meet the *Themis*."

"You can't make out her colours?"

"Not yet, sir, but when the sun's up . . ."

"Thank you, Lawrence."

Hayden sipped his steaming coffee and almost sighed. He had been killed half a dozen times over during the night, and here he was the next morning, drinking his morning coffee aboard a prize.

It had become apparent, during the dark hours, that his side stung and his shirt clung to his skin where the bayonet had run through his jacket. Finishing up his meal, Hayden stood, coffee in hand, and regarded the distant frigates. One was undoubtedly the *Themis*, and the second was almost as certainly British. Hayden couldn't imagine a French frigate sailing so boldly toward the *Themis*, knowing there was a second British ship in these waters.

The sun's limb touched the horizon, lifting slowly through the thin band of cloud.

"*On deck!* British colours at the mizzen," the lookout called down.

"Thank you, Mr Lawrence," answered Wickham. Seeing the first lieutenant had finished breaking his fast, the midshipman tipped his hat. "Your orders, sir?"

"You seem to have everything in hand, Mr Wickham. You might want to place me in irons before you take me aboard the *Themis*, but otherwise, carry on."

Hayden removed his jacket, unbuttoned his waistcoat, and found his shirt pasted to his side by a sticky mass of blood.

"Oh, sir, you're wounded!" Wickham said.

"Not compared with many another. Childers?" Hayden called the coxswain. "Is there some water on the boil?"

"There is, sir."

"May I have a bowl?"

"Aye, sir."

Hayden used the hot water to wash his wound as best he could, and found, to his relief, that it was a comparatively minor gash about three inches long. Childers bound it up for him and one of the men washed most of the blood from his shirt and waistcoat and hung them up to dry. A shirt was found among the dead French master's linen, and Hayden pulled it on, slipping a jacket over top, not unaware that his uniform now reflected his parentage—part English, part French.

The *Themis* scratched a small wake across the blue surface of the sea, barely rocking in the calm waters. She turned to starboard as the two ships closed, clewed up her main and fore-course, and backed her main topsail. It took Hayden some time to wear the transport, due to their small crew, but they were soon hove-to thirty yards from the frigate. One of their cutters was brought alongside, and leaving Franks in charge of the prize, Hayden and Wickham descended into the boat.

"Well, now I'm for it," Hayden said, feeling his resentment kindle.

"You just took a French prize, Mr Hayden. You should be cheered as you come aboard."

"I don't imagine huzzas are what Captain Hart has in mind."

They were soon alongside the frigate and Hayden clambered quickly up the side, feeling that no matter how much abuse was heaped upon him, he would, in some intangible way, have the upper hand in his struggle with Hart until the captain proved himself in battle. As he came over the rail he was met by silence from the crew, but Hawthorne gave him a hand, smiling broadly.

"Well done, Mr Hayden! Well done!"

"How went our mutiny?" Hayden asked quietly, glancing fore and aft. There were more marines than usual stationed about the deck, but otherwise all seemed quiet.

"There were some floggings, sir, but it amounted to very little," Hawthorne said quietly, but looked worried all the same. "We shall speak of it later."

Mr Barthe came smiling down the deck and shook his hand. "Our first prize of the war," he said warmly, "and all on your account, Mr Hayden." He shook Wickham's hand as well. "What is aboard her?"

"Grain," Wickham said.

Barthe's smile broadened. "Let the sailors of Brest go without their mealy French bread," he said. "Their misfortune is our fortune."

Landry was standing nearby, hands clasped behind his back. "The captain would see you in his cabin, Mr Hayden."

Hayden nodded, glanced at Hawthorne, who raised an eyebrow and shook his head. The first lieutenant walked toward the quarterdeck companionway, sure his court-martial would be announced momentarily. As he went below, he glimpsed the other frigate ranging up under a press of sail.

A marine at the captain's door announced him and Hayden doffed his hat and stepped into the great cabin. Hart stood by the stern windows, hands behind his back, staring out at the sun-dappled sea. Hayden waited for some time before Hart finally turned toward him. Instead of the anger he expected, Hart's features were composed, even aloof, as though he had been put upon by some other and had retreated into exaggerated dignity.

"Never in my years of service have I had an officer disregard my orders so thoroughly as did you last night. Nor have I had a lieutenant under my command wilfully put my ship and her people into such peril." The look of haughty disdain disappeared, and the hazy eyes narrowed. "The courts-martial shall put an end to your capers, sir. Try to make me look the fool! It is nothing but damned luck that you did not wreck the *Themis* and drown my crew." He slammed his fist down on the paper-strewn table. "Damn your eyes, sir! You shall not serve aboard a ship in the King's Navy again! I will see to it!"

Through the open window came a hail from another ship. The second frigate had ranged alongside.

Hart looked around as though confused, then gathered his wits. "You shall take the prize to Portsmouth and, upon my return, face a court-martial. Now remove yourself from my sight."

Hayden made a small bow, and left the cabin. It was no worse than he had expected. Hart had much influence with the Admiralty, so his threat was not empty, prize or no prize.

Very little aboard a ship was secret, and Hart's threat would have been heard. Within the hour everyone would know. Well, at least he would be off the ship. He would return to Portsmouth and make his report to Philip Stephens. One could hardly say he had fulfilled his commission, and he didn't believe the First Secretary would think so either.

Up in the sunlight, Hayden could see the men gathered along the rail, and the masts of the frigate beyond. Hart appeared on the deck almost immediately, and went to the rail, where the midshipmen and warrant officers parted before him, everyone sensing his anger. Hayden pushed through the men and found himself looking at the *Tenacious*, her captain standing on the rail, holding on to the mizzen shrouds with one hand.

"Hart, you young fire-breather!" Henry Bourne called across the calm water. "That was as neat a piece of work as I have ever seen! It took some bottom to slip in there with gunboats and frigates threatening, wind dying away, darkness approaching—not to speak of Les Fillettes! I feel avaricious to claim my share . . . but my crew do not agree." A charming grin spread over his face. "I could not see all that happened in the dark. We could just make out the Frenchman hauling down his colours and then we heard musket fire and some hot work, or so it seemed. What was it that transpired?"

Hart hesitated a second and then answered, "They hauled down their colours, but then the captain found his courage when the wind died."

"The scoundrel!" Bourne cried, still grinning. "Well, I shall take the greatest pleasure in writing my report for the Admiralty. This is one action where I shall not have to exaggerate the courage or enterprise of the men involved. Who led the boarding party?"

"One of my lieutenants," Hart said casually.

"Tell me who it was so that I might mention him by name . . ."

"No need, Bourne. I shall see he gets all that he deserves," Hart answered.

Bourne turned his gaze to the crew gathered at the *Themis*' rail, then shaded his eyes. "Is that Mr Hayden?"

The first lieutenant doffed his hat and raised a hand.

"Well, now I understand!" Bourne continued. "You had aboard a pilot. There is no man in His Majesty's Navy who knows the port of Brest more thoroughly." He glanced down. "My boat is launched. Let me come across to you. There is a matter I wish to speak of."

Hart gave a little bow and a wave of the hand. The agile Bourne was down into his cutter in a moment. Marines were quickly lined up and the bosun's mate piped the captain aboard. The marines stamped the deck and presented arms.

The genial Bourne shook Hart by the hand, offering his congratulations again. He turned to Hayden. "It wasn't you who led the boats, was it, Mr Hayden?"

"It was, sir. The men did not shrink from the danger in the least. It was an honour to lead them."

"Spoken like the gifted officer you are," Bourne said, then turned to Hart.

"You are a fortunate man indeed to have Mr Hayden as your first. Were it within my power to grant, he would have made his post by now."

Hart hid his reaction to this, but neither did he make any sign of agreement.

The officers were introduced, and Bourne, who was a man of great charm, won them all over with little more than a smile and his apparently genuine pleasure to make the acquaintance of each one of them. He took special notice of Wickham when told that he had been in the boarding party that had taken the prize.

"I believe Mr Wickham saved my life," Hayden told him.

"For that you have my thanks," Bourne said, "for Mr Hayden is dear to me."

They repaired below, Bourne sweeping Hayden, Wickham, Landry, and Barthe up in his wake. The table in the captain's cabin was soon set with a light meal, and Bourne spread his particular charm and good-will over the gathering. The company, aware of his reputation, hung on his every word. In a moment he was telling stories, some featuring exploits in which Hayden had played some small part—though Bourne did much to exaggerate this and to sing his praises.

As the meal came to an end, Bourne asked Hart if they might have a word.

"Certainly Mr Hayden may stay," Bourne said, as the gathered officers began to file out.

When the door was closed, Bourne turned to Hart, fixed him with that natural smile, and asked, "I don't know whom you would send home with the prize, but I have a second lieutenant who has a pressing need to see England. His wife gave birth to a new daughter but ten days past. He is a thorough sea-going officer. Were you to grant him the command, your prize would arrive in Portsmouth in good order, I have no doubt."

"I had planned to send Hayden," Hart said, not looking too pleased.

"I know it is a great favour I ask, and somewhat irregular, but the young man's heart is not upon the sea at the moment, and it will allow you to keep your first lieutenant with you, which I'm sure would meet with your approval. Let me assure you, Hart, I am not seeking in any way to claim even the smallest part of the honour you deserve for your bold endeavour. You may be assured of that. And I should be forever in your debt."

Hayden could see that Hart had no wish to comply, and certainly did not give a damn for any second lieutenant with a newborn child. "Who will make up the prize crew, then?"

"If you wish it," Bourne offered, "I will make up half the muster from my own men. Will that answer?"

"I *am* short of crew . . ." Hart mused, then nodded reluctantly.

Bourne patted Hayden on the shoulder. "Then you and Mr Hayden will be left to harry the unsuspecting French. Wait till I inform the Lords of the Admiralty that you sailed into the Goulet so far that I thought you would touch jib-booms with the ships in the anchorage. Not much further and the batteries would have had you in their sights. That took some nerve!"

Hart nodded graciously and rose to his feet. "I suppose we should be about our duties, then."

Hayden followed Hart and Bourne up to the deck.

"If you can spare Lieutenant Hayden for a brief interval," Bourne said to Hart as they reached the rail, "there are several of his former ship-mates who I'm certain would like to see his handsome face again."

"Mr Hayden has duties aboard the *Themis*," Hart said curtly.

The smile on Bourne's face barely wavered. "Quite right," he said. Bourne made his good-byes, thanked Hart again, and went nimbly down the ladder and into his cutter.

As soon as Bourne was out of earshot, Hart turned to his first lieu-tenant but did not meet his eye. "It seems, Mr Hayden, you shall have a reprieve," he said quietly, "due to the intervention of your friend Bourne. I hope you will endeavour to earn my approval in the future."

"I have never done anything but, sir," Hayden answered.

This caused Hart to raise an eyebrow. "Take yourself over to the prize and make a complete inventory of the ship. I don't want to find we've been cheated in any way when we reach the Prize Court."

Hayden drew himself up. "Sir, Captain Bourne is a man of unim-peachable honour."

Hart fixed him with a dark look, and Hayden touched his hat.

"A boat, if you please, Mr Archer," the lieutenant called out.

Hayden swiftly assembled a few men who could both count and write, and bore them over to the French transport.

As the only one perfectly fluent in French, Hayden took on the task of going over the ship's papers, searching for the manifest and bills of lading. The captain, whose name had been La Fontaine, was a man who had believed in order, and Hayden quickly found what he was looking for. In a drawer he also found a letter, unfinished and dated the day previous.

It read:

> *Ma chère Marie,*
>
> *Je t'écris en toute hâte, car alors même que nous pénétrons dans Le Goulet qui mène à la Rade de Brest, une frégate anglaise est pratiquement sur nous. Les vents ne nous permettent d'espérer les secours d'aucun navire. Nous nous rendrons s'il le faut, mais nous nous battrons si nous avons une chance. J'ignore ce que nous réservent les prochaines heures. Mon destin est entre les mains de Dieu et si je dois me présenter devant Lui, je n'aurai d'autre regret que la perte des jours que j'espérais passer auprès de toi.**

A quick search revealed a box of private correspondence. The lieutenant added the unfinished letter to this, found what other personal belongings he could, and carried them up into the sunlight.

"What have we there, Mr Hayden?" Franks asked, a yellowed smile appearing. "A bit of treasure?"

"The personal effects of the ship's master. I will send them on to his widow."

---

* My Darling Marie:

I write in great haste, for though we are entering the Goulet that leads into the Rade de Brest, an English frigate is all but upon us and the wind will not allow any ships to come to our aid. We will surrender if we must, but fight if we can. I do not know what the next hours will hold. My fate is in the hands of God, and if I meet Him I will regret nothing in this life but the loss of the days I had hoped to share with you.

The smile disappeared from the bosun's face. "Very kind of you, Mr Hayden. Very 'genteel,' as the French would say. That is what they say, isn't it, sir?"

"*Très gentil.*"

"Just as I said . . ."

A boat came alongside from the *Tenacious*, and with his second lieutenant, Captain Bourne appeared on the transport's deck.

Hayden gave the young second the appropriate papers, and left him to go over the ship on his own. No officer would take command of a vessel without ascertaining her seaworthiness and the general state of her gear. As he expected, the second lieutenant was exacting, efficient, and amiable.

"That was a most agreeable luncheon," Bourne ventured once they were alone. He then took Hayden by the sleeve. "Let us repair below a moment, if I will not disrupt your labours."

"You will not."

In a moment they were in the master's cabin, seated at a little table.

"So tell me, Charles, what really transpired in the dark? We heard shouts ordering you to return to the ship . . ."

"Could you make those out? We weren't sure ourselves," Hayden answered.

Bourne smiled. "So you plunged ahead and carried the transport by force majeure?"

"More or less, yes."

"And where was our intrepid Captain Hart during all this?"

"In his cabin, suffering from migraine. I believe the doctor had given him a soporific. We were away in the boats when the captain came on deck."

Bourne sat back a little in his chair, his face betraying that he had guessed as much. "He had no notion of what went on?"

"Not until we fired the bow-chaser to bring the transport to."

Bourne was quiet a moment, his look troubled. He drummed his fingers on the table.

"I owe you a great debt, sir," Hayden said quietly. "I was to be court-martialled before you appeared this morning."

Bourne blew out through his lips. "Court-martialled! On what charge? Immoderate bravery?" He shook his head in disgust. "How did you ever land aboard Hart's ship? I thought you were to be made Master and Commander when you left me."

"It did seem that such an appointment was in the offing when I left the *Tenacious*, but it did not come to pass. I was ashore without prospects when the First Secretary honoured me with the offer of this position."

"Stephens?"

"Yes, sir."

"Well, let us not be disingenuous; it is a bad situation, Mr Hayden. Hart has a particular character within the Service. Even so, he has his supporters among the Lords Commissioners of the Admiralty. But you will not prosper under his command. I will send my report, and not be coy in revealing your part in the business, but even so, Hart will receive the credit." Bourne sat, lost in thought a moment, then looked up at his former lieutenant. "Don't get yourself killed trying to gain the attention of the Admiralty by daring. It is likely that they will never hear of it from Hart, unless, like last night, there are other witnesses."

"I was not trying to get myself killed. I merely saw the chance of taking an enemy vessel, judged the risks to be acceptable, and did my duty. I knew the waters. The ebb was bound to carry us out to safety, even if the offshore breeze did not fill in. What else was I to do?"

"Exactly, Charles, and I did not mean to imply that you exhibited less than proper caution. You weighed everything to a nicety and acted without hesitation—as I would have expected. Many another would have dithered until the chance was lost. But you've shown Hart to be less than stout-hearted before his crew, not that they did not realize it, but even so . . . Hart will feel the sting of it."

"There is not a thing I might do that would please Captain Hart. The second lieutenant does nothing but capitulate to him in every little thing and Hart despises him as much as the next man. I shall face a court-martial before I will become another Landry."

"And that is completely understandable. But men such as . . ." Bourne hesitated, and then leaned over the table and spoke quietly but earnestly. "Men who secretly know of their own shyness—they hate officers such as you, Charles. Your very existence is nothing less than a constant threat to reveal the horrid truth about them. That is their greatest fear of all—that the world will learn the truth."

Hayden lowered his voice as well. "But as you have said, everyone in the Service knows of the man's character."

Bourne held up both his hands. "Indeed, that is true. But our good captain fantasies that this is not so, that the world has been deceived. He would like nothing better than to be thought the most valiant man in the Royal Navy, but he will never even attempt the deeds that would gain him such a reputation."

"Did you not always tell us, 'Do not seek acclaim; deserve it'?"

Bourne smiled. "So I did, and you have taken it to *heart*, I see."

Hayden laughed. "Poor man. His name lends itself too easily to such wit."

"I am only saying, Charles, that you should be wary of this man. He will do you damage, if he can—at least destroy your reputation."

"I have no reputation. I was fortunate to be offered even a situation such as this."

"Apparently you do have a reputation. Philip Stephens did not choose you because you were a blunderer. He chose you because he knew you were a man of great ability, but without any interest to speak of."

"At least the latter is true, unfortunately."

Bourne rose to his feet, looked down at his former lieutenant, a great deal of concern creasing his noble face. "It is only my intention, Charles, as a friend, to caution you. If Hart cannot break your will, and I don't believe for a moment that he can, then he will attempt to ruin you. Do not underestimate him. His kind have a vast genius for vindictiveness. A vast genius."

Fifteen

The French transport was soon small on the horizon in a moderate sou'west wind; beyond the reach of French privateers, Hayden hoped, many of whom lurked nearby in the hole-in-the-wall harbour of Conquet. Hart had sent along his official report of the action, as had Captain Bourne. A letter to Hayden's particular friend, Thomas Banks, Esq., had also been included in the home-going mail, detailing the lieutenant's singular view of the events.

Writing the initial missives to the First Secretary had made Hayden feel like a traitor—loyalty to his captain had always been reflexive with him—but after witnessing Hart's dereliction of duty, not to mention the way he treated his first lieutenant and the rest of his crew, Hayden felt more like a conspirator than an informer. The man inspired loyalty in no one—except Landry, apparently.

Hayden was not sure what Philip Stephens would do with his letters, but if they would in any way undermine Hart within the Admiralty, Hayden had decided he would not trouble his conscience over it. Fear that his letters would not be kept secret did trouble him, however; informers were despised in the service. If Stephens was not very masterful in his attempts to discredit Hart, and discreet about the source of his information, Hayden would face a future of ostracization; remaining in the service would become impossible. Indeed, he would almost certainly have no choice but to quit the country altogether. The idea of being disdained by his fellow officers distressed him terribly—especially late at night—but he had made his devil's bargain with Stephens and only hoped it would never come to light.

Despite all this, he wondered what Hart had written about the action. He did not need to speculate about what Captain Bourne had communicated to the Lords Commissioners; discreetly, his old champion had sent a copy of his letter to Hayden while still aboard the transport. It had been an utterly fair account and did not make use of any information gained in private conversation with Hayden, but only things he could have known from his position out at sea, and from what he had been told aboard the *Themis*. Even so, Hayden did come off as the hero of the action, and though Hart was praised for his nerve in going into the Goulet after the transports, Bourne had also noted that First Lieutenant Charles Hayden had intimate knowledge of the harbour and its surrounding waters. He let the Lords Commissioners draw their own conclusions from that. Tactfully, Hart's order for the boats to return to the ship before they had reached the transport was overlooked. Only Philip Stephens had that information.

Hayden lowered his glass, brushing the prize from his mind, though he did carry a little buoyant feeling for the prize money that would be due upon some future date. Money was not something Hayden had ever possessed in abundance, and a small windfall would not go amiss.

A general throat-clearing came softly from behind.

Hayden turned. "Mr Archer. May I be of some service?"

"The captain sends his compliments and asks that you attend him in his cabin, Mr Hayden."

Hayden rather doubted that Hart had phrased his request in quite those words, but appreciated Archer's adjustment of the language. "I shall go down immediately, thank you, Mr Archer."

Archer smiled. "My compliments on the prize, Mr Hayden. It was nobly done, sir."

"I'm not sure how nobly it was managed, but we did take the damned ship and that was worth something. Is anyone taking up a subscription for the dead men's families?"

The young lieutenant glanced down, brushing at some detritus on the planks with a polished boot. "Yes, sir. Mr Hawthorne. He asked that everyone contribute one twentieth of their prize money to the widows, but some of the men refused. Others would contribute some share of their money to one man's family but not to another's. It is all a bit of a muddle, sir."

"I'm sorry to hear it. Please tell Mr Hawthorne that he can count on me in the amount of one twentieth. If you will excuse me . . ."

"Certainly, sir. Thank you."

Only aboard the *Themis* would such meanness have occurred in the matter of widows and children. The first lieutenant shook his head, feeling his spirits plunge as he descended the stair. The marine at the door announced him and he found Captain Hart toiling at his table, a pair of spectacles perched upon his nose. The captain's hands were small and fleshy, the knuckles wrinkled little rings joining sections of bloated sausage. Childishly tiny fingernails brought the ends of his stubby fingers to near points—the hands of a gnome or stunted troll. As Hayden watched, Hart gripped his pen awkwardly between thumb and rigid forefinger and stuttered down marks upon the innocent page. He looked up at Hayden over the small lenses.

"I understand you're half a Frenchman, Mr Hayden."

"I am an Englishman, sir. It is my mother who is French."

"You speak the language like a Frenchman, though?"

"I do."

"Good." He slid a sheet of paper out of a neat pile and pushed it across the table toward Hayden. "I am not satisfied with your assessment of the French fleet, Lieutenant," he said. "Without greater confidence, I dare not send such an account to the Admiralty."

Hayden was taken aback. The numbers were Landry's, which he almost explained, but then realized that Hart would likely know this already as the assessment had been written in the second lieutenant's hand.

"There is also the anchorage inside Île Longue, which we have not looked into at all. You can manage a much more thorough survey from the land. I will put you ashore this night and retrieve you on the morrow, one hour after midnight at the northern-most end of the beach below Crozon. Is that clear?"

"It is, sir . . . but Brittany is hardly a safe place for Englishmen, even for those who can pass for French. If *The Times* is to be believed, the province was near to insurrection as recently as July. The people are said to be hiding priests who have refused to sign the civil constitution of the clergy. Not long before we sailed, I read that it was believed several bishops were being hidden near Brest."

Hart eyed him, pushing up the centre of his lower lip so that his chin dimpled oddly. "I will hear no excuses, sir. You will be put ashore and I will tolerate no arguments." For a moment he struggled to find his train of thought, and then went on. "Mr Landry was clever enough to salvage some clothes from the French transport. We'll put you and Lieutenant Hawthorne ashore once it is dark."

"Mr Hawthorne doesn't speak French, sir," Hayden blurted out.

Hart fixed Hayden with the same glare over the top of his spectacles. "Some French money was found aboard the transport and I retained it for just such an excursion." He unlocked a small iron box and took out some French monies that he then slid over to Hayden. "Tomorrow morning, one hour after midnight."

"I understand, sir."

"That will be all."

Hayden found Hawthorne and spent the rest of the afternoon drilling him on a few words and phrases in the French language. If luck favoured them they would stay out of sight by day and speak with no one, but if they were unlucky it would be best, even if Hayden did all the talking, if Hawthorne could not appear to be a mute. He gave the marine lieutenant a French name and tried to explain the manners of their enemy. It was not an entirely successful exercise, though he did feel that Hawthorne's *"Bonjour,"* if mumbled, would almost pass muster.

After some hours of attempted French, Hayden sensed a respite was needed, and poured poor Hawthorne a glass of wine.

"Tell, me," Hayden said, passing the marine a glass, "what finally transpired with our little mutiny on the gun-deck?"

Hawthorne closed his eyes and massaged his temples, as though their language studies had left a residue of pain in his overworked mind. He reached inside his jacket, which hung over the back of a chair, and removed a folded sheet of paper. "I have been trying to give you this."

Hayden unfolded it, and found two columns of names written within. He glanced up at the marine. "It signifies what, Mr Hawthorne?"

"It seemed to me at the time that the gun crews had divided into two camps. No. That is not precisely true. Most of the men at the guns remained aloof from what was happening, but these two groups of men were at odds, though I know not why. It was nearly dark and the whole matter caught me off guard, I am ashamed to admit, so I was not thinking clearly nor were my powers of observation engaged as they should have been . . . but even so, I feel this list cannot be far wrong."

Hayden examined the list of men again.

"But were they mutinous or just two factions who did not care for each other? I have seen crews where one group of men had greater hatred for some other than they ever had for the French."

"I cannot rightly say, Mr Hayden. They were at odds, and I think if you had not deployed my marines so quickly we would have had blood spilt, I truly do—even with an action looming."

"And you heard nothing said? No words shouted in anger, which would give us any indication of the nature of this dispute?"

"Oh, there was a great deal of name-calling and damning each other to hell and the like, but it was the general sort of cursing such as you might hear at any time among provoked seamen."

"And Hart flogged some men this morning?"

"Yes, a rather random collection after he had spoken to myself and a number of midshipmen and the master-at-arms. I'm quite certain that if any ringleaders were punished it was utterly by providence."

Hayden sat back, ran his fingers into his hair, and eyed the marine. "You say the majority of the men were not involved. That is a good sign, at least."

Hawthorne ground his teeth together. "I did say that, and it is more or less true, but . . . it seemed to me that the men who watched were weighing things up . . . I can't rightly explain, but they looked like gents at a cockfight, trying to decide where they would lay their money."

"I had that same feeling at Plymouth, when it appeared the hands might refuse to sail; some were merely waiting to see which direction events might take." Hayden applied himself to his wine. "The men don't understand the risk they run, Hawthorne. 'Mutinous assembly,' 'concealment of mutinous designs'—even 'mutinous language'—can all be punished by death."

"What of cowardice in the face of the enemy?" Hawthorne countered. "How should that be punished?"

"Our positions do not give us the luxury of seeking justice in all things, Mr Hawthorne, as you well know. It is our sworn duty to prosecute a war against the enemies of England, and a ship of war cannot be governed by elected assembly, no matter how much we might wish it could."

Hawthorne sat back and regarded him. "So, men might hang who are in the right, and officers might be promoted who have shied from the enemy at every turn?"

Hayden wondered what perverse twist of fate had landed him in this position—defending a man like Hart. "If you want to live in a just world, Mr Hawthorne, you will have to remove to America, where I'm told all is now perfection."

Hawthorne smiled. "You sound like Aldrich, our foremast philosopher."

"Yes, and Aldrich should learn to be more circumspect or he shall pay a heavy price, I fear."

The smile disappeared from the marine's face. "I have told him the same thing, but Aldrich believes that if one speaks the truth any man capable of reason will eventually have to agree . . . bloody fool."

A little before sunset, Hart ordered the ship to fall in with the coast. The helm was put over, yards shifted, and sails trimmed with a certain alacrity. Men had been flogged that day for insubordination, but Hayden did not think that was what inspired the crew's unusually efficient work. They had taken a prize, and not only was every man aboard materially richer, but their spirits had been enlivened as well. Granted, the prize was only a transport, but they had taken her under circumstances that any sea-going man would have to admit required bottom—many had heard Bourne himself say it. They no longer would be the butt of jests in any anchorage where British ships might gather, and such would raise the spirits of any man.

The wind fell away until it was nothing but whispers of its former glory, and the little frigate barely disturbed the waters as it passed, lifting only a little on the breathing sea. When it became clear that they would not close the coast that night, Hart ordered a cutter over the side.

"You will have to pull for shore," he said. "Carry the French our compliments, Mr Hayden." It was the only attempt at a jest Hayden had yet heard pass the man's lips.

"But we are several miles distant," Hayden objected. "The boat will never make the beach and return to the ship before dawn. The French will suspect you've put men ashore."

"They will never guess it," Hart said. "You can pass for a Frenchman, in any case. Get on with it. Don't waste the night left you."

Hayden and the marine lieutenant went over the side and down into the cutter.

"Away boat," the coxswain said quietly, and the men bent to their sweeps.

Hayden glanced over at Hawthorne, just visible in the stern-sheets.

"How do I look?" Hawthorne inquired, clearly uncomfortable in his French rig.

"Like an Englishman decked over with a Frenchman's clothing."

"I thought as much. Let us hope we meet no one." He was quiet a moment, and in the faint moonlight Hayden could just make out the concern on his face. Leaning toward Hayden, he whispered, "Do you think this endeavour has been designed to be shut of us?"

Hayden made a warning sign to the marine.

"Oh, you needn't worry about Childers." Hawthorne jerked a chin toward the coxswain.

The same thought had crossed Hayden's mind, and secretly he wondered if Hawthorne was not right. "We chose duty in Plymouth. Can we choose differently now?"

"Exactly so," answered Hawthorne, and they fell silent.

The little boat rocked over the low swell, and as the thole-pins had been muffled with rags, there was barely a sound to be heard but the water hissing past the hull and whirling off astern. Hayden was struck by the beauty of the unseasonably warm night—the moon waning toward new, stars hanging bright and crisp in the heavens' dark depths. He felt a strange excitement at returning to France; excitement and trepidation—like meeting again a woman one still loved after a long separation. Feelings washed through him like a running sea, though he could not name them. In vain he tried to push these emotions down, to focus his mind on the task at hand; he had Hawthorne to keep safe, after all. The Brittany where they were about to set foot was not the land of his youth—it was a dangerous place now, and for many reasons.

The pull to shore was long, and as Hayden had predicted, it was near to dawn when they finally slid up on the sand beneath the village of Crozon. Hayden had caused them to be landed at the northern end of the beach, as distant from the small jetty as possible. As Hayden and the marine lieutenant splashed ashore, sailors jumped over the side to push the boat off, knowing that if it were seen by morning and the French could guess from where they had come, a search would certainly follow.

"Good luck to you, sir," Childers whispered as the boat was pushed astern into the lapping waves.

"And you," said Hayden.

The men shoved the boat bodily out until they were waist-deep, then clambered aboard. The long, shadowy oars flashed out against a moon-silvered sea.

"Double time," Hayden said, starting down the beach. "Sun will be up soon."

"Aye, sir," came a voice from behind, "we've not a moment to lose."

Hayden spun around. "Wickham!"

"Aye, sir. I thought you might need another who can speak to the natives. I found some French clothes that fit, do you see?" The boy's face was barely visible in the moonlight, but even so, he looked terribly sheepish.

"You are returning to the ship . . ." But when Hayden turned out to sea, the cutter was already beyond hailing without him calling out loudly. He rounded on the little midshipman.

"Mr Wickham, this is the second time you've come away in the boats without anyone's sanction. Hart will be in a fury when he learns of it."

"You needn't worry, Mr Hayden," Wickham said softly, and only slightly abashed, "the captain will never miss me. You'll see. And last time I saved your life, or so you said."

"And this time we might all lose ours."

"There is nothing for it," Hawthorne said, touching Hayden's sleeve. "Come. We must be on our way. Perhaps Lord Arthur will be an addition to our little *ruse da gar.*"

Hayden was torn between relief to have another who could pass for a Frenchman—or French boy—and his very real vexation at Wickham's cavalier attitude toward discipline.

"*Ruse de guerre,*" Hayden corrected as he began to trot along the margin of the sea where the sand was firmest and they could make the best time.

"Just so," whispered Hawthorne and fell in behind Wickham.

They found the little jetty where a fire burned on the beach, illuminating boats drawn up above the tide line. There were, no doubt, men there, but they were asleep by the fire, Hayden was certain. The Englishmen struck the path that wound up the bank and hurried on.

"Were those guards of some sort?" Wickham whispered as they stumbled up the path.

"So I would guess. Some French variant of Sea Fencibles or Militia. Perhaps even soldiers. I hope we meet no more. Shh . . ."

The noise of them tripping up the path had attracted attention, and someone challenged them in French.

"Shall we make a run for it?"

"Only if you can swim to the *Themis*."

Hayden answered the challenge in French, and led his companions forward.

At the head of the path they were met by two men in matching tunics and round hats—local militia, Hayden suspected. They pointed their muskets at the strangers, though they did not seem to be overly worried that they would meet the enemy here.

"And who are you?" one of the men demanded. "We don't know you."

Hayden knew the accent immediately and answered them not in French but in the local language. At the mere sound of their own speech, the muskets were lowered.

Hayden introduced his companions and rapid-fire conversation took place, some money changed hands, and the three Englishmen were off into the darkness.

When they had gone a hundred yards, Wickham whispered, "That wasn't French . . . was it?"

"Breton," Hayden answered. "They think you are my son, despite the fact that I would have sired you at eight, and they believe Mr Hawthorne is an English smuggler. They look forward to a long and lucrative friendship."

"They knew me as English!" Hawthorne whispered indignantly. "I said only a single word: *bonjour*."

"Yes, well . . ." Hayden responded, and led them on without further comment.

The seaward side of the narrow peninsula was barren and treeless—a heath battered by winter gales off the cold Atlantic. But over the crest of the hill, facing Brest Harbour, the landscape changed to fertile pastures and luxurious woods, as though they had passed into another land entire.

Cottages were avoided, as was the tiny hamlet of Crozon, its church spire visible among the stars. They kept to narrow lanes and fields whenever possible, stealing through the shadows of trees and hedges. Hayden's boyhood memories let him down, now and then, but for the most part they served tolerably well, allowing him to guide his companions if not unerringly, at least tangentially to the place he wished to go. Unfortunately everything looked different by night—all moonlight and shadow. He was forced to stop frequently and match the stark shards of visible landscape with his store of memories.

Dawn was upon them too soon, and they went to ground in a stand of trees, eating a little of the ship's biscuit they bore. Hayden also carried a collapsible telescope and a pistol in his satchel. He had added a book he possessed, on the birds and other animals of eastern Europe, hoping it would suffice as explanation for the glass, if not the flintlock: a natural philosopher observing the miracle of botanical and avian life. By luck, the book had been written in Italian, not English.

In truth the wood was alive with many examples of this miracle: chaffinch, wood lark, blue tit, wren. The men lounged in the morning sunlight, which swam over them, broken and dappled by wind-shivered leaves.

"How much further might it be?" Wickham asked.

"Not more than a mile." Hayden shifted to one side to avoid a root that dug deep into his buttock, but landed upon another. "I think we should stay here most of the day. No sense wandering about in daylight more than is required. People here are curious of strangers, and we don't want to set them to talking or asking questions. If we break cover an hour before sunset that will allow us to reach the point of land where we can reconnoitre Brest Roads, then make our way back toward Crozon through the dusk . . . and starlight, if need be. We shall bribe our friends, the French militiamen, and be on the beach before midnight."

"As easy as rolling downhill," Hawthorne agreed, but his grin said otherwise. "I must say, I don't think much of their agricultural practices. Have they never heard of planting clover? Of rotation? Did you see that patch of abandoned cabbages? Runty and infested. A cobbler could grow better."

Hayden laughed. "We shall not have time for you to improve their methods along scientific lines, I'm afraid, Mr Hawthorne." He looked around. "We are fairly well hidden here and should sleep by turns. It could be another long night. Mr Wickham—"

"I will stand first watch, sir," the midshipman interrupted.

Hayden smiled, and lay down upon the hard ground. "And Mr Hawthorne? I strongly advise against snoring. It will give you away as English."

"I shall sleep like a Frenchman, Mr Hayden. You may count on it."

For a while Hayden lay awake, breathing in the forest scent, which kindled strangely powerful childhood emotions. He had spent a good part of his youth not far from this place, had once played in this very wood with his cousin. The happiness he had known then, the contentment and feeling that the world was both safe and just, flooded back. How much that world had changed! As a boy he had been either French or English by turn, depending upon which country he was in, but circumstances and age would no longer allow that. One must choose—but it was like a child choosing between one's mother or one's father, an unbearable loss either way.

He remembered telling Henrietta that in France he felt like an Englishman masquerading as French. When had that begun? For the life of him he couldn't remember. Of course he never expected it to be so true as it was that night.

Hayden did not know how long he'd slept, but wakened from a deep slumber to a hand on his shoulder. He opened his eyes to find himself in a patch of unseasonably warm sun, overly hot in his French cloak. "Is it my watch?"

"Not yet, sir," Wickham whispered, "but there are people nearby."

Hayden sat up, boiling warm, muddle-headed, and dizzy. He shook his head and tore open his cloak, allowing the small wind to reach him.

"Where away?"

Wickham rose to a crouch and crept through the sparse underwood, pressed aside a branch, and pointed silently. Two young ladies and a throng of children were in the throes of doing what could only be described as gambolling.

"Damn . . ." Hayden whispered.

"What are they about?" Wickham asked.

"Out for a frolic, I would say." He noticed the older girls carried baskets over their arms. "Collecting mushrooms, perhaps."

"I don't suppose they're cousins of yours?"

"No. My uncle's family removed to Arcachon some years ago."

"Bad luck."

Hayden gazed with a certain sadness at the scene; two pretty young women beneath ribboned straw bonnets, aglow with youth and high spirits. The children skipped and ran about them, like a little moving sea, overwhelmed now and then by gales of laughter. How far removed these innocents seemed from the *sans-culottes* of the Paris mob. It was a shock to think that he warred against these people, too.

"If they come into the wood we shall have to slip out the other side, which I do not much favour, as there is a lane and a large farmhouse in that direction and we shall almost certainly be noticed."

"Do you think they'll come into the wood?"

"Very likely, yes. It is a warm day to sit in the sun, and if they're seeking mushrooms, they will come looking in the shade."

"Then I suppose we can only wait," Wickham said, letting the branch go slowly back into place.

"Yes. Better wake Hawthorne. I can hear him snoring from here."

"Aye, sir." Wickham slipped quietly away, leaving the lieutenant to listen to the children's laughter.

Wickham and the marine were back in a moment, Hawthorne looking decidedly out of sorts.

"A drum, Mr Hayden, from the sou'west."

The lieutenant trotted as quickly as he could through the stand of trees, and, crouching behind a fallen log and some low bushes, saw a company of French Regulars heave into view. They marched in perfect columns, rows of blue coats, their officers seated on horseback.

"The forces of the revolution," Hayden whispered. "How they would like to seize some English spies."

"We're not spies," Wickham protested, sounding a little offended. "We're officers of the British Navy."

"In uniform, that is true. Dressed as we are, they would declare us spies, and condemn us as such."

Wickham looked surprised. "What is the penalty for spying in France?"

"The guillotine is the punishment currently favoured." He saw the look on the boy's face grow dark. "But you needn't worry, Lord Arthur. Your father sits in the House of Lords. You they would exchange. Hawthorne and me . . ." He shrugged. "English spies are not their interest at the moment, I suspect. Many in Brittany do not support the convention, and as good papists, they have been hiding reactionary members of the clergy. A military presence here has very little to do with the English."

At that moment the lieutenant of marines blundered through the bush.

"There you are," he whispered, falling down beside them. "One of the children came into the wood, unbeknownst to me. I was observed."

"Jesus, Mary, and Joseph!" Hayden crawled backwards from the log for two yards. "What did they do?"

"I don't know. The child sped off, screaming like an Irish banshee."

"Stay here—both of you." Hayden crawled another few yards into the wood, then was on his feet, running as lightly as he could over the moss and roots. Sunlight from the meadow appeared through the branches, and then the anxious young faces of the ladies. Hayden retrieved his glass from his satchel, and the book as well, smiled broadly, and stepped out of the trees.

"*Bonjour, bonjour, mesdemoiselles.*" He then switched to Breton. "What a perfect day God has granted us! Sunlit and warm, all His creatures abroad." He held up his glass and book, smiling as though a bit embarrassed. "Excuse us for skulking, my friends and me; we were seeking the Sardinian warbler, *Scorbutus cani*, leagues beyond its natural range. You cannot hope to observe one by any strategy but unworldly stealth. He is wary, mesdemoiselles. That little bird is wary."

He could see the apprehension changing to amusement.

"But I have not introduced myself." He made an elaborate, even comic, bow. "Yves Saint Almond at your service."

The children tittered, and the young women smiled. His Breton accent and his clownish manner put them at ease.

"You are not from around here," one of the boys said, eyeing him suspiciously.

"How perceptive you are," Hayden congratulated the child. "But when I was your age I visited this place often. My uncle lived only a short walk away."

"Who might that have been, monsieur?" one of the girls asked. They were much alike, the two of them: willow leaf–shaped eyes, with a little archipelago of faint freckles scattered across their cheeks. They looked as though they had been well fed on farm victuals all their short lives, and were all milky skin and corn-silk hair, supple and tall.

"Gabriel Saint Almond."

"Ah!" the taller said. "The Saint Almonds moved away."

"To Arcachon," Hayden said, and saw all doubt disappear from their faces.

"Marie was heartbroken," the other girl said, and laughed, receiving a cuff on the arm from her friend.

"You knew Guillaume?" Hayden said innocently.

The girls both giggled. "I am Anne Petit," the tall girl offered, "and this is my cousin, Marie. These little brats are a pack of wild wolves, seeking innocent lambs to devour."

"I thought they looked very fierce," Hayden declared gravely. "My friend, he said to me, 'Yves! I was set upon by a pack of wild wolves!' He was almost mad with terror."

The children giggled.

"Guillaume had an English cousin, too, did you know?" Anne asked; she regarded him oddly. "He, too, had differently coloured eyes, monsieur."

"My cousin Charles!" He waved a hand at his face. "It is a family trait, the eyes. But he is in America now, where his mother married a wealthy merchant, and they all live in a big house where they have grown fat and contented."

Anne nodded as though this were what she expected. "We met him, when he was young and we were just children."

"He was not so handsome as Guillaume," Marie said wistfully.

"But wittier," Hayden pronounced. He suddenly pricked up his ears, turning his head from side to side. "Did you hear that? My Sardinian warbler! It calls. If I may beg your leave . . . ?"

The young women smiled and waved for him to go. Hayden slunk back into the trees, pausing just before he disappeared, to raise his glass and examine the high branches of an oak. He waved once and entered the shady hallways of the wood. A few moments later, he found his companions still watching the French soldiers march by.

"You should come away from there, before someone remarks your pale, English faces," Hayden whispered.

"What about the children?" Hawthorne asked.

"I think I have convinced them we are innocent, if somewhat ridiculous, natural philosophers, seeking the rare Sardinian warbler."

"What in God's name is a Sardinian warbler?" Hawthorne demanded.

"A bird that eats sardines, for all I know. There, the tail of the French serpent, at last."

The final soldiers passed, the blue-backed company snaking down the road. Hayden took a long breath and felt his knotted shoulder-muscles relax. And then a French officer on horseback, a young boy up before him, came trotting back and left the road to pass east of them.

"Apparently we are not out of the wood yet," Hawthorne said unhappily. "That is the boy who discovered me."

"They did not tell me he had run off after the soldiers." Hayden stood. "Bloody hell."

Wickham leapt to his feet. "Shall we make a run for it?"

"With two hundred French soldiers around the bend? I don't think it would answer." Hayden wiped away the sweat on his brow with a rough sleeve. "I will have to speak with the officer, though I doubt he'll be as credulous as the young ladies. Damn; I wish I had not named my uncle now."

Hayden ran quickly back across the small wood, emerging on the other side to find the officer, head bent, listening to the ladies. The English lieutenant erupted from the wood, waved his telescoping glass, and cheerfully greeted the officer in Breton.

The Frenchman fixed him with a serious, measuring gaze, and answered in French. Hayden repeated his greeting in that language.

"Oh, here he is," announced Anne. "But we know him, it turns out. He came here often as a boy, to visit his uncle, Gabriel Saint Almond, who was our neighbour."

"And what is your business here, monsieur, if you will permit me to ask?" The officer did not seem overly suspicious, but rather a man performing his duty with admirable thoroughness.

"I am here for reasons of sentiment, monsieur, to see once again the place where I spent many childhood summers. Today I am taking note of the birds." He held up his glass and removed the book from his satchel.

"He is looking for the Sardinian warbler," Anne offered.

The officer's face did not change, but his tone did. "The Sardinian warbler makes its home upon the shores of the Mediterranean, if I am not mistaken, and flies south for the winter."

Hayden cursed his foolishness—mentioning a bird of which he knew nothing. "That is true, monsieur, so you can imagine my surprise to hear one singing in this wood so late in the year. But of course they have been known to wander even further north. A pair was collected in the Low Countries not two years past."

"You sound like a man of education, monsieur . . ."

"He speaks Latin," Marie said, as if this had made a particular impression on her.

"Do you indeed?" the officer asked, his interest piqued.

"Not with the fluency I would like," Hayden said modestly, realizing how imprudent it had been to have uttered a word in the tongue of the clerics.

"And what other languages might so learned a man speak?" the officer asked.

"A bit of High German; Italian, to a degree; Spanish, but only a lit-tle better than my Latin."

"Do you speak English, as well?"

"I can ask my way and order a meal."

"We are looking for English spies. Three men came ashore last night near Crozon, we believe, and are now at large in the countryside."

"And what did they look like?" Hayden asked, narrowing his eyes.

"Why do you ask?"

"I saw three men upon the road to Folgoit, early this morning. They hurried along unnaturally, as though pursued."

"I shall have enquiries made in Folgoit. Where are your friends, monsieur?"

"In the wood, seeking our warbler."

"I would be remiss in my duties if I did not speak with them, as well. I hope you will forgive my intrusion."

"Duty is a cruel mistress, monsieur," Hayden answered brightly, "but you may rely on us to offer every assistance." He favoured the officer with a smile, though he felt his heart sink. He had failed to divert the man's curiosity, and one word from Hawthorne would give them away. Hayden was not sure he could bring himself to shoot the officer, here, before two young ladies and a mob of children. Hawthorne, however, might not share his misgivings.

Hayden turned toward the wood, but, before he had taken a step, the officer said, "Let one of these children bring your friends, monsieur."

"If you wish." Hayden stopped and tried his best to look both unconcerned and of mild disposition. He hoped he would not have to open his satchel, because his pistol, he now realized, was of English manufacture.

Two boys were detached and sent running into the wood, fearless now with the French officer nearby. In a moment they returned with Wickham in tow.

"May I introduce my nephew, Pierre le Pennec," Hayden said, resting a hand on Wickham's shoulder.

"Monsieur," Wickham said, making an appropriate bow.

"And where is it you hail from?" the officer asked, his face a carefully composed mask of neutrality.

"Arcachon, monsieur."

"I see. And what is it your father does in Arcachon?"

"My father is dead, monsieur, but he was a barrister."

"My condolences, but I must ask—how did he die?"

"The doctors called it consumption, but I think they did not really know, monsieur. He took very ill and hovered at death's door for several weeks." Wickham cast down his gaze, as though the memory were painful to him.

The officer regarded the boy a moment, still showing no sign of emotion.

"Is there not another?" He searched among the children until he spotted the boy who had brought him there. "Is this the large man who frightened you?"

The boy shook his head, still too fearful to speak.

"My uncle's servant crossed over the road, chasing a bird he hoped to collect."

"Then let us go find him," the officer said. He doffed his hat to the young ladies. "Mesdemoiselles."

With two English spies beside him, the Frenchman rode slowly around the wood. Although he showed no outward signs of fear, when he thought no one looked he loosened one of the pistols holstered on his saddle.

Hayden wondered if he thought him a cleric in hiding, or a nobleman sent to raise the population of Brittany in rebellion. Perhaps he even believed them to be English spies. Each of these prospects was as dangerous as the other.

They slipped down a steep, grassy embankment to the road below— two greyish tracks separated by a swath of trampled green. A dry-stone wall topped the southern slope, and the little wood where they had hidden overshadowed the north. Birds called in the quiet afternoon and the low drone of insects all but drowned out the retreating beat of the drum.

"Where is your servant, monsieur?" the officer asked, his voice perhaps betraying a bit of anxiety.

"I don't know," Hayden answered truthfully. "If he is off after a warbler it might lead him some distance."

The officer twisted about to look north and something flew out of the southern forest and drove the man from his saddle. Hawthorne and the officer tumbled in a writhing heap, the Englishman on top for a moment, the French officer trying to call out.

Hawthorne attempted to choke off the man's windpipe, but a strangled cry did escape. The horse leapt clear of this, trotting a few yards. Hardly realizing what he did, Hayden leapt at the pile of thrashing limbs, grabbed an arm he hoped was French, and wrestled it to the ground. Another muffled cry escaped the man, and then something large and heavy was driven down from above. A horrible impact, and then a second, and the officer lay still, the arm Hayden pinned limp as a cable.

Wickham stood over them, holding a stone the size of a twenty-four-pound ball, a look of keen distress on his young face. Hayden leapt to his feet, casting his gaze desperately down the road, left then right. He saw no one in either direction.

Hawthorne, who was half under the dead Frenchman, disentangled himself and got to his knees, gasping for breath, his nose bleeding. He put a hand to his eye, blinking quickly.

"Are you injured, Hawthorne?"

"Struck me twice in the eye." He shook his head as if to clear his vision. "Nothing to speak of."

Hayden looked again down the road in the direction the company had disappeared. Wickham still stood, staring at the body in horror, the bloody rock in his hands.

"What shall we do, sir?" he almost whispered. "We're spies and murderers now. I wouldn't have killed him, but flailing around, he found your pistol."

For the first time Hayden noticed, almost beneath his feet, his own flintlock lying but a few inches from the officer's limp hand.

"Bloody hell!" Hayden muttered, retrieving the gun. Doing so, he looked, accidentally, into the dead man's blue eyes. The Frenchman lay, mouth agape, staring blindly up at the sky, his skull shattered and bloody, arms and legs thrown out unnaturally.

Hayden rose and gazed at the little tableau.

"They're going to be after us now, Mr Hayden," Hawthorne said. "As soon as they find this Frenchie."

"Not if we keep our wits about us." He looked desperately about as though there might be something lying nearby that might be used to save them. Pointing down at the depression of damp earth from which Wickham had clearly pried his stone, he said, "Set your stone back down there, Mr Wickham, if you please. Have a care to place it just as it lay when you snatched it up—the dirt-coated side down. Just so, yes."

Wickham carefully replaced the stone and Hayden knelt and pressed the turf close around it. He was back on his feet in a moment, examining the ground. "We must all march here, in the dirt track, to cover our boot-prints. Do you see? It must look like a company of soldiers has passed. No marks of anyone standing or moving about the dead man. But don't overstep any of the horse's hoof-marks. He came after the soldiers." Hayden pointed. "Something spooked the horse, here, and he threw his master. Do you see, where Hawthorne threw himself from the trees? The horse's hoofs dug in as though he sprang forward, frightened. The Frenchman was thrown from his saddle and by the worst luck struck his head on this stone. It is all plain as morning."

He began marching over the dirt, and the others fell in behind. They covered their boot-prints with others heading in the same direction as the soldiers. Hayden quickly ran his eye over the ground in the area, walking up the lane to where they had joined the path, and marching over their prints so that it seemed only the French officer had passed this way. The horse had come trotting back and stood grazing a few yards from its master, who lay, a mass of blue and white, fallen like a bit of cloud and sky.

"Let us hope the girls and their charges do not learn of this man's fate before the day is out," Hayden muttered. He waved down the road. "Come. This way."

He set off after the French troops, trotting along the road's grassy marge.

"But Mr Hayden . . ." Wickham said, catching up with the lieutenant and jogging alongside. "The soldiers went this direction. Surely they will send a rider back to find out what has become of their comrade."

"Yes, but we cannot go back the other way without risking discovery. On that tack lie houses. And this is where we must go to view the Rade. Pray the soldiers do not miss their officer for a few moments yet."

Luck, which had been running against them, reached slack then, and they managed to find a little hollow where they could leave the road without being observed. They crossed a pasture, liberally littered with sheep droppings, and dove into a thick hedge of chestnut and oak, a dense underwood beneath. But as Hayden suspected, down the centre ran a narrow path, shaded and hidden from hostile eyes.

"This is rather snug," Hawthorne observed as they hurried along.

"Not an uncommon feature in this part of France," Hayden answered, "but these paths are well used and we'll be fortunate not to meet the locals abroad upon the same track. Hurry on."

Two hours' time found them peering out of a thicket at a small company of blue-coated soldiers beating the bush beyond a wide, sloping meadow.

"Are they looking for murderers?" Wickham asked, "or just some possible English spies who came in from the sea this evening last?"

Hayden shook his head. "Let us hope it is some bishop still loyal to Rome."

"Damn Hart for sending us forth so close to dawn!" Hawthorne cursed. "I swear, he did not intend us to return." The man's face was red with anger and drawn with fear. "The countryside is awash with French soldiers hunting our poor British hides. I should turn myself in before I give us all away. The two of you can pass for French without me."

"I will not hear of it," Hayden said firmly. "We will swim together or sink as one."

Wickham immediately echoed Hayden and the marine nodded, grateful but uncertain.

The party of soldiers disappeared over a small rise, and Hayden waved his companions forward. "Now, before others appear."

They ran, bent low, over an open meadow, along a shattered, dry-stone wall, then down into a wood. The Rade de Brest was visible through the trees, the blue waters broken by small whitecaps whipped up by a sudden breeze.

"It is a miniature sea," Wickham observed.

"Five leagues, or thereabout, from south to north, with three sizeable rivers spilling their waters into the harbour. It would contain our entire fleet, and never see an anchor fouled."

They broke out of the trees, and the Rade opened before them, en-closed within the battered, ancient cliffs, though here and there the green sloped down to the water's edge. Brown tidal flats spread, smooth as skin, along the distant shore and inside Île Longue, which was below them and some distance to the left. Across the bay, to the north-east, the French fleet lay at anchor, the ships barely rocking in the wind.

"Well, sir," Wickham said, staring out over the harbour, "there are no ships anchored inside Île Longue."

"No. I didn't expect there would be," Hayden answered. Open pas-ture angled down toward the cliff top perhaps a quarter-mile distant, with only a few hedges and meandering, low stone walls breaking up the sward. With his glass, Hayden carefully examined the open area and the edges of the wood.

"I think we're alone here, for a few moments," he said. "Let us make a count of the ships, and be off. The sun will set in two hours, and there will be no moon until after midnight, so we would be wise to reach the coast before darkness is complete. We don't want to miss our boat."

"If only someone would cut down that stand of chestnuts." Hawthorne pointed. "It is spoiling our view."

Hayden looked around. "Mr Wickham . . . you like to climb trees, don't you?"

The boy smiled, knowing what came next. "More than pudding, sir."

The lieutenant gestured at a tree. "Up you go, then."

The two men boosted the midshipman up to the lowest branches and he made his way to a high vantage point.

"Keep a sharp eye for any sardine-eating warblers, will you, Mr Wickham?" Hawthorne whispered up.

"I will, Mr Hawthorne," the midshipman said seriously. "There's a big three decker with her topmasts housed, Mr Hayden. A hundred guns, perhaps one hundred twenty."

"Yes, I see her. *La Côte-d'Or*, I think," Hayden said, gazing through his own glass. Hawthorne scratched the numbers down on a sheet of paper. Thirty minutes later Wickham dropped out of the branches and brushed lichen from his hair and coat.

"What do you think, sir?" he asked as Hayden finished the tallies.

"I think these are precisely the same numbers Landry gave Hart."

Hawthorne shook his head, unable to disguise his dismay. "Fucking hell," he muttered. "We've risked our necks for nothing."

Wickham gave him a bitter smile. "The moon is not on our side, is she?"

Hayden considered their surroundings. "No, she will not rise for some time. We will have to travel by dusk, and trust to luck. Either that, or swim out to the *Themis*."

"Which we might be doing anyway," Hawthorne added resentfully.

"Whatever do you mean?" Wickham turned his innocent gaze on the marine.

Hawthorne glanced at Hayden, suddenly awkward. "Only that I wonder if Hart did not put Mr Hayden and me ashore to be rid of us."

Wickham nodded seriously. "I don't think my father would much approve of such a plan," the boy said.

Hayden looked at the boy with new-found appreciation. "Is that why you slipped ashore with us?"

"Not at all, Mr Hayden. It is unthinkable that a captain in the King's Navy would strand officers on a hostile shore. I came to appraise the agriculture."

"And does it meet with your approval?" Hawthorne wondered, breaking into a broad smile.

"Well, I do not comprehend scientific agriculture as some gentlemen do, but the hedgerows are unequalled in all of Surrey."

They made their way back through the trees, and paused to search the margins of the pasture with a glass.

"I think it is all clear, Mr Hayden," Hawthorne said, passing the lieutenant the glass.

"Quickly, then." Hayden set out at a trot, bending low and making as little noise as he could.

They were just scrambling over a low stone wall when a cry broke the quiet evening. A French soldier emerged from a hedge to the south and gestured frantically, pointing at the Englishmen caught out in the open.

"Damned luck!" Hawthorne said.

"I don't think we'll bluff them this time," Hayden said to Hawthorne, and the marine nodded, understanding immediately: his French would give them away.

The three began to run. Glancing back, Hayden saw the French soldier raise his musket. The dull *crack* of a firearm sounded, but the ball missed its mark. They redoubled their speed just as more cries reached them. Hayden dug a hand into his satchel as he pounded across the grass. Drawing out his pistol, he wondered how long he could keep up such a pace. Life aboard ship did not build up one's stamina for a foot-race, and to make matters worse, he was sure he'd opened the gash on his side, which stung like he'd been flogged.

More gunfire broke the quiet, and as they finally reached the hedge, a blue coat appeared out of the trees ten feet away. Hayden shot the man before he could raise his musket. Three more French soldiers appeared behind the first. Hawthorne and Wickham each counted for a man with their pistols and Hayden clubbed the last man to the ground with his gun, hammering him repeatedly until he lay still. The Englishman could hardly catch his breath, and his heart felt as though it would break out of his chest.

Hawthorne snatched up a musket, took careful aim, and shot the lead soldier crossing the field. Immediately he threw that gun aside, seized another, and fired again. The soldiers threw themselves down behind a stone wall and began to return fire. Putting a tree between himself and the enemy gunfire, Hayden loaded his pistol with shaking hands.

"Take these!" Hawthorne ordered Wickham as he stripped a dead soldier of his powder and shot. The midshipman barely hesitated, unbuckling a fallen man's shoulder straps, even as he lay moaning, blood oozing from a wound. The muskets were quickly loaded and the Englishmen were off again at a run, each bearing a French gun and a freshly loaded pistol.

They took to a path that ran down the centre of a hedge, shouts and calls breaking in on all sides. Unable to keep up the pace, the three slowed to a jog, gasping for breath. A sharp pain stabbed into Hayden's side, and Hawthorne was forced to stop for a moment, almost reeling.

"Go on," he gasped. "I'll keep them at . . . bay."

"We leave no one behind," Hayden managed, bent double, hands on his knees. Over the sound of three men struggling to breathe, he could hear the cries of French soldiers, though it was difficult to gauge their direction. Within the hedgerow, shadows were thickening, spreading out from beneath jumbled limbs.

"Sun should set in a few moments," Wickham observed. The midshipman was the least affected by the run, standing upright, pulling aside branches in an attempt to look out into the surrounding fields.

"A hay field to the sou'east, Mr Hayden," he whispered.

"How long are the grasses?"

"Well tasselled, sir, but I don't think there's half a fathom over the bottom. About two foot, I would wager."

"Who leaves hay standing this late in the season?" Hawthorne muttered.

A drumming reached them, and Hayden stood upright, listening.

"They're coming!" Hawthorne whispered urgently, and the fugitives dove into a thick bramble, forcing their way through and leaving bits of clothing and skin behind.

They were on their bellies, snaking forward through the shallows of the hay field. As the French soldiers thundered by, led by an officer on horseback, the Englishmen lay still. Hayden thumbed the flint on his musket, expecting to hear a cry of discovery, but the company passed. Hayden began crawling again, no thoughts for knees or elbows. It took an ungodly long time to cross the field, the sweet smell of dry grass and clover all around them in the gathering dusk. When finally they surfaced on the field's far shore, they lay for a few moments, listening, letting the darkness grow and deepen.

Finally, Hayden sat up and whispered for the others, who were not too distant. They all rose from the whispering hay, and slipped into the dark hedge. Hawthorne's large, pale face appeared in the dimness.

"Mr Hayden?"

"Here, Hawthorne. Where is Wickham?"

"Behind you, sir."

"Glad you accompanied us now, Wickham?" Hayden asked pointedly.

"Aye, sir," the boy said quickly.

Hayden shook his head. "This hedge is tending in the right direction, but I'm a bit lost. We have a good distance to travel before our boat arrives, so we cannot creep along too quietly. We must risk some noise, for if we are stranded in this country it will be only a matter of time until the French run us down."

He could barely make out the others' faces nodding in the dark. Good night-vision allowed Wickham to lead the others to a narrow path out onto the field beyond. Staying to the shadows, they made their way at a slow trot, stumbling now and then in the poor light.

Even without the ship's bell, Hayden was aware of the time passing by. Midnight would be upon them before they knew it. He was not sure what they would do if they missed their meeting with the boat. Go to the same beach one hour after midnight the next night and hope Hart would not give up on them, he supposed.

A road opened before them, and Hayden gathered the others into the darkness beneath an overhanging tree. Unfortunately, they could not afford to wait the time that Hayden would have preferred, and after ten minutes he waved them on. A call broke the stillness a hundred feet off, and they scrambled over a low wall and raced across an open field, the light of the stars casting faint but frantic shadows before them.

Musket fire cracked and Hayden pressed himself on, Wickham ten feet ahead and Mr Hawthorne two yards to his left. The marine stumbled, and Hayden dragged him up. Hawthorne dropped his musket and clutched his arm as they ran.

"Hawthorne's been shot!" Hayden called.

Without hesitation, Wickham stopped, took careful aim, and fired, then fell in behind them—the last place Hayden wanted the boy. They tumbled over a stone wall, and Wickham took the lieutenant's musket and fired at their pursuers again.

"Where were you shot?" Hayden demanded of Hawthorne, who was ripping awkwardly at a hole in his cloak.

"I cannot see—there, behind the meat of my arm," he spat out through clenched teeth.

Hayden tore the coarse cotton away, feeling it warm and sticky with blood.

"Lean this way so I can see." Hayden stared at the wound in the cool starlight. "An angel was apparently watching over you. It is barely a scrape. I don't think there is a musket ball lodged there at all." Taking his knife, he cut and then ripped a strip off the tail of his shirt and used this to bind the wound. All the while Wickham had been keeping up a constant fire, moving down the wall and then back, so that no two shots came from the same place. He had the French pinned down across the field, not by the rapidity of his fire but because he seldom missed. He crawled quickly up, as Hayden finished his ministrations.

"How's your patient, sir?"

"He should live, but he'll never have children. How goes it with you?"

"I think I've felled four, sir. Three for certain."

"Oh, a knighthood for you, without question!" Hawthorne said.

Hayden tried to gather his wits about him. "This gunfire will, undoubtedly, draw more soldiers. We have to move. Can you travel, Mr Hawthorne? Not too light-headed?"

"I'll keep up, Mr Hayden. You needn't worry."

"We're going forth on all fours, anyway. Give you a moment to regain your equilibrium. This way." He pointed and they set off crawling on the damp grass along the base of the wall.

A hedge loomed out of the darkness, and they trotted along in its shadow, Hayden in the rear. Hawthorne had definitely slowed and was no longer so sure-footed, wandering from side to side and stumbling. It worried Hayden more than a little.

Small companies of French soldiers could be seen in the distance, searching the hedgerows, calling one to another. Shooting broke out some distance off and drew both infantry and horsemen at a gallop.

"There's a bit of luck," Hawthorne whispered. They had stopped beneath a tree to catch their breath. "Whom are they shooting at, do you think?"

"Likely each other," Hayden answered quietly.

"One can always hope," Wickham said.

Expecting this distraction would draw most of the soldiers in the vicinity, the Englishmen slunk off, making the best speed they could.

Two hundred yards, and they paused in another shadow, surveying their surroundings. A little spring flowed here, and Hayden was doubly happy to find it, as he now knew exactly where they were. The three slaked their thirst, which was considerable after all their exertion.

"Are we not north of our destination?" Wickham asked.

"We are," Hayden answered, keeping his voice low. "I'm sure they will be watching for us at the head of the path below Crozon."

"But the western shore is cliffs for many miles!" Hawthorne said, clearly distressed.

"Yes, but there is another way down. It will require a bit of climbing, though nerve rather than strength will be called for. How is your arm, Hawthorne?"

The marine lifted the wounded limb and worked it back and forth a little. "A bit crank, but it will serve."

"Then we should be off. The cliff is not distant, but time grows short."

A final dash and they found themselves gazing down onto the beach below, the ocean spreading out to a distant horizon. Small, pale crests could be seen throwing themselves on the shore, and a salt wind rustled their clothes.

"It seems a long way down," Wickham said, staring at the beach below.

"It appears farther at night, for some reason," Hayden answered, thinking that the fall was much longer than he remembered.

"Where is the path down?" Hawthorne asked.

Hayden pointed to their right. "Along here. Not far, I think."

They made their way along the cliff edge, Hayden crouching low here and there to look at various crevices leading down. Each time he shook his head and passed on. After ten minutes of searching he stopped, thoroughly confused.

"What is it, sir?" Wickham asked.

"The way down should have been here," Hayden answered. "I must have passed it in the dark."

He looked both north and south along the cliff, hoping to see some landmark that would tell him where he was, but there was nothing. Unsettled, he turned back the way they had come, examining the cliff top carefully. A shout echoed over the wind, and Hayden stood up.

"There, sir!" Wickham pointed south along the cliff.

Though still some distance off, a small party of men came trotting toward them.

"They're armed, sir," Wickham warned.

Hayden called out to them in Breton, but the answer was in French.

"Well, Mr Hayden," Hawthorne said. "There are more Frenchmen than Englishmen here. If we have no line of retreat, I suggest we draw them as near as we can and then open fire." He held a pistol in his good hand, cocking it with a thumb.

Hayden looked around desperately. "Here!" he said. "This looks to be it . . ." The uncertainty in his voice gave him away.

Hawthorne cast a cynical eye at the narrow fissure in the rock. "Are you sure, Mr Hayden? I'd rather die fighting than falling."

"Not entirely certain, but come. It has to be here."

Hayden threw down his musket, turned, and went backwards over the edge, his boots finding footholds on the battered rock. Ten feet down he struck a ledge, more than two feet wide, which ran almost level in both directions. "Climb down! Climb down!" he called up. "This is the way."

A flash from above, and the report of a musket. A second shot, and then answering fire from the French. Wickham scrambled nimbly down and then Hawthorne lumbered down behind, both looking more frightened than he had seen them so far.

"This way." Hayden led them along the ledge, and fortunately around a little point in the rock and out of sight of the French. A few shots still sounded.

"They're killing shadows now," Hawthorne hissed. A wide crevice opened before them.

"The steepest bit is at the top," Hayden explained, pointing down. "Stay to the near side. There is no shortage of handholds or footholds, but test them well. I have had more than one chunk of rock break away under foot, or torn it off easily with a hand." He looked at his companions. "Arm holding up, Mr Hawthorne?"

"Good as gold, sir."

Hayden nodded at Wickham, then began to climb down. The faint starlight illuminated the cliff in patches, which was both good and bad. They were in shadow, which would make them harder to shoot from above, but the climbing was doubly dangerous. Hayden felt his way down, scraping his boots over the stone, searching for a toehold, a place where one might place a foot. Handholds were more easily found, but he had not gone far before one of these broke free and went tumbling down the cliff face. Hayden put his forehead against the cool stone and tried to calm his breathing.

"Everything all right, Mr Hayden?" Wickham asked from above.

He could just make out the midshipman above.

"Yes, broke off a bit of rock, that's all." He made himself go on, well aware that if his companions had the same misfortune the rock would come hurtling down on him. He knew that imagination was fertile ground for fear, and tried to concentrate on climbing. Moving one foot down, while maintaining two handholds and one solid foothold. Then moving a hand. Progress was slow and uncertain. Sometimes he searched for a foothold for a long moment before finding one, and had to treat with the panic that would ensue.

"I can hear them above us," Wickham whispered.

Hayden looked up at the cliff top, black against the stars.

Hayden could almost feel the eyes searching for them, examining each little projection. He tried to mould himself into the narrow fissure, then willed himself to be still as stone. A trickle of dirt sprayed over his face and down his collar. Hayden closed his eyes and wondered if that was from one of his own men or if it was sent down by some Frenchman's boot.

The voices faded and Hayden felt himself relax a little, but then they grew louder again. The soldiers had moved down the cliff top to the north and were now discussing what might be a man and what might only be an irregularity in the cliff face. A flash and almost simultaneous report, and a musket ball glanced off the stone ten feet away. He heard Hawthorne curse under his breath.

"They're sniping at Mr Hawthorne, sir," Wickham whispered.

Hayden cursed as well. "Tell him not to move . . . And to stay quiet."

Steeling his nerve, Hayden began to climb down as rapidly as he dared. A shout from the cliffs and a musket ball exploded two feet away, shards of stone showering Hayden's face.

A second ball sailed by his back. Hayden reached a platform of stone and traversed quickly to the right and into the lee of a little point where he was out of sight of the marksmen. Much shouting in French rained down from above, and he heard the soldiers running along the cliff, looking for a vantage from which to shoot at him again. Hayden hoped they had not left a man behind, because he traversed back a few feet, found secure footing, and fished his pistol out of his belt. He balanced it on a little projection of stone and took aim for the cliff top. A bit further away than he would like, but he allowed for the distance and a little for the wind as well.

The second the Frenchmen appeared, Hayden fired, and was gratified to see the lot of them retreat from the cliff top. "Climb!" he whispered, and when he was sure that the others followed, he thrust the
pistol into his belt at his back and began down again. In ten minutes he
came to a little triangular landing large enough for his party entire.
The cliff top was not in view from here, so they would be safe for the
time being.

Wickham was down in a moment, and then, more slowly, Hawthorne appeared. Hayden had used the time to reload and prime his
pistol.

"I think you hit one of them," Hawthorne reported when he reached
the landing.

"I don't think it likely," the lieutenant admitted, "but I drove them
back for a moment. Come, this way."

He clambered down about two feet and followed a narrow ledge
around a point to the north. He waited there with his pistol raised. As
he feared, a shot was fired from the cliff face as Wickham came into
view, but Hayden fired back and hoped that would give Hawthorne a
moment.

"Did they find you, Wickham?"

"No, sir," the boy reported. "Holed my satchel, but came no nearer."

"That's near enough."

As Hawthorne rounded the point, three shots were fired, but the
large man escaped unharmed.

"I think we are safe from them now unless they climb down after us,
which I fear they might do."

"I think they sent a man running south, Mr Hayden, so we will likely
have men coming at us along the beach from Crozon."

"We will be down long before they can reach the spot. Let us not
tarry. The way down is not so formidable now."

In a few moments they were on the sand beach. Hayden kept them in
the shadow of the cliff, scanning the sea with his glass, looking for the
Themis or her cutter.

"Difficult to pick out a boat without a moon in the west, sir," Wickham offered.

"Yes. How is your arm, Mr Hawthorne?"

"A good climb was just the tonic it required, Mr Hayden. It is on the mend."

Hayden smiled. He searched the long arc of the beach, picking out the fire by the quay where the fencibles would be guarding the fishing boats hauled up on the beach.

"What hour would you estimate?" Hayden asked.

Hawthorne looked up at the sky. "Near to midnight, by the stars."

"Then where is Mr Childers and our boat?"

"If he is late I shall flense him, render his fat, and light my lamp by it," Hawthorne growled.

"And a fitting lesson that shall be," Hayden replied.

Wickham came up then. He had been scavenging along the cliff base, and now held up a musket triumphantly.

"Is that one of ours?"

"I threw them off the cliff before I climbed down," the boy said, a bit smugly. "One had its lock shattered on the rocks, but this one will fire again. A bit of sand in the barrel, that's all." He cocked the gun and pulled the trigger. "There. You see? Good as new." He crouched down and began cleaning and loading the flintlock, and when he was finished, did the same with Hayden's pistol.

"May I have a look, Mr Hayden?" Hawthorne asked. He was trying not to appear anxious or impatient, but failing.

Hayden passed the marine his glass, and Hawthorne took a moment to search the secret sea. "Dark as Madeira out there, sir."

"I'm afraid you're right. Can you see any Frenchmen trotting up the beach?"

Hawthorne turned the glass down the curving sand and shook his head. "No, sir, but it is very dark and I can't say for certain."

The lieutenant cast his gaze around the beach, then more anxiously out to sea. "We will be in a bit of a bind if Childers' cutter does not soon appear. I don't think we dare climb up again. Men will be waiting at the top. If the fencibles come along the beach it will be fight or swim, and I don't think there is much profit in either."

Wickham stood gazing at the horizon, putting his hard-gained knowledge of the heavens to use. "I should hazard a guess that the hour of midnight has passed, sir." He said it calmly, no tone of despair to be heard.

"Mr Hayden . . . ? I believe I see men coming along the beach—double time."

Hayden cursed. Hawthorne passed him the glass.

"They did not tarry, did they?" Hayden said. He searched the sea desperately one last time, and then pointed his glass down the beach where the French were advancing. He glanced up once. "There will be shadow along the cliff base until the moon rises and shifts into the west. With a little boost from luck we will hide here and let these Frenchmen pass. We'll have to seize a boat and get out to sea. Tide is past slack, but the fall will not be great; even so, there is not a moment to squander."

They set out along the base of the cliff, their boots muffled by the soft, dry sand. When the French came huffing along the margin of the sea, small waves breaking around their feet, Hayden and his company lay down at the cliff's base and hid their pale faces. The party, three soldiers and several fencibles, passed them by without a glance, eyes fixed on the end of the beach, where the English had managed their descent.

When the French were well past, Hayden and his mates leapt up and continued jogging along in the cliff's shadow, which grew narrower as the bluff became less steep. Very soon they were crouched in a thin ribbon of jagged shadow, staring out at the watchman's fire burning near the foot of the jetty.

"How many men can you make out?" Hayden whispered to Wickham.

"I count three, sir."

"I could shoot one from here," Hawthorne offered, "then charge and overwhelm the others with pistol fire."

"All three will be needed to launch a boat. We are too few to manage it alone." Hayden thought a moment. "Go down the beach beyond the fire. There is enough shadow left. When you are in place, I shall walk out and speak to them in Breton, as though I have just come down the path from Crozon. When I have their attention, come at them from behind and train your pistols on them. Are we in agreement?"

"Aye, sir," Wickham said, and Hawthorne nodded. The two crept off, leaving Hayden crouched at the cliff base, watching the men by the fire. He fervently hoped there were no more asleep on the ground but reasoned the French soldiers had taken most of the guards with them down the beach, and any who remained would be awake and either too wary or too ashamed to go back to sleep.

Waiting what he hoped would be the proper time, Hayden went to the path leading to Crozon, slipped up it a dozen feet, and called out in Breton, emerging from the path a moment later. The silhouettes by the fire raised their fowling pieces and aimed them at the stranger. Hayden dearly hoped these were not the men he had met at the head of the path the previous night.

"Where have they cornered these foolish English spies?" he asked jovially. "I promised madam I would shoot one and bring her home a fat reward."

The guns were not lowered, nor were the men reassured by his Breton. He guessed they had been warned that there was a Breton-speaking Englishman abroad in their little corner of Brittany.

"You'll take her home your fat ass," one man said. "They have been cornered down the beach, or so they say. Who are you?"

"Pierre Laviolette," Hayden said. "And behind you are my two friends."

The men glanced back, confused, and found Wickham and Hawthorne aiming guns at their backs.

Hayden raised his own pistol, and the three Frenchmen looked suddenly very anxious.

"Put your muskets on the ground, if you please," Hayden said civilly. "We will need your help to launch a boat." Hayden looked at the boats drawn up on the sand and chose the largest one he thought could be launched by five men—twenty feet or so, bluff-bowed and deep-bodied with a sweet curving sheer and a square little transom. It lay with its stern already in the water, a short, deep little fishing boat that looked much like an English pilchard driver and with a similarly proportioned two-masted rig. A brisk inventory indicated that she had all her gear aboard, and to this was added a quarter-cask of wine from the beach and all the guards' food.

The Frenchmen went sullenly to work, Wickham and Hayden helping while Hawthorne stood with a musket to his shoulder. It was a risky venture, the odds even and only one man holding a gun, but none of the Frenchmen seemed willing to risk their lives over another man's boat.

The burdensome little boat resisted their efforts to make it waterborne, but finally broke free of the sand and slid into the shallows. Hayden put his shoulder to the hard planking, and pressed the boat up and out into the lapping waves.

"Take up all the weapons and load them aboard," Hayden ordered the marine, who complied swiftly. "And now you, Mr Hawthorne."

The man tumbled over the side, quickly training his musket on the Frenchmen again. Wickham went aboard next, then Hayden. He forced the men to push the boat until the water was around their shoulders, then sent them back. Oars went into place and the three Englishmen pulled out into Douarnenez Bay. They had not gone thirty yards when they heard the guards calling out, and then there was a crack of gunfire and a flash of powder near the beach fire. The shot struck the topsides with a *thwack*.

"My apologies, Mr Hayden," Hawthorne said, putting his back into the work. "I thought I had accounted for all their weapons."

Wickham unshipped his sweep, snatched up one of the muskets, and returned fire, emptying all the guns before setting his oar between the thole-pins again. There were no more shots, and they were soon lost in the darkness, small rollers sweeping under them. As the others manned the oars, Hayden sorted out and bent the sails, shipped the rudder, and soon had them under way.

He glanced back once at the dark shore, receding quickly, and felt such a terrible sense of loss—utterly at odds with his situation. A father leaving behind a child could hardly have been more disconsolate. For a moment he thought he might weep. But their circumstances would not allow this, and he turned his mind away.

Hawthorne breathed a long, audible sigh. "That was a little closer than I would have liked," he said. And then: "Do you think it would be an inappropriate time for a meal?"

"I think we shall suspend etiquette for the moment, Mr Hawthorne," Hayden said from the helm, forcing a jocular tone, "and perhaps indulge in a small luncheon—nothing immoderate, just enough to break our fasts."

"Just so," Hawthorne answered, "a small repast. I wonder what our hosts have so kindly provided?" He began to search through the food-stuffs, some wrapped in paper, some in small satchels. "Bread we have, of the French variety. Some small portion of cold pork, wine, a few stunted apples, and quite capital carrots. Hardly a feast, but . . ."

"Well, it is a beggars' banquet, Mr Hawthorne, so we cannot properly complain. I have a prodigious thirst, if there is a cup of wine to be had?"

They ate and drank beneath the starlight, as Hayden piloted them out of the bay toward the open sea. The little craft was not weatherly, and making considerable leeway, much to Hayden's distress. They were actually sailing back into the bay on this sou'west wind, though the next board would allow them to shape a course seaward. He sensed a change in the weather coming. A gale from the south-west, he expected. The wind was already making.

When Hawthorne remarked upon this change in weather, both Hayden and Wickham were suitably grave, which gave the marine pause.

"Is this cause for concern?" he asked, apprehension appearing where there had previously been elation at their narrow escape.

"We need to gain some sea room," Hayden said. He pointed with a stick of bread. "If we can weather Cap de la Chèvre in good order, cross the Outer Water, and slip by Ushant, we will have the entire Channel before us and all the sea room we shall likely need. But if we are blown back on the shore here," he waved his bread toward the cliffs, "we might be in some difficulty. This little tub makes such terrible leeway, and the tide does not favour us . . . yet." He looked around the boat. "Mr Wickham, would you be so kind as to take the helm?"

A small fish room was roughly formed by boards tree-nailed to frames athwart ships. Hayden managed to kick the longest plank free, and with a liberal use of the available rope fashioned a crude lee-board and thrust it vertically down into the water.

"Why, Mr Hayden," Wickham marvelled, "that eased the helm wonderfully."

"You may thank the Dutch," Hayden said, "who, as far as I know, contrived the first lee-boards, though others make the claim for the Chinese."

Exhausted by their flight across country, Wickham and Hawthorne lay down upon the nets and fishing gear and were soon fast asleep. Hayden, who knew they must escape the bay, kept to the helm, shaking his head often and even pinching and slapping his cheeks in an attempt to stay awake. Overhead, the stars began to founder in the blear, their light much diminished. The sou'wester grew in strength and though they were still within the protection of a long peninsula to the south, the fetch of some six miles allowed the seas to mount, small crests soon breaking around them.

Hayden stood several times to peer into the darkness, and finally woke Wickham to help put the boat about. The main was a dipping lug and could not be readily tacked by one man. Wickham was fuzzy-headed and stiff, but managed his part of the little evolution all the same. He took the helm while Hayden transferred the makeshift board to the starboard side, doubling the lines as he did so. They decided then to tie reefs in both sails, and woke Hawthorne to help. It was not an easy task on a strange boat in utter darkness, and took some little while.

"There!" Hawthorne declared, and then, showing a frightening disregard for sailors' superstition, added, "Now damn the wind!"

The midshipman lay down and was asleep immediately, indeed Hayden was not certain the boy had been awake. Even reefed, the little boat lay over on her side with every gust, and Hayden kept the main-sheet in his hand in the event it must be cast off to avoid a knockdown. Hawthorne sat with his back to weather, still as ballast. Hayden could sense the heavy exhaustion that weighed the marine down.

Spray came over the rail, soaking the lieutenant and sloshing about in the bottom. Wickham was wakened by the cold slap of a wave and sat up, shaking his head. He cursed with an eloquence Hayden had seldom heard from one so young.

"Is there a bucket, Mr Wickham?" Hayden asked. "I think a little bailing is in order."

"Aye, sir."

Hayden could hear the boy searching around in the dark.

"Two buckets and a tin cup, Mr Hayden," he reported.

"Good news. Let's not let too much water accumulate or it could be the ruin of us." Hayden knew that water shifting could quickly destabilize a small boat. He heard the sound of metal scraping over wood, and water being spilled—into the bucket, he assumed. In a few moments the bucket was emptied to leeward, and the scraping commenced again.

Two more boards were needed before Chèvre Point passed their lee and Hayden heaved a sigh of relief, though he knew their situation was only marginally improved. A long ground-swell reached them then, pre-saging a sou'westerly gale. He feared daylight would reveal their circum-stance as desperate—set either to be driven into the cliffs or into the harbour of Brest itself.

The moon, not long risen, slipped behind dense cloud, leaving the English sailors in darkness. Hayden had no compass and could only nav-igate by the wind, keeping the little boat full and by. The ropes he had used to construct his lee-board creaked and he wondered if they would hold in the deteriorating conditions. Chèvre Point was somewhere in the gloom—off his starboard quarter, he hoped, but it was impossible to tell; the other shore of the Outer Waters lay somewhere ahead. He

strained to hear the crash of surf, but with the wind rising it was difficult to discern surf from the general din of the gathering gale.

"Damn, it's close," Hawthorne said. "Will the *Themis* carry her
lanterns?"

"I believe so. *Tenacious* might still be in these waters and there is any
amount of coastal traffic."

"Do you think we can find her? The *Themis*, I mean."

Hayden shrugged. A gust of wind forced him to let the sheet run. For
a moment the wind battered them, pressing the boat over, but then it
eased.

"We might find her come daybreak," Hayden answered. If she hasn't
left us utterly, he thought to himself. "Time for a change of duties, I
think. If you would be so kind as to take over the bailing, Mr Hawthorne.
I will pass the mainsheet to Wickham, and I will take the mizzen sheet.
No sleeping on duty, Wickham. If you fail to let the sheet run when a
gust strikes we will be on our beam ends of an instant."

"Aye, sir. I'm fully awake now."

"I'm glad to hear it. Take only a half-turn around cleat and keep the
sheet in your hand. You can't see a gust coming in this darkness."

The wind seemed to be increasing and the seas piled up now that
there was no shelter from the land. Hayden wanted to hang on to as
much sail as he could for as long as possible; the shore could not be
far off in the dark. He was afraid they might even be losing their battle,
and being set to leeward. Another dollop of sea slapped him across the
face and chest, and he heard Hawthorne dutifully bailing. The lines
holding his lee-board creaked loudly, and the wind moaned. Seas came
hissing at them out of the dark, lifting them and carrying them a little to
leeward, or so Hayden imagined. He hoped the little flax sail would
hold.

In his mind the lieutenant was constantly calculating their position,
keeping a running dead-reckoning. The speed of the boat could be estimated with reasonable certainty, and he knew their position when they
passed Cap de la Chèvre. Their course he roughly guessed. Leeway must
be allowed for—greater than he'd like. And this gave him a crude posi-

tion. He feared that they were being pushed back toward the Goulet or the cliffs to its north.

Rain came hard on the wind, slatting against the planks, though the three sailors could not have been any wetter.

"I don't think we'll weather Ushant," Wickham said, letting the sheet run as a gust struck them.

"No. In this darkness, we don't even dare draw near."

"Do you have any notion of our position, Mr Hayden?"

"Somewhere north and a little west of Cap de la Chèvre. I will be forced to go about soon, and with the leeway we are making we will be set toward the cliffs north of Chèvre or perhaps Pointe de Penhir. With a little ill luck we could be driven back into the bay from which we set out, though I don't plan to go so far south."

Seas began to break dangerously about them, and with some difficulty they tied the second reef in their sails, shifting tack and clew, for the sails were without booms. The clew of a thrashing sail struck Hayden on the cheek, and the side of his face immediately began to swell and pained him terribly. It did, however, draw his mind from the painful gash in his side.

"I think there were only two sets of reef points," Wickham observed as the three men resumed their places.

"We shall have to try to scandalize the sails if the gale grows worse," Hayden yelled over the wind.

They came about and ranged now south and a little east, heading back toward the long peninsula that made up the southern shore of the Outer Waters. It could not be helped; to the north lay shoals and islands, with the Island of Ushant some miles beyond. Their little boat would be dashed to pieces there. In these winds and seas, Hayden would not dare venture there even by daylight.

Twice crests broke over them, and they were forced to bail for their lives. They tacked again, setting course by wind—nor'west by north, Hayden guessed, and hoped he was not being too optimistic.

The world began to shade toward grey from black, pale crests now visible at a little distance. They were, all three, drenched and chilled by cool October wind. Hayden had them bail by turn, which warmed them a little. Wickham was a good helmsman, but Hawthorne could not keep them by the wind for all his efforts, and the two sailors were forced to share the helm between them, watch and watch. The little boat had no business out in such a sea, and was only kept afloat by the skill and vigilance of her crew.

"I think we shall have proper daylight within the hour, Mr Hayden," Wickham observed. The midshipman wrestled with the helm, the scene being slowly revealed around them all of white-streaked seas, higher and steeper than they had guessed in the dark.

"I think you're right," Hayden said and twisted around to stare east. They were on the larboard tack now, heading roughly north-west. A dark shadow, jagged and ominous, could just be made out through the rain. It was impossible to be sure it was land, or to discern how distant it might be.

An hour saw the world change, the coast appearing, perhaps three miles distant.

"It's blowing a full gale now," Wickham called over the wind. His hair was plastered about his face, his skin glistening and translucent, a deep blue beneath. He looked cold and unwell, but the determination in his eyes had not diminished. Hawthorne was seasick, but kept to his bailing without a word of complaint. The motion of a small boat was so much different than that of a ship that many men who were never ill aboard a frigate would turn green aboard a cutter when but a little sea kicked up. Hayden had seen it many times and was thankful that mal de mer had never descended upon him.

"We have more offing than I dared hope," Hayden observed. He smacked the gunnel with the flat of his hand. "This little driver has done herself proud."

"It was your lee-board that did the trick, Mr Hayden," Wickham said.

Hayden stood, holding on to the mizzen, and peered out to sea, searching for a sail among the white crests.

"Any sign of her, Mr Hayden?" Hawthorne asked. He had slumped back against the side of the boat, taking a rest from his bailing.

Hayden scanned the great expanse of sea, and shook his head.

"I shall take my trick at the helm now," Hayden offered, lowering himself to the aftermost thwart. He relieved Wickham of the tiller, exchanging mainsheet for mizzen sheet. The boy slipped forward and slumped down beside the marine. They were a sorry sight, and Hayden suspected he looked no better.

"I fear we are dicing with our lives out here," Wickham said.

Hayden nodded. The boy was right. It would be safer perhaps to scud, but the land lay too close to leeward for them to run off.

"If we could gain a little more sea room we might slip in behind Ushant. There is a small nook there—the Baie du Stiff—in which a little protection might be found. It would not be without risks, for people dwell there and might offer us aid."

"It seems a great risk," Wickham said, "even if there were no people. There are islands and shoals aplenty between ourselves and Ushant."

That stopped the conversation for a moment.

"What do you think has become of Hart?" Hawthorne wondered.

"That would be dependent upon his position before the gale struck. He would have tried to put as much distance between himself and France as he could if he found himself south of the Raz. If he were north of Ushant he would lie-to and try to preserve his westing."

"If he did not cross the Channel, perhaps all the way back to Torbay," Wickham said. The boy had the dull, blank look of exhaustion and chill. Men could die in such conditions. The wet and the cold wind drew off the heat from their bodies. There was little he could do for them, however.

"Both of you should eat," the lieutenant ordered.

Hayden wondered if he should turn about and run back into Brest Harbour. Would they be noted as anything but fishermen returning from the sea? No doubt, it was known that the English spies had escaped in a fishing boat, so there was a danger that a cutter would be sent to question them.

They stood out to sea all that morning, bailing constantly, Hayden and the midshipman exchanging tricks at the helm. Mercifully, the rain abated, except for the occasional squall that would loom up to windward like a black ghost. The wind both chilled and dried them. Sitting at the tiller was the worst—in the full blast of the wind—but tending the mainsheet, even hunkered down in the boat, condemned one to inactivity, and the cold would get a hold of that man too. Bailing seemed to help, but after one's turn at the bucket, they would soon be shivering. Hayden kept them all eating small amounts of food and drinking wine or water.

After one such refreshment, Hawthorne put his head over the lee rail and was horribly ill. He slumped back in the boat, wiping a hand across his mouth.

"Fish were hungry," he offered, and closed his eyes. A moment later he roused himself and went back to bailing, fighting off the lethargy that he knew might be his death.

Late in the forenoon the wind began to take off, and the seas soon grew less steep and threatening, but a low, heavy swell still ran. Though the immediate danger was now much reduced, Hayden was still unsure of their course of action. Much of their bread had been ruined by the spray and the crests that broke aboard, and they would soon have no provisions at all. To sail back to the English coast at the three knots they would make under the best conditions would be an undertaking. A good nor'easter might blow them out into the Atlantic.

"Sail, Mr Hayden!" Wickham pointed sou-sou'west. "It looks like a two-sticker. A little brig, or a snow."

Hayden had taken his turn with the bailing cup and raised himself up to look over the long, green swell. A patch of white could be seen, riding over the big seas, perhaps five miles distant.

"Do you think she's one of ours?" Hawthorne asked, though his tone suggested he thought such a thing unlikely.

"I can't tell," Hayden admitted. "If she is French they'll likely think us fishermen caught out in a blow. Not a common occurrence in a little boat like this, but not unheard of either. I'll beg some food, if they draw near." Hayden began a careful search of the surrounding waters, and then he swore.

Wickham twisted around to look nor'east. "Looks like a Chase Mary, sir."

Hayden dropped his tin cup into the bilge. "Yes, and she's a damn sight nearer than the brig."

"You don't think she's after us . . . ?" Hawthorne looked up from his place, hunkered down out of the wind, his head drawn down into his collar like a turtle.

"What shall I do, sir?" Wickham asked, his hand holding the tiller a little tentatively.

"Stay your course, Mr Wickham. If the brig is English she might make for the *chasse marée*, hoping to catch a privateer. Then we'll know whether to try to reach her or stay clear."

"Has the brig seen the *chasse* yet?" Wickham wondered.

Hayden estimated the distance of the two ships. "I don't think so. The *chasse* is closer but the brig has the wind in her favour. It will be a close-run thing, that is certain. Come up a little, Mr Wickham, as close to the wind as you dare. We shall try to intercept the brig . . . and hope."

For some time it seemed the brig would reach them first, though whether this would prove good or ill they still could not know. But when half of the hour had passed Hayden began to think that the *chasse marée* would win the race. Clearly, she was intent on catching them.

"That's a fast lugger, Mr Hayden, and that's for sure," Wickham observed. "I dare say, those are cannon on her deck."

"I believe you're right," he said, turning toward the brig, which was making sail in an attempt to reach them first, suggesting to Hayden that perhaps she *was* English. "The *chasse* is hoping to snatch us, go about, and make all sail possible to gain the harbour before the brig can effect our rescue. Mr Wickham, would you mind very much if I took a trick at the helm?"

"No, sir," and the midshipman gave up the tiller with obvious relief. Both reefs were shaken out as the wind fell away, and the boat picked up a little speed, bobbing over the long, emerald swell.

The *chasse marée* was directly astern of them now, close enough that Hayden could make out the faces of the French crew gathered on the foredeck. The little ship was painted a deep blue, and as she rode over each swell, arcs of white were thrown from her bow. Her canvas was full and taut, as they sailed her by the wind, heeled well down. A mushroom of smoke appeared before her, and a ball splashed into the sea two dozen feet to windward. The report of the cannon was ominous on the empty sea.

Wickham raised one of the muskets he had been busy loading and returned fire, to little effect, apparently, as no one left the foredeck or even recoiled.

The English ship—they could see her colours now—fired a warning shot, the ball holing a wave between the *chasse* and the fleeing Englishmen.

"'Lodged in the middle' has taken on new meaning," Wickham observed. "If the French don't sink us the British might."

"But who do the British think we are?" the marine lieutenant wondered aloud. "Three men in French kit in a French boat . . . but pursued by a privateer."

"They might not be giving us much thought. It is the privateer that interests them."

A second shot was fired by the French and this one sailed so close overhead that Hayden and his companions threw themselves down.

"Bloody hell!" yelled Hawthorne.

A musket cracked then, and the Englishmen all kept themselves low; only Hayden had his head up to steer. Hawthorne overcame his sore arm and he and Wickham began firing back, though found the little fishing boat an unstable gun platform. Another ball was fired and the yard on the mizzen was shattered, the sail thrown down over the men, splinters spinning everywhere.

The boat yawed terribly, but then Hayden recovered and kept her going, though he was forced to pay off, for the balance was lost. Their speed was reduced to a crawl, and the crew of the privateer gave out a shout. The lugger was almost upon them.

"Don't fire!" Hayden warned Wickham as the boy emerged, flailing, from beneath the fallen sail. He had a musket in one hand and more than a little rage in his eye. "If we shoot now they will return fire and almost certainly kill us."

A succession of reports came from the English ship just then, for she had turned to larboard and fired a broadside. Several shots found the chase, and sails came crashing down upon the deck. Of an instant, the *chasse marée* was in flight, her stern lifting high to the following sea. It was the turn of the English to cheer then, and the men in the little fishing boat joined them. The brig drew up a few moments later, and Hayden and Wickham shipped oars and brought their boat alongside as the brig backed sails.

Hayden sent the midshipman up the side first, then Hawthorne. He looked back once at the fleeing privateer and gave his head a shake. Pushing their little boat clear with a foot, Hayden climbed up the side of the heaving ship and scrambled over the rail.

"I see they've finally given you a ship, Hayden," someone said, and the lieutenant looked up to find the concerned face of his friend Robert Hertle hovering nearby. The two clasped hands.

"I am even happier than usual to see you, Robert," Hayden said warmly.

"I have no doubt that you are." Robert glanced at the other newcomers. "And who are your French friends?"

"Nary a Frenchman among us. Lieutenant of Marines Colin Hawthorne and Midshipman Lord Arthur Wickham."

Robert shook them by the hand. "You have a story to tell, I can see. Come down to my cabin and we shall get you into some dry clothes, then eat and drink to your escape. I have my own tale to tell."

Sixteen

The gale had broken and the brig lifted to the low swell, a breeze filling her sails and the sun angling in through the stern windows. The men from the *Themis* sat in their crumpled French dress, now dry, trying to exhibit some self-control as they devoured the food on the table before them. Captain Robert Hertle merely picked at his meal—a show of politeness.

" 'Tis the greatest wonder we are sitting here," Hayden concluded, and lifted his glass of claret. "To Lady Luck."

"Lady Luck," the others echoed.

"I shall drink to the aforementioned Lady, and gladly," said Hertle, "but your exploit took a great deal of pluck and enterprise. I should not want to climb down that cliff in the dark."

"There was starlight," Wickham said, attempting to sound casual.

"Well, that makes it a walk in the park, doesn't it?" Hertle said, smiling. But then his face grew serious. "Now it is my turn for a story, though not so full of daring as your own." He fell silent a moment, troubled and thoughtful. "As we travelled north, bearing dispatches from Gibraltar, we met this morning a frigate. Immediately, we made the private signal, to which she in turn responded, convincing us that she was one of ours. We spoke the ship at about eight in the forenoon. Realizing that this was none other than your own *Themis*, Charles, I enquired of Captain Hart as to your well-being. To my great distress, I was told that you and another man had been put ashore to assess the strength of the French fleet in the harbour of Brest, but you had not made your appointed rendezvous with the ship's boat and were assumed captured. I asked if they had not gone back the next night at the same time and was told that they had sent a boat for you but one night only. There was some other small exchange, and then she proceeded south."

"There was no boat," Hawthorne broke in indignantly, "at least not at the appointed hour."

"He must have sent a boat," Hertle objected softly. "There were officers aboard, young gentlemen."

"It might have been sent to a different place," Wickham said, looking up from his food, something he had barely done this last hour.

"A misunderstanding . . ." Hertle said. "You're suggesting it was a misunderstanding?"

Wickham looked wary. "Perhaps, sir."

Hertle turned to Hayden. "What did Hart say you, Charles?"

"That we would be met one hour after midnight, at the north end of the beach below Crozon."

A crease formed between Captain Hertle's eyebrows. "To me he said 'south,' not 'north.' In fact he made a point of saying this twice, which I thought odd at the time."

"We were put ashore at the beach's most northern end," Hayden said, "and were to return to that spot." He had been wondering about this very thing for some hours. What had become of the cutter that was to have met them?

Hawthorne glanced at him darkly, raising an eyebrow.

Hertle shook his head, as though unwilling to consider the possibilities, and continued his story. "After parting with the *Themis*, I ordered my ship on, determined to send a cutter ashore this night. And what strange sight should meet us as we closed on the coast south of Brest? A little lugger sailing away from the coast into the final gasps of a gale, and with what appeared to be a privateer in hot pursuit." Hertle smiled. "I have heard it said that French privateers will go after anything that floats, but this prize seemed a bit inconsequential even for them. As we have no liking of privateers, we thought we might look into this matter. And here you are—not captives of the French after all, and there are three of you, not two, as Captain Hart had stated."

"That is another story," Hayden said, glancing at the midshipman, who concentrated all his energies on his victuals.

"Well, by whatever strange paths you have come, you are now guests of mine and I shall carry you back to England with me."

The guests having eaten and drunk their fill, servants cleared away. Hawthorne stood, hunching beneath the low deckhead. "Come along, Mr Wickham. I'm sure Mr Hayden and Captain Hertle would like to speak in private."

The two excused themselves, though not without profuse thanks to Robert Hertle for their delivery, and for the recent, much needed, meal. Once the cabin was empty, the two friends regarded each other a moment.

"It would seem that good Captain Hart made very little effort to recover his first lieutenant and lieutenant of marines," Hertle observed. "Only enough to satisfy any enquiries that might be made by the Admiralty."

"Neither Hawthorne nor myself have enough interest at the Admiralty to warrant any enquiries at all."

Robert sat back in his chair and stretched his legs out before him. "But one could not say the same of young Lord Arthur Wickham, whose father is a man of influence."

"Hart didn't know Wickham had come ashore with us. The boy stowed away in the cutter, and only revealed himself when it was too late for me to send him back. His mates in the midshipmen's mess were to conceal his absence, if it became necessary."

"I should like to see Hart's face when he discovers that he abandoned the son of the Earl of Westmoor ashore without so much as a backward glance, let alone a concerted effort to learn what had become of him." Hertle chuckled. "And now that I've recovered you, his lack of action shall look doubly derelict. I almost feel sorry for the man. Mrs Hart might have some influence among the Lords of the Admiralty, but I should think that an aggrieved Earl of Westmoor will have more. What say you?"

"*On deck,*" came a call from above. "Sail, due south. A frigate, by the looks."

Hertle raised an eyebrow. "I will wager that is Captain Hart, in something of a lather, having discovered that he's marooned the son of an earl on a French beach."

The two men went on deck, and after a cursory examination with a glass, agreed that this was the *Themis*, making all possible sail in her effort to get north. Hertle ordered his ship hove-to and the two friends retired below again, and as quietly as he could, Hayden related all that had transpired since he had gone aboard the *Themis*. Hertle heard him out, his face growing darker and more grave by the moment.

"You have been deucedly lucky, Charles," Hertle said when Hayden had finished. "First Bourne and now myself. You cannot count on a friend coming to your rescue again."

"I know that only too well." Hayden gazed out over the now sunlit ocean, gulls and gannets swinging and wheeling in their wake. "I wish Hart had gone off south and you could carry us home."

"As do I, but it is not within my power." Hertle sat at the small table, gazing at his friend, lost in thought.

"Will you carry a letter back home for me?" Hayden asked.

"Let me find you ink and paper."

Pen and ink were produced and a few clean sheets of hot-pressed paper. Hayden applied himself with a will, and before the *Themis* had ranged up and, at a signal from Hertle, hove-to, the lieutenant had completed his letter to "Mr Banks" detailing all that had happened and written in such a way that the First Secretary could hardly help but understand their stranding had been almost certainly intentional. When Hayden turned the letter over to Robert Hertle, his friend had the goodness to ask no questions.

Joining his shipmates on deck, Hayden watched as Hertle's crew quickly and expertly lowered a boat. Hayden could not help but wish his own crew were so adept. The three climbed down and in a moment were aboard the *Themis*. Hayden turned and raised a hand to his friend Robert as he stepped onto the deck of his own ship again. Robert waved back, and then turned to his duties.

The crew of the *Themis* were gathered about, but there were no huzzas or indeed any words of welcome at all. Only an unnatural and uncomfortable silence. The men all knew what had transpired, and if Hayden needed any proof, this was it.

He led his small party down the gangway to the quarterdeck, where Hart stood, a little distant from his officers. Only Barthe and the surgeon had a smile for the men returned. The others would hardly meet Hayden's eye.

Hart did not feign pleasure at his lieutenant's deliverance. "What do you mean, sir!" he began, addressing Hayden in the most belligerent tone, "taking Mr Wickham on a dangerous sortie without so much as asking my leave?"

Wickham stepped forward. "If you please, Captain Hart, Mr Hayden did not know I was ashore. I stowed away on the boat without any being aware of it."

Hart was taken aback for a moment. "Mr Wickham, your loyalty is misplaced. You cannot intervene. Mr Hayden must accept responsibility for your presence—"

"I do accept it," Hayden interrupted.

Hart was surprised, but a little gleam of triumph glittered in his eye. The corner of his mouth raised just perceptibly. "Then you admit you knew of his presence . . ."

"I was not aware, but it was my responsibility all the same. If Lord Westmoor wishes to hold anyone accountable, then it will be me. Mr Barthe may write it in the log and I will sign it."

Hart looked, for a moment, confused, as though Hayden must be playing him some trick. The first lieutenant tried not to smile. Wickham, he was sure, would tell his father the true story of their adventure—and Hayden would receive no admonishment from that quarter.

"You might also write in the log," Hayden continued, "that we were at the arranged rendezvous point at the proper time, but no boat appeared."

"What? Damn your eyes, sir!" Hart blustered. "What do you mean by that? Damn your impudence! Are you accusing me of . . . of—"

"I'm making no accusations, sir," Hayden said evenly, "only stating a fact. The boat did not arrive as it should—though I know not why."

"It was sent to the south end of the beach below Crozon, as we arranged!" Hart thundered. "And no one can deny it. Childers will tell you the same himself."

"It was to have fetched us from the beach's northern end, sir. That was our arrangement."

"You are mistaken!" Hart said. "Very much mistaken. Is that not true, Landry? Did you not hear me tell Mr Hayden to meet the boat on the beach's southern extreme?"

"That is true," Landry said, meeting no one's eye. "I heard it most clearly, sir."

"You were not even present," Hayden said with disdain.

"No, sir, but by happenstance I arrived at the captain's door as he spoke his instructions. Realizing he had you with him, I went away, intending to have my word with the captain when he had concluded with you."

Hawthorne snorted, almost pawing at a plank with his foot, head shaking in disbelief.

"Have you something to say, Mr Hawthorne?" Hart demanded.

"Yes, sir. Mr Landry was on deck seeing to some small damage done to one of the boats in the taking of the prize. He did not leave the deck until Mr Hayden emerged from speaking with you. I was present myself, as were others, and can attest to this."

Hart's face turned crimson. Hayden thought he might strike the marine with his balled-up fist. "Are you calling Mr Landry a liar, sir? Clearly you misapprehend what occurred."

"I am not mistaken, sir. Mr Franks and one of his mates were with Mr Landry at the time. You might ask them."

"It is not necessary for me to ask them," Hart bellowed. "I know what I said, sir! Mr Hayden misheard me, and almost brought his shipmates to ruin as a result. Now get about your duties. I shall have you question me no more!" Hart spun around and retreated below, muttering to himself.

Landry started to back away.

"Running off, Landry?" Hawthorne asked quietly. "Just when I think you can sink no lower, you surprise even me with your cravenness."

Having nothing to say for himself, and being too cowardly to challenge Hawthorne, the second lieutenant slunk off. Hayden and his companions slipped below to wash and change into uniform.

Barthe came in almost immediately, shaking his head, his lips pressed into a tight line, manner stiff. "It is an outrage," he hissed, "the way the man treats you, Mr Hayden. Strands you on the beach and then, when you have the audacity not to be captured and executed as spies, he assails your dignity and all but accuses you of insubordination." Barthe threw himself down in a chair and raised his hands in a gesture of helplessness.

"Mr Barthe," Hayden entreated the master, "I might remind you to be more circumspect."

"This is very good advice, I'm sure," the master said, "and I should heed it, were I not offended beyond all—"

Wickham burst in at that moment without even a knock on the door. His face was pale and though he opened his mouth to speak, no words came.

"Lord Arthur," Hayden said, concerned. "What has happened, sir?"

Wickham worked his jaw soundlessly for a moment and then managed, "He flogged Aldrich while we were ashore, sir."

"Aldrich . . . ! Whatever for?"

"For having possessed Mr Paine's pamphlets," Barthe interjected, "and for preaching unrest among the crew."

Hayden sat down hard in a chair. "But what proof had he of that? I have the pamphlets in my trunk."

"Hart had no proof at all," Barthe said, "but he questioned Aldrich and the man admitted to having possessed the pamphlets."

Hayden reeled back as though struck. "Has Aldrich no sense at all?"

"He is an honest man, poor fool. Two dozen lashes he took for it. The best able seaman aboard. He's in the care of Doctor, for his back was slashed to ribbons."

Hayden hurried down to the orlop and into the small space partitioned off for the use of Dr Griffiths. Half a dozen cots swung here, their occupants all but invisible behind weather clothes. The surgeon's apothecary-chest stood against one bulkhead, its locking doors ajar, squeaking softly as the ship rolled. In the dim light, Hayden could see Griffiths bent over a cot, his mate holding aloft a smoke-stained lantern.

"Doctor," Hayden said softly, and Griffiths looked up, nodded perfunctorily, and went back to his ministrations. The mate made a knuckle with his free hand.

Drawing near, Hayden found Aldrich, stretched out upon his stomach, eyes closed and face bathed in sweat. Even in the poor light, Hayden could see Aldrich's cheeks were crimson, almost glowing. Very gently the surgeon tugged free the dressing, revealing a back that appeared to have been slashed with a razor. Hayden recoiled from the sight, then regained his self-possession.

"May I help in any way, Doctor?" Hayden asked.

"Is that you, sir?" Aldrich asked between teeth clamped tight.

"It is, Aldrich, and terribly distressed I am to see you in such a state. It was not my doing in any way, Aldrich. I want you to know that."

"I never thought for a moment that it could be, sir. Never for a moment . . ." He grunted to cover a cry of pain.

"Mr Hayden," Griffiths said. "If you would be so kind . . ."

Hayden nodded, retreating quickly from the sick-berth.

For a few moments he lingered at the foot of the ladder, pacing back and forth, his rage barely under control. The doctor finally came to him, wiping his hands on a cloth.

"What is his condition, Doctor?" Hayden whispered.

"You saw, Mr Hayden," Griffiths answered, his tone almost hostile. "Two dozen lashes. Cut near to the bone in places." He removed his spectacles and leaned back against the ladder stringer, his anger dissolving visibly. "He is in much pain, though makes every effort to hide it." Griffiths spoke so low Hayden could barely make out his words, and the lieutenant answered in kind.

"And this was over pamphlets that Aldrich did not even have in his possession?"

The surgeon looked up at him sharply. "You must not misunderstand this, Mr Hayden. Hart did not give a damn about Aldrich and his pamphlets. This was a message to the crew. Any who supported you will be at pains to hide it now, for Aldrich's punishment will be fresh in their minds." He drew a long breath. "And it is a message to you. Any man whom you befriend is in danger. That is the corner he has you in."

"How did Hart even know about these pamphlets?"

Griffiths raised an open hand, his gaze moving just perceptibly toward the gunroom.

Hayden should not have needed to ask. "Please, keep me informed of his condition, Dr Griffiths."

The surgeon nodded, and Hayden climbed up to the berth-deck, where the young gentlemen regarded him with troubled, silent faces. As he entered the gunroom, Hayden slammed the door behind him. He spotted Landry in his cabin, the door half-open. Barthe and Hawthorne sat either side of the table.

"I should like a word with Mr Landry," Hayden said, and the two men scrambled up from the table, retreating quickly toward the door. "Mr Barthe? Ask the middies to find themselves some duty upon the deck."

"I will, sir."

Landry looked as though he would bolt after the master, but Hayden blocked his way.

"You know that Aldrich is the finest able seaman aboard this ship, and yet you had him flogged . . ."

Landry looked left and right, then stepped back against the wooden bulkhead. "The captain had him flogged. Not me."

"Only because you've been reporting gunroom conversations to him, Landry."

The little lieutenant drew himself up. "Sir, I am a gentleman—"

Hayden snorted. "You are an embarrassment to the service, running to the captain with every little thing that's said, currying his favour at any cost. Have you never thought what becoming Hart's protégé will mean to your career?" The letters to Mr Banks came unaccountably to mind—a dash of cooling rain on Hayden's rage.

Landry's indignation dissolved visibly and he sank into one of the chairs. "I do not have a career, nor do you, Hayden. We both gave that up the day we stepped aboard the *Themis*." His gaze flicked toward the deck beams, the captain's cabin overhead. For a moment Hayden thought the man would weep. "He . . . he is the ruin of us, with his shyness and his petty tyranny. But what am I to do? No other captain will have me now. And yet the sea is all I know. I am not fit for any other life. Hart has taken everything from me, and I can do nothing now but acquiesce to his every bidding, submit to each indignity, for without him I am lost." He glanced up at Hayden almost imploringly. "I am like a man fallen into the sea, clinging to some bit of wreckage, knowing that in but a short time even that will fail and I shall go under. And that is you, as well, Hayden, though you do not know it yet. Hart will break you. I see a crack in your pride already, where Hart applied his lash to Aldrich. The captain knows your weakness now. The crew will be held hostage, and if you dare defy him he will flog another innocent man, and yet another after that, until you come to heel. And then one morning you will gaze into your looking-glass, Mr Hayden, and find *me* staring back."

The first lieutenant was at a loss for words. Was there a man buried deep inside Landry, after all?

He leaned closer to Landry. "Does Hart not know how close this crew is to mutiny?"

Landry shook his head. "He believes the lash protects him."

Hayden slumped down in a chair. "Aldrich was the voice of moderation before the mast. Flog another like him and Hart will find the deck beneath his feet is paper-thin."

Landry regarded him evenly, almost a look of sympathy, of brotherhood. "Do not overvalue the bravery of this crew, Mr Hayden. They have been forced into cowardice for so many years they no longer know where to find their courage."

"They took the transport in the Goulet," Hayden retorted.

"A poorly defended transport is not a frigate, Mr Hayden. Take them into a real battle and you will soon see what they're made of." Landry rose, bobbed his head to Hayden, and stepped toward the door. "You fight in a lost cause, Hayden. The *Themis* is full of rot. She crumbles around us, and one day will take every man Jack aboard down to the lightless depths. And we shall not be missed." Landry went quickly out.

Hayden sat a moment, staring at the empty table, his thoughts awhirl. Was it possible that Landry had once been like him, full of zeal and the desire to make his way in the service? That the rot that spread throughout the ship had crept into him, eating away until he was but an empty shell—the Landry Hayden knew? If that were true, what would prevent it from happening to him? Certainly, if Hart flogged some innocent member of the crew every time he wished to punish Hayden the lieutenant would be brought up short. The crew would not misunderstand why these floggings were being applied and would quickly come to despise him. He would have no allies then.

During the early months of the French Revolution a number of noblemen had taken up the side of the revolutionaries, turning against their king and, in some cases, their families. Most had been farsighted men—men of conscience—but others had stood by king and caste against the voice of their conscience. Hayden felt like one of these men now—but in Hayden's case conscience pulled him in both directions. Hart was a tyrant, but Hayden believed the English cause—officially, *Hart's* cause—was right. The grievances of the men were legitimate— just, in many ways—but this was not the time to protest or refuse to perform one's duties. England was at war, after all. Never in his life had Hayden felt himself so torn. His poor brain was being distorted by its inability to make peace among all the contradictions. He wanted to scream with the frustration of it.

And then there were the letters to Mr Banks . . . How he now wished he had let that scrap of paper lie on Philip Stephens' desk. Better to have no ship and keep one's honour intact—one's future! For surely Landry was right: no captain would have him now.

He took up his hat and climbed onto the deck, into the sunshine. There were no greetings, or even a friendly face. The Jacks seemed to gaze at him blankly, distantly, as though they were condemned men and he but a bystander watching the hangman's cart roll by.

He turned to find Hart standing by the rail, and he was gazing at Hayden as well. The captain smiled.

"Is it not a perfect day, Mr Hayden? The storm brought the rains, sweeping away all that God did not deign good, and now the world is made anew. And I . . . I am content with it."

Hayden lay in his swinging cot, still deeply fatigued from his exertions ashore, much of his body stiff and aching. The door to his cabin was closed, and he ignored the sounds of conversation in the gunroom beyond. The slow pitching of the *Themis* as she made her way south would have soothed him had his indignation not been so inflamed. The creaking of the wooden ship as she worked in the small seas, the dull thud of a barrel rocking in the hold below—all familiar, even comforting, sounds, but there was no solace for Hayden that night.

In his hands he gripped Mr Paine's pamphlets that had caused such trouble of late. He read *The Rights of Man*.

All hereditary government is in its nature tyranny. An heritable crown, or an heritable throne, or by what other fanciful name such things may be called, have no other significant explanation than that mankind are heritable property. To inherit a government is to inherit the people, as if they were flocks and herds.

Seventeen

The gun boomed and was thrown back, the wooden slide screaming along the iron frame, thudding to a percussive halt. Hayden put a hand on the iron frame and found it surprisingly warm.

"I'm still fearful of sparks," the gun captain muttered unhappily. His opinion of the new gun was not in doubt.

"Never a spark!" Muhlhauser answered brightly. The little man from the Ordnance Board was so happy to see his gun finally fired that he hardly took notice of the crew's reaction.

A good number of the watch below had gathered to witness this spectacle and stood about, shaking their heads and speaking low among themselves, a few grinning vacantly at the sheer novelty of this contraption.

"Iron is too brittle to take this battering," Barthe observed. "It will break at last, I fear."

"Not were you to fire a hundred rounds a day," Muhlhauser assured him. "We have not brought it to sea without first testing it thoroughly on land. You will see, Mr Barthe, there will be no sparks, no sudden failure of the structure. And do you note how quickly it can be reloaded and run out? Faster than a standard eighteen-pounder. I shall not be surprised to see this new gun replace many of the long Blomefields in the near future."

Before the gun could be fired again, the cry of "sail ho" propelled Hayden up onto the quarterdeck, into the golden sunlight of Biscay Bay, glass in hand, cocked hat slapped roughly in place. It was another warm fall day, as though the headlong rush of summer had gained too much momentum to be stopped by mere numbers on a calendar.

"Where away?" he asked Archer, who indicated sou-sou'east.

A small gathering of seamen aimed the Cyclops eyes of their various glasses toward that point of the compass, and Hayden joined them at the rail.

"It looks to be a brig," Wickham suggested.

"Or a snow," the master added as he followed Hayden to the rail.

Hayden found the angular dab of stained white among the small, cresting seas. Whether brig or snow, she was still hull-down and her colours, if they were flying, obscured.

"Do you think she's one of ours, Mr Hayden?" Wickham asked.

"All I see, Mr Wickham, is a bit of sail. Whether the cloth is British I cannot say."

"So near to the coast, she is very likely French," Hart pronounced, "an outlier to a squadron, most likely." He lowered his glass. "Mr Barthe? Alter our course to west-by-north, if she will lay it."

"But what if she is one of ours, sir?" Barthe asked.

Hart turned on him, his volatile temper flushing crimson into his face. "Mr Barthe, when you are captain of this ship you may give the orders. Until such time the duty still falls to me. West-by-north."

"I did not mean to question your authority, sir," Barthe stated evenly, unwilling to be intimidated. "I'm merely suggesting that this is a bold little brig to be sailing directly for us . . . unless she is British, in which case she might have need of our assistance."

"She is sailing hard," Wickham chimed in. "She might have a Frenchie in her wake."

"Perhaps I should go aloft," Hayden said softly, "and see if I can make her out . . ."

Hart did not hide his frustration well and glanced at Landry, who looked quickly away. The captain's officers were united against him.

"Lay aloft, then, Hayden," the captain ordered, "but I will not endanger my ship if you are less than certain."

Hayden touched his hat and hurried forward toward the main shrouds.

"Shall we beat to quarters?" Archer asked.

"Aye," the captain said reluctantly. "But stand ready to alter course, Mr Barthe, and to make all sail, if required."

Hayden went quickly up to the main-top and found Wickham already there; the boy had slipped up the starboard shrouds.

"And what do you make of her, Mr Wickham?"

The midshipman did not lower his glass but kept it fixed upon the distant sail. "I cannot tell, sir. Her hull is just now coming into view."

Hayden raised his own glass as the vessel fired a cannon to starboard and ran up a hoist of flags.

"On deck," Hayden called down. "I believe she is one of ours, unless some Frenchman has penetrated our signals."

Hart reluctantly altered his course to meet the brig but required Hayden remain aloft in case she turned out to be an enemy practising a bit of subterfuge. As the ship drew closer it was clear she was not being chased; she was, however, almost certainly British.

In less than an hour she ranged alongside—an old-style brig-sloop replete with raised quarterdeck—backed sails, and quickly lowered a boat. Her commander came over the rail in haste, touching his hat, hardly a moment to be civil. He was younger than Hayden by several years and wore only a lieutenant's epaulette. Small and neat with precise movements, like a little automaton.

"Herald Philpott, at your service, Captain Hart," he announced, "acting commander of the sloop *Lucy*. Captain Bourne has sent me to request your aid, sir. He has four transports, a brig, and a French frigate at bay in the roadstead east of Belle Île. With the wind in the sou'west, sir, no ships from L'Orient can yet come to their aid. He respectfully requests that you rendezvous with him a league north-west of Belle Île, where he endeavours to tempt the French into making a run for L'Orient. Captain Bourne believes, with your aid, some or all of these ships can be taken or destroyed before their rescue can be effected."

"Are these Frenchmen not anchored beneath the batteries on the island?" Hart asked.

"I believe they are, sir."

"Then what does Bourne expect me to do?" Hart demanded indignantly. "Place my ship within range of twenty-four-pounders?"

The little man's face hardened, and his stiff manner became more so. "I'm sure Captain Bourne has weighed the risks most judiciously, Captain Hart."

"Has he, now? Well, all events must occur once, as they say." Hart stepped away from the visitor, turning his gaze out to sea.

"Shall I inform Captain Bourne that you refused him aid in this action, Captain Hart?"

Hayden almost smiled. Certainly Bourne had instructed the young lieutenant to say precisely this. Refusing to aid a British ship in anything but the most ill-conceived endeavour—one certain to lose an officer his command—would result in court-martial. If Bourne was even partially successful without Hart's help, then Hart would appear shy. If Bourne failed, but could make an argument that he might have succeeded if Hart had joined the action . . .

"I did not say I refused," Hart replied quietly, perhaps realizing that the young commander had chosen to have this exchange on deck, attended by numerous witnesses, not all of them in Hart's camp. Seeing Hart receive a measure of his own physic gave Hayden great pleasure.

"I fear, Captain Hart," the young officer stated softly, "that I must insist you do one or the other: come to Captain Bourne's aid or refuse."

Hart's anger flared—the lack of respect being shown him was scandalous—but he looked quickly around like a man trapped, and then, with great self-control, nodded. "I shall meet with Bourne and try to dissuade him from pursuing such a hazardous endeavour. Mr Barthe, shape our course for Belle Île."

Lieutenant Philpott glanced over at Hayden, revealing, for the briefest instant, a little smile of triumph. He quickly took his leave and clambered down into his boat, the toes of his polished shoes rapping against the topsides as he descended.

The deck came to life then; men were called to their stations to trim sail, yards were shifted, the helm put over. In a moment they were heeling to a healthy beam wind, and making seven knots toward the little French island that had, for several years during a previous war, been under the control of the British.

Wickham ranged up beside Hayden, who had shifted to the forecastle, largely to put the length of the deck between himself and Hart, who was at his worst when both angry and frightened.

"Have you been to Belle Île, sir?" Wickham asked.

"Twice," Hayden said. "It is well named, for there is hardly a more charming island that I can think of."

"Perhaps we should have kept it?"

Hayden laughed. "I don't think its present inhabitants would welcome our return. I understand that a goodly number of them are Acadians—Canadians who would not submit to English rule. They were moved here after the Treaty of Paris, and hold no love for us, I fear."

Hayden raised a glass. The distant horizon was awash in a white haze, and the lieutenant could not be sure if he perceived a dark mass within or if it were merely his imagination.

Wickham looked quickly around, then stepped a bit nearer, saying quietly, "What will Hart do? He cannot tell Bourne that they are not French ships, or that they are three deckers we dare not engage."

"Oh no," Hayden whispered. "Bourne will not let Hart wriggle free, as he knows full well Hart will attempt to do. No, he has set the hook deep, and our good captain can do nothing but flop up onto the deck. It's the fish room for him."

Boot-steps from behind ended the conversation and Hayden turned to see who approached.

"Mr Muhlhauser. Were you satisfied with your trial, sir?"

"Most satisfied, Mr Hayden, though it would have been even better had we had the opportunity to fire another two dozen rounds. But now I am given to understand there is some small chance my gun might finally get an honest trial?"

"Honest trials are rare in this age, Mr Muhlhauser, but we shall soon see. How is your gun crew? Are you pleased with their efforts?"

Muhlhauser looked like a man asked a most embarrassing question. "Well, Mr Hayden, if they do not mutiny I think they will answer."

"What do you mean, sir? Have you cause to doubt their loyalty?" Hayden asked.

"No more cause than I have to doubt any of the Jacks, but that leaves reason enough, don't it?"

"I'm afraid you're right, Mr Muhlhauser. Perhaps I shall see you issued a pistol."

"I have a brace in my cabin, thank you." The man said this without bluster; in fact he looked a little frightened.

"Then you are well set up. We shall trust in Mr Hawthorne and his marines to assure the devotion of the crew, and all go about our duties."

Muhlhauser nodded.

Another joined them on the forecastle then.

"Dr Griffiths, how fares Mr Aldrich?" Muhlhauser asked.

"As well as a man can be who has had his flesh torn to ribbons."

This brought an unhappy silence to the forecastle, but then Muhlhauser spoke up, raising his hand to indicate a bird that hung in the air not distant from the frigate's side, almost motionless on some eddy caused by the sails. "What species of bird might that be, Doctor? Can you tell?"

"Why, it is *Avis albi*, Mr Muhlhauser," Griffiths answered. "Very common in this part of the world."

"Ah," Muhlhauser responded. "I had wondered . . ." He then crossed the forecastle at the behest of the gunner, to see to one of the chase guns.

"*Avis albi*, Doctor?" Hayden repeated quietly.

"Is it not a bird, Mr Hayden? Was I not correct?"

"It is indeed a bird."

"And is it not white? for so it appears to my eye."

"White as a ship's wake, Doctor."

"Then *Avis Albi* would seem to be an accurate description, would it not?"

"I cannot deny it, and it is my hope that our guest will always find this description satisfactory."

The doctor gave a small bow and quit the foredeck.

Hayden had not forgotten Muhlhauser's reaction when he had believed himself mocked by Mr Hawthorne; how would he respond when he found out Griffiths was practising upon him?

Not ten minutes later Hayden overheard Muhlhauser speaking to Mr Barthe.

"Do you see this white bird . . . ?" Muhlhauser asked.

"I do," Mr Barthe answered.

"*Avis albi* it is called."

"Well, I know not what the Romans named it," the sailing master replied, "but we ignorant seamen call it a gannet."

Sometime later Griffiths reappeared and stood by Hayden. For a moment he regarded the eastern horizon, as many did aboard the *Themis* that afternoon. "So, your friend Bourne will draw us into an action?"

"It seems likely."

"Is he as rash as the men say?"

Hayden shook his head. "In all of his endeavours, he thinks first how he might preserve the lives of his crew. His actions only seem rash to those who do not have his imagination, for he perceives weaknesses in the enemy others do not and devises the most ingenious methods to exploit them. No, if Bourne has a plan it will be thoroughly thought out."

"But what will he do about the shore batteries?"

"Oh, Bourne is not much concerned about shore batteries. Once we have laid our ship alongside a Frenchman they will be unable to fire for fear of killing their own. As long as there is wind to keep us moving we shall pass through their cannonade in short order, though not without some damage. Although you would hardly know it aboard the *Themis*, it is a war. A little risk cannot be avoided."

Griffiths turned to regard him, his look quizzical. "Mr Hayden, the prospect of action invariably seems to cheer you."

"And how could it not, Doctor? If not for the odd bit of actual warfare, this would be the most tedious career in the world. One might better be a banker or a law clerk. After all, look at you, Doctor. Certainly you could have opened a surgery in Bath and spent all your days listening to old ladies complain of infirmities innumerable and afflictions too ghastly to name, but you chose the Navy. There must have been a reason."

"I was endeavouring to escape my family, Mr Hayden."

The lieutenant laughed. "It is this regard for the sacred bond of family that is responsible for almost the entire officers' corps in His Majesty's Navy, Dr Griffiths. But most of us were sent to sea to be shut of us. Your case is somewhat singular." Hayden raised his glass and announced, "The beautiful isle."

Bourne bent over the table in what had been his cabin before the carpenter's mates had knocked down the bulkheads. All the others clustered around. A stained and worn chart of the waters surrounding Belle Île had been spread for their viewing, and the host tapped the paper with a crooked finger. "The French frigate lies to her anchor here, at the southern end of the anchored ships. The transports are arranged, more or less, in a line north, the one nearest the frigate having lost her main and foremast. The frigate towed her in last night, and we damned near caught her, too." He looked up at the others, a smile overspreading his face as he recalled the chase. "All six ships had sustained some damage . . . in the recent gale, no doubt. But now they are in difficulties, aren't they? One ship is disabled, though I think they will abandon her without much of a fight if the others think they can make L'Orient."

The young commander of the brig was also present, as were Bourne's two senior lieutenants and his sailing master; all as excited as Hayden himself.

"I will round the island from the south and engage the frigate. There is a little brig to the north—I think she might once have been ours. I have marked her place. We shall put the *Lucy* on her, then I'll have no worries of being raked by her guns while I board the frigate, for even six-pounders are deadly when fired through the stern gallery at close range. Once we have engaged the first ships, the others could cut their cables and run for L'Orient, so we might have to chase them down. I should hate to sink any of them, for they are valuable as they are and I don't like to murder Frenchmen any more than I must." He glanced quickly at Hayden, then back to his chart.

Hart shook his head. "I am touched by your concern for the lives of Frenchmen when our own English crews shall be subjected to much worse from the guns ashore. Forgive me, Bourne, but it is not a serviceable plan. Come, you must admit, there will be much loss of life aboard our ships."

Bourne straightened as much as the low deckhead would allow. "I am not much afraid of the fortress guns, for we will slip in at dusk, if this wind holds. It will take the gunners ashore just that much longer to find us, for it will be difficult for them to perceive where their first few shots strike the water. Once we have laid our ships alongside the enemy's the shore gunners will be unable to fire upon us for fear of striking their own. But the shore batteries should not much concern you, Hart, for it is my suggestion that you lie off the northern tip of the island, in plain view, to discourage the transports running for port."

Hart could not completely conceal his surprise. "It is a small part you ask me to play," he grumbled, as though he were not delighted with the prospect of prize money for so little effort.

"Well, my crew profited from your enterprise at Brest. We shall repay you in kind. It is my hope that the mere sight of the *Themis* will stop the French transports from attempting to make L'Orient, but they might fool us and cut their cables, thinking that you cannot intercept all three. We shall see. If the *Lucy* can disable the brig quickly without sustaining substantial damage, then there will be two British ships for the chase."

"The *Lucy* is more than equal to a French brig, sir," Lieutenant Philpott offered. "I am confident of it."

Bourne smiled kindly upon the young man, but then turned his attention to Hart. "I do have one other request, Hart. Although Lieutenant Philpott is prepared to take on a French three decker if I would allow it, I have decided to override his enthusiasm. With all due respect to Lieutenant Philpott, who is an excellent officer, and as acting commander of the *Lucy* has performed admirably, it is my preference to have a man of more experience in charge of the *Lucy*. Would you allow Lieutenant Hayden to take command of the brig?"

Hart glanced at Hayden, then back to Bourne. "What happened to the brig's original captain?"

"As we chased these ships in behind Belle Île, Captain Wilson had the terrible misfortune to have been struck by one of the French frigate's eighteen-pound balls, which killed him instantly, may God rest his soul."

Hart shivered visibly. "Have you not a lieutenant of your own to whom you can grant command of the *Lucy*?"

"Neither is as experienced as Mr Hayden, and I should like to have them aboard when we engage the frigate."

Hart appeared to dither a moment and then nodded. "Then I shall put Mr Hayden temporarily under your command, and may we all be the richer for it. Eh?" He laughed, as though they were all brothers sharing equally in the enterprise.

But Bourne laughed, too, no sign of censure upon his pleasant face. "I might also ask if you could spare a dozen good men to crew the *Lucy*, for she is not over-manned and might well find the French resistant to her intentions."

Hart nodded. Hayden thought Bourne might ask anything of Hart as long as he spared him taking the *Themis* into action. Bourne must have known Hart would resist any attempt to put him in danger, so devised this ancillary role for the *Themis*. Hart had, rather quickly, given up his argument that the shore guns would kill too many Englishmen, once his own valuable life had been exempted from that particular risk.

"My plan is simple," Bourne began, "and I'm sure you will all see that immediately. I will take my ship and beat down the seaward side of Belle Île—there is just enough daylight left for me to manage it. Take your ships around the northern tip and into the channel between Quiberon and Belle Île. When I round the southern end of the island I will have the wind behind me, and come up rather quickly on the French frigate. Once I have engaged her, both of your ships should make for the little French brig, but the *Themis* will sheer off and stay just out of effective range of the guns ashore. It is my hope that the guns will waste some time firing at the *Themis*, allowing the *Lucy* to come alongside the French brig and board or disable her. If my crew can do the same to the frigate, the transports will all be ours, and they will know it, too." He looked up from his chart where he had been watching the battle play out in his mind's eye. "If the transports cut their cables and try to run, their capture will fall to you, Hart. Are we in accord?"

All the officers present gave their assent.

"Darkness will fall not long after you have engaged the frigate," Hayden observed. "If we are to chase the transports—and maybe the frigate too, if she runs—we should have some means to tell friend from foe."

"Two lanterns, one above the other, on the main topmast," Bourne offered, "and a blue flare shewn on the stern every five minutes for half a minute. Will that answer?"

The others nodded. There was no time for even a toast, as there was only enough daylight left to manage the affair.

Hayden returned to the *Themis* with Hart, to find his dozen men and retrieve his pistols. Neither man spoke as the barge made its way quickly back to their ship, hove-to nearby. Hayden found himself regarding the distracted captain as the Jacks plied their sweeps. The lieutenant had known incompetent officers in his time. He'd met men of limited understanding—too many, in truth—and captains who could manage a ship in the most desperate conditions but had not the least notion of how to fight her. But outright cowards were very rare in His Majesty's Navy. For the briefest moment he almost felt pity for the man—but then he remembered Aldrich, face-down in the surgeon's cot.

Hayden followed Hart over the side of their ship, where the captain called for the officers to join him in his cabin.

As he passed, Hawthorne drew Hayden aside. "Will we fight? Has Hart agreed?"

"Yes and no. Hart will no doubt explain your part in a moment. As for me, I am for the brig-sloop, and I will take a dozen good men with me."

The hastily called council of war convened in the captain's cabin, a place few were invited for anything but ship's business. Hart quickly laid out Bourne's plan, presenting it as though he had played a significant part in its creation. A chart was laid on the table, and with the reflected sunlight playing on the deck beams overhead, Hart sketched in the positions of the anchored French ships.

"Should we not attack the transports when Captain Bourne and Mr Hayden take their ships into action?" Barthe asked. "We could put our ship between two of the transports, anchor, and force them both to haul down their colours. The third ship could be dealt with thereafter, and the last is disabled."

"Bourne and I have considered all eventualities, Mr Barthe," Hart said, "and agree that this plan is the best. It is too late to change it now, at any rate." The florid-faced captain looked around at his gathered officers. "We will, of course, go to Captain Bourne's or Mr Hayden's aid should it be required. After all, a few guns ashore will not unnerve the likes of us, eh?" He chuckled a bit too loudly. "A night's work, gentlemen, and we shall all have some coins to rattle in our purses. Are we cleared and in all respects ready for action, Mr Landry?"

"We are, sir."

"Mr Archer, will you find a dozen men to accompany Mr Hayden aboard the brig?"

"I will, sir."

Hayden thought Hart was doing a passable imitation of a decisive commander—an imitation of Bourne, to be more precise. It was a wonder how greatly the man's spirits had lifted when it had become clear he would not be involved in the actual fighting.

An hour later Hayden climbed down into one of the cutters, and as soon as he settled himself in the stern sheets, picked out Lord Arthur Wickham seated in the bow.

"Mr Wickham," Hayden began sternly, "I hope you have no designs to even set foot upon the deck of the *Lucy*."

"I have the captain's sanction, Mr Hayden!" Wickham countered.

"Why does that seem so very unlikely to me?"

"Truly, sir. I approached Captain Hart, arguing that it was not possible to go safely to war, and he said I might as well proceed with his blessing as I would likely swim over to the *Lucy* anyway."

"If past experience is accounted for, this would seem to be true."

"You had need of another, anyway, sir," Wickham said as the boat pushed off. "A dozen plus yourself made thirteen—a most unpropitious number. Now we are fourteen, and fortune sails with us."

"We have been relying too frequently on having fortune aboard, Wickham, but I hope you're correct."

Eighteen

They were piped smartly aboard the brig, Lieutenant Philpott tipping his hat to the new acting commander. Hayden immediately took Philpott aside.

"I hope, Lieutenant, that you harbour no resentment over my appointment, which was as much a surprise to me as to you, I must say."

Philpott nodded in his precise manner. "It was not a surprise to me, Mr Hayden. Captain Bourne had made his intentions known to me before meeting with Hart. I have had the deuced bad luck of never having fought in a significant action in my short career. I agreed entirely with Bourne that, for the safety of the *Lucy*'s crew, a more experienced officer should have his hand on the helm. Do not devote a moment to concern over my pride, Mr Hayden. It has taken far greater blows than this and staggered but an instant."

Hayden smiled in spite of himself. "You are a protégé of Bourne's, I see."

Philpott looked slightly embarrassed, the automaton becoming more human. "It is difficult to be around such a man and not see the wisdom of his methods."

"Yes, if we become half the seaman Captain Bourne is, we shall be all right, I think." Hayden glanced up at the sun. "We haven't a great deal of time. I should like to look over the ship and see for myself your preparations."

The *Lucy* was not large and Hayden quickly had the measure of her. Twenty six-pounder guns constituted her armament, along with two swivel guns that could be moved either fore or aft or to either side of the deck. She was an odd little vessel, neither fish nor fowl—larger than a single-decked brig; almost a ship sloop but for her double-masted rig. Her guns sat higher above the water than on a conventional brig, and her quarterdeck looked very old-fashioned, though handsome in its own way—like a well-turned-out dowager, Hayden thought.

"She's uncommonly handy, sir, and I think you'll find her crew more than willing, though hardly more experienced than myself in close action."

As they rounded the tip of Belle Île, Hayden and Philpott stood at the rail, gazing out over the French ships in the roadstead beyond Le Palais. The French two-master could be seen swinging to her anchor behind the transports, the sleek frigate just visible beyond. Outside the village of Le Palais, a citadel stood upon the heights, and Hayden could see the mouths of the big guns, staring like unblinking eyes down at the British ships.

"Strike a course east-sou'east, Mr Philpott. It is my intention to sail toward the Île de Hœdic, then come about when Bourne appears around the southern cape. It is about one league from the southern point to the Rade du Palais, where the ships lie. On this wind, it will take Captain Bourne half of the hour to reach the French frigate. I would like to engage the brig just before Bourne arrives, to draw fire away from him, if possible. We will have the wind on our beam and can make or shorten sail as needed, but either way, shall make straight for the Frenchman." He glanced up at the pennant flying from the top. "If the wind does not shift, we shall be forced to take some fire as we approach, but it is my intention to sail across her stern and rake her once, then range alongside and fire another broadside. Can your crew work their guns so smartly?"

"I believe they can, Mr Hayden." Philpott said this with certainty, which gave Hayden confidence.

"Then we'll board and, if God wills it, carry her."

Philpott's concentration creased his brow like a ploughed field. "I shall hold your men in reserve for boarding, Mr Hayden, if that suits you, though we may require a few hands temporarily to assist in reducing sail."

"They shall be yours, Mr Philpott."

The ship was put on the desired course and sailed freely toward the small Île de Hœdic, the low peninsula of Quiberon licking out toward them from the north-east, Île d'Houat off their larboard bow. On their starboard quarter, the *Themis* took up her place under reduced sail. There was no doubt in Hayden's mind that the crews of the French ships, and the gunners on the heights above, had their eye on the British frigate; the little two-sticker that scurried along before, like a lapdog on a leash, was hardly worthy of regard.

Timing the appearance of Bourne would be critical. The great seaman had told them how long he believed it would take, given sea, wind, and tide, and Hayden did not think he would be far wrong. It was incumbent upon him and Philpott to be within striking distance of the French brig at that moment—about two and a half miles or a little less, they both calculated. This meant they would have to come about and take up the course of their attack before Bourne actually appeared, which was a bit of a risk, but there was nothing for it.

Wickham came up then. "Is this your first action, Mr Philpott?"

"I must admit that it is, Lord Arthur, though we did take some fire chasing the transports here, and damned unlucky that proved for Captain Wilson. Rest his soul. Is it your first, as well?"

"No, sir, though until recently I was in the same position as yourself. Mr Hayden contrived to take a transport right in the throat of Brest Harbour—an enterprise I had the good fortune to join—and then we went ashore, where we fought several small actions with French regulars and fencibles."

The young lieutenant was clearly impressed. "It sounds as if you've had quite a time of it lately, Lord Arthur."

"Entirely due to Mr Hayden," Wickham said. "He'd rather fight than drink gin, the Jacks say."

Hayden laughed. "I'd much prefer the gin, Mr Wickham," he said. "Which proves you should never trust the wisdom of the foremast hands."

"Excepting Mr Aldrich, sir," Wickham answered earnestly.

"Aldrich is the exception to all rules," Hayden agreed, his spirits brought low by the thought of the able seaman lying wretchedly in Griffiths' sick-bay, his back flayed and bloody.

From the fortifications on the Île d'Houat, a bloom of smoke mushroomed, followed by the sound of an iron ball scraping the sky. Twenty yards before the *Lucy,* it threw up a spout of water, alarming a little whale, which sounded with a splash. The first shot was quickly followed by another. For the next half hour the French kept up a fairly consistent cannonade, one ball passing through the fore-topsail of the *Themis,* but doing remarkably little damage otherwise. Hayden held his course and was somewhat surprised to see that Hart did the same. The lieutenant was taking some satisfaction from subjecting Hart to enemy fire, for it would be difficult for Hart to turn his more powerful frigate away while a lowly brig-sloop sailed through. The little ship was already taking the frigate's rightful place in the action—Hart's rightful place—and the least Hart could do would be to play his small part without shrinking.

They held their course until they judged the time right, then put the ship about. The battery on Île d'Houat did not give up its cannonade, and as the *Lucy* tacked, a ball pierced the sea so close alongside that it soaked the officers standing at the rail.

Hayden wiped the salt water from his eyes with a sleeve, looked at Philpott, who was as wet as he, and they both began to laugh.

"Damned Frenchmen . . ." Philpott managed. "They could see I wore my new coat!"

The two lieutenants and the midshipman all doffed their coats and hats, which were taken away by Philpott's servant. As Hayden had no second coat with him, all three gentlemen agreed they would have to fight in waistcoats.

"The men aboard the *Tenacious* will think we have removed our coats out of fear of snipers," Philpott said.

"Then we shall be at pains to prove we are not shy," Hayden replied.

"On deck!" the lookout called. "Sail. South-by-east."

"It is Captain Bourne," Wickham said excitedly, giving a little boyish jump.

"And so it is," Hayden said, scrutinizing the ship rounding Pointe de Kerdonis, the island's south-eastern tip.

As he watched, the *Tenacious* slipped into the shadow of the island, making sail as the wind took off a little with the setting sun. She looked ominous and formidable in the failing light, Hayden thought, and was happy he was not aboard the French frigate watching her bear down under a press of sail.

"The French ships all have boarding nets rigged, Mr Hayden," Wickham observed. He stood with his glass screwed into his eye, gazing toward the anchored vessels.

"Bourne's carronades will make short work of those." Hayden raised his own glass. "Is that an anchor cable I see ranging from the stern quarter of the frigate?"

Wickham shifted his attention to the southern-most ship. "I think it is, sir. Why have they done that?"

"So they can veer more cable to their bower and let the head of the ship fall off, bringing their broadside to bear on Captain Bourne no matter how he approaches."

"That is clever, sir," Wickham said. "Will Captain Bourne be aware of their design?"

"I don't know." Hayden looked to the west, where the sun was quickly descending. Already Belle Île cast a long shadow out toward the anchored vessels. A single cable would soon be invisible, even at a short distance.

The fortress guns on Belle Île, which had fallen silent briefly, began to fire, throwing shot beyond the anchored frigate, even though Bourne was not quite within their range.

"They will not so easily scare off Bourne," Philpott said confidently.

"That is the oddest thing . . ." Wickham declared, still looking through his glass. "I could swear I saw a French regular, like the soldiers we met ashore, emerge from the frigate's companionway, only to be chased back down by an officer."

Hayden fixed his glass upon the frigate but could see no sign of blue coats. "Are you certain, Mr Wickham?"

"Most certain, sir."

"Damn!" Hayden lowered his glass. *Tenacious* was now only a few cable-lengths from the French frigate. "Alter course for the frigate, Mr Philpott, and make the signal to break off the engagement."

"Whatever are you saying, Mr Hayden?" Philpott stood staring at him, utterly confused.

Hayden turned on the smaller man. "While Bourne was west of the island, French troops must have been ferried out to the frigate, and now lie hidden below, waiting for Bourne to board. They hope to carry the *Tenacious* by main force."

"But how can—"

Hayden turned away from the lieutenant. "Who has charge of the signals?" he demanded loudly.

A midshipman stepped quickly forward. "I do, sir."

"Make the signal to break off the engagement. Quick as you can!"

"I shall fetch my signal book," he said and ran for the companionway.

Wickham went directly to the cabinet where the signal flags were stored, and began pulling them out, spreading them carefully in order. As if to make up for his obstinance, Philpott pulled the flag halyard from its pin and began attaching the flags himself.

"Mr Harland?" Philpott called. "Make ready to fire a gun to larboard."

Hayden turned back to the frigate, now in shadow but for the tips of her masts. A sail ran up from the end of her jib-boom, luffed sharply, and then was backed to starboard, setting the ship's head off on the opposite tack.

"*On deck!*" a lookout called. "The Frenchman's making sail, sir."

Philpott glanced up at Hayden from his signal flags.

"Only backing a jib and paying off on the starboard tack," Hayden told him. "They'll veer cable and bring a broadside to bear on Bourne.

Damn! Gun captains! Make ready to fire the larboard battery. Helmsman, I want to luff up off her stern and rake her the length of her gun-deck."

Philpott ran up the hoist of flags and ordered a single gun fired.

Everyone watched the *Tenacious* anxiously.

"She is ignoring our signal, Mr Hayden."

"I feared she would. Bourne is not one to give up a fight."

Tenacious had swung out to the east, planning to do as Hayden had intended with the *Lucy*—cut across the enemy's stern, rake her, then luff up alongside, pour in a broadside, then grapple and board. The Frenchman had foiled him, though, paying out his bower cable.

Shot from the fortress began to fall around them in earnest; the fearsome, unforgettable scream as it passed overhead. Hayden tried to ignore it. A ball either had his name on it or did not. Cowering would not change that.

He wondered what Bourne would do now. The French captain was paying out his cable slowly, keeping his broadside aimed toward the approaching British ship. The man's coolness was to be admired, as he did not waste his shot on a distant target.

Philpott ranged up alongside. "It looks as if *Tenacious* will beat us to the Frenchman by a good five minutes."

"I fear you're right. It is my guess that Bourne will pass downwind of the Frenchman, exchange broadsides, luff up across her stern, fire again if time will allow, carry his way forward, turn to larboard, and let his ship drift down on the Frenchmen, intending to board." He turned to find Wickham, who stood a few paces off. "Where is the *Themis*, Wickham?"

"To the north-east, sir. Half a league or a little less. She's still taking fire."

"Difficult to believe they've spared any for her," Hayden said. "I don't think the Frenchman will let his ship go much beyond beam-on to the wind. By the time we reach her she should have the *Tenacious* alongside, and be in the process of boarding their attacker, much to Bourne's surprise. I don't imagine they'll reload their larboard battery, which means we may pass by without much fear of their guns."

"Shall we pour in a broadside as we pass?" Philpott asked.

"No, our little six-pounders can be better employed, I think. Let us luff up across her stern and fire, each gun in turn, the length of her gun-deck. If there is a company of French soldiers aboard we might do much damage. We'll then throw our grapnels over the sterns of both ships and board the Frenchman over the taffrail. All more easily said than done. I shall ask you to bring the *Lucy* up along the Frenchman's stern, as I do not know how far she will carry her way."

"Leave that to me, Mr Hayden." Hurrying immediately to the wheel, Philpott relieved the helmsman and bore off just a little.

A tremendous explosion, and the French frigate was enveloped in a dark, roiling cloud. *Tenacious* seemed to stagger, losing her rhythm with the sea, but then she bore up again, and pressed on, her rig and sails much shot away, spars hanging, shattered, in their gear, swaying forth and back. Hayden could see the men rising to their feet, throwing torn canvas and fallen cordage over the side so the guns could be worked. Two men gently slid the limp and bloodied body of a ship's boy over the rail, and for an instant Hayden closed his eyes, though the sight did not go away.

When Hayden raised his glass, Bourne appeared amid the wreckage, gesturing, calling out orders, his hat gone and the left side of his face a smear of red. Tentacles of smoke wafted down on the *Tenacious*, but still Bourne held his fire. Hayden could see him standing on the gangway, his cutlass raised, gun captains bent over their cannon. The instant a gun was run out on the enemy frigate, the cutlass swept down, and the English broadside boomed, echoing back from the cliffs of Belle Île.

Splinters scythed up through the smoke, humming as they spun. Bourne was by before the French had recovered, and their ragged broadside was fired into the pall of smoke, striking nothing. Hayden could see the Jacks aboard *Tenacious* furiously swabbing, then ramming home powder cartridges.

Tenacious swung slowly up into the wind, topsails shaking for a moment, then pressing back against the masts and rigging as the yards were squared. Quickly, the yards were shifted again and the ship came through the wind, and was blown down on the Frenchman's starboard side. At less than ten yards the two ships fired their broadsides and the sharp *crack* of musket fire began. In a moment the two vessels thudded dully together, and the crews of both sides sent up a cheer. British sailors leapt the distance from rail to rail, brandishing their tomahawks and cutlasses. They fell upon the French crew just as blue jackets erupted from the companionways fore and aft. As the infantry massed, they began to push the British back, but they were hindered climbing out the companionways by the smallness of the ladders and lack of room on the deck. Hayden could see the crew of the *Tenacious* fighting furiously at the bulwark, but in a moment the blue jackets would be like a great wave, throwing them back, breaking over the rail and pouring onto the British deck.

Through his glass, Hayden could see the English Jacks being bayoneted, and falling upon their own mates. He lost sight of Bourne and wondered if the indomitable commander had finally overreached. Men on the *Lucy's* fore-top began firing their muskets, and though Hayden was not sure of the effect, he did not stop them. To stand by and watch the slaughter was more than anyone could bear.

As the *Lucy* passed by the French frigate, Hayden braced himself to take a broadside, but only the muzzle of a single gun stood proud, and it did not speak. There was a deathly silence on the brig until they passed, and then a sigh seemed to course through the entire ship.

"I'm going to bring her up, sir," Philpott announced, and spun the helm.

Hayden made his way quickly to the forward gun, saying to each gun captain as he passed, "Do not fire until I give you the command."

He found Wickham a few feet behind and waved him up. The boy had a cutlass in one hand and a pistol in the other.

"Mr Wickham, if I am shot you must take command of our guns. Fire as the frigate bears, one gun at a time down the length of her gun-deck. Kill as many blue coats as you can."

The boy nodded grimly, his face flour-pale. "Aye, sir."

The little sloop carried her way for some distance in the failing wind, but Philpott knew his ship and she just barely maintained steerage as they ranged up along the Frenchman's stern. Men stood on the rail with their grapnels in hand, ready to lock the ships together.

"Wait until she loses headway," Hayden cautioned them over the din. The sound of fighting was loud. Muskets cracked in the rigging and the clash of steel rang in the evening air.

Smoke still lingered on the decks and stung Hayden's eyes and nose. He looked upon the scene before him—a frenzy of violence and brutality—and for a moment felt such utter repulsion he was almost ill upon the deck.

"We're going to pass the Frenchman, sir," the gun captain warned him.

"Be patient," Hayden responded, clearing the images from his mind. He stared at the shuttered windows of the frigate's stern gallery. When they were all but up with the last window, Hayden tapped the gun captain on the shoulder.

"Fire," he shouted over the chaos.

The gun jumped back, its ball smashing the dead-light and glass beyond. Hayden moved to the next gun and waited a few seconds until the same window was open to them. Through the shattered frame he could see light stabbing down into the frigate's waist, twenty yards away. Blue coats were still mustered there, but had been thrown into disarray.

"Fire," Hayden ordered, and the second gun reared back, a deafening explosion battering his ears. The third gun came to bear and fired in its turn, shattering another of the stern windows.

The *Lucy* slowed to a near stop and Philpott put the helm over as the men threw their grappling hooks over the frigate's stern, bringing the *Lucy*'s raised quarterdeck level with the frigate's stern gallery. Due to the height of the quarterdeck, the guns mounted there could fire directly the length of the gun-deck.

"Load the guns with grape," Hayden ordered. "Rake the gun-deck."

In a moment they were climbing up over the rail and running along the deck. Hayden realized that Wickham and Philpott were to either side, and then they threw themselves on the rear of the mass of blue as the *Lucy*'s gunners fired again down the length of the gun-deck below.

Hayden shot a man, who turned, startled to find the British behind him. Throwing away his pistol, Hayden dove into the fray, thrusting with his sword, feeling it slide horribly into flesh.

Hayden fought his way to the rail and clambered up, preparing to jump across to the *Tenacious*, when a gun sounded, and a crowd of Frenchmen before him were scythed down like wheat. Wickham leapt up on the rail beside him and pointed with a bloody cutlass.

"Our men have one of the quarterdeck guns," the boy shouted. And sure enough, Hayden could see through the smoke members of his own crew madly loading one of the *Tenacious'* guns. Hayden held up the man beside him, and the gun was fired again, to equal effect, though it reared back, smashed into the stern rail, and turned on its side.

Hayden leapt across the chasm, grabbing the frayed end of a broken shroud. Bounding down on the deck, he slipped and fell in the blood, and was dragged up by Philpott.

They dove into the fight, overwhelming the French soldiers and sailors, who were not expecting to be attacked from behind, and in a moment they were throwing down their weapons, though on the forecastle the fighting was still fierce and undecided.

In the growing twilight Hayden gathered some of the *Lucy's* crew and charged into the melee on the foredeck. In five minutes they tipped the balance, and the enemy cast down their arms.

Leaving Philpott in charge of the forecastle, Hayden hurried back along the gangway, stepping over many fallen. The cries and moans of the wounded came to him now, as the sounds of battle were all but extinguished. Hayden found Bourne standing by the jury-rigged wheel, a cloth pressed to his bleeding face.

"Hayden! I thought you would be overrunning the French brig, but here you are . . . delivering us from certain destruction. However did you know to come?"

"Wickham observed a French regular stick his head up the frigate's companionway only to be chased back down by an officer. I surmised they had reinforced the ships with troops from the garrison, and was fortunate to have been proven right."

"You penetrated their deception when we did not. Wickham . . . Was he the young middy with whom we dined?"

"The very one."

"I shall thank him most profoundly. Will you do me a service, Hayden? See if you can find if the French captain is alive. I desire the honour of accepting his surrender."

"Mr Hayden!" It was Wickham calling from thirty feet up the shrouds. "The transports have cut their cables, sir. And so has the brig, I believe. They're making sail."

Bourne looked at Hayden. "Do you think Hart has the bottom to take on a little brig and some transports?" he asked quietly.

"Not if he thinks they've been reinforced by infantry."

"How shot up is the *Lucy*?" Bourne asked, casting his glance over the rigging of the brig-sloop.

"She's virtually untouched, as you can see."

"Then let us quickly secure the prisoners and get you under way. My own ship is too damaged, I fear." Bourne looked about the deck. "We've paid dearly for this Frenchman. If you can keep even a single transport from reaching harbour I shall regret it less."

Hayden nodded. "Mr Wickham?"

The boy answered from the shrouds, where he was clambering quickly down.

"Gather up our crew . . . and find Mr Philpott if you can."

"I'm here, Mr Hayden," Philpott called as he appeared in the after companionway.

Hayden cast his gaze around, assessing their situation in the gathering gloom as Philpott crossed the bloody deck to him.

"Are you uninjured, Mr Philpott?"

"Barely a scratch, sir."

"I'm happy to hear it. We are swinging around head to wind, which makes me think the frigate's stern cable has parted. Gather up all the men who are fit to serve. We will make sail and give chase."

All the *Lucy*'s crew fit for action were collected from the decks of the two frigates. Hayden and Philpott led them down a boarding net onto the gun-deck of the French frigate, thinking it would be somewhat easier to climb aboard the *Lucy* through the stern gallery. Upon the gun-deck the effect of the *Lucy*'s fire could be seen. Their cannonade had caught a large company of French infantry unawares, and the blue coats lay everywhere, their bodies ripped apart. The Englishmen stopped, frozen by the sight.

A young infantryman moved, causing Hayden to whirl, raising the sword he still carried, but the man, hardly older than Wickham, only reached out silently, as though appealing for aid. Wickham turned aside to go to the man, but Hayden caught the midshipman's shoulder.

"You cannot help him," Hayden rasped, and then Wickham recoiled in horror.

The infantryman, partly covered by his fallen comrades, had been blown nearly in half, his glistening entrails spreading out from his blue jacket.

Wickham pressed a sleeve across his powder-stained mouth, eyes wide. "Good God, sir," came his voice, muffled and choked. "How many widows have we made this hour?"

Gently, Hayden drew the midshipman away.

Philpott caught his eye. The lieutenant's face was waxy-pale. "Our gunners raked the deck with grape," he whispered. "Smashed the ladders. They had no place to hide."

Hayden tried to fix his eyes to the fore, and stumbled toward the shattered stern gallery. He had ordered this terrible cannonade, had even directed its fire to inflict the most damage. The thought came to him that it was almost a sin for him to look away.

Afterward Hayden had no memory of climbing out the stern window and onto the bloodless deck of the *Lucy*. All he could recall was standing by the wheel, drawing in great draughts of clear air, darkness settling around them, the stench of carnage and powder smoke drifting down from the two frigates. He made his way to the wheel, and when he turned, discovered he'd left behind a trail of bloody footprints, growing less distinct with each step but never gone.

Nineteen

Hart flinched as a shot screamed overhead, half throwing up an arm as though it would ward off an iron ball. He recovered himself quickly and stared off toward the *Lucy*.

"What is Mr Hayden doing?" Barthe asked aloud.

The officers stood at the *Themis'* rail, watching *Tenacious* converge on the anchored French frigate. To their amazement, the *Lucy* had changed course and appeared to have given up her intention to attack the French brig.

"Oh, you know our Mr Hayden. He comprehends a great deal more than Captain Bourne or myself. So he has ignored his orders and is going to the aid of the *Tenacious*, as though a captain as capable as Bourne has need of him."

"Shall we go after the brig ourselves?" Barthe asked. "I mean, if the *Lucy* will not?"

Hart shook his head and made a sour face, though he did not deem to look at his sailing master. "By no means. We will lie off here, to keep the transports at anchor, as was planned. I wonder what Bourne will have to say to his precious protégé after this?"

"There must be some reason for Mr Hayden to disregard his orders so," Archer stated firmly. He had his glass fixed on the British ships approaching the French frigate in the lengthening shadow of Belle Île.

"Mr Hayden has nothing but disregard for orders," Hart said disdainfully. "And now he is displaying his incompetence for all to see. Imagine, our fire-eating first lieutenant afraid to attack a little brig . . ."

Hart might have said more, but at that moment the French captain fired his broadside all at once. Smoke enveloped the anchored frigate and at that range the effect on the *Tenacious* was tremendous. Gear and sails fell, the main-topgallant mast toppled slowly over the side, and yet the ship only seemed to stagger, then bore on.

"You see," Hart announced, waving a hand at the ships, "Bourne has not faltered. He has no need of Mr Hayden, whose efforts will only cause offence."

The two frigates appeared to draw so near that surely they would soon collide, yet there was no reply from the British guns.

"Why does Bourne not fire?" Archer muttered.

"Because he knows his business thoroughly," Mr Barthe answered. "He will wait until he can inflict the greatest damage—until the Frenchman is about to fire again, and then he will give them the whole weight of iron at once."

"The Frenchman's run out a gun," Landry cried.

And as he said this the *Tenacious* herself was enveloped in smoke, the deep boom of the cannon echoing off the island, as though the first cannonade was followed immediately by a second.

"There, do you see, Mr Archer?" Barthe asked. "That is how it is done. Never for a moment would Bourne lose his nerve. Never for a moment."

Tenacious ranged up past the frigate's stern, but before her guns could be reloaded. Smoke veiled the French ship, only the tips of her masts visible through the dark cloud.

"There, too late for the Frenchman to fire again now. Bourne is by."

Tenacious carried her way past the French ship's gallery, backed sails, shifted her yards, and came through the wind. But instead of gathering way the backed sails pushed her down on the French frigate. For a moment she seemed to hang there, and then both ships fired their broadsides at once.

Barthe reeled back from the rail, lowering his glass. "My God! They cannot have been ten yards distant. The butcher's bill from that broadside alone will be too painful to tally."

"And look . . ." Hart pointed. "There is our foolish Mr Hayden, who cannot give up his misguided enterprise, now."

The two frigates came together in a cloud of smoke, and the cheers of the crews carried over the water. Musket fire broke out, but little could be seen in the smoke. The *Lucy*, almost in Bourne's wake, ranged alongside the frigates, passing into the cloud as it detached itself from the larger ships.

"Now Hayden will get his comeuppance," Hart all but gloated. "A deck of eighteen-pounders at that range will teach him a lesson long overdue."

The men on the quarterdeck all held their breath, watching the little brig-sloop half-obscured by the drifting cloud. But the French did not fire. The British sloop passed by, put her helm over, and came head to wind across the Frenchman's stern.

"Well, he is either damned lucky or bloody astute," Landry announced, half in admiration. "I cannot say which."

Hawthorne, who stood a few paces back from the officers at the rail, felt a little smile spread over his face. Hart could barely contain his fury that Hayden had not suffered a cannonade at close range. What matter that the entire crew of the *Lucy* would have been slaughtered into the bargain?

As the smoke swept away, sections of the frigates' decks were revealed, and an unholy melee was under way there.

"Sir," Archer said, surprised. "There is infantry aboard that French ship! Do you see?"

"That is our explanation," Hawthorne muttered, as surprised as Archer.

"Now, how in God's name did Hayden know that?" Barthe asked loudly.

Hart swept up his glass and gazed at the terrible scene just as the *Lucy* fired a gun, and then another.

"Mr Hayden has not arrived a moment too early," Archer observed. "Poor Bourne is getting the worst of it." And indeed it was true; by sheer numbers, the blue-coated infantry were driving the British crew back onto their own decks.

Even without a glass, Hawthorne saw Hayden climb over the rail onto the deck of the French ship, cutlass in one hand, pistol in the other. Wickham was right behind, both officers in waistcoats, and then in their wake, a swarm of *Lucies*. A cheer went up from the crew of the *Themis*, and Hawthorne joined in before he knew it, earning a black look from Hart.

"Three cheers for Mr Hayden!" a crewman yelled from somewhere down the deck, and the rest of the men *"huzzaed"* with a will.

A ball from the battery on Belle Île chose that moment to tear a hole in the mizzen, not twenty feet above the officers' heads. Hart all but dropped his glass, but Barthe looked up calmly, and then turned back to the battle on the frigates, his face an admirable mask of calm.

"And we've just restitched that sail from foot to peak," he observed.

"Cut our grappling lines, Mr Philpott," Hayden said, clearing his throat, struggling to master his reaction to the carnage on the gun-deck. "Make sail. We have a brig and some transports to chase."

Axes were taken to the grappling lines, and the ship began to drift north-west, beam on to the wind. Hayden ordered the helm put over as the sail loosers scrambled aloft. In a moment the little ship began to make headway, her bow turning slowly to the north. Gulls passed over as they made their way out to sea, lamenting sadly. The smoke of twilight hung in the air; Belle Île, jagged and dark, silhouetted against the faint light still clinging to the western sky.

Hayden took his night glass and climbed the foremast shrouds. Bracing himself in the fore-top, he gazed into the gloom ahead. Far off, the lights of L'Orient glimmered, and in between the inky, rippled sea spread before the dying wind.

"*On deck,*" Hayden called just loud enough to be heard. "A point to starboard. I see a ship. Send the men to their guns, Mr Philpott—quiet as you can."

"The wind is going light," Philpott whispered, "shall I call for stun-sails?"

Wickham clambered onto the platform at that moment.

"If you please, Mr Philpott," Hayden answered.

The midshipman gazed into the darkness with his glass. He was the only midshipman aboard the *Themis* to possess a night glass, and his eyes were famously sharp.

"There is a second ship, I think, Mr Hayden. Almost dead ahead, but further off than the first."

Hayden searched the darkness. "Yes. I see it. Is that the brig, do you think?"

"Perhaps so, sir. I can't make out a mizzen."

Sailors scrambled up past them and onto the yards, running out the stunsail booms. The tip of Belle Île passed to larboard, and on the western horizon the last gasp of light was drawn in like a breath. Low across the sky, a few clouds charcoaled haphazardly. Overhead, stars winked into being, casting their cold, faint light down onto the darkened sea.

"Will these transports have infantry aboard, sir?" Wickham asked.

"I don't know if the garrison on Belle Île is that large, but it is possible."

"We haven't enough men aboard the *Lucy* to carry ships so heavily manned."

"No."

Wickham lowered his glass and turned to Hayden in the faint light. "Then what shall we do, sir?"

"We'll try to bring them to. Force them to surrender."

"But the Frenchman in the Goulet hauled down his colours then attacked our boarding party."

"And now you see how ill-advised a course that truly was. We are far more likely to fire upon a ship until much of her crew is dead than trust them again. Damned, villainous master! He has put his own countrymen in peril."

Hayden cupped his hands and whispered down to the deck. "Have you our blue flare in readiness, Mr Philpott?"

"I have, Mr Hayden. To be shewn for half a minute every five once darkness is complete. I'll order it displayed now, sir."

A blue flame appeared at the stern, the seaman who held it dimly illuminated in the garish light. And then it winked out.

Hayden raised his glass and searched all of the sea that was not hidden by the *Lucy*'s sails. "Bloody wind," he whispered. "Just when the French run for port, it takes off."

Clearly offended by Hayden's impudence, the wind died altogether, to much muttering from the deck below. The *Themis'* lieutenant slung his glass over a shoulder, swung out, grasped the backstay, and went, hand over hand, down to the deck. He found Philpott on the darkened quarterdeck.

"Extinguish all lanterns," came the whisper. "Captain Hart's orders. No lights to be shewn." The master-at-arms stood at the head of the stairs leading down into the waist, and Hawthorne passed his order on without question. On the quarterdeck, however, the marine could hear an argument as he ascended the ladder.

"But it was agreed we would carry lanterns on the mainmast and burn a blue flare," Barthe said firmly, his frustration barely in check.

"It was Mr Hayden's idea," Hart shot back, "and a bloody foolish one, as you would expect."

Hawthorne could barely make out the captain and master in the gathering darkness. A glance overhead told him the stars were succumbing to a high overcast.

"But we might be fired upon by our own ships," Barthe contended.

"Damn your eyes, Mr Barthe," the captain swore. "The *Tenacious* and the *Lucy* have a French prize to deal with, not to mention substantial damage to hull and rig. We share these waters with four French ships, and lights and flares will only make us known to them. We shall be fired upon in the darkness, without warning. There will be no lights. That is my order."

Hawthorne took himself forward along the larboard gangway. For a moment he gazed down into the darkened waist where the gun crews were at their stations. He wondered if there would be trouble down there beneath the cover of darkness.

A man bumped him, and the marine almost tumbled from the gangway. A knuckle was made, an apology muttered. Hawthorne had no idea who it was. He carried on, feeling his way along the bulwark, finding his sentries in their places.

"I thought I saw something, sir," a corporal whispered to him. "There. Almost abeam. Perhaps a half-point forward."

Hawthorne stared into the hushed dark. The distant light on Île de Groix provided the faintest illumination, but a fog appeared to be setting in from the sea, obscuring everything.

"Do you see it, sir? A light, maybe . . . ?"

"I'm not certain. Let me inform the captain."

He hurried back to the quarterdeck and found Hart on the starboard side, pacing. The wind had died away to a whisper, and Hawthorne was sure they were all but stationary on the water.

"One of my sentries thought he saw a light—to larboard. Almost abeam. Maybe half a point forward."

Hart crossed to the larboard rail, Landry in tow, or so Hawthorne thought. The night was becoming so close that almost nothing could be seen. The captain and his lackey stood gazing into the night, their anxiety palpable.

"I think it is a light," Landry said. "For a moment I saw it."

The fog crept in from the west, silent, unyielding. It cast itself over them like some amoebic creature, absorbing man and ship into its limpid mass.

"Do you think they know we're here?" Landry whispered, his voice breaking.

"We will know if a six-pound ball cuts you in half," came the sailing master's voice out of the dark and liquid night.

"We will fire a broadside," Hart announced suddenly.

"But Captain," remonstrated Barthe, "we can't be sure it is even a French ship."

"We are in French waters," Hart contended, "it can be nothing else. Mr Landry, prepare to fire the larboard battery."

"But where is our target?"

"Helmsman," Hart ordered, "give her a spoke to starboard. Our target will be directly abeam. Now jump to it."

Hawthorne heard Landry stumble forward to give the orders.

"The sky grows hazy, Mr Hayden," Philpott observed. A damp, cold mist washed slowly over the rail at that moment.

Hayden glanced up to find the stars reduced to blurs. "As if we weren't having enough trouble finding our quarry." He leaned close to Philpott and whispered so that only the lieutenant could hear: "Under any other circumstances I would put the men into boats and attempt to board that ship in the offing, but there is no way to know if they have infantry aboard. I must say, it seems unlikely. How many men could the garrison on Belle Île spare?"

Philpott nodded in the darkness. "That is the question. There were a goodly number aboard the French frigate: no fewer than an hundred, I should think. They can't have reinforced four transports and the brig as well. It seems a defensible risk. I will lead the boarding party, gladly."

Hayden was impressed with the younger man's pluck. There was no hesitation there. This was no Captain Hart in the making.

"If I am to send men to fight a shipload of French infantry I will lead them myself. You will assume command of the *Lucy* in my absence."

Philpott nodded, genuinely disappointed, Hayden thought.

"I shall put all your own men from the *Themis* in the boats, and as many as I think we can spare."

"Mr Hayden?" came Wickham's whisper from above. "Is that a ship to starboard? Do you see? Half a point aft of amidships."

Hayden went to the rail and peered into the thick night. "Can you make her out, Philpott?"

The lieutenant's answer was lost in an explosion of long guns, and Hayden was hurled to the deck. For a moment he lay, dazed, debris spread both over and around him. Propping himself up on an elbow, he shook his head.

"Mr Philpott?" he whispered, then looked up at the ruined rigging. "Wickham, there?"

"I'm here, sir," Wickham called down, "but I think the rigging is badly damaged, sir."

"I'm sure it is. Are you whole, Mr Wickham? Can you climb up and extinguish the lanterns?"

"I can, sir."

Hayden searched the shadowed deck with his eyes. "Mr Philpott?"

Someone moved a few feet away, and Hayden scrambled over and found Philpott on his back, limbs writhing unconsciously. He saw another shape rise up a few feet away—the helmsman, he guessed. "Find the surgeon," Hayden ordered. "Mr Philpott has been wounded."

A moment later, Wickham appeared at his side.

"Are you injured?" he asked the middy.

"A splinter or two. Not worth a surgeon's attention."

Hayden forced himself to stand, dizzy. "Those were not the brig's six-pounder guns," he declared. "Look at the ruin they made of us . . ."

A second broadside roared, but only a single shot struck forward. The rest screamed off into the darkness, holing the sea some distance off.

A man began to cry out in pain.

"Silence that man," Hayden ordered. "Quiet on the deck."

"Mr Hayden . . . ?" Philpott tried to sit up but was unable to.

"Carry Mr Philpott below," Hayden whispered to two men who appeared out of the darkness.

"No . . ." Philpott breathed. "No. I don't believe I'm injured. Just . . . dazed." In the blackness Hayden could make out the lieutenant's pale hands brushing limbs and torso, searching for wounds. "I appear to be whole, as remarkable as that seems."

The two men helped him to his feet, where he stood a moment, wavering like a stalk of wheat in the wind, but then he found his balance. "What in hell's name was that?" the man managed.

"Eighteen-pounders," Hayden whispered. "Or so I would judge."

"Where did a French frigate come from?" Wickham asked.

"It's not French," Hayden said firmly. "I'll wager it's the *Themis*."

Someone cursed in the darkness, and low muttering spread forward.

"Then we should hail her," Philpott said quickly.

"No," Hayden answered just as quickly. "If we're wrong it would invite another broadside."

Guns boomed again, lighting up the water two hundred yards away, illuminating for an instant the rigging of a ship. The report rolled across the water, like a wave, but the shots were aimed some distance ahead of the *Lucy* now.

"What do they shoot at?"

"Phantoms," Hayden said. "Shadows. We must not show a light that any can see."

"But we are much damaged and the starlight is quickly fading."

A little breeze from the east touched them then, backing the rolling sails.

"Asleep at last," Philpott whispered, looking up as the sails pushed against the mast and rigging.

Hayden went to the helm, spinning it quickly. "We are caught aback, Mr Philpott. We must shift our yards."

"What course shall we make?"

"I should still like to catch us a Frenchman—north toward L'Orient." He stared off into the darkness. "Send men aloft to survey the damage. We shall make what repairs we can. Is there water in the hold, Mr Wickham?"

"I will go down and see for myself, Mr Hayden." And Wickham disappeared toward the companionway.

Sailors padded quickly around the deck, throwing aside torn sails and broken gear. Others went aloft as fast as darkness would allow. Whispers began to seep down from above.

"Fore-topsail brace, larboard side, shot away."

"Main topsail hanging in her gear, Mr Philpott."

"Main starboard shrouds in a hell of a mess, sir," whispered the bosun.

"Will they stand, Mr Plym?" Philpott asked.

"May'est, in this little breeze, sir."

"We'll jury-rig what we can, Mr Plym. Reeve a new fore-topsail brace, to begin. That sail will be needed."

"Lash the main topsail yard to the rigging," Hayden whispered up to the men. "Let's not have it coming down on our heads."

The yards were braced around and the sails filled. The ship seemed to hover, like a gull on the wind, and then began to make headway. In a moment there was a burble of water along her hull—three knots, or so Hayden guessed. He kept glancing up nervously at the main, expecting it to go over the side at any moment.

Wickham popped out of the after companionway. "We're making no water, Mr Hayden, as far as the carpenter can tell." He came and stood by the wheel. "But we've one sizeable hole in the hull, three feet above the water line."

"Tell the carpenter to show no lights while he makes his repairs, even if we have to hang some old sails over the side."

"I already did, sir. He grumbled, but I explained that if our light were seen he'd have a few more holes to bung, maybe in his gut."

"Well said. Now take yourself out to the end of the jib-boom with a night glass, if you please. See if there is a brig or a transport somewhere before us. It wouldn't do to collide with one in the dark."

Wickham jogged forward, disappearing in a few paces. Hayden could no longer see the bow of his own ship, for the stars sank into cloud and the fog was growing thicker by the moment. The breeze now was off the shore—almost due east—perfect for the Frenchman trying to make L'Orient before the British ships could overhaul them. Hayden took off his waistcoat and half-covered the binnacle, smothering what little light there was. He could only just make out one of the compasses now, but was steering by the wind largely, anyway.

"Now, if my waistcoat doesn't catch fire," he muttered.

One of the midshipmen appeared, his arm in a sling. "We have a bit of coloured glass we can slip into the binnacle, Mr Hayden. I'll put the other light out. Can't be seen at ten yard, then."

"Yes. Do that. How fares your arm?"

"A few stitches. The doctor says not to use it for a week. Be right as rain, I'm sure."

Overhead, he could hear men working in the rigging. A line was carried aloft to haul up cables to replace the main shrouds that had been shot away. The men were working in almost complete darkness, but knew their little ship from keel to truck. Monkey fists thudded to the deck and crewmen fastened to these the materials needed for repairs, the bundles disappearing up into the darkness.

A shadow with Mr Philpott's voice appeared. "Shall I have you relieved at the helm, Mr Hayden?"

"If you please, Mr Philpott."

A quartermaster's mate took the helm, and Hayden fetched his waistcoat from the binnacle, where the middy had shipped a piece of smoke-stained glass to dim the compass light.

"Where is the frigate that fired upon us?" Hayden asked. "Can any see her?"

The lookouts all reported that she had been lost in the darkness and fog. A distant glow, bearing north-west by north, was almost certainly a light upon the Île de Groix.

"Are you familiar with these waters?" Hayden asked Philpott.

"Moderately so. Presently, we are in open water, perhaps six leagues south of L'Orient. The glow in the north-west is the light on the southern tip of the Île de Groix. There are sizeable fortifications there. To the east, the coast forms a long arc tending north then curving round to the west. But then, you likely know all this."

"On such a close night it is reassuring to hear another agree with one's own perceptions. If we do not catch a Frenchman in the next two hours, Mr Philpott, I fear we shall be forced to give up this business." Hayden searched the sky for a moment. "It seems we are in for a change of weather. This land breeze will die away and I would expect a wind from the south-east—perhaps a small gale. A little sea room would be welcomed."

Hayden made his way forward along the darkened deck. A distinct *thud* sounded a few feet ahead, followed by many curses and much muttering by the men on deck. It was a mallet fallen from above, it appeared.

"You up there!" one of the waisters hissed. "Drop another like it and I'll be up to pound your little toes to flats. Do you hear?"

"Captain on deck," a man near Hayden announced, and the argument died away.

Hayden stepped carefully among the men working in the waist, and in a moment was on the forecastle. They seemed to have sailed out of the fog—or perhaps the land breeze was driving it back. "Wickham?" he whispered.

"Here, Mr Hayden," came the middy's voice from somewhere out in the dark.

"Any sign of our quarry?"

Wickham came in along the bowsprit, landing nimbly on the deck, his natural agility unhampered by the darkness.

"Can you see in the dark, Wickham?"

Wickham chuckled. "Not quite, sir, but I flatter myself that I manage better than most. I think there is something in the distance. Do you see? Half a point to starboard and perhaps a third of a league distant . . ."

Hayden tried to part the darkness, first with his naked eye, then with his night glass. "A lantern," Hayden said. "Is it a lantern?"

"That's what I thought, sir. It blinks in and out as though obscured from time to time by sails or rigging."

"Or men upon a deck," Hayden said.

"That would likely mean she's coming our way, sir."

"Precisely so."

"Is it the *Themis*, do you think?"

"I don't know, Wickham. If it was the *Themis* that fired on us, Hart was not carrying two lanterns high on the main mast, so perhaps this is he."

"He's turned back, then."

"So it would seem, unless a ship from L'Orient could have been carried here on this wind."

"It's been blowing two hour, sir. At four knots that's eight miles."

"Slip back along the deck. Tell everyone to make not a sound. Enemy ship in the offing. Ask Mr Philpott to alter course to the west."

Wickham reached out and grabbed his shoulder. "Ship dead ahead!"

Hayden whirled around. "Go, take the helm. Not a word of English from anyone."

Hayden cupped his hands to his mouth and called out, *"Navire droit devant! À tribord toute!"**

From out of the darkness came shouts in French, and as the *Lucy* veered to larboard, the bow of a large ship loomed over them. Hayden began cursing the ship in his most colourful French.

An officer with a lantern in hand appeared at the rail.

"Pourquoi voguez-vous toutes lumières éteintes?"† he demanded in a broad Provençal accent.

"Une frégate anglaise nous a tiré dessus," Hayden complained. "Look what a ruin she left us in."

"Where is she now, this frigate?" the man called.

"Lost in the darkness two leagues astern, thank God."

As the ship passed, the man hastened along the deck so that they still might speak. Hayden kept pace, hurrying aft. At the taffrail the Frenchman stopped, still holding his lantern aloft.

"How many were there? How many frigates?"

---

*"Ship dead ahead! Alter course to larboard!"
†"Why are you showing no lights?"

"Two or three, a sloop, and a sixty-four-gun ship," Hayden called.

The officer swore, and in a moment the gloom swallowed him whole.

There was not a sound on the *Lucy* for a long time, and then Philpott said under his breath, "Bless your linguistic gifts, Mr Hayden. They had guns run out."

"Yes," Hayden answered. "They'd heard the cannon fire, no doubt. I think we should stand out to sea, Mr Philpott. Who knows how many French ships have put out from L'Orient."

Men were sent to their stations to trim sail and brace the yards, course set to take them out into the deep Atlantic.

Twenty

The sun cleared the horizon, pressing back the cool night. A small breeze, east-south-east, brought the ships beneath the transitory shade of a passing cloud. Around the horizon, a dense, distant fog hung low over the sea, obscuring all but the highest terrain of the French shore. The *Lucy* appeared at the centre of a bubble of blue—sea and sky—surrounded by a thick, frosty haze. At the rail of the little brig-sloop stood Philpott, commander again, watching Hayden's cutter rise on the dimpled swell as it made its way toward the *Tenacious*. In the raw light of the new sun, Philpott's face appeared haggard and pensive. It had been the kind of night that aged a man—even a very young one.

Philpott's crew swarmed over the little brig-sloop, putting her shattered rigging to rights as she rolled and heaved on the slow, ocean swell. To the east, a similar scene of feverish activity was being re-enacted aboard the *Tenacious*, and upon the French frigate as well, for Bourne had put a prize crew aboard and taken her out to sea.

"She looks a crack ship," Wickham offered, waving a hand at the French vessel. "Not long off the stocks, I would wager."

Before Hayden could agree, the boat came alongside the British frigate and Hayden stood, balancing, waiting for the sea to lift him—ship and cutter not of one mind in their motion. Upon the crest, he grasped the ladder and swung his foot nimbly up as he had done many hundreds of times. In a moment he came over the rail, followed by Wickham, met there by a row of marines and a bosun smartly piping them aboard. The marines raised their muskets and fired a salute just as guns rang out from both the *Lucy* and the prize. Aboard all three ships Hayden was given a loud *"huzza."*

Bourne pumped his hand and a great smile spread over the captain's face. "Welcome aboard, Mr Hayden. I believe I speak for all my officers and crew in expressing my most profound gratitude for delivering us from the French, for certainly we should all be prisoners upon Belle Île this morning if not for your swift action."

"The credit should be shared by Mr Philpott and the crew of the *Lucy*," Hayden responded, a bit flustered by the praise. "And Mr Wickham, here, who detected the infantryman emerging from below the Frenchman's deck only to be chased back down again."

Bourne shook Wickham by the hand. "You have my thanks, as well, Mr Wickham. Great powers of observation will stand you in good stead for a life at sea." Bourne waved a hand aft. "Come down to my cabin, both of you. There are decisions to be made and I would hear your thoughts on these matters."

To be so included by such an officer left Wickham almost transported, but he managed to put one foot before the other. As they made their way along the deck, Bourne turned to Hayden. "I gather that was not your cannon fire last night sinking a French transport?"

"No, sir. It was the poor *Lucy* receiving a broadside; we lost a man, too."

"I am sorry to hear it," Bourne declared. "The brig seems quite heavily damaged for the victim of a few six-pounders . . ."

"Doesn't she though?" Hayden replied.

Bourne's look turned very sour, but he said nothing more.

In the captain's pleasant cabin the men were all seated and food and drink served by efficient servants. Hayden could not fail to note how happily these men went about their work, in contrast to the crew aboard the *Themis*, who all crept about in fear of undeserved censure and ceaseless humiliation.

"Here is our present situation, gentlemen," Bourne began, setting down his glass after offering a toast to their success and another to the King. "We are two leagues and a half distant from the French coast with an enemy frigate in our possession. Hart is nowhere in sight, though my lookout thought he detected a ship sailing north just before sunrise. She was lost in fog before any other saw her."

"North?" Hayden said. "That can't have been the *Themis*. She was to sail south, down the coast of France and Spain all the way to Gibraltar."

"Well, then my man was wrong," Bourne replied, "but Hart is still nowhere in sight and I fear has gone off about his own business and left you gentlemen behind. I can think of no other explanation for it."

Wickham glanced at Hayden, who had no answer for the unspoken question. Hayden was certain that Hart would leave him behind without an instant's hesitation, but Wickham . . . That seemed unlikely in the extreme.

"At least one French warship sailed from L'Orient last night. It passed us in the dark. Do you think the *Themis* might have been taken?" Wickham asked.

"If she was," Bourne replied, "Hart surrendered without even a pistol being fired, for we heard no cannonade other than the broadsides that apparently damaged the *Lucy*. Now, here is what I propose," Bourne continued, not overly concerned with the fate of Captain Hart, apparently. "You will take the French ship *Dragoon* back to Plymouth. We will have to make up a prize crew as best we can. You have your dozen men from the *Themis*, and Mr Wickham, of course. I hate to take any men from the *Lucy* as she is undermanned as it is . . ." Bourne raised his hands. "I will have to make up the rest, in the absence of Captain Hart."

"Who will expect his share of the prize money all the same," Hayden observed.

Bourne's benevolent look did not falter. "Well, Hart is gone and there is nothing for it. There are, aboard the French ship, many prisoners, though no small number took to the boats when the battle turned in our favour. But even so, there are still well over a hundred, though we killed as many."

"They lost a hundred men?" Wickham exclaimed.

"Seventy-some infantrymen—many of whom were caught on the gun-deck by your fire—and then another sixty-odd from the ship's crew. An awful tally, I fear, for such a short little action. And that does not take into account the wounded, all of whom are under the care of the French surgeon and his mates—about fifty men on the sick-and-hurt list, some most grievously injured."

"I have never heard the like . . ." Hayden said, almost at a loss for words.

Bourne nodded, his manner now sober. "It was hot work and our broadsides at such short range took their toll."

"Even so . . ." Hayden put down his fork, his appetite gone.

"We have little time to mourn the losses—on either side," Bourne observed. "I would like to see the *Dragoon* safely back in England. She is a good, sound ship, though lightly built as these Frenchmen tend to be. Even so, I can't think of any reason why she should not be bought into the service."

"I will gladly sail the prize home, but I wish Hart were present to give me this commission himself. He will likely be vexed when he finds I have gone off and taken Lord Arthur with me."

"Hart put you under my command. In his absence, and as we cannot know if we shall meet him again, I will give you orders to take command of the captured vessel and return her to Plymouth. Hart might complain as he likes, but I will take all responsibilities, and if the Admiralty have anything to say it will be me who answers. I wish to get you under way as quickly as possible. There is, yet, a French squadron in L'Orient and they might decide to come out and take their frigate back." Bourne turned to the midshipman. "Mr Wickham, would you mind terribly if I had a word alone with Mr Hayden?"

Wickham almost leapt to his feet. "Not at all, Captain Bourne." The young middy was out the door in an instant.

"What do you make of him?" Bourne asked, nodding to the just-closed door.

"I think he'll be a fine officer one day."

"That is what I think, as well." Bourne sat back in his chair and regarded his former first lieutenant seriously. "You believe it was Hart fired on you last night, not a Frenchman?"

"It is difficult to be certain, but I don't think a French ship could have reached us so soon. The wind had not long turned."

"You carried your lights as we agreed?"

"We did."

Bourne looked troubled, confused. "It is a damned unpleasant business, though of course not unheard of. I've seen friend fire upon friend of a dark night, but even so . . ." Bourne shook his head. "Perhaps Hart has proceeded south and you are shut of him—you and young Wickham."

"But when I return to England I will be without a ship once again."

Bourne's expressive face showed real dismay. "I will do what I can for you, Charles. Perhaps we can find you a first lieutenant's position, at the very least. Less than you deserve, but upon a good ship with a fighting captain the opportunity to distinguish yourself in action will become a possibility."

"It would be a relief to have a captain eager to fight the enemy, rather than a captain I have to contest with to engage even a lowly transport."

"You did the best you could in a bad situation. Taking the transport at Brest and bringing the *Lucy* to our rescue should gain you some attention within the Admiralty. I shall do my part to see that they do, you may rely on that."

"You have ever been my greatest champion, Captain Bourne, for which I thank you."

"It is unfortunate that I have so little influence among the Lords Commissioners. Has not one of them a daughter you might marry?" A broad smile spread over the captain's face. "Love, pure and true, might profit you greatly."

"Alas, the Lords of the Admiralty do not troll their daughters at the depths I swim."

Bourne laughed. "Alas for us both. I have my second lieutenant on the *Dragoon*. She sustained some damage to both hull and rig. Not so much that we will not all receive a pretty penny when she is bought into His Majesty's Navy." Bourne went to a diminutive writing-desk and took up some papers lying there. He passed Hayden a sheet. "Your orders." This was followed by several letters. "I have written the Admiralty saying that, having lost contact with Captain Hart, and having no way of knowing when he might be met again, I have commissioned you to return with our prize to Plymouth. I have also given a full accounting of our battle at Belle Île, though saying nothing of your adventures during the night. I will leave that for you to report, though you might be circumspect regarding who fired on you in the darkness. Hart's own log should tell the tale, not that it will matter. Such things happen and are seldom grounds for even the mildest sanction. An accident of war—regrettable but impossible to prevent. I'm sure you are anxious to be aboard your command." Bourne touched a hand unconsciously to his wounded skull, his look of benevolent pleasure wavering.

"How is it with your wound?" Hayden asked.

Bourne returned from his thoughts, his smile reappearing. "Oh, it's nothing. I've sustained worse wounds during my morning skirmish with the razor."

Hayden followed Bourne onto the deck into a blue Biscay day.

"A fine morning to set sail for England. My crew are most anxious that you not neglect our mail, Mr Hayden."

"Not for a moment." He shook hands with Bourne. "I cannot thank you enough for your kindness."

Bourne looked almost perplexed. "Kindness? I should never grant you more credit than you deserve, Mr Hayden. The Admiralty might promote the careers of men who are undeserving, but I would never do it. Luck to you, Mr Hayden."

Hayden went quickly over the side and down into the cutter. The French ship had no boats, as some of her crew had escaped in them to Belle Île, so Bourne had given them one of his cutters—a great sacrifice on his part. If fortune did not favour Hayden, having a ship's boat might save his vessel and the lives of his crew.

As he was rowed over the slowly heaving sea, Hayden found himself staring at the captured frigate—a lovely-looking vessel, all told. If he had remained in France, with his training and background, he might have just such a command now. It was an unsettling thought, in part because the idea was as attractive as it was repellent. It was with some trepidation that he took hold of the ladder rung and scaled the topsides.

Unlike his reception aboard the *Tenacious*, little fuss was made when he reached the deck of the French prize. Bourne's acting second lieutenant congratulated him heartily, but then Hayden's disquiet was thrust down so that he could attend to business. His own men from the *Themis* were ferried over from the *Lucy*, and he made Wickham his acting first (and only) lieutenant. The ship was surveyed from stem to stern and keel to truck, all her damage assessed.

Forward on the orlop-deck, substantial bulkheads had been erected to curtail the liberty of the French prisoners. Hayden called for the master-at-arms to unlock and open the door. The low murmuring of his mother's tongue died away as he ducked into the dim chamber. A little light and air funnelled down from a grated scuttle, but the air was musty and noisome all the same. The prisoners lounged about the cramped space, staring darkly at the Englishmen who had suddenly appeared in their midst. They had a dolorous, aggrieved air about them, as though they had somehow been falsely accused and imprisoned unjustly. Hayden was about to speak, but his mouth went suddenly dry, and he backed quickly out the door, nodding to the sentry who threw the bolts and clapped the lock in place. He had a desperate need for air, but before he could retreat toward the ladder, Bourne's lieutenant spoke.

"There is one among the prisoners who appears to be shunned by the others," the man informed him. "He has been trying to speak to us, but we have not enough French among us to fathom what he is saying. The only Frenchman who appears to speak a little civilized English will only shrug when we ask what the man is saying. Likely a pederast, I would think. The French crew call him something that sounds like *'Le Boho,'* whatever that might mean."

"Boho?" Hayden repeated, surprised. "Do you know the man's name?"

The young officer stopped and gazed at Hayden. "He calls himself Fournier, I believe, but the prisoners name him Sanson." And then, seeing Hayden's reaction, "Have you heard of him?"

"Sanson is a name not unknown among the French. Can you bring the man out to me?"

"I can." The young lieutenant hurried off.

Hayden retreated to the light and air of the quarterdeck, where Wickham found him.

"Stores are adequate to see us to England, Mr Hayden," the newly minted officer reported, "though little further. Powder, shot, cordage all sufficient to our needs. The only commodity we seem to lack is grog, sir, though this appears to have been made up for by a surplus of wine."

"The poor hands shall have to make do with French claret, then," Hayden answered, not without a smile, "and French victuals, too."

Bourne's lieutenant appeared in the companionway, accompanied by a man with his hands bound, watched over by two sailors with muskets. Hayden took the measure of this Frenchman, feeling both repulsion and intrigue. He was young, early twenties, and darkly handsome, though of small stature. His manner was grave, wounded, as though he expected to be badly used, yet he carried himself with some pride all the same, or perhaps defiance.

"Monsieur," Hayden said.

"*Capitaine*," the man replied, making a deferential nod, a slight raising of the bound hands as though in supplication. "I am Giles . . . Sanson," he said in the French of an educated Parisian. "It might be of little consequence to you, monsieur, but if I am left among my own countrymen they will likely do me harm, for the few junior officers who remain have not the authority to restrain them."

"And why would they do this, Monsieur Sanson?"

The man hesitated only an instant—a quick glance into Hayden's eyes. "Though I have tried to hide it," he replied, "they have learned that my family have been . . . executioners for many generations. We are disdained, monsieur, and though I have never so much as assisted at an execution—in truth, have endeavoured to separate myself from the occupation of my family—they hate me all the same. I must throw myself upon your mercy, *Capitaine*, and beg for your protection. Without it I believe I will be gravely harmed, perhaps murdered."

Hayden regarded the young man. He had heard of *les bourreaux* during his time spent in France, but like most of the inhabitants of that country, he knew little about them. A small cadre of families had been the executioners for several centuries; despised, feared, ostracized. They married among themselves, lived often in proximity to one another, and maintained a mysterious little society of their own, keeping the guillotine and passing the secrets of their trade down from one generation to the next. Hayden's uncle had told him that some individuals had conducted several hundred executions during their tenure. And here stood a child of such a family, hands bound, appealing to him for protection.

"I can keep you separate from your countrymen, Monsieur Sanson, but I will have to put you in leg irons while you remain aboard ship."

"*Capitaine*, I will accept this gladly rather than stay among my countrymen, but if there is any small service I might perform I will give you my oath that I shall not attempt to escape, or cause you the least distress."

Hayden regarded the man's eyes, trying to sense a lie. "What was your position aboard ship?"

"I assisted the chef until it was discovered who I was, and then the men would not deign to touch food I had prepared. The *capitaine* allowed me to act as his servant, though I believe that secretly his feelings toward me were no different from the others'."

"Then you will be my servant, though if you make any trouble I will toss you back in with your countrymen in a moment. At night you will be put in leg irons."

The man bowed his head. "I shall do everything within my power to repay your kindness, and I swear, I will act, under any circumstances, as an Englishman would."

Hayden waved a hand at the Frenchman and said in English, "Release him. The man will act as my servant until we reach Plymouth."

Sanson's bonds were removed, and he chafed his wrists, his eyes glistening with tears barely held back.

"I have come aboard ship with no kit. Not even a razor," Hayden stated to the Frenchman. "I shall have to scavenge what I can from among the French officers' belongings."

"The late *capitaine* has no need of his effects now," Sanson replied. "I will see if they are still in order, if you wish."

"Yes, go down into his cabin and find what you can. We will speak later."

The man bobbed his head, and then with a glance at the two seamen who still trained their muskets on him, he slunk away.

"I trust you know what you're doing, Mr Hayden," Bourne's lieutenant observed.

"That is my hope as well."

"Who is he, Mr Hayden?" the man asked. "Why do his fellows treat him so?"

"They think him a gypsy," Hayden lied.

"Ah," the lieutenant said, "he has a dark countenance, doesn't he? Don't you worry that he'll steal from you?"

"He won't steal from me."

The lieutenant looked a bit embarrassed, uncertain of Hayden's blunt response. "I'm sure you know what you do," he repeated. "I'll take myself back to the *Tenacious* if you have no further use for my services."

Hayden thanked the lieutenant for his assistance, and shook his hand as he climbed over the rail.

He turned to Wickham then. "Did you understand the conversation I had with the Frenchman?"

Wickham took off his hat and wiped a sleeve across his brow. "I did, Mr Hayden. How . . . remarkable."

"I would ask that you repeat it to no one. The man appears to have been persecuted enough."

Wickham nodded. "Of course, sir. Not a word. But when we reach England it will be into the hulks for him. You won't be able to protect him then."

"No, but for the next few days he can live without fear. That I can manage. Come, we have much work to do. I want to be under way before the sun reaches its zenith."

But the sun's zenith had passed, if only by a little, before Hayden had his ship under sail. He gazed out over his new command, the tiny crew—forty men—running about the deck and scrambling aloft. He prayed the winds would be fair all the way to England, for he had hardly men enough to reduce sail, let alone deliver them from a gale of wind.

"Does she not move handsomely through the water?" Wickham asked. The young midshipman stood by the man at the wheel, gazing over their ship, eyes fairly gleaming. His first commission as acting lieutenant. It did not matter that he had only received it due to a terrible shortage of officers and because his own ship had sailed off and left him. He was an officer—at least for a few days.

"That she does, Mr Wickham."

"I think she is making better speed than would the *Themis* in the same wind and sea."

"Very possibly," Hayden answered, suppressing a smile. He went to the stern rail and looked about the horizon. The *Tenacious* and the *Lucy* were both dropping astern, and in toward the French coast he could just make out some specks of sail half-submerged in the low fog—coasters or fishermen, hardly worth his notice even if he had enough crew to fight his ship, which he certainly did not. If they encountered the enemy he would be forced to subterfuge and prayers, for his tiny crew could not hope to man even a few guns and at the same time handle sail.

Hayden patted the rail—French oak. Although the ship was only distinguishable from an English frigate in her details, she felt both familiar and terribly alien.

"*On deck!*" came the familiar cry. "Open boats, point and a half off the starboard bow."

Hayden gave his head a shake and turned to his duties. "Are they fishermen, Price?"

"Don't appear so, sir. Look like ship's boats. Cutters, mayhap."

"Run aloft and see what you make of them, if you please, Mr Wickham."

"Sir." The midshipman hurried forward and scrambled up the shrouds with the same energy he always displayed, and Hayden was glad to see his temporary rise in status had not gone to his head, making him feel that such a task was beneath him.

A moment later Wickham stood in the foretop, looking down at Hayden, who had made his way forward. "I would wager that Price knows his business, Mr Hayden. These are ship's boats or I'm a blackfish."

"Alter course to starboard, if you please," Hayden called back to the man at the wheel, "a point and a half. Sail trimmers to their stations."

Crewmen were in such short supply that Hayden helped slack the sheet of a foresail himself, almost having forgotten what salt-hardened hemp felt like. He called for his glass and stood at the bow a moment gazing at the distant boats, too far off to make out clearly as they were swallowed and then bobbed up to the top of a wave. He swung the leather strap of his glass over a shoulder and joined Wickham on the foretop. The acting lieutenant had his glass trained on the sea almost dead ahead.

"Do you know, sir, there is a man sitting in the bow of the nearer boat that looks for all the world like Mr Barthe. I swear I can see his red hair, grey strands and all."

Hayden fixed his glass on the closest boat. "You have better eyes than I, Wickham. I can make out the boats, but little more, though I did think I detected a flash of red in the further boat."

Wickham moved his glass a little, and for a moment concentrated silently to focus his glass on the moving boat, trying to allow for the motion of his own ship as well. "There *are* men in red jackets, I think," the boy said. "Do you suppose a French ship might have sunk out here?"

"Perhaps, but those boats are travelling north with the wind, not toward the shore as you would expect. Do they wave a jacket or do anything at all to gain our attention?"

"They don't appear to, Mr Hayden. They are an uncharacteristically retiring assembly of castaways, I should say. Perhaps they've mistaken us for an Englishman . . ."

"Which would be no mistake, but I take your meaning. We shall have our answer by and by."

Hayden was about to set out for the deck, when Wickham exclaimed, "Sir! Those are British marines; I swear to it."

Hayden returned to his position, braced himself against the roll of the ship, and tried to fix his glass on the distant boat. To keep the tiny object centred in the lens was maddingly difficult, but after a few moments he at least agreed that there were a number of people dressed in red. Whether they were marines, or even men, he could not say, but Wickham had better eyes than he.

Hayden climbed down to the deck, though a strange feeling of disquiet began to overtake him. During the course of the next half hour he twice made the journey forward with his glass, where he paused to gaze at the distant boats, their white oars flashing rhythmically in the bright summer light. As he stood by the bow-chaser the second time, trying to hold the little boats in the wavering eye of his glass, Wickham called from aloft.

"That *is* Mr Barthe, Mr Hayden! Those boats are from the *Themis*. I can see Mr Hawthorne, I'm sure."

A small breeze of whispers passed among the men on the deck, and more than a few hurried to the rail and leaned out to peer forward. A half hour crept slowly by. The boats crested a wave and the dispirited— some, bloodied—faces of Hayden's crew mates became unmistakable. Wickham raced down the shrouds and appeared beside Hayden, who stood at the forward rail.

"What has happened?" the midshipman wondered, but Hayden had no answer.

The lieutenant could hardly remember seeing such looks of dejection. The boats, overcrowded in the extreme, were brought alongside, their occupants silent as mourners. Mr Barthe stood in the bow of one cutter and addressed the ship in broken French.

"You may speak the King's English here, Mr Barthe," Hayden answered. The sailing master was, for a satisfying moment, held speechless.

"Mr Hayden?" he finally managed. "This is the French prize! God be praised."

This revelation raised the men's spirits noticeably, and they began to scale the ladder. A good number required assistance and a few wanted slings, too injured to climb. Almost all the men were bruised and powder-stained, their clothing torn and soiled.

Barthe came over the rail stiffly, and collapsed against the hammock netting. He gathered in a long, ragged breath and closed his eyes a moment. Hawthorne reached the deck, showing great concern for his fellows, and Mr Barthe in particular.

"What has happened, Mr Barthe?" Hayden asked, feeling deeply shocked to see his own crew mates in such a state. "You look as though you've had a terrible battle."

"Where is the *Themis*?" Wickham interrupted. "Is she lost?"

Hawthorne himself looked as though speech would fail him, but then he managed in a harsh, parched voice, "No, Mr Wickham. And yes. There was a mutiny, and we are the men loyal to the King. They put us into boats—out of fear, I think—and sailed off toward Brest, where I assume they intend to offer our frigate to the French."

Hayden heard himself curse, and the men gathered round filled the air with muttered oaths.

"Quiet on the deck!" Wickham called out.

"Have a care there!" Griffiths called out from one of the cutters. "Captain coming aboard."

The tackles creaked, and, barely able to keep himself in the bosun's chair, Captain Hart was slung aboard. Landry scrambled over the rail at the same moment and eased the captain down onto the deck, Hart moaning terribly as he did so. The captain's coat, thrown over his shoulders, slipped off as he was lowered, and silence washed over the gathering like a cold sea. Hart's back was flayed to bloody ribbons.

Landry looked up, his face powder-burned and eyes sunken into dark pits. "Two dozen lashes," Landry declared, "applied with a will."

"Who did this?"

"It was Stuckey who swung the cat . . ."

"Stuckey . . . ?" Hayden heard himself echo.

Griffiths came onto the deck then, needing a little help to stand steady. "We must get Captain Hart below," he said, wiping the back of a hand across his unshaven face.

"The French surgeon has a sick-berth rigged forward," Hayden instructed.

"I will treat him myself," Griffiths insisted.

"Of course." Hayden bent to help lift the captain. "Take him up gently, now. Gently."

Hart was eased below and settled into a cot, where Griffiths began to converse with the ship's surgeon in halting French. Hayden left them, hearing the sounds of Hart crying out and demanding succour, as he retreated.

A moment later he was on the deck, calling for Hawthorne and Barthe. At moments like this a fierce determination came over him, and his mind seemed to focus utterly. All his years of training under able captains like Bourne came to the fore, and he made decisions with exceptional rapidity, weighing a thousand pieces of information with an uncanny kind of intuition.

"Tell me the number of men who came away in the boats?" he asked them.

"Fifty-one," Hawthorne answered promptly. "But O'Connor departed this life and we put him over the side."

"How many can fight or work a ship?"

Hawthorne glanced at Barthe.

"Eight in ten, Mr Hayden," Barthe replied, "though they are all hungry, thirsty, and in need of rest."

"Food and drink we have. There is no time for rest. How many were left aboard the *Themis*?"

"Dr Griffiths estimated that there were thirty killed and about half again that many too injured to stand watch. You were fourteen that set out for the *Lucy*. By my count that leaves near to eighty able-bodied men aboard the *Themis*, though a good number of them landsmen."

"We have roughly the same numbers," Hayden said. "Mr Barthe, will you be our sailing master?"

The man reached up to touch his hat but had none. "If you are captain, Mr Hayden, I am your sailing master."

"Mr Wickham?" Hayden called.

"Here, Mr Hayden," the boy said, coming forward. He had been passing among the castaways, who were sprawled on the deck. Hayden realized that he had quill and paper.

"What have you there?" Hayden asked him.

"I'm making a list of who came away in the boats and of the men who are hurt. We're moving the wounded down to the doctors as they can receive them, sir."

"Mr Wickham, if you become any more efficient you will be the next First Lord. We must arrange the crew as best we can. Feed the men from the *Themis*, then make up watches." He turned to Barthe. "How far ahead do you think the *Themis* might be?"

"Not so far as you might think; they were a long time arguing among themselves over what was to be done, both with the ship and with the deposed officers and loyal crew." Barthe ran a hand through his unbound hair in thought. "Perhaps three leagues, but under reduced canvas for want of able seamen."

"Then it is top-gallants, Mr Barthe, and stunsails, too, if you please. We might not catch the *Themis*, but it will not be for lack of will. As soon as the men are fed and their places made known, we will clear for action."

Hayden climbed the mainmast himself and loosed the gaskets on the top-gallant. In a moment he was down to haul away on the halliard, and the men could hardly have done it without him.

"Begging your pardon, sir," said one of Bourne's crew, making a knuckle, "but that's the first time I've hauled a top-gallant halliard home shoulder-to-shoulder with the ship's captain."

"I only hope I have acquitted myself passably," Hayden said.

"Oh, managed most handsomely, sir," the man assured him, to laughter from his mates.

"What is your name?" Hayden asked.

"John Lawrence, sir; rated able."

"Well, Mr Lawrence, you are captain of the main-top now. Can you manage it?"

"I will not disappoint your confidence, sir," the man mumbled. "That is to say, your confidence is not misapplied. Not one whit."

"I am glad to hear it."

A few moments later Hayden was on the quarterdeck, where he found Barthe and Wickham bent over a chart. They had sailed into the fog, which was patchy and varied in density—here thick as a sheep's coat, a moment later thinner than gauze.

"What see you there, gentlemen?" Hayden asked.

Barthe looked up, touched his invisible hat, and then laid a finger on the chart. "Before we plunged into the fog, Mr Wickham and I agreed our position was in this vicinity if not precisely at the tip of my fingernail. I have estimated the position of the *Themis* at the time we were set adrift. She was still hove-to when we lost her in this damnable fog, so it is impossible to predict her course or speed over the bottom. It was the impression of both the doctor and myself that the faction favouring sailing into Brest Harbour and turning the ship over to the French would carry the day, and the flogging of the captain made that almost certain, I would venture. Be that as it may, the *Themis* cannot be far ahead, though one must admit that in this fog they could be easily missed. One could sail past them within pistol shot and not know it, if they had the common sense to stay silent."

Hayden regarded the chart a moment. "We can do nothing, Mr Barthe, other than shape our course for Brest. If we happen upon the *Themis*, all the better. If not, we may pray we arrive off that harbour before the mutineers. We will hold our position there as long as we are able and await their arrival, where we'll welcome them into the revolutionary fold with a great cannonade."

"You have my agreement there, Mr Hayden. They mistreated us terribly after they'd taken the ship, and killed many a good man in their bloody coup. I would like nothing better than to catch Bill Stuckey with a sharp blade, that I would." He made another hatless salute. "If you please, sir, the fore-topsail yard is not braced to my liking." The corpulent little master hurried forward, calling out for hands to aid him.

"Mr Barthe is much distressed by the loss of one of his mates . . . and many another friend."

Hayden turned to find the marine lieutenant watching the master disappear forward.

"So it would seem, Mr Hawthorne. But you can't have more than a dozen marines remaining. I assume none of them joined the mutineers, which means you lost nigh on twenty men yourself . . ."

Hawthorne nodded, his gaze drifting off toward the luminescent fog. "Yes. They caught us unawares—no rolling cannon-balls or anything like. Six bells and they jumped the men guarding the armourer's stores and the forward magazine. One of the crew—the loyal crew—raised the cry and then it was pistols and muskets. We were driven back onto the quarterdeck and into the aft section of the ship. Landry and a few of the middies and servants held the gunroom for some time, making the bastards pay dearly, though Albert Williams and my corporal were killed. I had rushed on deck as soon as I was roused, in my night-shirt, cutlass in one hand, pistol the other. We were poorly armed or I think we might have prevailed, but the crew had pikes and hatchets and finally muskets too, and most of all they had powder, while we soon ran dry." Hawthorne paused, swallowed, could not continue, then found his voice again. "No one shirked, though, or surrendered without a fight—excepting maybe Hart, though I can't say what befell him in the darkness. It was a bloody business; men knocked to the deck suing for mercy were beaten to death—crewman fighting crewman—but finally it was lost and the few of us who remained on the quarterdeck threw down our arms. They herded us together like cattle and made us lie face-down on the gangways, half atop one another, while they debated what was to be done. Once the ship was taken there was little among the mutineers to make common cause—hatred of Hart, perhaps, was all that had bound them together. Some, led by Stuckey, were for sailing the ship into Brest and offering her to the French in return for asylum. Others thought they should set out for foreign parts, though there were a good many who looked deeply remorseful and dismayed by what they had done. Setting aside Hart had been their intention, with little thought to what would come after, I fear. But then Stuckey and his followers, who held the captain, lit upon the idea of flogging him, 'on Mr Aldrich's account,' they claimed. Before anyone realized what went on Hart was seized up to the grating and Stuckey near tore his arm out, such was his fury. I've never seen such a savage flogging. Stuckey fell down to the deck afterward and couldn't catch his breath for a few moments. And that was that—it was Brest then, for the Admiralty would spare no energy to hunt them down and they all knew it. There was talk of flogging Franks and Landry, but Aldrich came up on the deck, out of the doctor's care, and admonished the men to do no more flogging, and certainly none on his account. He would have said more, but he fell in a dead swoon and was carried below."

"What became of him?" Hayden asked.

"The mutineers would not give him up, saying he was one of them, though I am not sure that was true. We were much bullied as we lay there, every Jack who had a score to settle, or was still in a rage, found some helpless man to ballyrag. It was a relief when it was decided we would be put into boats, for the prospect of staying among those brutes was enough to unnerve the strongest among us."

"I'm surprised they did not take you with them so the French could imprison you."

"We were surprised as well, but Stuckey wanted us put into the boats, as though he were afraid to keep us aboard."

"With his mutineers divided he might well have been wise to do so—if one can call such a man wise."

"Yes, well, he took *us* by surprise."

"And for good reason. Stuckey was one of the men who stood against the disaffected in Plymouth."

This seemed to trouble Hawthorne. "So he did, but it must now be said that Stuckey and a few others were trying to stop the petition because they had larger designs. They did not want Hart removed, for he was the greatest aid to their cause, provoking the hands so that Stuckey and the others might prey upon their indignation. Once Aldrich had been flogged without reason, the crew's resentment was easily worked up. He made fools of us all."

Hayden felt enormous distress at this. He had misread the situation entirely. "You will have to put your head together with Mr Barthe and the doctor and make a list of all the men killed, on both sides, the mutineers, the men who stayed loyal to Hart, and any, like Aldrich, who were ill and could take no side."

"Yes, we'll do that. There is one man who will have a list of his own—a division of one."

"Who was that?"

"Giles."

"Young Giles? The giant?"

Hawthorne nodded. "He fought neither for nor against the mutineers. In fact he seems to have hidden himself away, and would have come away in the boats but Stuckey would not allow it, saying a man who had murdered his crew mate had better stay among the mutineers, though he was much cuffed and kicked for not coming to the mutineers' aid. 'Let him come away in the boats if he wants to,' argued Mr Barthe, but Stuckey would have none of it. 'You don't want him,' old Bill says, a sneering grin on his ugly face. 'It was him 'at killed Penrith. Him and no other, though unlucky McBride swung for it.' "

This silenced Hayden for a moment. "And did you believe him?"

"Not for a moment, but then I saw the way the boy hung his head. 'Tell them you didn't do it,' one of the middies said to him, for they like the boy overly, but he couldn't answer. 'Oh, he did it all right,' Stuckey said. 'Old Penrith got Giles to put his name to the petition and when Giles came to his senses there was no taking his name off. Giles and Penrith had a little conversation up on the main yard, and Penrith went for a swim, didn't he?' Thought he was quite a wit, apparently. They kept Giles with them, anyway, and he looked like a guilty man."

Hayden felt distress lay her cold hand upon him. "Well, the boy is like not to speak up on his own behalf. I should not take the word of Bill

Stuckey, who might have committed the murder himself and only blamed it on Giles."

Hawthorne did not look convinced by this. "Hard to imagine why he'd bother. Stuckey's going to hang if the Navy ever lay hands on him, anyway."

"True enough; still, the man is a liar and a coward. The good news is, if they have elected a landsman like Stuckey as captain the ship will not be well sailed."

Wickham came hurrying along the deck. "Mr Hayden . . . Captain Hart is asking for you, sir."

Hayden glanced over at the marine lieutenant, who raised an eyebrow. "If you will excuse me, Mr Hawthorne . . ."

Hawthorne gave a little bow of the head.

The sick-berth had been made up on the forward gun-deck beneath the forecastle, though it would have to be moved when the ship cleared for action—a regrettable nuisance. The stench of the place struck Hayden as he descended the forward companionway: the pungent odour of alcohol and physic mixed with the meat-rotting reek of septic wounds. The cots hung in neat rows, so close the surgeons and their mates could barely make their way among them. Overhead, a grated hatch let twenty little squares of light play over the slowly swaying cots, skittering from one side to the other as the ship rolled. Lamps brought a little more light to the darker recesses, from which came inhuman moans and occasional cries of agony.

Hayden spotted Landry forward and made his way along the row of cots, trying to smile at the men and look full of hope, hiding the horror he felt, pressing down his own desire to flee the place out into the pure sunlight and clean air.

Hayden found Griffiths standing by the cot of Captain Hart, separated from the rest of the sick by a makeshift bulkhead of sailcloth. The surgeon applied a glistening film of some liquid, perhaps oil of olives, over the captain's flayed back. Hart grunted and moaned at brief intervals, muttering curses and prayers that could hardly be distinguished one from the other. A pale-faced Landry moved aside to let him pass.

Griffiths finished his application and, looking up, nodded. "Captain Hayden," he said.

Hart shifted so that he could bring Hayden into the corner of his vision, his usually florid face now utterly crimson. "What is this I hear, Hayden, that you intend to chase the *Themis*?"

"That is correct, Captain Hart. I hope to overhaul her before she can reach the harbour of Brest."

"You will do nothing of the sort!" Hart stormed. "Do you want to see us all killed? We few were lucky to get away with our lives. You will proceed to Plymouth with all speed."

"With all respect," Hayden said evenly, "it is my intention to chase down the mutineers and, if it is at all possible, either sink or take their ship."

"Damn your impudence, sir!" Hart thundered. "I am your superior officer. You will take my orders or I will have you removed from your post."

"You put me under the command of Captain Bourne, sir, who granted me command of this vessel. You are my guest, and in no state to take command or even the deck, were it your place to do—"

"Damn your eyes, sir! Mr Landry, you will assume command of this ship and proceed to Plymouth, forthwith."

Landry squared up his narrow shoulders and cleared his throat. "Begging your pardon, Captain Hart, but I believe Mr Hayden is in the right—we are guests aboard his ship. Castaways rescued and under his protection. To attempt to seize control, were it possible, would be mutiny . . . sir."

"Blast you to hell, Landry!" the captain said, shifting about so that he fixed his clouded eye upon his second lieutenant. "I will see you court-martialled with Mr Hayden, broken of rank, and drummed out of the service!"

"Perhaps you will, sir," Landry said mildly, "but even that will hardly be more harm than has been done by my past years of service. I will do my duty and support Mr Hayden's attempt to retake the *Themis*." The little lieutenant made a stilted bow and disappeared behind the sailcloth wall, where his shadow could be seen walking stiffly away.

"Landry!" Hart called, but there was no answer.

The captain let out a moan of pain, and then, shifting about so that his squinty eye fixed upon Hayden, he whispered, "You cannot even imagine the harm I shall do you, Hayden. When we return to England—"

But Hayden interrupted. "Threatening the captain of a ship, sir; I might caution you that it contravenes the Articles of War. Good day to you."

Hayden could hear Hart cursing and crying out in pain as the acting captain made his way back among the wounded, all of whom had heard every word that had been said. There would be no lack of witnesses to his refusal to obey Hart's orders . . . but Hayden had taken all the orders from that man he could stomach, and refusing to take more was like throwing a carcass off his back.

As he mounted the steps he heard himself mutter *"Fucking Englishman!"* and was rather taken aback.

Landry stood waiting for him as he emerged onto the deck, diffuse sunlight throwing faint shadows onto the worn planks. The second lieutenant touched his hat.

"I am not certain, Landry, the Admiralty will agree that Bourne's commission overrides Hart's authority. You would be safer not to throw in your lot with me."

"Mr Hayden, after what has happened, I have no doubt that this will be my last voyage aboard a ship of His Majesty's Navy. As a last act, I would dearly like to retake the *Themis*, a ship lost due to incompetence of command, in which I played no small part. I have done nothing to earn your confidence, Mr Hayden, but if you will allow it I will endeavour to change that." The little man looked so earnest, so needing of his approval that Hayden felt some part of his dislike for the lieutenant melt away.

"Come, Mr Landry," Hayden said. "We have much to do."

On the quarterdeck Hayden called all his officers together: Barthe, Landry, Archer, and Franks, as well as the midshipmen.

"Where is Mr Wickham?" Hayden asked.

"He's only just found out about Williams, sir," Madison answered.

"Ah . . . a terrible loss," Hayden said softly, a strange tightness across his chest.

"I'll fetch him," Hobson offered, disappearing down the companion-way.

In a moment a sober and red-eyed Wickham arrived on the deck, attempting mightily to regain his acting-officer dignity. "Captain," he said, touching his hat, "now that you have two commissioned lieu-tenants aboard I must give up my position as acting first lieutenant."

"I'm afraid you must, Mr Wickham," Hayden agreed with real regret. "I will make you acting third lieutenant. Mr Landry and Mr Archer will be first and second officers. Mr Barthe, sailing master. Franks, bosun. Have we watches set?"

"Aye, sir." Wickham withdrew a folded sheet of paper from his jacket and tactfully gave it to Landry to pass on.

Hayden glanced over the list, largely to be sure the small number of men were distributed as intelligently as possible. "Well done, Wickham. How fare the castaways?" he asked of the men in general.

"They are being fed now, sir, and look all the better for it," Landry answered up smartly.

"Mr Archer, gather a crew and move the sick-bay down to the orlop-deck. I know there is little room, but it will have to be done all the same. I would move them into my cabin, but it is no place for wounded men and doctors in an action. Mind you attend to Dr Griffiths' instructions, and take great care with the wounded. Once that is done we will clear for action. We haven't enough men to sail the ship and man the guns, so the gun crews shall go a man shy and we will keep the most able seamen on deck to handle sail. I should think it would be best to put Bourne's crew on deck as they work together well."

Landry reached out an open hand, nodding to the watch and station bill Wickham had made up. "I will organize the crew, if you like, Mr Hayden."

"If you please, Mr Landry. I have another task for Mr Wickham." Hayden turned to the young acting-lieutenant. "Back to the masthead for you, I fear; the curse of having the sharpest eyes on the ship. I'd rather we spotted the *Themis* before they us."

"I won't allow that, sir," Wickham said, touching his hat and hurrying off.

The wind, which had blown with great consistency, but faintly, all through the forenoon, now began to sigh, then hold its breath, only to sigh again. The ship would steady as her sails filled, then lose her wind and all her gear would slat terribly on the low swell. Even at this stammering pace they soon sailed into the bright, frosty mist that clung low to the ocean. Lookouts were posted in various places about the ship, even a man out on the end of the jib-boom. The fog, which fairly glowed a snowy, crystalline white, thinned to wisps at times, then gathered its powers and pressed close again.

Hayden paced about the deck, observing the efforts of the crew, speaking now and then with Mr Barthe about the set of the sails, for the inconstant wind forced them to tend sheets with frustrating regularity if they were to keep the ship moving.

"Mr Hayden, sir . . ." Wickham called from aloft, interrupting his circling of the deck.

Hayden turned his attention upward, and found the acting third lieutenant perched upon the topmast trestle-trees, glass in hand, gazing down at the deck.

"I can see the tops of several masts, sir. Three or four large ships of war, I would guess."

"Are they showing colours?"

"Not so I can see, sir, but they appear to be seventy-fours. One, perhaps, larger. They pass south, and seem unaware of us." Wickham peered off into the mists again, then leaned over and called down, "Gone, sir."

"You might want to rid yourself of your British jacket, Mr Wickham," Hayden called up, and then to Archer nearby, "We might all do the same, in the event that we must pass for Frenchmen." He looked around the deck. "Monsieur Sanson? Where is my servant?"

"Ici, mon capitaine."

"Can you find us coats and hats from the French officers?" Hayden enquired in French.

"I believe so, monsieur." The Frenchman inclined his head in a precise motion.

"We will keep them ready to hand in case we need them. Find yourself an officer's uniform as well. I might need another who can speak French."

Hayden continued his rounds, finding the men adapting easily to the new ship. He spoke with several members of the *Themis'* crew, almost all of whom appeared deeply distressed by what had happened. Hayden had never been forced to kill a member of his own crew, so he could only imagine what a whirl of confusion must be going on inside them. And now they were hunting the *Themis* and would engage her people again, if Hayden had his way.

As he detached from a small knot of men, Hayden found Barthe gazing at him thoughtfully, a purple cheek, shiny and swollen, contrasting with his brick-coloured hair.

"You look very pensive, Mr Barthe, as do most of the castaways, I note."

"To be ill-used by your own crew mates. To see your friends murdered at the hands of these very same men . . . It is enough to send a sound mind spinning into melancholy, that is certain."

Hayden felt himself nodding. "Yes, I'm sure you're right. And now I wonder . . . will the men who came away with you in the boats fight their fellows, do you think? Have they the heart for it?"

"No one's heart will be in it, but I think we will fight all the same. You will see. They are stout fellows, though Hart did everything he could to unman them."

The ship passed into fog, and was then becalmed within its unearthly grasp. A fanciful world of wafting mist and invisible, oscillating sea.

"It could be a level of Hades, could it not?" Hawthorne observed as he and Hayden drank coffee on the quarterdeck. "A hell where seamen are stranded—cast away—until the end of the world. Look, we appear to be afloat in roiling mist."

"As infernos go it is rather dank," Hayden answered, surprised by the marine lieutenant's seriousness. "But we are not the men in hell. Not this day. It is Bill Stuckey and his confederates who must feel the nearness of the flame. I have no sympathy for Hart, who brought this calamity upon himself, but the poor sods who suffered under him are almost certain to find justice, and a terrible sentence it will be."

"Perhaps we should pray not to overhaul them . . ." Hawthorne ventured, watching Hayden's reaction.

The lieutenant shook his head. "No, despite all the sympathy I feel for every man who endured beneath Hart's boot, we cannot win a war without ships, even ships under the command of tyrants."

"What of shy tyrants?" Hawthorne said quickly. "Men too cowardly to meet the enemy?"

"Hart should have been removed from his command—you will get no argument from me on that point—but it was the place of the Admiralty to do it. Not the crew."

"Unfortunately the Admiralty were not fulfilling their trust, but supporting their man instead."

"Mr Hawthorne, I agree it is a moral morass, but we will only compound it by taking matters into our own hands. It is our duty to take the *Themis* if we can do it by any means short of our complete destruction. That is what I will attempt and I will draw my pistol against any man who will not follow those orders."

"And I will draw mine beside you, Mr Hayden, but it is all a muddle. The only justice that has been done since I boarded that ship was the flogging of Hart, and that was done by a mutineer."

"Mr Hawthorne . . ." Hayden cautioned.

At that moment the wind filled in, the sails bellied, and the ship slowly gathered way. Sun, obscured in a watery haze, began to burn through the mist, which thinned visibly around them. Even so, their world was only reduced to an irregular circle, two leagues broad and circumscribed by a bright, crystalline fog.

Hayden could not help but notice that the middies were a melancholy lot, having lost the well-loved Albert Williams, the Bert of "Trist and Bert." Tristram Stock was red-eyed and embarrassed for it, though he looked to commence weeping again as Hayden spoke with him.

"I will tell you this, Mr Hayden," he whispered, "most of the men did not want the mutiny but the captain drove them to it. You could see it in their faces once it was all over. I'm sure they are a sorry lot this day. Many had wives and children whom they'll never see again. We mayn't have had a crack crew, like the *Tenacious*, but they were mostly good-hearted men, good-hearted men driven to folly."

They spoke a little of Williams, of how he liked to use the word *eloquent* to describe the most unlikely things ("I have the most eloquent little course change for you, Dryden." "An eloquent measure of grog for you, sir"), and his love of debate, having been known to reverse his opinion completely upon another conceding he was in the right. They agreed that he would have made a fine officer one day, as one always did of young gentlemen who departed this life too soon.

The fog edged away all that long afternoon and the dusk seemed to press in as the mist finally disappeared altogether.

"I don't know how we'll ever find her now," Barthe complained. "Fog all day and now the night is setting in. Unless we overhaul them in the darkness and arrive at the harbour of Brest before them, they have slipped away, Mr Hayden."

"Sail ho," Wickham called from aloft. "Hull down and dead before us."

Hayden hurried forward to a place where he could see the midshipman high above. "Is it the *Themis*?"

"I cannot say that, Mr Hayden, but I cannot claim it is any other ship, either."

By the time Hayden reached the top-gallant trestle-trees the dusk had grown all but impenetrable. A faint, pale patch, possibly angular, was all that Hayden could make out even with a night glass, but he had no doubt Wickham was right—it was a ship. But was it their ship? That was the question everyone asked.

"They are on our exact course, sir," Wickham noted, "and not carrying top-gallants in a fine top-gallant breeze, indicating that she might well be undermanned."

"My hunches have never paid me much at the gaming table, but perhaps at sea my luck is better. I think this is our ship, Mr Wickham. Keep us in her wake as long as you can." As Hayden descended to the deck, the stars began to fill the sky, a great river of luminosity passing overhead, stars so densely packed that no one could rightly explain it.

Despite Wickham's gifted night vision, Hayden knew the most likely method of overhauling the ship was to keep their course diligently. He and Mr Barthe arranged tricks at the wheel for the most capable helmsmen, and with their small muster, that left both the master and acting captain to stand a trick themselves. Hayden did not mind. Truth was, he liked to take the helm now and then, but as an officer this small pleasure was denied him. Once he had the spokes in his hand, Hayden imagined he could feel the sea breathing beneath him, could feel each rise of the ocean's breast as the wave carried them forward, and then left them settling into the trough. The wind caressed his neck, whispering its origin on the compass rose, and he steered, feeling the billowing sails draw them on.

The ship's bell sounded the night's depths. Midshipmen heaved the log, noting their progress and marking a position upon the chart.

Landry approached him at the wheel. "Idlers and watch below are in their hammocks, sir."

"Thank you, Mr Landry." Hayden finished his trick at the wheel and was relieved by Mr Barthe. Leaving the deck to Landry, he went below to the dead captain's cabin, a place he had been avoiding for reasons he did not quite fathom.

Five tapers in a silver candelabra illuminated the table. The white overhead spread this soft light to all corners of the cabin, which was revealed to be much damaged by the *Lucy*'s cannonade. An elaborate place-setting lay upon the table and it occurred to Hayden that Williams would have termed it "eloquent," as though it spoke. All but one of the gallery windows had been destroyed by cannon fire and were covered now by stout planks, caulked and payed. Before the undamaged window sat Giles Sanson—the executioner's son. In his hands he held something angular, bringing Hayden up sharp.

"Monsieur Sanson?"

"*Capitaine* Hayden," the man responded, but his gaze remained on the object he held. "I believe I told you that my *capitaine* protected me from my countrymen . . . And yet I betrayed him. Is that not strange? Perhaps it is as the others say—I am tainted, my blood impure from the thousand murders of my family. I am inherently an evil being, cursed in the sight of God."

"A man is defined by his deeds, not his blood," Hayden said. "Is that not why your countrymen deposed their king and nobles?"

"Yes . . . perhaps." He was silent a moment. "When I reach England what will become of me?"

"You will be imprisoned, likely in a hulk."

"With my countrymen?"

"Yes, until you can be exchanged. And I'm sorry for it."

The young man nodded, as though he had known this all along. "My father told me that I could not escape what I was. That I would be driven back, and perhaps he was right, at least in part." He held up the object he contemplated. "The signal book of my *capitaine*, monsieur. I was charged with throwing it into the sea, but I did not, hoping that I might trade it, use it to buy protection from my fellow citizens." He stood and gently placed the book on the table. "For your kindness. Do not turn the ship around on my account, *Capitaine* Hayden," he said softly, "my pockets are filled with grape." With that he lifted the window sash and, without hesitation, threw himself into the obsidian sea, the window slicing closed behind him. Hayden rushed to raise the sash and thrust his head out. There was nothing to be seen but the slightly luminescent wake scratched upon the glassy waters.

"Poor, sad bastard," Hayden muttered. He knew it was his duty to put the ship about and search for the man but he also knew that he would find nothing. Sanson had joined the thousand victims of his family.

A knock sounded on his door, and the marine posted there let Archer in at a word from Hayden.

"Sir," the young man said, flushed from having run down the ladder, "quarterdeck watch said that something fell from your cabin. There was a splash."

"It was Sanson."

Archer looked confused. "The gypsy, sir?"

Hayden nodded. "He threw himself out the window."

"Shall I have the ship put about, sir . . . ?"

"No, Mr Archer. Sanson weighted his pockets with grapeshot. He will not be found in this life. Have Mr Barthe write it in the log . . . the French captain's servant, one Giles Sanson, likely of Paris, self-murdered. Due to the circumstances of his death, which I have just explained you, no search was made."

"Aye, sir." Archer started to back out the door but then stopped. "Why did he do it, Mr Hayden?"

"Because he was a good man unjustly persecuted due to the circumstances of his birth."

"Because he was a gypsy, you mean?"

"Something like that, yes."

"So much for liberty, equality, and fraternity."

"Yes, so much for all three."

Archer reached up and tipped his French hat, and backed out, closing the door. Hayden took up the volume left on his table. It was heavy due to its lead covers. Inside he found the signals of the enemy—something that the Admiralty would be very happy to possess even if the advantage provided would be brief.

He collapsed into a seat, realizing suddenly that he was exhausted beyond measure. Too much had happened in the last twenty-four hours and he'd had hardly a wink of sleep to bolster his defences. And now this melancholic Frenchman had brought death into the cabin. It occurred to him then that he would be overwhelmingly relieved to have this cursed voyage over.

A soft rap at the door was followed by his writer, Perseverance Gilhooly, bearing a tray of food.

"It's French food, sir," the boy said with distaste, "but Mr Wickham said you might not mind."

"I will manage, Perse. You were not injured in the mutiny, I take it?"

"Hardly, sir, though I fought alongside the middies and Mr Barthe in the gunroom."

"Good for you, Perse."

"Thank you, sir. Will you be needing anything else?"

"No, thank you . . . Where is Joshua?"

The boy hesitated, hovering by the door, his face suddenly pale and drawn. "He . . . he departed this life, Mr Hayden."

Hayden felt a hand go to his forehead, though he had not commanded it do so. "I am so sorry," he replied softly. "What became him?"

"I did not see it, sir, but was told one of the mutineers threw him over the side."

"My God! The child could not swim a stroke . . ."

Perseverance choked back a single sob, nodded, then stepped out of the cabin.

Hayden ignored the meal upon the table and went to the window, staring out over the dark, moving sea. Here he was aboard a French frigate, wearing a French captain's coat and hanging his hammock in his cabin. A feeling of kinship came over him at that moment for the poor Frenchman who had thrown himself into the bottomless waters. Hayden, too, could not escape his family or his heritage, it seemed. This strange masquerade appeared to have been contrived to make this point unavoidable.

"And now am I an Englishman in a Frenchman's coat?" he whispered.

Though he had no appetite, the acting captain forced himself to eat, tasting nothing, but knowing his body had need of sustenance. He lay fully clothed in the former captain's cot and slept for an hour—a haunted hour—and woke feeling utterly unrefreshed.

Twenty-one

Four bells—midpoint of the middle-watch—two of a morning upon the land. Hayden mounted to the quarterdeck and gazed around all points of the compass, assuring himself that the weather was much unchanged, the stars still alight in a pitchy sky.

"All is well, Mr Landry?"

The first lieutenant was a shadow figure, eyes lost in black pools, his diminutive chin all but invisible in the dark.

"It is, Mr Hayden, but for some thick little patches of fog and a weak-willed breeze."

"Biscay will always demand her pound of flesh. Our chase?"

"Wickham is on the forecastle, sir, and says he saw a light some time ago. I could not see it myself, but his eyes are more cunning than mine."

"Indeed. You may take some rest, Mr Landry," Hayden said. "Two hours in a cot and some victuals will not go amiss, I should think."

"They would not, Mr Hayden."

The shadow figure tipped its French officer's hat and retired. Hayden made a tour of the ship, assuring himself that Mr Hawthorne's marines had the prisoners secure, although he did not have the door opened this time. To see his mother's people so confined and defeated was not a sight he bore easily.

Upon the foredeck he found Wickham, his night glass trained forward.

"I understand there was a light . . . ?"

Wickham, decked out in a too-large French lieutenant's coat, like a child playing grown-up, lowered his glass and touched his hat. "For the briefest instant, Mr Hayden. And twice since, I've seen the same. Whoever she is we are in her wake, sir."

"Let us hope it is the *Themis*, for having heard what befell my servant, I should, myself, like to hang the man who flung poor Joshua into the sea."

Wickham nodded. "Mr Hawthorne told me, sir. It saddened me terribly." A moment's silence. "And now this papist, Sanson, has followed behind, I am told . . . ?"

"Yes. A whole family too intimate with death, I think, though Sanson certainly was melancholic, and such people often take their own lives."

"I had a great-aunt did the same, sir, much to everyone's sorrow." Then his arm shot up. "There! Did you see? Just a dull flash, almost dead ahead."

Hayden squinted into the dark, attempting to force a light to appear, without success. For ten minutes he stood on the foredeck, staring into the night, but then he gave it up with a shake of his head, a heave of his taut shoulders.

"Keep me informed of any sightings, Mr Wickham. It torments me to think that she might be sensible to our presence and drop back in darkness to give us a broadside."

"I shall never allow that, sir."

As Wickham made this vow, the ship sailed into a dank cloud. In a moment, beads formed on the bulwarks and darkened the deck.

"Damned bloody fog," Barthe growled as he joined the others on the foredeck. "Thick as molasses where you find it, but hanging low over the sea, hardly stretching to the masthead. Aloft there," he cried. "Are you above this deuced fog?"

"We're in the thick of it, Mr Barthe."

"Well, it is still low to the sea," Barthe intoned, "you can be certain of that." The corpulent sailing master had a dwarf-like silhouette due to the slight stoop in his carriage.

"I have no doubt you're in the right, Mr Barthe," Hayden assured him. He gestured at the slowly swirling fog. "In this we could ram the *Themis* before we knew she was there."

Barthe stood by the starboard rail, staring anxiously into the night. "I will be more pleased to see the dawn than I am commonly, and that is saying a great deal."

"A few hours, Mr Barthe, and we shall have a shred of light." Hayden made a slow circuit of the deck.

Wind and sea, the two things sailors discussed with greater frequency than even the fairer sex, proved that indecision was not exclusively a human distinction. The wind would make for a time, sending the ship rushing through the waters, and then would take off to a mere zephyr. A ground-swell would reach them out of the darkness, and see the men rushing aloft to reduce canvas, expecting the wind that such seas foretell, but the wind would not materialize and the seas would die, mysteriously, away, leaving the old salts to mutter and shake their heads. Stunsails were not reset, though top gallants were held to.

The watch crept on, bell by bell, until the morning watch was called. Two hours more and a meagre brightening of the eastern sky marked the advance of the autumnal morning. Hayden was standing by the taffrail when he heard the sailing master's deeply felt sigh.

"Your much-longed-for daylight at last, Mr Barthe," Hayden remarked.

Barthe gazed a moment more, then turned his bruised face toward the acting captain. "It was a damned long night given the number of hours encompassed." Barthe looked around. "Where is Mr Wickham? Has he our chase in sight?"

"Lieutenant Wickham is on the foretop, Mr Barthe," Hobson reported.

"It is a bit close for even Wickham to see any distance. Would you join me for a breakfast, Mr Barthe? Mr Landry will take the deck in a moment, I'm sure."

"Sail ho!" Wickham shouted from high up among the rigging. "On the starboard beam."

Hayden went to the rail and a glass was placed in his hand, but all he could discern was a landscape of varied grey—fog and sea—a scene that reminded him, inexplicably, of winter London. The ship rose and fell, parting the mist and sending it spinning in little dervishes behind. He felt his breath coming in short gasps and endeavoured to master it.

"Mr Franks," Hayden addressed the bosun softly. "Go to quarters . . . but with as little noise as can be managed. Mr Archer? There you are. Silence fore and aft; pass the word."

"Aye, Mr Hayden," Archer whispered.

Breakfast was forgotten. The watch below was roused quietly—no piping up hammocks—and bleary-eyed sailors crept onto the deck. The bulkheads had been taken down the previous day, and the gun-deck was clear but for the captain's cabin, which Hayden could hear the men dismantling as silently as could be done. Landry popped out of the companionway aft, glanced around, and came immediately to the rail.

"Is it the *Themis*, Mr Hayden?"

"We don't know, Mr Landry, but very likely."

Guns were run out, sails dampened, the boats streamed aft. Glancing one to the other, men shifted about, saying nothing—anxious and excited, wondering if today would make their fortune or see them dead. A tired-looking Wickham materialized at the rail.

"Did she appear to be the *Themis*, Mr Wickham?" Hayden asked the acting lieutenant, who was a little out of breath.

"I think it was, Mr Hayden, but couldn't be certain. She keeps to the same heading or very nearly so."

Hayden nodded and was silent a moment, calming his mind so that he might weigh their situation. "Mr Barthe? Prepare to wear ship. Send the men to their stations and stand ready to shift our yards."

"What have you in mind?" Landry asked.

"We will wear and try to range up astern of them. Before they know we're there, we'll rake them once."

"Sail, sir!" Wickham's arm shot up and he pointed into the mist.

Slowly, a ship began to take shape, sails and rigging, the dark smudge of a hull—impossible even to count the gunports.

"She is the *Themis*!" someone blurted.

"Silence, there," Landry cautioned. And then to Hayden: "I do think the man was right. That is our ship . . . is it not?"

Whoever she was, Hayden was certain she was a frigate. She lay about an English mile distant, under lowers, topsails, and top-gallants, but the inconstant fog still obscured her sufficiently that Hayden could not be certain she bore the mutineers.

Wickham was gazing intently into his glass. "They're going to quarters, sir."

"And so passes our small advantage." Hayden raised his own glass, damning the fog.

"Men are at their stations, Mr Hayden," Barthe informed him. "Shall I give the order to wear?"

Hayden lowered his glass but did not take his eye from the distant vessel. "Wait but a moment, Mr Barthe. Let us be certain of this ship. We might want to slip off into the fog yet."

"She's running up her colours, Mr Hayden," Wickham said quietly.

Hayden raised his glass in time to see a flag jerk to the mizzen gaff, waft once, then spread against the grey. "That would appear to be the *tricolore* upon the canton," he said.

The silence was broken by whispering.

"She could easily be the *Themis*," Mr Barthe asserted. "We flew the French ensign to confuse our enemies many a time. Many a time."

Smoke blew out from the ship and a hoist of signals hauled aloft. An instant later the report reached them over the seas.

"If it is the *Themis* then they are hoping the fog will make that appear to be the French navy's private signal," Wickham ventured.

"Where is my writer?" Hayden asked. "Someone find Perse and send him down to my cabin for the book I had him put away this morning."

Barthe looked at Hayden oddly, as though he thought it a strange time to do a little reading.

A moment later Perseverance Gilhooly came running onto the deck and put the weighty, sailcloth-covered volume into his master's hand. Hayden tucked his glass under an arm and began thumbing the pages. After a moment he stopped at a loose page that had been inserted. "I fear, Mr Wickham, that these are not our mutineers. Either that, or they have learned the enemy's private signal." He turned and glanced around the quarterdeck. "Mr Archer? You read a little French?"

"I do, sir, though I do not speak it as well as yourself and Mr Wickham."

"It will not matter." Hayden gestured the young officer nearer, and showed him the book. "Here is the answer to the private signal. Run it up immediately, if you please."

"Aye, sir." Archer took the offered book. "Is this the French captain's signal book?"

"It is."

Archer stood a moment, stunned, then hurried to the flag cabinet.

"How in the world was that overlooked?" Barthe asked. "They had all the time in the world to throw it into the sea."

"So they did, but it was entrusted to Monsieur Sanson, who kindly passed it along to me."

"Three cheers for melancholy French gypsies, sir," Wickham declared, making Hayden smile.

A moment later Archer ordered a gun fired and he ran up a hoist of flags in reply. Hayden stared at the distant vessel, still half-obscured in the grey.

"What effect has that had, Mr Wickham?"

"Difficult to be certain, sir, but I would venture that they appear a little relieved."

"We will know if they answer our signal with a broadside," Barthe muttered.

"*On deck!*" the lookout cried. "Sail. Almost dead ahead."

"Mr Wickham. Would you hop forward and see if you can distinguish the nationality of this ship? I hope we're not in the middle of a

French squadron. Mr Landry. Give the order—no calls in English. Let us not give ourselves away."

Wickham jogged down the gangway, onto the forecastle, along with Hobson, and the two of them trained glasses forward. For a moment the middies made no move, and then Wickham whirled around.

"*Capitaine,*" he called out. "*C'est l'anglaise. La* Themis.*"

"Fucking hell," Barthe muttered. "Mutineers ahead and a French frigate on our beam—no doubt fully manned. We're in the fire now." The master worried the stay he held by one hand, unable to hide his alarm.

Hayden hurried the length of the ship, joining the two midshipmen on the foredeck. "You're certain, Mr Wickham?"

"I am, sir. The fog parted a moment and I could see her plainly. That is our ship, Captain. I know her."

Raising his glass, Hayden picked out the frigate in question. The mist obscured her somewhat while he watched, but not so much that he couldn't distinguish the French naval ensign as it was hoisted. A gun was fired and signals sent aloft, impossible to make out in the gloom.

"Well, they're not as foolish as one might hope," Hayden observed.

"Do you think they'll deceive the Frenchman, sir?"

"Difficult to know." Hayden glanced from the *Themis* to the French frigate. His situation had turned rather abruptly: two hostile ships, one fully manned, almost certainly. He wondered if he shouldn't use the thinning fog to slip away, but somehow Hart lying below in a fury at his chase of the mutineers made this seem craven—the course a man like Hart would choose.

"Mr Wickham, if we open fire on the *Themis* do you think the Frenchman will realize we're Englishmen in disguise?"

Wickham lowered his glass and gravely considered the question. "They will certainly presume that one of the two ships is British. What else could they think?"

An idea formed in Hayden's mind—a rash idea, certainly, an idea fraught with hazards . . . "Exactly so," he muttered. For a brief moment he hesitated—utterly unlike him—then turned to the other midshipman. "Mr Hobson, jump back to the quarterdeck and have Mr Archer make the signal for 'chasing enemy vessel' or whatever the French equivalent would be."

"I will, sir." The middy set off at a run.

Hayden stood for a moment, trying to regain his breath. It was a bold decision—and in very little time it might be proven foolish.

Wickham raised his glass again, but Hayden felt he was being regarded all the same.

"Is that not a dangerous game to begin, sir? The Frenchmen will almost certainly come to our aid."

"But if we engage the *Themis*—without explanation, as it were—they will almost as certainly decide the chasing ship is British and come to the aid of the mutineers. We have no other choice but to sail away and let Bill Stuckey and his company take our ship into Brest Harbour. But confronted by two French ships I believe the mutineers will haul down their colours—their false colours. We will board and take possession before they realize we are their former shipmates."

"But what will we do then, sir? That is what I wonder. That Frenchman will have a full muster. What do we do if she sends a boarding party to aid us?"

"There is a heavy fog. We will have to slip away or at least deceive them long enough to do so."

Wickham hesitated, lowered his glass, and turned toward Hayden. "Your experience is beyond mine, Mr Hayden, and your judgement is proven. But I fear this Frenchman might penetrate our disguise"—a glance at his over-large coat—"which is rather thin. Not everyone can pass for a Frenchman as you can."

Hayden turned to see Archer running up a hoist of signals. "We will have to keep some water between ourselves and this French frigate, then, Mr Wickham. Let us hope she is happy to stand off and let us do the fighting."

They were silent a moment, staring into the roiling grey. The

Themis—and Hayden was beginning to agree with Wickham regarding her identity—was under courses and topsails. This meagre suit of canvas was the only thing about her that would alert an observer to the truth that she was no longer a ship of His Majesty's Navy—but for her false colours. Her course was true, her too-few sails trimmed to a nicety, there appeared to be order on deck—not a scene of drunken anarchy, as one might expect. Four pale, colourless dabs at the taffrail were, no doubt, mutineers—peering through officers' stolen glasses.

"Are they clearing for action, Mr Wickham?"

"I believe they are. Starboard gunports are opening."

"They've only enough men to fight one side of the ship, and even then the gun crews will be short at least a man."

"What shall we do, sir?"

"Signal our sister ship to engage her starboard battery. We'll engage her to larboard, let the French pour in a broadside or two, and then we'll come alongside and board her, though I think she'll strike before then."

"They might strike and try to talk their way out of this—if they plan to turn themselves over to the authorities in Brest, why not do it at sea?"

"Because there is a very real danger that any French captain will claim them a prize anyway, and then it will be off to a French prison until the end of hostilities, whereupon they will be returned to English soil and an appointment with Jack Ketch."

"I have no doubt you're right, sir, but Stuckey and his gang are clearly not in the habit of looking so far ahead. Men are lying aloft, Mr Hayden . . . to set top-gallants, I believe."

It was not managed in a seaman-like manner, but eventually the main top-gallant yards were raised and the sails loosed to belly in the breeze.

"Well, that is plain. They're going to run for Brest and keep their French colours flying. Not an unwise decision. Do you still think this the faster ship, Mr Wickham?"

"Not to be disloyal to the *Themis*, but I do, sir."

"We shall soon see."

Hayden went quickly back to the quarterdeck, where he found

Landry and Barthe in conversation with Hawthorne. "Mr Barthe, are you content with the speed we're making? The *Themis* has decided to run for Brest. Can we overhaul her?"

"I shall have the stunsails reset in a moment, sir."

"Thank you, Mr Barthe." Hayden found Archer examining the French frigate through a glass. "Mr Archer, how goes our correspondence with the French?"

The second lieutenant lowered his glass and touched his hat. "Well enough, Mr Hayden. They hoisted their number a moment ago. They're the *La Rochelle*, sir. Mr Barthe says she's a new-built thirty-eight, but hasn't been seen in these waters for a year. She's been in the West Indies, he believes."

Hayden raised his glass and inspected the French frigate again—for as the day brightened she was a little easier to make out. She did have the look of a ship that had just crossed the Atlantic: paint dull and flaking, some seams in her topsides in need of a caulking mallet.

"Excellent," Hayden said to himself.

"Pardon, sir?"

"Let us hope Mr Barthe is right. If they've just crossed the Atlantic they likely won't have heard about the taking of the *Dragoon* by British seamen, and her bottom will be fouled, as well. It might be too much to hope that her crew are ill or depleted, but a foul bottom will let us slide away, especially in this slippery maiden." He patted the rail. "Let us hope the *Themis* does not outrun *La Rochelle*; I'm counting on her assistance."

"Shall I make our number in return, sir? I found it in the book."

"Yes. Do that, Mr Archer. We wouldn't want them to stop believing in us."

If *La Rochelle*'s bottom were foul there was little sign of it. She set as much canvas as Hayden's prize, and held her place in the little triangle that the three ships made on the grey sea.

As the sun warmed it began to burn away the fog, revealing the *Themis* in all her mutinous glory.

"When we curse the damned fog, it will not leave us," Barthe growled. "And now that we have need, it will abandon us."

"Helmsman," Hayden said, "half a spoke to larboard. Don't allow the Frenchman to narrow the distance between us." Wickham had planted a little worry in Hayden's mind. He was willing to take this risk with the Frenchman because he could pass for one himself, but the rest of the crew were not so able. Perhaps the French would penetrate their ruse if they drew near enough. Now that the fog had left them, Hayden had no intention of letting that happen.

He turned a slow circle, subjecting the sea to a cold scrutiny. The coast of France formed an undulating blue line to the east; a headland, he was certain, must be Pointe du Raz. Beyond *La Rochelle*, a few flecks of white and oak bark stood out against the azure sea—the sails of fishermen and small transports. The breeze was filling in a little from the south-west, though there were still no whitecaps to be seen—seven knots, he reckoned. Before them the *Themis* rocked gently on the Biscay swell, her top-gallants billowing. It was too soon to know if the *Dragoon* was gaining on her, but he imagined she was.

Dr Griffiths appeared at that moment.

"Good morning, Doctor. How fare our sick and hurt?" Hayden was a bit embarrassed by his good cheer, for the doctor looked very grim and pasty with fatigue.

Griffiths drew nearer and then spoke quietly. "We lost McLeod last night, Captain."

"Oh, I am sorry . . ."

"And Captain Hart's condition appears to be worsening. He needs a physician. A hospital. And physic that I do not possess." The doctor glanced around, noting the other ships. "Have you taken into consideration what might happen if Hart were to die? He has many friends in His Majesty's Navy, Mr Hayden. If it appears that he might have been saved but for your insistence—against Hart's wishes—that you would attempt to take the *Themis* . . ."

"We do not sail for England every time a man is injured, Dr Griffiths, as you well know—certainly Hart never made an effort to take a flogged man back to port. Men live or die according to the will of God and the skill of our surgeons. I will not make an exception for Hart when there is a British ship about to be turned over to the French." He pointed forward. "Not when that ship is this close."

"Yes, Mr Hayden, I know we do not return to port every time a man is injured, but Hart is a captain, a man of considerable interest within the Admiralty. There is a . . . *political* facet to this situation." Griffiths seemed a little ill himself—in humour as well as appearance.

"I am aware of it, thank you, Doctor, but I believe I know where my duties lie. I will have Mr Barthe note your concerns in the log in the event that Captain Hart's condition grows worse. You shall bear no part of the blame."

"I am less worried about my future in the navy than your own, Mr Hayden. Rushing Hart back to the care of a physician, and his loving wife, would do more to further your career than taking any number of mutinous vessels. But I will say no more." He glanced again at the not-so-distant ships. "I don't suppose Stuckey and his mates will surrender without a fight?"

"If we can convince them we are French, they might, but even then I am not so certain. They don't want their ship to become a prize and themselves made prisoners."

The doctor regarded him oddly. "There has been hardly a dull day since you found your way aboard our ship, Mr Hayden."

"Do you regret it, Doctor?"

Griffiths regarded him with his clear, intelligent eye. "I do, as a doctor, for our lists of injured and dead have grown considerably, and much suffering has come to us. But as an Englishman, I am rather proud of what we've accomplished."

"Well, Doctor, I shall, as always, try to limit our wounded to the smallest number possible."

A cannon fired at that moment and a ball found the water not far off their starboard bow.

"The *Themis* is firing at us, Captain," Hobson called, and was hushed by half a dozen for speaking out in English.

"I would say they don't mean to parley, or end as a French captain's prize. It will be a fight if we overhaul them, which I believe we will do in the next two hours."

Griffiths reached up to touch a hat that was not there. "I will ready my table. Send me as few as you can, Mr Hayden."

"I do not send any, Doctor, it is the French who perform that service."

Griffiths looked him up and down. "But are not you the French, sir? So it would appear." A small smile appeared and the doctor retreated below.

The forecastle gun crews were mustered and Hayden went forward. The *Themis* kept up a regular fire with her stern-chasers, balls landing very near.

"We're just out of range, sir," the captain of the starboard bow-chaser said as Hayden reached the forecastle.

"So it seems." Hayden turned his glass on the stern of the *Themis*, and there he could plainly make out Bill Stuckey—a man he'd once imagined he'd reformed—wearing a cutlass and a brace of pistols. Chagrin and anger coursed through him.

Hawthorne appeared, musket in hand. "Is that my darling Willy on the quarterdeck, sir?"

"I believe it is, Mr Hawthorne."

"Sadly, out of musket range."

"At the moment . . ." Hayden looked east, gauging the speed of *La Rochelle*. She appeared to be holding position, to Hayden's satisfaction. "Mr Hawthorne, when we come alongside the *Themis* I will put a few of your best marksmen up in the tops. Tell them to keep their faces hid as best they can. I want no one recognized until we are on their deck. The rest of your marines will be in the boarding party. I will need every man I can find if we hope to carry the *Themis*."

"My marines are yearning to have a bit of revenge, sir."

"Good. They have the greater numbers, so we must use our guns and the guns of *La Rochelle* to even the odds."

Despite the gravity of their situation, Hawthorne appeared to be suppressing a smile.

"What is it, Mr Hawthorne," Hayden asked, "that you find so divert-ing in our situation?"

Hawthorne's smile blossomed fully, and he took hold of the lapel of his French officer's coat. "When I told Muhlhauser that this crew would 'wear motley,' I did not comprehend my own wit."

Hayden shook his head, and laughed despite all.

The *Themis* fired again and the ball landed so near that a fine spray reached the tip of the jib-boom.

"I think it's time to return fire, Mr Baldwin, when you are ready. If you can dismount a stern-chaser I shall give you a half a crown."

"That is handsome of you, Mr Hayden." The gun captain made a knuckle and then turned to his crew. He bent over his gun with a great show of concentration, shifted it to larboard a few inches, sighted again, elevated the barrel a little, stepped clear, warned his crew, and jerked the firing lanyard.

The French gun was no quieter than an English one, and Hayden closed his eyes both from pain and from the caustic smoke. Immediately he forced lids open in hopes of seeing where the shot fell. Like the oth-ers, he held his breath, waiting for the breeze to carry some of the smoke away, which it did very ineffectively on this point of sail, for the ship was always sailing into the smoke as the wind carried it with them.

A white plume of water spouted in the wake of the *Themis*.

"The line is very true, Mr Baldwin," Hayden observed. "A little ele-vation and we'll see if these mutineers will stand upon the quarterdeck or scurry like rats."

The gun crew went into their familiar routine, swabbing, inserting the cartridge, and ramming it down the barrel.

"Home!" Baldwin announced, for he held a small wire in the prick hole to feel for the cartridge. He pricked it with a practised motion and waited for the wadding, followed by the shot, and then more wadding. Priming the pan and the shot hole was the work of a second. The lock was snapped-to, cocked, and the gun run out. Baldwin traversed it a lit-tle to starboard this time, pried the barrel up, and wedged it. A warning to his crew, and then a sharp tug on the lanyard.

Again the terrible assault on the ears. Hayden squinted through the smoke, watching for the plume of water, or, better, a spray of splinters. A moment of confusion.

"Through the mizzen topsail, Mr Baldwin!" Wickham announced. "Did you see?"

"You've the eyes of a hawk, Mr Wickham," Baldwin said in admiration. The gun crew jumped to their work, swabbing and ramming with a will. A jet of smoke at the stern of the *Themis* was quickly followed by the familiar, unnerving scream of a cannon-ball approaching. The fore-topsail dashed about, and there was the sound of shattering wood, splinters raining all around.

Hayden looked up to see the fore-course flapping and thrashing about.

"Mr Barthe. They've shot away the foreyard yardarm. We shall have to reeve a new brace and scandalize the sails. I should like to keep them set, if we can."

Sailors went aloft at a run, and before the *Themis* could fire again, a jury brace had been rove. The sails quieted, and there was near silence on the deck as the men waited for the next shot.

The *Themis* did fire again, but whether they had aimed wide or it was a trick of the sea, the shot landed in the water to larboard. Everyone aboard laughed, including Hayden, though he did not know why.

Their bow-chaser bucked again, and again Hayden grimaced at the report. A second's wait, and one of the *Themis'* gallery windows exploded into shards. The men cheered.

A distant shot drew Hayden's attention, and he saw smoke wafting over the bow of *La Rochelle*.

"Our countrymen are not shrinking from the fight, Mr Hayden," Hawthorne noted.

"They don't want to waste this advantage, Mr Hawthorne—two frigates against one. Our little *masquerade de guerre* is serving."

But *La Rochelle*'s shot fell short by a cable-length.

"Mr Wickham, I think it might be wise for you to climb to the fore-top and shout down to us in French as though you were the lookout."

Wickham grinned, touched his hat, and ran to the shrouds.

"Pass the word for Mr Barthe," Hayden said and then called out an order in French, expecting no one to understand or obey. Barthe appeared at the forward mast, speaking trumpet under his arm. "I hope you don't plan to use that—unless you speak French?"

"No sir, my mate brought it me and I took it out of habit."

"We are too swift. I don't wish to reach the *Themis* before the French frigate. Can you slow us a little without it seeming too overt?"

"I'll slack some sheets, Mr Hayden, and make ready to clew up our courses and take in our top-gallants."

"You can do that, Mr Barthe, but I don't believe the mutineers will offer battle. They will run until we disable their ship; that is what I think. Courses and top-gallants will be needed yet."

Barthe nodded, and was just turning away as something occurred to Hayden.

"Mr Barthe? You must find a hat, sir. Your red hair is far too distinctive. Tuck it away, if you please."

Barthe nodded, and sent his mate scurrying for a hat.

The next ball passed so close that Hawthorne swore he felt the wind from it. Striking the deck at a low angle, it bounced once and thundered the length of the deck, hitting no one and nothing, before sending up a spout in their wake.

Hayden turned and looked aft, where all the men stood at their stations, faces pale and grim.

Wickham called out something in French and Hayden answered at the top of his lungs only to have his words drowned by Baldwin's gun firing. The shot sailed just wide of its target and the gun captain looked up at Hayden, embarrassed.

"My apologies, Captain Hayden. The ship yawed a little unexpectedly."

"So it did, Mr Baldwin. I am on my way to the quarterdeck and I will have the helmsman relieved."

The gunner touched his forehead, and Hayden left them to it, making his way without hurrying along the gangway, showing no signs of fear to his men, even though there was a broken plank where the ball had struck the deck. Hayden stepped over the spot, exhibiting more indifference than he actually felt.

Hayden called for a new helmsman and the master's mate came to take the helm, though he was red-eyed and pale of face.

"Have you had any relief at all from this wheel, Mr Dryden?" Hayden asked him.

"A little, sir. Not to worry. She's very easy on the helm and keeps a true course with the least effort."

"I hope we shall take back our ship and return our crew to their stations by and by. Then I shall have Mr Barthe relieve you of duty for a watch to let you rest."

The man looked entirely grateful and made a quick knuckle, only taking a hand from the wheel for an instant. Hayden was certain that there were many men as tired as Dryden, and felt a wave of guilt that he had spent time in his cot earlier.

"Have we had any more signals from our sister ship, Mr Archer?"

"She acknowledged your request to engage the enem—the *Themis*, to starboard, sir." The usually recumbent Archer stood with a glass in his hand, the signal book tucked into his belt. "I've been watching them for signs of suspicion, sir. An officer does quiz us, now and again, with a glass, but so far I believe they have not penetrated our disguise."

The gun fired forward, a moment of anticipatory silence, and then a cheer from the men on the deck. Hayden turned his glass to their forward quarter and among the strands of fog he found a scene of chaos on the quarterdeck of the *Themis*.

"It would appear that I owe Mr Baldwin half a crown," Hayden observed with satisfaction.

The *Themis'* undamaged stern-chaser lobbed a ball that passed through all of their topsails without doing any other appreciable damage. The *Dragoon's* mizzen topsail, however, tore almost in two.

"Mr Barthe?" Hayden called, barely raising his voice.

"I will see to it, Mr Hayden," the master replied as he came hurrying along the gangway.

They were, ever so slowly, drawing up on the stern quarter of the *Themis*. Hayden could see the mutineers plainly now, and with his glass he could make out their individual faces—drained of colour and filled with apprehension. They set the stunsails in a manner Hayden could only call lubberly, but it did not matter; the *Dragoon* was overhauling her and the mutineers knew it.

"If the *Themis* sheers to larboard, Mr Dryden, we must do the same. We cannot allow them to loose a broadside on us without being able to reply."

"I have my eye on her, Mr Hayden. I won't let a lubber like Stuckey put one over on me."

Muhlhauser was standing by the taffrail to larboard, appearing like a deer about to spring to flight. Hayden realized that the man had placed himself such that the masts were between himself and the cannon fire of the *Themis*. It seemed a little odd to the acting captain that the man from the Ordnance Board, whose function it was to create guns more able to inflict damage and carnage, was so frightened to be on the receiving end of his own creations.

"How fare you, Mr Muhlhauser?" Hayden asked solicitously.

"The ball that struck the deck almost did for me, Mr Hayden. Had I taken another step I would have been in its path, I'm quite certain."

"Ah. Many a sailor can tell a similar story, Mr Muhlhauser. It forces one to contemplate how narrow the river between death and life." Hayden tried to smile in a kindly way. "It occurred to me that a man with your particular knowledge would be of great assistance on the gundeck. I'm sure any of the gun captains would welcome your aid, and we are, as you know, terribly short of able-bodied men."

Muhlhauser nodded. "I shall be happy to do what I can, Mr Hayden." He started away and then stopped. "It takes more nerve to stand on the quarterdeck when the great guns are firing than anyone can know who has not done it." He tipped his hat to Hayden and went briskly down the companionway.

Archer, who stood not far off, also tipped his hat to Hayden. "In the midst of an action, that you would have a kind word for a landsman . . ."

"It is not much of an action," Hayden answered. "Not yet, at least. Mr Archer, is there not, among the prisoners, a man who speaks a little English?"

"You could call it English, Mr Hayden. An officer named Marin-Marie."

"Have Mr Hawthorne dress him in an officer's coat and hat, and bring him onto the quarterdeck with an honour guard of two marines."

With a look of only slight mystification, Archer went in search of Hawthorne, who was assisting the gunners on the forecastle. A few moments later, an apprehensive-looking Frenchman was brought onto the quarterdeck.

"Lieutenant François Marin-Marie," Hawthorne announced. The man before him, slightly plump of face and form, could not have known the scrape of a razor, Hayden thought, for he was a mere boy—no older than Wickham. Even so, he made a graceful bow, and then stared at Hayden with a look of some disdain.

"Why 'ave you brought me 'ere?" he asked in English.

"I have need of your assistance, Lieutenant," Hayden answered in French. He pointed toward the *Themis*. "That is a British ship under the command of British mutineers. They believe your ship is still in possession of the French, which is why we are so dressed." He gestured to his clothes. "It is our intention to take back the ship from the mutineers, but as they are likely to recognize me and others of my crew, I would have you speak to them when we come within hailing distance."

The boy drew himself up. "And why would I do that?" he demanded, in French. "It is no affair of mine."

"Because your treatment when we reach England will depend on how well you have co-operated. It could be a very long war and I myself should not want to spend it in a hulk up some godforsaken backwater, my fate unknown to family and friends."

The boy's armour of disdain cracked a little, and he swallowed noticeably. He glanced around at the Englishmen surrounding him. "And what ship iz zat?" he enquired in English, nodding to the French frigate.

"Captain Bourne's *Tenacious*, under French colours."

Another quick glance at the less-than-friendly faces. "What would you 'ave me say? My English eez . . . poor."

"I will stand behind you and tell you what to say."

A ball struck the hull forward. Their own chase-piece answered. Another cheer from the men.

"Why do you do this?" the boy asked quietly in his own tongue. "You are French. I hear it in your voice."

"My mother was French, Lieutenant. I am an Englishman." Hayden turned away. "Mr Hawthorne? Have your men keep Lieutenant Marin-Marie here, on the quarterdeck, out of everyone's way. Unbind his hands. I will call for him at the appropriate time."

Hayden went to the rail and looked forward. The *Themis* was without her mizzen topsail, which had been shot away. Even with guns traversed to their utmost degree, Hayden was sure they could not strike the mutineers on this point of sail. If they came up a little to bring their broadside to bear, the *Themis* would foot away, and unless their shot managed to bring down some sails, they would have to make up that lost distance. Better to stay their course, and wait until they could fire on this point of sail. A dull crash as the mutineers fired, and a ball touched the top of a wave and skipped off across the ocean, like a spinning stone on a pond.

A small group of sailors had gathered by the quarterdeck barricade, where they were conversing with the marine sentry.

"What's this about, do you think?" Landry, who had found Hayden to report the gun crews standing by, nodded to the men. "Aren't they *Themis* men? I sent them down to the guns."

Hayden saw the sentry glance his way, and walked quickly down the deck, Landry by his side.

"These men are asking permission to speak with you, Captain," the sentry offered as they approached.

"They should all be at their stations," Landry observed pointedly. "What is this about, Lawrence?"

The gunner's mate, Lawrence, made a knuckle, then looked quickly at the five men who accompanied him. One of them nodded, as if to say, *You speak.*

Lawrence, who did not look overly comfortable with his role, glanced down at the deck. "Begging your pardon, Captain. It's just that we believe some of our mates aboard the *Themis* never meant it to go so far . . . to a mutiny, and all." He produced a piece of paper. "Mr Martin writ down their names for us, if you please, sir." He offered the scrap of paper to Hayden, who took it reluctantly.

"What do you expect me to do, Lawrence?"

"Well, sir . . ." He lost his train of thought a moment.

"Speak up, Lawrence. I'm not going to have you flogged, or even stop your grog."

"Well, Mr Hayden," he said in a small, dry voice. "It doesn't sit well with a goodly number of the men to be firing on shipmates who never meant harm to any."

Hayden glanced at the list—about twenty names, he guessed. "Did these men participate in the mutiny or did they not?"

Hawthorne ranged up alongside him, and Barthe appeared behind the gathered men. Reaching over their heads, Hayden passed the list to the sailing master.

"Well, sir," Lawrence stammered, "some participated more than others, but none of them meant to. Samuel Fowler stepped in and saved Roth's life when two of the foretop-men were about to split his pate." The man turned to Roth, who nodded concurrence, apparently. "And the same Samuel Fowler argued against flogging anyone, even Captain Hart, sir, though he got cuffed for it by some of his mates."

Barthe held up the list, pointing at it with a stubby finger. "All of these men were in the thick of it at the end. Palley was one of the men firing his musket into the gunroom. I saw him myself. Mayhap he killed Williams, too. King was—"

Hayden held up a hand. "Mr Barthe . . . We cannot convene a court-martial here." He regarded the men, who looked both unnerved and wretched. "It is not my place to grant anyone a pardon, Lawrence. Nor can I shirk my duty. You all had the good sense and loyalty to the King not to join the mutiny aboard the *Themis*. Do not start down that path now."

Men raised their hands in protest, and Lawrence spoke quickly. "Mr Hayden, we never meant for this to appear in the smallest degree mutinous—"

"Never for a moment did I think that, Lawrence. But let me tell you this: we are woefully short of men and I can excuse no one because of their conscience. You must all take your places at the guns and do your utmost to inflict damage upon men who were not long ago your shipmates . . . my shipmates. I will take this list, and if there is finally a court-martial, I will see that it is given due consideration. You may all have your say then. But today you must fight. There is no choice for any man aboard."

The Jacks all looked one to the other, faces drawn and lined from their suffering.

Lawrence gazed down at the deck, and nodded. "Aye, Mr Hayden, but it is a dark day. A miserable, dark day."

"So it is, Lawrence," Hayden replied. "Return to your places now, and no more will be said of this matter."

The men hung their heads, made quick knuckles, and turned to go down to the gun-deck.

Hayden watched them go, wondering how keenly they would fight if it came to that—which it almost certainly would. With this in mind, he crossed to the young French lieutenant, who stood at the taffrail, feigning indifference to both events and danger.

"Monsieur," Hayden said, touching his hat. "We shall stage a little play for these mutineers once we are within hailing distance, and you shall play the principal role—the only man aboard this French ship of war who speaks English." He addressed the two marines who guarded him. "Take him below. We can't afford to lose him to English fire, can we?"

"Monsieur," the man addressed him quietly in his own language. "You have made a mistake, taking the side of the English. But it is not too late. The French navy would embrace you. Find a way to release my crew mates; let us take back our ship, and you shall be a hero to your true country. You deceive yourself, *Capitaine*; in your heart you are a man of France. Look at you . . . Are you not more comfortable in that uniform than in your threadbare English lieutenant's jacket?"

"Take him below," Hayden said again, but as the man reached the companionway, he glanced back over his shoulder, a knowing look on his face. Hayden stood a moment, forgetting what he had been about, his hands finding the fabric of his crimson jacket.

A discharge of flame and smoke from the French frigate caught his attention. They were almost within range now, and their bow-chaser lobbed a ball that landed not far short of the *Themis*. That would give the mutineers pause, he thought; two French frigates chasing, and they with less than half a crew.

The *Themis* fired her stern gun at that moment, and sent an iron ball howling among the men at work in the rigging.

"Mr Landry. Pass the word to the forward gunner; tell him to load with chain shot and aim up into her rigging, if you please."

"I will, Mr Hayden." Landry found a middy to run his order forward; some of the reefers served on the quarterdeck in action to carry orders to disparate parts of the ship.

Wickham chose that moment to shout aloft in French, and Hayden called out in answer. He was not at all certain their voices would carry to the *Themis*, but the distance between the ships was growing small. Best to keep the ruse alive.

Wickham then pointed at *La Rochelle*, now near enough that she was emerging from the mists. A shaft of sunlight brightened her sails, and threw her black hull into relief against a tract of jade-green sea. "She is overhauling us now that we've had some sail shot away, Mr Hayden."

"Yes, I think she will catch the *Themis* almost as we do." Hayden turned to find his first lieutenant. "Mr Landry, I think we should steer to come right up alongside the *Themis*, load our deck-guns with grape, fire a broadside, grapple, and board her."

Landry considered a moment. "What about your English-speaking Frenchman?"

"I will have him call out for their surrender as we draw near. If they refuse we will board. There will be time to fire one broadside as we bear up alongside, then the men at the guns must take up their arms and join us on deck."

"Aye, sir. Shall I put Wickham on the gun-deck?"

"I would keep him with me, if I could. It will aid our cause to have orders shouted in French. Mr Archer shall have command of the gun-deck, and turn the signals over to Wickham." He turned to find the converted middy. "Mr Wickham? Did you hear?"

"Aye, sir."

The signal book was dutifully passed from Archer to Wickham, and Landry and the second lieutenant repaired to the gun-deck, from where Landry appeared but a few moments later.

Shot from the *Themis* continued to do small amounts of damage, but Bourne's gunners at the forward chase-piece were far more deadly. Hayden actually found himself a bit chagrined that his own men were so deficient—the result of Hart exercising his guns so infrequently, and firing them in anger never. He wondered how the captain fared—flogged by his own men. Hayden couldn't think of another incident like it. When word of it reached England great infamy would befall the *Themis*, her crew, and officers.

Hayden wondered if this was not what was driving him to attempt this mad venture—retaking the *Themis*, with a French frigate a few cable-lengths away. If he returned to England with the mutineers in irons, and the *Themis* again under the British flag, there was some paltry chance he might save his career. He glanced down at his French uniform. If Philip Stephens could see him now. So much for becoming Hart's nurse-maid. He could also put paid to the notion that the First Secretary would become his patron!

"This ship is a flyer, sir," Wickham pronounced from atop the rail, where he clung to the shrouds.

"Mr Wickham," Hayden responded, "I do appreciate your exuberance, but if you fall into the sea the French signal book will surely be lost. If you please, sir . . ."

Wickham leapt down from the rail, landing with a thump on bare planks.

"Is it not a curious and ironic fact, sir, that we came to sea to fight the French and here we are on a French ship, dressed as French officers, about to engage the English?"

"Exceedingly curious. Mr Dryden?" He turned to the man at the helm. "How fare you, sir?"

"Well enough, Captain," he said, one of the few who appeared to use the title without any hint of the self-conscious.

"Captain Bourne's gunners seem to be shooting away the *Themis'* rigging as quickly as it can be renewed, so we are gaining rather handsomely, I note. What I want you to do is come up on her stern quarter, but be prepared to luff if she attempts to do so. Come up on her stern quarter, then simply run us alongside."

The master's mate pulled his eye from the *Themis* for a second to glance quizzically at Hayden. "Carrying all this sail, sir?"

"Aye, the sea is small and we are barely making four knots as it is. We shall take some fire from their chase-stern, but we will have to endure it. Once alongside, no doubt, both ships shall fire a broadside, but then it will be cutlasses and pistols. It is possible we might convince them to surrender, unless they realize we are terribly undermanned or are not what we appear. But that will not change our tactics, we shall run our ship alongside even so. Is that perfectly understood?"

"It is, sir."

Hayden stood upon the quarterdeck with Landry and Wickham, watching the slow convergence of ships on the great, foggy sea. The small wind on their stern quarter appeared to be taking off, slowing the ships even more. Hayden ordered the crew fed, one gun crew at a time. Then a few men from the upper deck, followed by a few others. He, Landry, and Wickham would not leave the deck and plates were brought to them where they stood, which they addressed without ceremony or even much notice of what they ate.

The sun lifted and arced westward, but the snowy fog appeared to resist its warmth, and still clung to the sea in silvery patches. As they neared the *Themis*, her stern guns began to cause more damage and put everyone on deck and aloft into a state of nervous apprehension.

Tristram Stock appeared on the quarterdeck, having traversed the gangway at a brisk, purposeful trot. "If you please, Captain Hayden, the chase-gun captain asks permission to fire at the stern guns on the *Themis*."

"That seems a good bet, given his recent record. Carry him my permission, Mr Stock, but tell him also that I regret I cannot give him another half-crown if he succeeds."

Stock smiled. "He has been telling everyone about his 'half-crown shot.' He was very pleased about it."

"I'm sure he was, but I cannot be giving out half a crown to every gun captain who makes a lucky shot."

"You needn't worry, sir, the men have their prize money, and very content with it they are." Stock touched his hat and hurried forward.

The bow-chaser began a relentless cannonade of the *Themis'* stern, Bourne's gun-crew putting on a display of both accuracy and rapidity of fire. The stern gallery was soon a ruin and the quarterdeck a place of great danger. It became difficult to see through the clouds of smoke enveloping the stern of the mutineer's vessel and the bow of their own, but the guns finally fell silent on the *Themis* to a cheer from the men.

A solemn Perse delivered Hayden his pistols and cutlass. "Have you a station, Perse?"

"Mr Landry sent me down to run powder," the boy answered in his soft Irish brogue, "though I'm as strong as some who man the guns, sure."

"We all play the part asked of us and do not protest."

"I was not protesting, Mr Hayden . . . well, not much." The boy gave him a small bow, and slipped away.

Hayden pulled his sword from its scabbard and was pleased to find it polished to a high sheen.

"*Cultellus*," Hawthorne observed from two yards distant.

"Pardon me?" Hayden responded.

"Latin, sir. The word from which *cutlass* was derived. *Cultellus*."

Hayden smiled. "Your scholarship is a constant source of inspiration, Mr Hawthorne."

The marine laughed, as did Hayden.

"I hope to drive my *cultellus* into the arrogant throat of Mr William Stuckey," Hayden said.

"Do you find his throat arrogant?"

"Terribly. Do you not?"

"Not so much as his hair."

"Ah. Your marines are ready?"

"That they are, Captain." Hawthorne paused and met Hayden's eye. "I must tell you, Mr Hayden, it gives me great pleasure to call you *captain*."

"I am only a prize-captain, Mr Hawthorne, and with my prospects, you shall be addressing me as *lieutenant* by week's end."

"Captain Hayden, sir?" Dryden said from his place at the wheel. "I'm almost ready to bring her up, sir."

Hayden looked forward, the two ships were converging, and although the expert fire from the *Tenacious'* gunners had silenced the stern guns of the *Themis*, the crack of musket fire began in earnest. Hawthorne's own men returned fire from the tops and from the forecastle.

"Have a care, Mr Dryden. Do not run our jib-boom into their stern or tangle it in the mizzen shrouds."

"Baldwin is to alert me if I come too near, Captain."

Hayden turned to the marine lieutenant. "Have Monsieur Marin-Marie brought on deck, if you please, Mr Hawthorne."

Twenty-two

At the last possible moment, Baldwin leapt up onto the gun-truck and waved a shirt to Dryden, who spun his wheel. The ship began a sluggish turn. Before them, Hayden could see the mutineers, armed and stripped to the waist, watching them with a mixture of outrage and dire apprehension. The second French frigate, *La Rochelle*, ceased to fire, as she was afraid of striking what she believed was another vessel of her own service. Even with her guns silenced, she was quickly ranging up to a position where she might unload her entire broadside into the *Themis*, and the mutineers could not have been insensible to it.

"Now, Monsieur Marin-Marie," Hayden said to the prisoner, "repeat every word just as I say, and no tricks or Mr MacPherson will be obliged to put a blade in you. *Do you understand?*"

The Frenchman nodded once.

Hayden then turned to the others. "Not a word of English, now. And Mr Stock, kindly step behind the gunners, there, where you shan't be recognized." Hayden himself made a screen of Marin-Marie and the *Tenacious*' gun-crew.

"You do realize that we both wear the uniform of a *capitaine*?" the Frenchman observed softly.

"These cullies will never know the difference. Mr Baldwin, can you bring your gun to bear upon that carronade?"

The man made a saluting motion, strictly observing the order to speak no English. He dug his Samson's bar into the deck, and in quick little stages, pried the carriage to the right as far as it would go. Even so, it did not bear on the carronade, quite, but they would not now be killed by the carronade before they could fire. Hayden could see only a few men on the deck of the *Themis*—the rest certainly remained below at the great guns.

Hayden took hold of Marin-Marie's shoulder. "Now, as loud as you can: 'Surrender your ship. We know you have less than half a crew. Haul down your colours or we will board.' "

Marin-Marie played his part better than Hayden expected, his tone bold and commanding. And the words were not without impact. Mutineers on the quarterdeck began a fierce argument, but there was so little time.

One of the men—Jarvis—broke away from the group and came to the rail. "We are English mutineers," he called through cupped hands, though the distance between the ships could be measured in yards. "We have removed our officers and wish to take our ship into Brest Harbour. We wish to join you. Do you understand? Join the revolution . . ."

"Say: 'Lay down your weapons and we will talk,' " Hayden whispered to Marin-Marie.

"Lay down your weapons, monsieur, and we will parley," the French officer called. Then aside to Hayden in French, "Pardon, monsieur, I said *parley*."

But Hayden did not care. He could see the carronade coming to bear, the men bent over it. He knew the Jack who held the firing lanyard—a sailmaker's mate named Dalford Black, his bald head shining with sweat. There was indecision on the *Themis*, no agreement on a course of action . . . and then it was decided.

"And find ourselves in a French gaol?" cried one of the mutineers. "Not in this life!"

Hayden found the big landsman, Stuckey, among the crowd, just as he levelled a pistol and fired. Marin-Marie spun around and stumbled to the deck, clutching his arm.

"Fire," Hayden said to Baldwin, and the gun, hot from its work, jumped, blasting a section of the *Themis*' bulwark to splinters. "Off the fo'c'sle," Hayden ordered, pushing men before him and pulling Marin-Marie to his feet.

"Take him to the doctor," Hayden ordered the marines.

The carronade fired at that instant, showering them with splinters, but they were out of its direct line.

"Fire as she bears," Hayden said to Tristram Stock, who turned and gave the prearranged signal to a man standing on the gangway. The order passed below and to the gun crews on the quarterdeck. Hayden then drew his sword, raised it high, and repeated the same words loudly in French.

Below, the first gun fired, shaking the deck and splitting the air. The *Themis* replied, and at such short range the report was terrible. Smoke ballooned up from between the hulls and hid the enemy. Through the cloud, musket fire fell, striking randomly. A ball found the blade of Hayden's sword and sent it clattering to the deck, but he swept it up, apparently undamaged.

Sail-handlers began letting go sheets, and down-hauls brought stay-sails rippling deckward. Upper yards were lowered so that sails hung in their gear, and the main and foresail were quickly brailed up to be clear of fire. It was a neat job, handled by the *Tenacious*' crewmen, and those aloft came hand-over-hand down the stays to take up arms.

The boarding party mustered on the gangway and quarterdeck. Hayden could not count them in the smoke, but he climbed up on the rail as grapnels were thrown aboard the *Themis*. There he found himself staring at men he had served with hardly more than a day before—Jarvis, Clark, Freeman, and a gunner's mate named Pool.

As each of the great guns came to bear, both ships fired almost at once, smoke blasting up on a wave of heat, the crash of splintering timbers deafening. There was soon no way an order could be heard as the two ships fired away at each other from a distance measured in feet. Men began falling in earnest on the deck, and Hayden drew one of his pistols and, through the smoke, found himself staring at William Pool—a kindly man who had invariably treated Hayden with respect. Pool raised a pistol, his look startled, and Hayden killed him with its single shot.

The collision of the two ships propelled Hayden across the distance created by the vessels' tumble-home. A heel caught up in the hammock netting and he landed awkwardly almost atop Pool, who had been thrown down in an unmoving tangle of limbs. Scrambling up, Hayden realized that the only reason he lived was that there were so few men on the *Themis*' deck. But then they came streaming up from below, having fired their guns once.

His own crew came over the barricades and Hayden was, immediately, in the thick of it.

"We'll not be taken by any poxy Frenchmen!" a man yelled and ran at Hayden with a pike.

Throwing himself aside, Hayden felt the pike tear away the shoulder of his coat. He slashed horribly at the man's throat, but cut across both his eyes instead. As the man fell, Hayden was beset by yet another. The mutineers fought with a fierce desperation, but the outrage of their former victims quickly equalled it. For a time the fighting see-sawed back and forth, but the mutineers' surprise at finding they battled not Frenchmen but their former mates shook them a little. Slowly the exhausted Hayden began to realize they were pressing the attack. Mutineers retreated along the gangways, some leaping down to the gun-deck.

"Mr Hawthorne!" Hayden called, finding the marine but two yards distant. "We must secure the magazines."

Hawthorne nodded, and began gathering a small party around him. Hayden ran along the gangway, sweeping up a group of men in his wake. They jumped down onto the gun-deck, where they found a scene of terrible ruin and death, the smell of smoke and blood thick in the air.

As they approached the companionway, mutineers came pounding up the ladder. Hayden and his party threw themselves down behind the great guns as firearms were discharged and lead balls cracked and rang against iron and wood. Before the mutineers could reload, Hayden led

his men in a charge. The mutineers retreated to the top of the companionway, but there made a stand, fighting with a savage abandon, hardly
taking notice of wounds.

"There you are, Franklin Douglas," one of Hayden's men called. "I
owe you this, you bastard." And he stretched out the mutineer Douglas
with a single blow.

Fearing his men were pressed back, Hayden found his second pistol
and shot the most ferocious adversary—a topman named Michaels. His
ball caught the man in the mouth, and toppled him down the ladder in
a slump. The mutineers held their ground a moment more, then broke
and fled below. Hesitantly, Hayden went down the steps—crouched to
look into the dark corners, expecting at any second to be shot—but the
mutineers had retreated or lay on the deck. The sound of fighting had
ceased from all points. A strange, ominous silence pervaded the ship. A
group of his own men from the *Dragoon* appeared in the midshipmen's
berth and signalled all-clear.

Hayden led his men down onto the orlop-deck and the half-sunken
magazine, which he found swaddled in wet blankets against sparks. It was
nearly dark here, but a little glow spilled out a square of glass in the
light-room door, which had been so placed to provide illumination for
the powder-monkeys.

The magazine door hung slightly ajar, and Hayden tugged it open a
crack. Inside, lit by the stained glow emanating through the light-room
glass, he could see one man, hunched in pain. The boy-giant Giles
leaned heavily against the wall, one hand pressed to his side, the other
holding a pistol aimed down into an open powder barrel. Around him,
illuminated by the faint light, slowly swirled a fine cloud of motes—
powder dust.

"Giles . . ." Hayden said, trying to keep his voice soft and reasonable.
"What is it you do?"

The boy could not hide his surprise. "Mr Hayden? Is that you, sir?"

Hayden pressed the door open a few more inches so the two could
see each other. Giles was contorted in terrible pain, he could see, his face
pasty and slick with sweat.

"It is, Giles. Stay calm, now."

"Have you gone over to the French, sir?"

"Not at all, Giles," Hayden said, trying to keep all fear out of his voice, though his mouth and throat were parched. "I am sailing the French prize we took at Belle Île and have dressed as a Frenchman to confuse the enemy. We found the *Themis'* officers and some crew adrift in boats."

"They came to no harm, then?"

"None at all," Hayden said cheerfully, and smiled. "Mr Barthe told me that you did not join in the mutiny but Stuckey would not let you come away in the boats. He will say as much at the court-martial, and Mr Hawthorne will declare the same, for so he told me. You may put the pistol down. You will go free, I'm sure."

The boy shook his head, and in the saddest tone said, "Not the likes of me, Mr Hayden. Me they'll hang. Look what they did to McBride, and he wasn't even guilty . . ."

Hayden did not like the way this was said—as though Giles knew McBride was innocent. "But you didn't kill Penrith," Hayden stated firmly. "Stuckey was lying."

For a moment it looked as though the boy would weep, his gaze falling away. "I didn't mean it to go that way, Mr Hayden. I thought I could put a scare in him—get him to take me name off the petition—Stuckey told me I would hang for signing it—but Penrith pulled a knife . . ."

"And you let McBride hang for it . . ." Hayden said without thinking, appalled.

"He was a lying fucking landsman. No one mourned when he went up."

With difficulty, Hayden hid his revulsion. "Put the pistol up, Giles. You'll kill everyone aboard, yourself included."

"I'm shot through the gut, Mr Hayden. Blood and shit are leaking out of my arse." For a second he closed his eyes. The hand holding the pistol began to tremble perceptibly.

"I've seen the doctor patch up worse."

The boy shook his head. "Tell your men to lay down their arms, Mr Hayden, or I'll blow the *Themis* to flinders."

"You killed Penrith by accident, and you've been tortured by it ever since; I can see that. Are you really willing to murder two hundred?"

"I'm damned to hell already. What'll a few more murders mean on my ledger?"

Hayden saw him feel the lock with his thumb, assuring himself the gun was cocked.

"Giles . . . ?" came a soft voice from behind.

Hayden turned to find a gaunt and ghostly Aldrich making his way stiffly through the clot of men at Hayden's back. Every motion caused him agony, Hayden could see, but his eye was clear and determined. Stepping aside, Hayden let him pass, as though he were a superior officer. He almost reached for his hat.

"Haven't we had enough killing? We never intended this when we talked of sailing to America." Aldrich pulled the low door gently open and then slumped down to sit with his feet on the inside step, leaning heavily against the frame, hardly able to support himself.

"Mr Aldrich . . ." the boy said, and tears began to slip down his cheeks. "We are all dead men anyway . . ."

"Not all," Aldrich said softly, his voice filled with sadness, disappointment. "Not Mr Hayden or Mr Wickham, here. Not any number of your shipmates. I am not dead . . . yet." He held out his hand. "There's been enough killing among our own people, Giles."

The boy began to sob, his hand shaking terribly. A thrust of pain doubled him over and he cried out.

"I'm sorry, Mr Aldrich . . . but this is what was agreed to. I swore to fire the powder if our ship were taken. We'll all hang if I don't . . ."

Hayden realized that the sounds of fighting had ceased. A hollow, eerie silence pervaded the ship. Of an instant, he expected the silence would be shattered by an explosion more terrible than any he had witnessed, and Charles Saunders Hayden would depart this life.

Giles closed his eyes again from the pain. And Aldrich stepped silently forward, a pale hand reaching for the gun.

Hayden plunged into the magazine after the seaman.

Aldrich grabbed the gun, but Hayden knew that in his weakened state he was no match for Giles.

Clenching his fist, Hayden drove it into Giles' abdomen, doubling the boy over. He grabbed the giant with both hands and hauled him bodily out of the magazine, Aldrich still clinging tenaciously. They tumbled down in a heap and Hayden searched for the gun in the tangle, but Aldrich rolled free, lying still, exhausted, the pistol in hand, resting across his chest.

Someone had the sense to shut the magazine door. Hayden pushed the boy off him and scrambled to his knees.

Giles lay twisted, his shoulders heaving. Crouching quickly, Wickham rolled the giant over where he convulsed terribly, eyes rolled back. But then he lay still, releasing a long, slow sigh, as though he had found some unexpected satisfaction in the last second of his life.

"Aldrich? Are you hurt?" Hayden asked.

The man shook his head, paused, then nodded. He began to weep, releasing the pistol so that it bumped gently to the floor. He covered his eyes and rolled onto his side, his flayed back coming to view.

No one knew what to say, but stood mutely, embarrassed, moved by the grief of this man they all respected. It was a hard but brief squall, and then Aldrich staggered to his feet, wiping away tears with callused fingers. Men jumped forward to assist him.

"That was a great chance you took, Aldrich," Hayden said.

"I jammed my finger behind the trigger, Mr Hayden. He nearly crushed it, but the gun would not fire."

"It was a brave thing to do, and but for it we might all be dead." Hayden could see Aldrich was swaying on his feet. "Please take Mr Aldrich back to the sick-berth. And ask the doctor to attend him as soon as he is able." Like the crew, Hayden found himself calling Aldrich "Mr."

Hayden set three men as sentries over the magazine, climbed the stair, and made his way aft along the berth-deck. Near the gunroom he met Hawthorne emerging from the aft companionway.

"Have you secured the magazine, Mr Hawthorne?"

"I have, Mr Hayden, and an easy task it was, as there was no one near it."

"You've left some men you trust to stand sentry over it, I suppose?"

"So I have." The marine's hair was glued to his forehead from sweat, and one hand was wrapped in a crude bandage.

"Then will you take a company of men and search all the decks from stem to stern, and chase out any rats still hiding or they might do us some mischief yet."

"I will, sir."

Hayden returned to the deck, only to be met by a French officer climbing over the rail, naked sword in hand. The *Themis* men all stood about in dumb bewilderment. Thrusting down his sheer surprise, Hayden reached into his pocket, tore out a handkerchief, clapped it over his mouth, and said loudly in French: "Monsieur! Monsieur! You must not board this ship. These English have the fever, the yellow fever. That is why they are only half a crew; all the rest are dead. Get off! Get off!" He waved his free hand to chase the man from the deck. "Back into your boat—immediately!"

The officer hesitated only a second while his startled brain caught up with the meaning of the words being shouted at him, and then he scrambled over the rail, chasing the men who followed him back down the ladder.

Hayden went to the bulwark, and looked down at the Frenchmen in their boats.

"The fever," they were saying. "They have the fever." And these words galvanized them, set them to flight in a clumsy scramble of backing oars and thumping hulls.

As the lead boat cleared the *Themis*' stern, Hayden heard a lone voice call out in French. "They are English! You must listen. It is a ruse. They are English!" And then the voice was muffled. Hayden turned to find Marin-Marie being hauled bodily from the rail of the *Dragoon*, though he clung tenaciously to the shrouds.

"Return that madman to the doctor!" Hayden shouted in French. "Have we not enough troubles without his foolish delusions?" Hayden turned to the French officer. "We will do what we can here, and then tow the English ship into a quarantine berth. Will you go ahead and alert the harbour authorities so that no boats approach us, please?"

"Will you not require our assistance?" the officer called out, standing up in the stern sheets of his boat.

"No, thank you, Lieutenant. We will manage. I only hope you have not carried this terrible fever away with you."

Hayden thought he could see the man go pale even at that distance.

"Good luck to you," the man called, found his seat, and ordered his boat swiftly on.

"Mon Capitaine," Wickham addressed him in French. "What are your orders?"

"Round up the English prisoners, and separate the sick from the healthy. The wounded English must be kept apart from our wounded. Let their own doctor attend them." Hayden's eye found Mr Barthe. "We must make repairs and prepare to tow the prize into Brest." And then quietly in English: "We must repair the two ships, Mr Barthe, but not before night-fall. It is my intention to slip away as soon as darkness is complete."

Hayden looked around the deck for the first time. It was a scene of shocking carnage, dead and wounded lying in grisly tableaux here and there. A few cowed-looking mutineers, clutching bloody wounds, were held by Hawthorne's marines and armed seamen. Archer moved among the prostrate men with a pair of midshipmen, terribly dividing the dead from the living.

Ascertaining the distance to the French boats, Hayden spoke quietly in English: "What are our losses, Mr Landry? Do we know?"

"Mr Archer is making the tally, sir." The first lieutenant hesitated, his demeanour disintegrating a little, but then he mastered himself. "I fear it will be a terrible butcher's bill, sir. There aren't twenty mutineers left alive, and I dare say, they are all wounded, for they fought until they were killed or we subdued them. Not a one laid down his weapons of his own doing."

"They didn't intend to be taken prisoner—by anyone. We interrupted Giles, about to fire the magazine."

Landry ran his fingers back into his hair, this bit of news shaking him utterly. "And I felt lucky to have survived the fight . . ."

Hayden glanced up. "If you please, Mr Landry, send men aloft to quiet those sails or they shall flog themselves to rags."

Landry reached for the hat he'd lost in the fight, and then went rushing off.

With the *Dragoon* grappled to her larboard side, the *Themis* had swung slowly so that the wind now lay on her beam, causing her sails to slat about in their gear. Fortunately, both sea and wind were small.

Wounded were borne past to the doctor still aboard the *Dragoon*. A knot of sullen mutineers had been assembled just off the quarterdeck, and every few minutes another of their kind was added, flushed out of some hiding place below. Splinters lay everywhere, and the rigging hung in tatters.

"Captain Hayden!" The rather urgent tone of Wickham's voice interrupted his assessment of damages. Hayden found the acting lieutenant, not surprisingly, standing at the stern rail with a glass held up to his eye.

"The French captain still has his ship hove-to, and he's signalling, sir."

Hayden shaded his eyes and regarded the ship, which was not nearly as distant as he would have liked. "What has become of our signal book, Mr Wickham?"

"I'll fetch it, sir." In a moment, Wickham returned, quickly thumbing through the open signal book. "Here it is!" He jabbed a finger triumphantly at the page. "It is the signal for 'standing by to provide assistance.'"

"Damned interfering Frenchman," Hayden heard Hawthorne mutter, which expressed Hayden's sentiments with precision.

"Shall I make an answer, sir?" Wickham asked.

"Just acknowledge the signal. Set a man to keep watch on the French frigate, as well. I should like to think that they are only being helpful, but that damned Marin-Marie might have kindled some doubt in their minds—perhaps some little detail that struck them as being false, as being 'un-French.'" Hayden swept his eyes over the scene, wondering what it could have been.

But he had no time to dwell on that, or on the French ship hove-to nearby.

"Pass the word," he said. "No shouting from the tops or from the deck. Sounds can travel a great distance over water, as you all well know. Mr Barthe, you will have to make do with quiet commands or by sending men aloft with your orders."

Mr Barthe saluted.

"Mr Hawthorne, I think our mutineers deserve to be in irons."

To which Hawthorne grinned and nodded.

Hayden strode quickly forward. "When you are quite finished there, Mr Archer, we must see to the gun-deck. Men still lie there—too many—though I fear they have all departed this life."

A grim-looking second lieutenant glanced up at him. "Aye, Mr Hayden," he answered softly.

"Where is our carpenter?"

"In the hold, Captain," Stock reported.

"Just the man I'm looking for. Mr Stock, jump over to the *Dragoon*, if you please, and learn if she is making water."

The boy set off at a run.

On the gangway, Hayden stared down onto the gun-deck, and found Chettle emerging from below. "What is the verdict, Mr Chettle? Do we sink or swim?"

"Swim, sir, for the moment. There's a terrible mass of damage, Mr Hayden: smashed planking, hanging knees blown to splinters, cracked frames, and the like. But she's making very little water, all the same."

"All above the waterline, then. Have you seen to the *Dragoon*?"

The man squinted up at him. "I shall slide over there and have a look, Mr Hayden."

"I have sent Mr Stock to find if she's making water, but I would hear your more expert opinion."

Chettle made a knuckle, and then, followed by his mates, wormed his way stiffly out one of the shattered gunports and into the ship lying alongside. Hayden went down onto the gun-deck to take stock of the damage himself, but found it difficult to see anything for the carnage.

The two ships had been firing at each other from a few yards, and it looked it. Many of the gunports had been blasted and the rest ripped off in the collision. But the damage was not quite as bad as he had expected. The ship could be made more or less watertight. Enough to allow them to sail for England.

Wickham dropped down from the gangway, and could not hide his reaction to the sight.

"Where is Mr Franks, Wickham? Aloft?"

"He was taken to see the doctor, Mr Hayden."

"Not too bad a hurt, I hope?"

"I don't know, sir. I only just learned it myself from Holbek."

"I shall have to stand in for Mr Franks as best I can."

Hayden divided the crew, putting Landry, Barthe, and Archer on the *Themis*, while he did what he could with one of Franks' mates, a handful of able seamen, and an only slightly larger group of landsmen and ordinaries. The two ships were pulled apart to stop them from thudding heavily together and to allow the hulls to be crudely repaired. A shortage of skilled seamen and the relentless westering of the sun meant the work could not be done to Hayden's standards, but they had to slip away that night before any other French ships happened upon them. Hayden was not sure his yellow-fever bluff would work twice.

The sea, which had been almost calm, developed a noticeable lump originating from the south-west. A chill air reached them as a smoky grey spread from the western horizon across the clear blue vault.

"Pass the word for Mr Wickham, if you please." Hayden sent a ship's boy to find his only lieutenant.

A moment later, Wickham appeared, his overlarge uniform shifting about him oddly as he hurried along.

"There is a gale in the air, Mr Wickham, and the weather-glass appears to agree. Find the gunner and be sure all the guns are double-breeched where possible, and where the repairs will not allow it, lashed alongside. Coverings for all but the fore-hatch. We shall only have time to house the top-gallant masts, but the yards must be sent down. Lower the crossjack-yard. We shall double up tacks and braces, rig relieving tackles to the tiller, preventer braces to larboard on the lower yards." Hayden stopped to run through his mental list.

"Heave in the boats, sir?" Wickham prompted.

"That, too. And the topsail yard parrel was contrived by a landsman; be sure it is well slushed, for we haven't time to make it anew."

"We'll never have time to complete all the repairs before the gale strikes."

"I fear you're right." Hayden thought a moment. "Go down to the French prisoners with some marines, if you please, Mr Wickham. Find out if their carpenter and bosun and any of their mates are still among the living. We will release them under Mr Hawthorne's care. Better to have a skilled French seaman doing the job than a lubberly marine, who will be put to better use watching over them. I would let some of these prisoners up on the deck, a few at a time, for they have not had air the whole day, but that damned French ship is still too near."

Wickham left Hayden gazing out over a darkening sea. He consulted the weather-glass again and found it still falling. Men were taken off the hull repairs and scrambled aloft with paunch and thrum mats. Rounding was made up to guard against chafe, and the upper yards sent down in a seamanlike fashion, the men from the *Tenacious* working as efficient teams hardly in need of an order.

As the daylight waned, a boat came off from the French frigate, now at some distance, and made its way over a dull sea. Careful not to fall downwind, a surprisingly mature lieutenant stood in the stern sheets.

"*Capitaine,*" he called from just within hailing distance. "My *capitaine* asks if you have the materials to make repairs, and if your doctor has all the medical supplies he will need."

"Carry my most sincere gratitude to your captain, monsieur," Hayden answered in French, "but we will certainly make do with what we have. It is better if you do not come near. Many men have died of the fever on the English ship." Hayden pointed toward the distant coastline. "The Rade de Brest is not far."

"A gale is nearing, Capitaine. Your hull was much damaged by the English. You should get under way as soon as you can make sail."

"That we will, monsieur. That we will."

It seemed for a moment that the man would say more; he waved. "*Bonne chance, capitaine.* May God be with you." He found his seat and, to Hayden's horror, he ordered his coxswain over to the *Themis.* Too late, Hayden realized he should have called out that the English ship was well provided for as well, but now the man rowed nearer to the *Themis* and asked the same question.

Archer appeared at the rail and answered in French that they were making repairs and warned them to keep their distance due to fever.

The man in the ship cupped his hands to his mouth and shouted louder, a volume calculated to carry over the rising wind. "*Non, monsieur.* I inquired if you had the materials you needed to complete your repairs and if your doctor required any medicines that we might possess."

"We will make do, monsieur," Archer called, but not too loudly. "*Merci.* You are very kind."

Hayden breathed a sigh of relief. At a distance, and against the background of rising wind and sea, Archer's voice had been difficult to make out—enough to hide his imperfect accent, Hayden hoped. But then he saw the French lieutenant conferring intensely with his coxswain.

Hayden called for his glass, and found the French lieutenant, bent near to the other man. "Pass the word for Mr Wickham, if you please," he whispered to Tristram Stock.

A moment later the acting lieutenant appeared at his side.

"Mr Wickham, I fear we have been found out. Gather every man we can spare from the hull repairs and prepare to make sail. Bring aboard all stagings. Fire a gun and run signals aloft for the *Themis*—British signals. We must get under way at once."

Wickham did not wait to ask questions, but tore down the aft companionway, the soles of his shoes beating to quarters.

In a moment, men came padding onto the deck, but not nearly enough. Planks used for stages by the caulkers and carpenters were hauled aboard and thumped on the gangways.

The ship was hove-to under much-reduced sail—just enough to ease her motion—an aid to the men working aloft. Getting under way with such a small crew was laborious and slow. Hayden himself helped shift the yards, heaving on the braces, one eye on the French boat making its way over the rising sea. Darkness was closing in quickly, aided by gunpowder-black clouds.

Yards were squared and what sail they could prudently set, filled. The motion of the ship changed as she began to gather way.

"North-west by north, Mr Wickham."

"Aye, sir. I wonder if one of us shouldn't glance below, Mr Hayden? The hull repairs are not finished, and I fear we will be taking on water."

"I will do that, Mr Wickham. Have the pumps manned immediately."

Hayden took a last look at the distant French ship. The boat, all but invisible on the darkening sea, had almost reached her. He could see the white oars flashing among the pale horses.

In the gathering dusk he clambered down a makeshift companionway ladder, and found himself in near-darkness, lanterns swinging here and there, or being held aloft by boys to illuminate some particular place a cursing carpenter was working.

"Captain on deck," someone announced, and the men who did not have both hands full touched foreheads quickly. He had kept Chettle aboard the *Dragoon*, because her lighter structure had resulted in greater damage. A Frenchman, presumably a carpenter, was gesturing dramatically and speaking his own tongue at speed.

"I don't know anything about any damned *lay toop*," Chettle was answering, his tone not kindly.

"What seems to be the trouble, Mr Chettle?"

"This bloody Frenchman—begging your pardon, sir. This Frenchman, God bless his black papist heart, is shouting something that we can't fathom, sir."

Hayden addressed the Frenchman in his own tongue. Hayden almost laughed when the man finished.

"Well, I'm happy the man was only making a jest," Chettle grumbled.

Hayden turned to the carpenter. "He says your oakum—*l'étupe*—is driven too hard, and when the planks swell it will be pressed out."

"Mr Swinburn has been a caulker these twenty year, sir; I think he knows his business. He did drive it very hard, sir, but these particular planks were near green and won't swell enough to notice. We then payed with pitch and spiked batons over the seams. On the berth-deck we did the same, but we laid tarred canvas over the new planks and then batons over—an unholy mess, sir, but the best method under the circumstances. Plugs simply would not answer in some places, for the two ships being so close the damage was very great. She will seep a little, Mr Hayden, until the dry planks take up. Then I reckon she'll be as tight as any ship can be, given the time and materials at hand."

"As long as she'll see us through the gale."

Chettle gave something between a nod and a shrug in answer, which did not fill Hayden with confidence.

Quickly, he went down to the berth-deck, holding aloft a lantern. Half an inch of water was sloshing across the deck and water seeped in around the few plugs every time the boat began to lift to a sea.

"If this water on the deck increases, we will have to address it, Mr Chettle. Even a few inches of moving water can present a danger to a ship's stability."

Quickly, Hayden walked around the deck, examining what could be seen. The repairs had largely been effected to the outside of the hull, though shattered frames—roughly sistered—could be clearly seen. The work was crude, but Hayden thought it adequate.

They descended to the orlop and into the makeshift sick-berth. Hayden found his way among the swinging cots to find the hull untouched but water dripping down between the shrunken planks of the deck above. Buckets were scattered about to catch the drizzle, some hanging from the deckhead, but even so, the deck beneath was wet, and sailcloth awnings had been rigged over some of the cots.

"Can nothing be done about this water, Mr Hayden?" Griffiths enquired.

"She'll take up yet, Doctor," Chettle answered for Hayden. "Don't you worry."

"I believe Mr Chettle is right, Doctor. The wood will swell as it becomes soaked with water and the seams will grow tight. Until then, I will send men with moppats and buckets."

"Let us pray this swelling does not take all night," the doctor replied. "Are we in for a gale?"

"I'm afraid we are. How goes your work?"

Griffiths had made his way closer, and now said quietly: "All the worst is over, but we have so many wounded, with all the mutineers as well. Even with two surgeons—and Dr Bordaleau is very competent, especially with a bone-saw and amputating knife—we have all we can manage. More, in truth."

"We are all taxed to our limits at this moment. I have a gale coming and hardly enough crew to reef the mainsail. I trust you will do your utmost, and we shall all do the same. How fares Mr Franks?"

"In a great deal of pain. He had his foot crushed by a falling spar. I will almost certainly have to amputate but will wait for the swelling to diminish before I decide. If the foot can be saved, we shall do it."

"Poor Franks. I will try to visit him later, if I can. I must complete my inspection, if you don't mind, Doctor."

As he turned to go he saw a man seated in a chair with his head and half his face bandaged. A carefully dressed hand raised stiffly.

"Mr Muhlhauser?"

The man nodded. "I've been the victim of my own invention, Mr Hayden. I'm certain it was my very own gun that fired into the side near me, and look"—he gestured to arm and head with his good hand—"it was a smashing success!"

"So it appears. Not too serious, I hope?"

"Just a scratch, sir, thank you for asking. I shall be ready to man a gun on the morrow, if you require it."

"Let us hope that won't be necessary." Hayden could not help but think the man looked rather pleased with his wounds and having served in an action. He'd be wanting a knighthood next. Hayden refrained from telling him that his invention had been destroyed in the battle—or more likely had destroyed itself, the metal carriage having proved too brittle, as many had predicted.

He had the prisoners' berth opened, where the French were being held, and inspected the damage here as well. The prisoners looked frightened and angry, he thought. Hayden offered a few reassuring words in French, the men glancing one to the other when they heard their own tongue spoken without accent. Someone whispered, *"traître"* and then another, *"renégat"*—*turncoat*. Hayden stepped out of the lockup, his face burning, temper barely in check.

"Well done, Mr Chettle," Hayden mumbled, as they mounted the ladder to the berth-deck. "Sound the pump wells at each bell and report the depths to the officer of the watch, if you please. I will be on deck."

Hayden emerged into a harsh wind, the sea gathering and cresting about them. Darkness was not quite complete. He could see the dark bulk of the *Themis* on their port quarter, perhaps a few cables distant. Aloft, the men were finishing their gale preparations, and on deck the boats were being covered and lifelines stretched fore and aft.

"Where is our Frenchman, Mr Wickham?" he asked the middy.

Wickham pointed to the south-west. "I can just barely see her, sir. A lantern flickers now and again, if you watch carefully. She fired a gun and made a signal as we got under way: 'Heave-to.' I thought it best not to acknowledge, sir. I hope I didn't overstep my authority."

"I would have made the same decision. There is little she can do to us with this rising gale and night coming on, but if she is still with us by morning and the wind and sea take off, she might cause us some mischief yet."

Wickham gazed to windward and then made a slow circle. "I think this gale will carry us clear to England. Are we sound enough to weather it? That is what I wonder. I have never had to frap a ship, sir, but I suppose we can manage it even with so small a crew."

Hayden was glad the darkness hid his smile. "She is a sound, new-built vessel, Mr Wickham. Damaged, yes, but still strong. Frapping will not be necessary, I think."

"No, sir. I'm sure you're right."

"How often are you relieving the men at the pumps?"

"Every bell, sir. We haven't enough to do more than that."

"I think we shall have the Frenchmen man the pumps, Mr Wickham. Detail marines to watch over them, and have them relieve the Frenchmen often, for we have a goodly number and all might benefit from a spell of exertion."

"Aye, sir."

Hayden stood by the helm for a time, and rain began to fall, beating against his back. Perse appeared out of the darkness, bearing oilskins. "The cook has made some foreign-looking victuals for you, sir," the boy said in his soft Irish brogue. Hayden could almost see the scowl of disapproval in the dark.

Hayden pulled the coat on, thankfully. "Has he, now?"

"Aye, sir. I don't fathom what he's saying, but he made me to understand by pantomime that he thinks it will spoil if 'tis not eaten right smart, sir."

"I shall be down the moment Mr Wickham returns to the deck. Make certain no light escapes my cabin window, Perse, if you please. There is a French frigate out here and I do believe he's smoked us."

"I have it trussed up tight, sir, as Mr Hawthorne told me. And the quarter gallery windows are shaded as well."

"Well done."

As Hayden stood waiting for Wickham, Dryden appeared out of the darkness. He held an arm up against the wind-driven rain, and hunched over like a man trying to stay warm.

"I'm concerned for our mainsail, Mr Hayden," he hollered over the gale. "The yard is split for a fifth of its length. We fished it proper, sir, but I don't think it will take this." He waved a hand into the wind. "Perhaps if we reef the mainsail it might stand . . ."

"No, Mr Dryden, let us take it in. I don't want to send men aloft to reef, and then, an hour later, send them aloft again to take in the sail. If the yard gives way at an unpropitious moment, men will be killed. Take the sail in smartly, if you please, and then reef the main topsail as well."

Dryden's nod was barely visible in the dim lamplight. "Aye, sir. I took the liberty of rigging a quicksaver on the foresail. I hope that meets with your approval?"

"It does indeed, Mr Dryden."

The young master's mate hurried forward, searching out the acting bosun. For the next three quarters of an hour, Hayden found himself staring upward into the impenetrable gloom, worried that the yard would give way and the yardmen would be tumbled into the sea or down onto the deck. But finally the task was managed by the too-small crew, and Hayden breathed a sigh.

"Shall I take the deck until you have eaten your dinner, sir?"

"Very kind of you, Mr Wickham. We must keep to this heading to be sure we clear Ushant, but once we are confident the island has been weathered, we shall set a course for Plymouth, for we have a fair wind, if too much of it."

"We'll scud home, Mr Hayden."

"*Fuir devant le temps*, Mr Wickham."

"Pardon me, sir?"

"It is what the French say for *scud*: *fuir devant le temps*. Fly before the wind."

"If we are to dress as Frenchmen we might as well speak like them," Wickham ventured in French.

Hayden went below, shed his oilskins, and was relieved to find his cabin more or less dry. He then removed his French jacket as well, pulling on his worn blue wool, his lieutenant's epaulette gleaming dully in the light.

He folded the crimson silk coat carefully, and tucked it in the French captain's trunk. A second's contemplation, and he closed the trunk lid softly.

"A mere British lieutenant—with no future—again," he whispered, and went to the table.

His hen in brandy sauce with pickled champignons was utterly cold, as was everything that accompanied it. The French claret, he was happy to note, was nearly the perfect temperature and he savoured every sip—

a fragrant Bordeaux from Paulliac, he guessed, from the French captain's own supplies. A knock, and his marine sentry opened the door to reveal Dr Griffiths.

"Come, Doctor, a glass of this magnificent claret will put some colour back in your cheeks."

Griffiths nearly slumped in a chair. He removed his spectacles, and for a moment pinched the bridge of his nose with bony fingers, eyes tightly shut. Hayden held his peace until the doctor finally opened his eyes, crimson-veined and red at the rims. He received the offered wine with the softest thanks.

"It has been a difficult day in the sick-berth, I am sure, Doctor."

"The most difficult I have known, but then Hart never got into a scrap, so we had only incidental injuries incurred in the course of running the ship. Today . . ." The man raised a hand, palm-up, then took a sip of his wine. "I will tell you honestly, Mr Hayden, when men refuse to surrender they can be terribly cut up before they are subdued. I dressed the wounds of a man who was stabbed and cut more times than I could count. Only one or two wounds were of consequence, but the cumulation must have let all the blood he could afford."

"That is one patient you won't have to bleed, Doctor," Hayden offered.

Griffiths' eyes went wide and then he choked out a laugh. "How can you make a jest at such a time?"

"Have you not asked me that very question before? I can't quite remember." Hayden held up his glass so that the light of the lantern shone through the deep-crimson liquid. "Jests are like wine, Doctor, they help ease our burdens, and allow us to see the world as a better place than truly it is. We took back the *Themis*, and though I know the cost was great, we prevented a British frigate being lost to the enemy."

"Come have a closer look in my sick-berth and you will wonder if it was truly worth it."

"I'm sure from the cockpit, in the middle of an action, all battles seem pointless. I would feel no different. But we cannot win a war without injuries and wounds—even deaths. I will pay a visit to your sick-berth once we have weathered this gale. It is important for officers to understand the human cost of their endeavours so that they do not spend men's lives too freely."

Griffiths nodded his agreement. "And where is our French frigate, do you think?"

"I hope she shaped her course for Brest, but all we can say with any certainty is that she cannot be seen at the moment. I think we have shaken her, or so I hope."

Griffiths raised his glass. "Confusion to the enemy."

"Hear," Hayden said, and they both drank.

"I have one more morsel of news that you should hear before I leave you in peace," the doctor said. "Being informed that you did indeed overhaul and take the *Themis* sent Hart into a rage. I have been plying him with alcoholic tincture of opium—laudanum—and he has been not quite in his right senses. I fear, however, that what he is saying is more the truth than not, and among his cursing and muttering he repeatedly said, 'Thinks he will make me look the fool. He will see what I am made of when we reach England. I will do for him,' and much more in a similar tone. I think the thing Hart fears most in this world is having the truth about his character revealed, which you have done quite handily."

"Captain Bourne said much the same thing."

"Well, so you know; Hart's senses might be deranged for the moment, but his threats are not idle."

Hayden was too exhausted to feel the threat, but his tired brain told him that Griffiths was right. "I will bear that in mind, Doctor. Thank you."

In less than an hour, Hayden was back on the deck, wrapped in the dead captain's oilskins. There was no sign of the French ship now, but neither could he make out the *Themis*, partly because looking to windward was near impossible with the rain driving upon them. Landry would have the good sense to give them sea-room. A collision in the dark of a stormy night would bring both ships to ruin. The gale-driven rain pelted his back like gravel. As the seas and wind rose, Hayden ordered sail reduced until they were down to foresail and main topsail, both reefed—"a skirt and bonnet." The main topsail was clewed to the unsound mainsail yard, but Hayden hoped this sail, close-reefed, would not exert enough pressure to shatter the fished spar. He told Dryden to be certain the braces were carefully tended so that no undue pressure was put on one side or the other.

The night wore on and the gale freshened by the hour. Hayden set watches for his acting officers, but given the scarcity of able crew, condition of the ship, and severity of weather, he chose to keep the deck as long as he was able—through the night if necessary. Wickham was an exceptional middy, mature beyond his count, and with a grasp of seamanship that was rare in one so few years at sea, but he was still lacking in experience, and even a very dexterous mind would not make up for that.

The *Dragoon* rolled more heavily than he liked, and an increase in top-hamper would likely have aided her, but of course such spars were in danger in these conditions. She also had a strong tendency to yaw, which Hayden was sure could be corrected by stowing her hold to increase her draught aft.

Seas came hissing out of the darkness, lifting the stern high. They would carry the ship on their shoulder, and then disappear forward as the ship settled in the trough. Running before it could become dangerous if the seas mounted too high. Hayden had four men on the helm, as it was, and he paid careful attention to the ship's motion, noting that despite her tendency to yaw, the helmsmen were able to keep her more or less dead before it, though she slewed a little as each wave lifted her.

Occasionally a great, maned monster would take them from behind, thundering against her damaged stern, and Hayden would send a man below to be sure no harm had been done.

Dryden appeared out of the darkness, wrapped in a Frenchman's oilskins. He had been aloft, inspecting the mats and guarding the rigging against chafe.

"How fare your thrum mats, Mr Dryden?"

"Well enough, sir. Mr Barthe would not be too disheartened by the job we've done, if I do say so." Dryden was quiet a moment. "It is a prodigious sea, Mr Hayden, is it not?"

"Indeed it is, and will grow worse as we reach soundings. I hardly remember a late-summer gale more severe."

"No, sir, though I have not been at sea so very long. Mr Barthe would say it is no great sea compared to 'the grey beards of the southern ocean.'"

Hayden laughed. "And I'm sure he would be right, but with this damaged ship and her juried rig I do not want any more of it."

"Yes, sir, but the wind appears to be making yet. I think we have not seen quite the worst of it."

Dryden, it was soon revealed, was more prescient than usual. The gale did grow worse, and the sea more dangerous. The deck was awash more than once, and a particularly steep sea dumped green water over the stern, which almost washed the ship's captain off his feet. The ship, however, served them well, and Mr Chettle's repairs stood the test, though she was not as dry below as anyone would have liked.

Hayden relieved the helmsmen often, and after sending Wickham below for some rest and a time to dry and warm, he took a turn below himself. It was in the middle-watch, but Perseverance Gilhooly brought him a cold leg of mutton and a block of crumbling, only slightly mouldy cheese. Hayden chased it down with port.

For an hour he lay dozing in his cot, which he swung athwart-ship to accommodate the direction of the seas. It traced a great arc across the cabin, flinging him high, then swooping back down again. He had to remind himself that it was the ship moving in such furious gyrations, and the cot that remained more or less stationary. Sleep did not find him for more than a few moments at a time, and then dreaming and waking bled together, the sounds of the gale pressing into his fancies, until it was difficult to tell one from the other. Once he thought he heard whispering in French, and snapped awake, only to smile. The ship's bell rang, a glass was no doubt turned, and all was well.

Hayden stayed for a moment, his cot feeling uncommonly warm and snug. He listened to the sounds of the gale; the creaking of the ship, the high, shrill note of wind as it oscillated up and down in the gusts, the squeaking of the tiller as it moved. And then he heard the whisper again, *"Silence!"*—but pronounced by a Frenchman. Did he sleep or wake?

Disembarking from his cot was almost an adventure in itself, but long practice landed him upright on the deck. Quickly, he drew on his clothes, and snatched his cutlass from the rack. Outside his door he found the marine sentry slumped in the corner, head forward. Hayden stirred the man with his foot. Then crouched before him, as the marine, Jennings, shook himself from sleep, a stupid, indignant look upon his face.

"Not a sound, Jennings," Hayden warned him softly.

The man scrambled up, the indignation quickly replaced by consternation. Dereliction of duty would see a marine flogged.

But Hayden had not time for such matters now. He put a finger to his lips, and crept forward, bracing his bare feet against the ship's pitch and roll. The gale had not abated and the roar of seas and screaming wind remained loud. He made his way to the companionway, where for a moment he tarried, listening carefully. And then he heard it again—someone whispering; English this time but heavily accented.

"Move quickly; no sound."

"But I am the surgeon . . ." came the reply, firm but frustrated. "I don't have keys for the lockup or the armoury."

Griffiths!

Then a whisper, almost drowned by the crashing seas—though Hayden was left with the impression, due entirely to speech rhythms, that it was French, as was the answer.

He put his head close to the marine's ear. "Some Frenchmen are free on the berth-deck. Get yourself forward and find me some men. But keep them quiet."

The marine nodded, and set off into the near-darkness, slipping out the door onto the gun-deck. A little blast of wind fluttered the candle in the single lantern, and he thought he heard the men below pause in their movements, though above the thunder of waves, he could not be certain.

He lay on his stomach near the companionway, wondering what time it might be—how near it was to the change of watch. If only someone would ring the bell. Trying to still his breathing, he concentrated all his energies on the single act of listening. How many were there? Marin-Marie, and at least one other, for he had heard him speak to someone in his own tongue. Straining to hear in the lull between gusts and rushing seas, he could not distinguish the rhythmic creaking of the pumps. The prisoners must have overwhelmed their guards. Eight Frenchmen plus Marin-Marie, then, though the latter was wounded. Too many for him to confront alone—and then there was the doctor, presently hostage. This was the only reason he did not raise a cry; if the Frenchmen barricaded themselves in the gunroom with one or more hostages, the possibility of harm being done to one of his crew would be great.

Hayden could not, however, let them reach the armoury, release their countrymen, or take control of either of the magazines. They were on the berth-deck, he a deck above, and the armoury was one deck below them, on the orlop. The magazines, fore and aft, were half-sunken so that they extended below the orlop a small distance into the hold. By the sound of their whispers, Hayden believed the Frenchmen to be outside the gunroom by the companionway stair—essentially in the midshipmen's berth. Due to the small crew, fewer sentries stood their stations than would have been normal on a frigate of this rate. Hayden also knew that the men in their hammocks forward of the midshipmen's berth were all exhausted beyond measure and would not be roused easily—and the fury of the gale would mask many a sound.

The loud hiss of the great waves passing; in the rigging, a high, modulating moan; the rudder working forth and back like an old door; timbers strained and complaining. Amid all of this, bare feet, perhaps, descending the stair, hesitant in the dim light, and then the stumble of booted feet—Griffiths, who could never adjust his gate to the roll of a ship in a gale.

Hayden slid slowly forward, resting a hand on a stair so that he could peer down into the dimness below. Beneath him, shadows. Whitewashed bulkhead, planks soot-smeared from candle smoke. A door, crooked in its frame but shut; beyond, the silent gunroom. All angles and lines, no irregular shapes that might be men.

Hayden glanced up at the door the marine had taken, wondering where in hell he could be. Silently he climbed down the stair, using hands and feet on the treads, like a child. The gunroom door had a tendency to creak, so he timed its opening with a sea crashing aboard, the hinges' tell-tale shriek lost among the din.

Inside he was met by utter darkness. Chairs would have been removed to some place where they could be restrained; the table, though, was bolted to the floor. Groping forward, he found its hard edge, and made his way, hand by hand, along one side. Hawthorne preferred the centre cabin to starboard, and Hayden hoped he had managed to claim it here.

Pulling open the door, he whispered, "Mr Hawthorne! Mr Hawthorne, sir!"

A rustling, then a muttered "Fuck off. I've only just gone to sleep."

"Hawthorne, it's Hayden."

Louder rustling. "Mr Hayden? I beg you to forgive me, sir! I didn't—"

"Hawthorne. Some Frenchmen are loose in the dark and they have taken hostage the doctor."

He heard the marine lieutenant fumble out of bed, perhaps breeches being pulled on, a muttered "Where is my bloody sword?"

Hawthorne's hand found Hayden's shoulder in the dark. "Dryden slings his cot across the way, if he's not on deck."

In a moment they'd roused a muddled Dryden and went as three blind men out the creaking gunroom door. A marine almost shot them as they emerged into the dim light of a watch lantern.

"There you are, Jennings," Hayden whispered. "It appears there are nine of them, gone down onto the orlop with the doctor as hostage."

Four men lurked behind Jennings—two marines and two hands, the former with muskets, though perhaps too wet to fire, and the latter with handspikes. He and Hawthorne had cutlasses and Dryden was unarmed.

"We cannot let them release the prisoners or break into the armoury," Hayden whispered. "I shall try to negotiate their surrender, but we might have to fight.

"Shall I raise the off-watch, sir?" Dryden asked.

"Only a few men you can trust, Dryden. Too much noise will tip our hand." Hayden crouched down by the companionway, listening, then lay down and leaned his head and upper body into the opening. He could hear no sounds of men, see no lurking shadows or movement. The cockpit was below; forward, the cable tiers; various storerooms, including the armoury; and right forward, in place of the sailroom, the temporary prisoners' lockup. Abaft this was situated the forward magazine.

There were two guards stationed there, though not necessarily marines, as there were so few of them aboard. From the deckhead between them, a lantern swung; a damnably sooty one, which cast only a frail circle of squalid light.

A grunt. The rasp of a strangled cry. Two bodies thudding dully to the deck. Whispers.

The Frenchmen would have two muskets now, and though the guards did not possess keys for the lockup, the locks or hinges could be prised, given time. The near-constant clamour of the gale would make such efforts almost undetectable. A sentry would begin his rounds at some point, the watch would change, but the Frenchmen would be free and likely have broken into the armoury by then. Once they were armed, the ship would be theirs.

Hayden found Hawthorne in the dark. "We must take them by stealth. If detected, we must charge. The doctor will have to look out for himself."

Hawthorne put his mouth near to Hayden's ear. "We must be mindful of the powder-room."

"Inform your musketeers," Hayden whispered, and led them down to the orlop.

They crept forward, around the hatchway to the hold, keeping low, hiding behind the cable tiers, over the coils of massive cable for the anchors, the stench of salt and mud. Hayden could see the escaped prisoners, bent before the lockup door. A clatter to his right.

"*Merde*," a voice muttered.

Hayden found himself face-to-face with a dark shape and without thinking drove the heel of his sword hilt into the man's temple, collapsing him like a tent. Hayden lowered the man to the planks and struck him once more to be certain he was gone.

They crouched behind the noisome coils, watching for an instant. A grating squeal as iron fittings were drawn through wood.

"As she lifts . . ." Hayden said, and as the stern began to rise, he vaulted over the cable. Crouching to clear the low deckhead, they crossed the few yards with as much stealth as speed would allow. The dim light, half hidden by the Frenchmen gathered about the lockup door, and the pounding seas, masked their attack. Only at the last second did they have the ill luck for one man to stumble, causing the prisoners to turn.

Hayden drove his blade into a man raising a musket, and it discharged harmlessly into the deck. Cries all around, both French and English. A desperate melee erupted as men were thrown forward by the motion of the ship.

Someone still prised urgently at the lockup door. Inside men threw their weight against it repeatedly. Another musket fired, dropping the sailor to Hayden's left. He slashed at a man bent before the door.

An explosion of light and pain and Hayden staggered back, stumbling down onto his haunches. A confused moment when the world reeled and he lurched onto his side. Above, shadow men locked in struggle; he was dimly aware of a flash, and then another. Men dropped from above, beating down the French, crouching over them and driving hard, callused fists into chests and faces. Then a voice—Hawthorne—shouting, "Enough. Enough!"

"Mr Hayden?" a voice was saying, and not for the first time, Hayden suspected. "Mr Hayden? Are you hurt, sir? Are you bleeding?"

"No . . . I don't believe so," he mumbled, attempting to raise himself. "Just a bit . . . dazed. A blow to the head." Hayden tried to stand on the rolling deck, but the darkness seemed to press in, and he lost balance.

"Catch him! Don't let him fall." And hands gripped his shoulders, lowering him gently.

"I require light!" a voice demanded loudly.

"Aye, Doctor."

Hayden was laid on the deck, the world swaying and wobbling this way and that. He thought he might be ill. Dark shapes of men, some lying, others moving with exaggerated slowness. Men kept appearing from somewhere. Someone bent over him.

"Doctor! It's Mr Hayden."

"Yes, I see that, Mr Wickham, but I can also see that he is not bleeding to death, as is this man. I need anything that can be used for a tourniquet. Yes, that will do nicely. Hold this arm up like so. Do not swoon, sir. Think of it as red wine."

The lights went dim and when they slowly swam back into focus Hayden felt himself borne up, passed man-to-man up the companionway, into the light. The men who bore him staggered like drunks along the berth-deck among the off-watch, who were all roused now, empty hammocks swaying, oddly slack and lifeless, like shed skins.

"I believe I might stand," Hayden said, making some effort to form the words.

"Doctor said to carry you to your cot, Mr Hayden. He'll be along by the by."

He felt himself being handed again up a stair, then into his swinging cot. After a time he realized Hawthorne stood over him.

"Did you just recently pass for a surgeon, Mr Hawthorne?"

Hawthorne chuckled. "This very morning. Feeling better, sir?"

"A little, yes. The world is still swaying about, but I think these sways are natural, given the gale. We prevailed, I take it?"

"That we did, Mr Hayden, but at the cost of three wounded and two killed. The French fared worse. Marin-Marie will not put his English to our service again."

Hayden propped himself more upright and felt the side of his head. There was a great, prodigious swelling behind his ear, and a sticky bit of blood. It was painful to the touch.

Hawthorne drew in a whistle. "You did catch one, didn't you?" He parted Hayden's hair so that he could see the wound. "I've had worse from a brother," the marine observed.

"You must come of a genteel family—"

A knock and Wickham opened the door, peering in. "How fare you, sir?" he asked, clearly relieved to see Hayden sitting up.

"I have the blackest headache I have ever known, but otherwise, I am unharmed. Others did not fare as well, I am told . . . ?"

"No, sir. Marshall and Burchfield are both dead, and Jennings and White have beastly wounds. Jennings has lost a terrible quantity of blood."

"Then we shall delay flogging the man for sleeping on duty," Hayden replied.

"Was he really sleeping?" Hawthorne asked.

"Yes. Asleep with enemy prisoners aboard. Unforgivable, I'm afraid, no matter how great his wound."

Hawthorne cursed. "How did you know the Frenchmen were loose?"

Hayden pressed fingers to his forehead. He had not been exaggerating the ache in his skull. "It was the strangest thing . . . I was dozing fitfully. Do you know that odd state where sleeping and waking mix and dreams become confused with the real? I dreamt that someone was whispering in French—and then it occurred to me that I was not sleeping. For a moment I was unsure if I had dreamt it, and then I heard it again, or so I thought. I was out of my cot, grabbed my cutlass. It was then I discovered my sentry, Jennings, slumped in the corner, snoring peacefully."

"There is no excuse," Hawthorne declared. "Many were exhausted and still did their duty."

"I sent him for reinforcements . . ." Hayden quickly told them the rest of the story. As he spoke, Griffiths came in quietly and examined his wound without interrupting.

"Why were you about, Doctor?" Hayden asked as he finished.

"I was worried about Freeman, and as the motion of the ship made sleep all but impossible, I decided to look in on him. As I left the gun-room I was met by Frenchmen, two bearing muskets."

"They overpowered the two quartermaster's mates who were guarding them as they worked the pumps," Hawthorne said.

"Marin-Marie was among them," Griffiths went on. "I fear he was not as badly wounded as I had supposed, and he must have slipped out of the sick-berth. They took me down to the orlop with them . . . and the rest you know. It was a miracle I was not killed in the action, but they had made me lie on the deck and as soon as the French were attacked I began shouting in clear English."

"I do recall someone cursing and blaspheming . . ." Hawthorne mused, trying to keep from smiling.

"I cannot recall my exact words, Mr Hawthorne, but they were, by necessity, of an urgent nature."

"We were fortunate not to have lost more men than we did," Hayden observed. "And I am very happy to see you unharmed, Doctor."

"Mr Hayden did twice warn all of us that you were prisoner," Hawthorne said.

"Tell me the state of our ship," Hayden said to Wickham.

"The gale has not grown worse this two hour, sir, and we hope it will soon begin to abate. Mr Chettle's repairs have taken up and barely weep a tear now. Constant pumping is no longer the order, as we pumped the wells dry and the water flows in now but slowly. I think we shall see the wind begin to take off before sunrise. If the wind does not back, we might see England on the morrow."

"Let us hope that is true, Mr Wickham. Perhaps I will take a tour of the deck . . ."

"I don't think that would be advisable, Mr Hayden," the doctor said firmly. "All appears to be in hand. It would be best if you rested for a few hours. Let us see what comes of the pain in your skull. After such a blow as you received, there can be bleeding within the cranial cavity, and exercise will only increase the flow."

"Yes, no need to keep the ship flying," Hawthorne commented. "Once home we shall all face the court-martial, anyway . . . for the loss of our ship. No need to hurry that."

Twenty-three

An odd, hollow silence, indescribable in nature, had invaded Hayden's mind. Or perhaps it was a want of the usual patterns of thought, the normal business of the mind. Certainly the blow to his skull had altered whatever process of reason had normally occurred, though Griffiths assured him this would not be a permanent state. The order of his mind would return in the fullness of time.

His mental state was not helped by a repeating dream that he walked through the streets of Plymouth dressed in the French captain's silk coat, which he had only recently shed. Everywhere he went people would stop and stare in silent loathing. Waking from the dream was little relief as the feelings it engendered lingered, and like as not, he would fall into the same dream when he slept again. Dr Griffiths had no physic for this, and Hayden could only hope that the dream would cease when his mind recovered.

The *Themis* swung to her anchor in Plymouth Sound among the men-of-war, transports, and merchant vessels—a constant traffic of small boats, under both oar and sail, swarming among the great ships. Lighters and luggers weaving their wakes among the hoys and barges, cutters and smacks.

Their prize, the French frigate *Dragoon*, had been warped into a dry-dock and was undergoing repairs as well as being carefully surveyed.

There were great hopes that she would be bought into the service, and Hayden was rightfully joyful because of it.

His report to the Admiralty of the voyage of the French prize, *Dragoon*, had, in his present mental state, been something of a trial, and his long letter to his particular friend, Mr Banks, had been more difficult still. How to write such a missive preserving the truth while not appearing to disparage Hart and serve his own cause was a dance whose steps only the most adept could master—and he was not feeling particularly light of foot.

Hayden was in temporary command of the *Themis*, as Hart had gone ashore some days before to be admitted into the care of a noted physician. The frigate was only lightly manned—the Jacks who had been aboard the prize with Hayden at the time of the mutiny, and those loyal to Hart (or perhaps Britain) who had been put off in the boats. Eighty men in all, twenty of whom would be returned to the *Tenacious* as soon as was practical. Landry and Archer had begged leave to go ashore, and Barthe was on and off the ship, as his wife and daughters had taken rooms in the town—an impossible luxury ordinarily, had it not been for the prize money that would almost certainly be his. During the day the sailing master came aboard to see to the work being done on the ship.

Most of the middies, including Wickham, had been allowed to visit their families, though all visits would be brief—there was to be a court-martial as soon as Hart was deemed recovered enough to bear it.

A few of the sick and hurt were taken ashore to be seen by a physician, but most were under the care of Dr Griffiths, including Franks, who still had his foot, though the doctor believed there were several fractured bones, and the bosun was in not-inconsiderable pain.

"Captain approaching!" one of the sentries cried.

Hayden picked out a barge being smartly rowed toward them, an officer of apparent post rank sitting in the stern sheets. He called for his glass and in a moment had fixed a beaming Robert Hertle in the lens.

Hayden had him piped aboard, a hastily gathered line of marines presenting arms sharply.

"I see you have made your post in fact, now," Hayden said, doffing his hat and shaking his friend's hand.

"The Lords of the Admiralty have seen fit to honour me with the command of a new frigate. She is anchored in the Hamoaze at this very moment, being fitted for sea."

Hayden's congratulations were both effusive and heartfelt, with barely a trace of envy. The two men repaired below to the captain's cabin. Hart had sent for all his belongings, clearly having no intention of setting foot on the *Themis* again.

"So, you are hanging your cot in the great cabin, in anticipation of promotion, I collect?" Hertle took one of the chairs.

"No, I'm still in my cabin in the gunroom. If Hart returned he would deem it an unpardonable trespass if he were to find I occupied his cabin. Even though he has called for all his belongings, I should never presume. I have, however, been using it for ship's business."

"I am most anxious to hear your tale, Charles," Hertle said, lowering his voice and glancing up at the open skylight. "Plymouth is awash in rumours; mutiny, murder, captains flogged, enemy frigates taken, revenge, and confusion to the French. Last I saw you we had plucked you out of the jaws of a French privateer, and you were returning to an uncertain welcome from your captain. Pray, what followed?"

Coffee was delivered by the gunroom steward, and Hayden waited until he had gone before beginning his tale.

"We had hardly set out south to continue our cruise when an old-fashioned brig-sloop appeared, carrying all sail, intending to intercept us. Immediately Hart named her an enemy vessel, outlier to a French squadron, but his officers protested just enough to delay his flight, and allow the brig to make the private signal. She proved to be under the command of a lieutenant, having lost her commander the previous day chasing stragglers from a French convoy scattered by the recent gale. Bourne had sent her in hopes of finding us or some other British ship that might help him take the transports which had sought refuge beneath the guns inshore of Belle Île."

Hayden told his coffee-fuelled story, leaving out no relevant detail. When he was done, Hertle smiled.

"So you were not even aboard the *Themis* when the mutiny took place?"

"I was in command of the prize."

"Then you will not be part of the court-martial at all," Hertle said in obvious relief.

"It is possible that I will be called to give evidence, but neither Wickham, the midshipman who went with me into the prize, nor myself will be named in the proceedings, for which I am greatly thankful. Even though Hart and his officers will almost certainly be acquitted of any wrongdoing, such an incident can't help but tarnish a man's career, even so."

"Hart's career is already tarnished. His character within the service could hardly be lower. One would hope that even his patrons in the Admiralty will withdraw their support at last, else they be stained themselves for championing such a man."

"So do I hope." Hayden's mind turned for an instant to the despised correspondence with "Mr Banks."

His friend regarded him a moment. "You look out of sorts, Charles; I would say *melancholy*, if I did not know you better."

Hayden tried to smile and failed. "I do feel . . . strange. Perhaps it was the blow to the head, but I feel oddly removed from things, as though I have sunk a little deeper into my own poor mind." For a moment words failed him. "It was a peculiar cruise. I began as an English lieutenant contending with my captain for the privilege of making war on the French; then, for a time, I was a French *capitaine* chasing and taking an English ship of war; and now I am, once again, a mere lieutenant with no future in the British Navy." He shook his head, glancing at his friend, who regarded him thoughtfully. "I would be happier about my return to British cloth if the British themselves showed the slightest signs of welcome. Instead, I am a traitor to my mother's people, and spurned by my father's. But here I am, all the same, the only officer in the fleet who celebrates an English victory while at the same instant mourning the French defeat. I am torn in half, Robert, and don't know how long I can bear it."

Robert shifted in his chair, leaning forward and placing an arm upon the table. "You cannot make a decision to side with the British with your head alone, Charles—your heart, for want of a better word, must do the same. It is rather like choosing a wife—one might make the most reasonable, intelligent match in the world, but if your heart is not engaged as well you will never be happy. In truth, I believe you will always be in misery."

"Perhaps you are right, but how does one make one's heart follow? That is what I do not know. The heart—at least my heart—has never been much governed by what my mind thought it *ought* to do."

A knock on the door interrupted their conversation. Hobson stuck his head in.

"Begging your pardon, Mr Hayden. A boat bearing two ladies lies alongside. It appears one is Mrs Hertle, sir. I have ordered them to be brought aboard. I hope I have done the right thing."

"I'm quite certain you have," Hayden said, rising from his seat. A look of joy passed over his friend's face, prompting Hayden to observe, "Well, it is apparent *your* heart and brain are in complete agreement, Robert— at least when it comes to your choice of mate. Let us go up."

He followed Robert up to the quarterdeck, where they found not only Mrs Hertle but her cousin Miss Henrietta Carthew, looking about in charmed bewilderment. They were both pink-cheeked from sun and wind, despite parasols and bonnets, and blushed when they saw the two gentlemen, heightening the effect.

Hayden felt his lowered spirits take a sudden lift, as though a cool breeze had suddenly filled his sails after languishing for weeks in the doldrums.

As a captain aboard ship, Robert Hertle's greeting had not the affection he would normally have bestowed upon his dear wife, especially after so long a separation, but his pleasure could not be hidden. Henrietta curtsied elegantly, and greeted them by order of rank.

"Lieutenant Quixote," she said, a smile half-suppressed in the most engaging manner.

"Miss Henrietta, how pleased I am for this opportunity to thank you for the kind loan of your book."

"You may reward me with a tour of the deck, Mr Hayden, if that is permissible?"

"Certainly it is. Mrs Hertle? would you care to tour the deck?"

"Would I be impossibly rude if I begged your indulgence, Lieutenant Hayden? I feel I have had too much of this warm autumn sun . . ."

"By all means, would you care to repair below to the great cabin? It is much cooler there, and a noble breeze has found its way down the skylight all morning."

Captain Hertle accompanied his wife below, and Henrietta favoured Hayden with a conspiratorial smile. A leisurely tour of the deck followed, many questions asked and answered. Upon the forecastle, Henrietta shaded her eyes and gazed up into the labyrinthine rigging.

"It is a regular cat's cradle, is it not, Lieutenant?"

"Indeed it is."

"And each rope has a different function and some obscure nautical designation—such as *brace-girdle* or *top-slumper*?"

"Very much like that," Hayden said, forced to smile. His present mental state made him feel very much her inferior in both reason and cleverness.

"And pray tell, Mr Hayden, who are these ropes here?" She nodded toward cables slanting down to the boom.

"Stays, Miss Henrietta."

"Do they draw in the ship's waist?"

"Very much so."

"And does the ship complain?"

"Only after supper."

"That must be what is meant by a ship being *well-mannered*."

Their tour circled the ship, bringing them back to the quarterdeck by the larboard gangway. The sailors working about the deck hid their fascination with this creature who had found her way into their little world—rather unlike most of the ladies of their acquaintance.

"Mr Hayden . . ." Henrietta regarded him with a tilt of her lovely head. "I dare say, this dressing about your head is not some nautical fashion?"

"A rather ungrateful Frenchman struck me quite a blow, Miss Henri-etta. I fear it has made me something of a dullard . . . though only tem-porarily, I hope."

"I am sorry to see you injured, Lieutenant Hayden," she said, a strange look that might have been anxiety spreading over her face—though quickly mastered. "Our little circle would be much diminished by the loss of your thoughtful observations," she added.

"It is the kindest thing anyone has said to me in a month."

"The Navy apparently does not properly value your talents, Mr Hayden."

Hayden feared he did not hide his reaction to this statement well. "So I have often thought." They had come to the wheel, and Hayden asked loudly, so that his voice would carry down the skylight, "Shall we join Captain and Mrs Hertle?"

"I should like nothing better," Henrietta answered almost as loudly.

They made quite a show of laughing and other polite noises as they descended the aft companionway, and Hayden knocked on the door, even awaiting a summons, before opening it.

"Is this your cabin, Mr Hayden?" Henrietta asked, looking around with a sense of approval, even surprise. "It is much more commodious than I expected."

"It is not my cabin, I regret to say, but the captain's, which I am mak-ing use of as he has quit the ship and I am, very temporarily, the senior officer."

"It should be Mr Hayden's cabin," Mrs Hertle stated firmly. "I'm sure such a cabin will be yours one day, Charles."

Hayden bowed at this compliment, but then noticed his friend Robert's face was quite dark.

"Is something amiss?" he asked.

Robert held out a copy of *The Times* of London. "You have not seen this, I collect—*The Times* of two days past?"

"I have not."

"Nor had I. Mrs Hertle brought it. Perhaps we should all sit down to tea."

Indeed, there was a tea spread upon the table, a white table-cloth and the best china from the gunroom on apparent loan.

Henrietta rather noticeably took on the duty of pouring tea, which would have pleased Hayden no end had he not been put into a complete state of alarm by Robert's manner.

Robert Hertle opened the paper and reduced the creases with a single shake. "Allow me to pass over the preamble," he began. "'There can hardly have been a more eventful cruise than that of His Majesty's Ship *Themis*, a frigate of thirty-two guns sent this past month to harass the enemy upon her Atlantic coast. Under the able command of Captain Josiah Hart, the *Themis* began her cruise by taking a transport in the very entrance to the harbour of Brest, notwithstanding concentrated fire from the enemy's shore batteries, pursuit by gunboats, and the threat of two French frigates that weighed anchor to give chase. The entire enterprise was witnessed by Captain Bourne of the frigate *Tenacious*, who wrote that it was "an exploit of great boldness carried out with a coolness and purpose that all true seamen must admire."

"'The courageous Captain Hart was, a few days later, called upon by the able Bourne, who had chased four French transports, a brig, and a frigate into the lee of Belle Île, where they lay at anchor beneath the batteries. Not to be turned away by mere shore guns, the two dauntless captains devised a plan to cut out the ships. With the aid of the *Lucy*, a brig-sloop of twenty guns under the acting command of Lieutenant Herald Philpott, the two frigates set upon the French at dusk. Astutely observing a French infantryman, who appeared upon the French frigate's deck only to be chased below by an officer, Hart deduced that troops had been carried aboard from the garrison on Belle Île and were waiting to surprise the British boarders. Unable to reach the French frigate before the *Tenacious* did so, Hart signalled the nearer *Lucy*, sending her to the aid of Captain Bourne. Without this timely assistance, Bourne admitted, he would have been overwhelmed, his ship lost, but with the aid of the *Lucy* he carried the enemy frigate.

"'The remaining French ships cut their cables and ran for L'Orient, escaping under the cover of darkness. As a French squadron put out from this port on a fair wind, the *Lucy* receiving a broadside from one, the British ships turned out to sea, but not before securing their prize, and taking the French frigate, *Dragoon*, as a spoil of war.

"'After this auspicious beginning, Captain Hart's cruise took a turn unlooked for by any, as his crew, no doubt influenced by French agents and republican sympathizers, mutinied during the night. Having put many of his best and most loyal sailors aboard the prizes, the noble captain was taken by surprise, and after a spirited fight and many wounded and killed, was forced to surrender his ship to a sorry collection of treacherous revolutionaries. Their passion for republican ideals was such that they flogged Captain Hart for the damage he had done to their chosen cause, and putting Hart and his loyal crew into boats, as had been done to the unfortunate Captain Bligh only a few years past, vowed to sail the *Themis* into the harbour of Brest and surrender her to the French authorities.

"'But Captain Hart could not be so easily undone. Despite the thirty-six lashes he had endured, he intercepted the French prize, *Dragoon*, as it sailed toward Plymouth, and taking command from a lieutenant, ordered the frigate to pursue the *Themis*. They managed to overhaul the mutineers the day next, and dressing themselves in French uniforms and flying the hated tricolour ensign, deceived a French man-of-war into offering some nominal support in the retaking of the *Themis*. With this French ship standing by to offer aid, Hart overhauled and boarded the *Themis*, taking the ship after a desperate fight during which all but twenty of the mutineers were killed. Hart then made fools of the French, whose captain never discovered that the *Dragoon* was manned by a British prize crew numbering only eighty men! Under cover of darkness, the *Dragoon* and *Themis*, again under British flags, sailed for Plymouth in a rising gale, which place they reached not without further adventures. Although it is the policy of the Admiralty to hold a court-martial over the officers and crew of any ship lost by whatsoever means, knowledgeable gentlemen assure that Hart's hearing will be brief and he shall be exonerated of any blame in the affair, especially as the lost ship was taken back by his own efforts. There is much talk around London that the deserving captain will receive a knighthood for his efforts, and given the circumstances, His Majesty might not wait until the court-martial has been held, as its outcome is not in question.' "

Robert looked up from the paper.

"There is not a word of truth in the entire account!" Hayden protested, still stunned by what he had just heard. "Certainly, the public may be deceived by such invention, but the Lords of the Admiralty know better." A thought occurred to him. "You don't think this is in any way a reflection of Hart's report to the Admiralty? There is the ship's log, officers' journals. Captain Bourne witnessed many of these events. He'd quickly put the lie to this."

"Captain Bourne is far away, Charles, and not likely to return before the attention of the public has been engaged elsewhere."

Some attempt was made to divert the flow of conversation into an-other channel, but to little avail. Hayden was unable to draw his mind from the damned litany of lies so recently recited, and the others were, all in their own ways, unsettled as well. After extending an invitation to dine that night, the guests excused themselves, leaving Hayden to watch the retreating boat. Mr Barthe emerged from the bowels of the ship, where he had been overseeing the shifting of several tons of shingle in an attempt to make the ship trim a little more by the stern when next she was stowed. Hayden invited the master down to the great cabin and spread the odious paper before him.

As the sailing master read, a blush of crimson appeared on his neck. It radiated out to his face, growing, by the sentence, deeper in colour until finally his skin glowed beneath his fiery hair like an overheated stove. The master's hands began to shake so that the edge of the paper trembled.

Barthe slammed the paper down on the table, his choler boiling over into several moments of near-incoherent bluster punctuated by extremes of profanity: "The pusillanimous, cunt-ridden, goat-fucking . . ." But even the master's encyclopaedic vocabulary failed to delineate adequately the charac-ter of Captain Hart and his unnatural villainy—at least Hayden assumed it was Hart to whom Barthe referred.

After a few moments more of this volcanic outpouring, Barthe regained some semblance of sanity, and reverted to mild ejaculations of invective, interspersed throughout more or less coherent speech.

"Never in this life, Mr Hayden, never in this life have I read such a self-serving pack of vile lies! Hart should be flogged again, the fart-catcher!" Barthe's colour tempered so that it did not appear quite so alarming.

"You dishonour the profession of valet," Hayden said, for *fart-catcher* was a crude term for a gentleman's valet, derived from the valet's practice of walking behind his master. "But you assume this account had its origin with Hart. It might have been concocted by some Fleet Street flat who knit it together from rumours."

"Oh, you give our glorious captain too much credit, Mr Hayden. Hart or some confederate fed this yarn to a cully at *The Times*." He jabbed the paper with a finger. "Do you see here? They quoted Captain Bourne, and assuming those were the good captain's own words, they could have come from no other source but the Admiralty. No, Hart wanted to get his broadside in first, before the court-martial might bring any guns to bear. Hard to find guilty such an ink-and-paper hero. Captain Sir Josiah Hart will be exonerated of all responsibility for the loss of his ship, and heartily praised for his sudden dedication to heroism, after a lifetime of infamous shyness. Bloody, craven martinet. And to think he has taken credit for all your enterprises, Mr Hayden; capturing the transport at Brest when he ordered the boats back to the ship, even spotting the infantry aboard the *Dragoon*, which he certainly did not. I stood on the quarterdeck beside him and heard him say about you the most infamous things! He all but named you a coward for going to Bourne's aid."

"Well, it is only a newspaper account, after all, Mr Barthe. No one gives such things much credence, for they are inaccurate more often than not."

"I will be glad of my chance to address the captains of the court, for my log and memory are accurate in every detail, you may be sure. Hart shall be exposed at least there, if not in the popular perception."

"Do not count on that, Mr Barthe. You recall the court-martial of Breadfruit Bligh? The captains who sat in judgement wished only to ascertain that each officer and crewman had resisted the mutineers as best his situation allowed. And though no one appeared to have offered any resistance at all, they were acquitted, even so. When you consider all the men killed and wounded during the *Themis* mutiny, the judges of the court will be sure to hold no one responsible for the loss of the ship. Hart's contribution to the crew's resentment and disaffection will not be spoken of, nor will it be allowed to be spoken of. You may count on it."

Hayden set out for the home of Robert's aunt in good time, not wishing to be a moment late. It was here that Mrs Hertle and Miss Henrietta resided while in Plymouth, an arrangement of great happiness to all, for Robert Hertle's aunt, Lady Wilhelmina Hertle—known as Aunt Bill, though not to her face—was the widow of Admiral Sir Sidney Hertle and lived alone but for a sickly, spinster cousin upon whom she had taken pity. To her great sorrow, Lady Hertle's children had all predeceased her: a daughter in extreme youth; another of some unnamed fever; and her only son—Robert's older and much-admired cousin— who died at sea, a promising young lieutenant whose service was cut short while trying to secure a gun that had broken loose in a gale.

Hayden was much surprised and relieved by the material improvement in his spirits at finding not only the Hertles in Plymouth, but also the engaging Henrietta Carthew. All recent confusion and resentments were pushed aft in his thoughts, and his mind, for the most part, was given over to the contemplation of far more pleasant matters.

Aunt Hertle stood in odd relation to both Robert and his wife, as well as Mrs Robert Hertle's cousin, Henrietta Carthew. Admiral Sir Sidney Hertle had been the eldest brother of Robert's father, thus Lady Hertle was Robert's aunt. Lady Hertle's father had, in addition to the future Lady Hertle and her siblings, several children by a second and much-younger wife. Of these, one daughter married a certain Mr Carthew and brought the lovely Henrietta into the world. Another bore a daughter who grew up to marry Hayden's good friend, Robert Hertle. Divided by both blood and geography, Robert and Elizabeth lived in complete innocence of one another until the age of twenty, when they met by chance on a country house outing.

Thus Aunt Bill had the pleasure of counting among her nieces and nephews Robert, Elizabeth, and Henrietta.

Aunt Bill lived upon the rise above Plymouth Hoe, in a fine house with an overlook of the entire sound. Hayden found the address, and was greeted by a footman whom he recognized immediately as an old seaman, likely a servant who had attended the admiral. His hat was taken, and Robert Hertle came out to greet him.

"Charles, we are so happy you could escape your duties. Do come in; Aunt Bill awaits. I related the narrative of your recent cruise and she is very keen to make your acquaintance."

Aunt Bill was something of a revelation, for she defied her years with astonishing vigour. Despite having passed her eightieth year, her dark hair was barely streaked with grey, and one had to look more closely than was polite to discern the almost invisibly fine lines around her mouth and eyes. She was tall, though to Hayden's eye too thin, not given to plumpness either in figure or in face, and her posture was almost military in its erectness. She had a clear, measuring eye, which she fixed upon Hayden.

"Lady Hertle," he said, making a leg. "It is a great pleasure to meet you at last."

"And I you, Lieutenant, though I am much distressed to learn of your foul treatment at the hands of the Lords Commissioners."

Hayden did not want to appear a grumbler, and so smiled and waved a hand. "A few gales are common in every voyage, Lady Hertle. I cannot complain of mine when so many have met with evil weather before me."

"But gales are made by God, Mr Hayden, and therefore serve a divine purpose. Nepotism and interest are contrivances of men, and serve only the narrow designs of a few, not even the wider aspirations of a nation." She led him to a chair and took the seat next. "My late husband, Admiral Hertle, valued capable, enterprising officers above all things and did much to promote their careers. Were he alive now he would come to your aid, I am certain, for injustice was abhorrent to him."

"The good opinion of such a respected officer would be reward enough, Lady Hertle."

She favoured him with a youthful smile.

"He is not habitually so charming," observed a voice, and Hayden turned to find Mrs Robert Hertle and her cousin returning from the terrace. "He has no small talk at all, I warn you."

"I am very used to Navy men, Elizabeth, and know their ways as well as any. It should be noted that I have very little small talk myself, thank God, nor have either of you." She apparently referred to the younger women.

"Why, Aunt, I am shocked to hear you say it. I can talk a great deal about fashion, carriages, events of no importance, engagements, foibles—"

" 'She said this's; he said that's,' " added Henrietta.

"And I know all the latest court gossip."

"There is a false claim if ever I have heard one."

Henrietta threw herself down in a chair. "I feel quite exhausted by all this small talk."

"Oh, so do I," agreed Mrs Hertle. "Shall we ever have supper, Aunt, or do you mean to starve us?"

"Is my niece's behaviour not quite scandalous, Lieutenant Hayden? And Henrietta, to whom I am related in some vague and distant way, is just the same. In my day such behaviour would have begun the whispering. Do you know what they call me behind my back?"

"I do not, Lady Hertle," Hayden lied.

"Aunt Bill! Can you believe the impertinence? I, the widow of an admiral who had the honour of being a Grand Commander of the Order of the Bath!"

"Shocking."

"Oh, Aunt," Mrs Hertle managed, laughing. "Henrietta tells me that the ton, the ladies within the circle of the Prince of Wales, are completely brazen. Why, they wear gowns so revealing that every man in London knows what only a husband once knew. You cannot name our behaviour scandalous when weighed against what has now become . . . common."

Lady Hertle fanned herself affectedly. "I am so glad to have retired to my small house far from such spectacles." A servant entered, bowing to the mistress. "Apparently I do have a supper for you, after all, Elizabeth. Starvation has been staved off once again."

The dining room was capacious, though fell well short of being grand. Even so, it was a comfortable, elegantly appointed room, with a large dining table of teak wood, clearly brought back from somewhere in the Far East. A sizeable glass case displayed silver plate, much of it bestowed upon the late admiral for his many services.

Dinner was rather typically British, or more specifically English, something Hayden had learned to endure. Certainly, it was better than Navy food; soup, a course of fish, a roast duckling served with asparagus and peas, venison, plovers' eggs in aspic jelly—all served *à la russe*. Sherry. Madeira. A chocolate confection. Coffee. Walnuts.

The footmen varied in their skill, and Hayden suspected one was actually the gardener dressed in livery for the occasion. The party was so small that there was little chance for a tête-à-tête, though he had happily been seated beside Henrietta, whose presence he could actually feel, as though she glowed like coals.

Lady Hertle was a skilled and gracious conversationalist, and clearly had been a Navy wife, for she soon revealed a great store of knowledge regarding the character of Lords Commissioners and admirals; more than Hayden could ever hope to know. When Hart's name came up she tactfully steered the conversation away.

Like Mrs Hertle and Henrietta, she read widely, and spoke with equal knowledge of poetry, the plays of Shakespeare, the histories of Rome. In her youth, she had accompanied her husband to many a post where his function had been as much diplomatic as military, and clearly had a great love of travel. She encouraged Hayden and Robert to speak of the many places they had visited, and this was no small number, given their chosen careers.

Hayden thought her eyes rather like the sea: shining one moment, then shadowed by a cloud of sadness, quickly dispatched by a little breeze of laughter—only to return again.

Hayden believed that his own conversation was dull and without wit, but if this were true, and not merely his perception, no one seemed to mark it. Indeed, it appeared that Henrietta attended to his words with particular care.

The Hertle family seemed to be distinguished by a studied disregard for convention, which made them natural allies to the Carthews, Hayden thought. He also noted that Henrietta treated Lady Hertle with great respect, and was at pains to hide her greater understanding of several topics of conversation, choosing her words with care so that no great contradiction was offered.

Roman historians were discussed with varying degrees of knowledge, and finally republicanism, traced from its earliest roots in ancient Greece to present-day America and the folly that took place across the Channel.

"Do you know," Hayden said, "that I have aboard the *Themis* an able seaman who has read, I believe, every book, pamphlet, or scrap of writing aboard ship to which he has been allowed access? He read all the doctor's medical books with a high degree of understanding, as well as recent writings by Burke and this man Paine. Among the midshipmen, who have made their berth into a kind of reading-and-debating club, he is much esteemed and they never seem to mention his name without attaching *Mister*, and spoken with a high degree of respect, too."

Lady Hertle appeared very charmed by this. "Why, I should like to meet this man," she pronounced, to Hayden's surprise. "Will he soon become a warrant officer, Mr Hayden? Admiral Hertle believed that the very best officers began their careers before the mast."

"More than one officer has proposed to put his name forward for master's mate or bosun's mate, but at all times he has refused, saying, as he did to me, that he does not desire authority over others. You see, he believes in man's equality and his fondest desire is to dwell one day in America."

"He was not one of your mutineers, I hope?" Lady Hertle asked.

"Not at all. He used the high regard accorded him by the other Jacks to intercede during the mutiny and stop the flogging of officers, though not until Hart had suffered this fate. It was also Mr Aldrich, for that is his name, who again used his influence to stop the boy who had been charged with igniting the magazine aboard the *Themis*, a singular act of bravery, which I witnessed myself."

"Was this not the same Aldrich whom Hart had flogged for possessing Mr Paine's pamphlets?" Robert asked.

"It was, though no one else aboard the ship believed the punishment was justified, and it engendered much resentment among the crew, for Aldrich had the respect and love of almost all aboard but for a few jealous of his learning and the great regard bestowed upon him."

"For every genius, no matter how small," Lady Hertle offered, "there is another whose pettiness and jealousy cannot bear it. How many great men have been hounded by others, inferior in every way?"

A moment's silence followed, or perhaps was observed, the cloud of sadness passing over Lady Hertle's eyes again.

"Did you know, Mr Hayden, that Lady Hertle met Rousseau?" Elizabeth Hertle remarked.

"I did not know."

Lady Hertle smiled and shook her head. "He was a genius but a scoundrel, Mr Hayden. A complete scoundrel. How anyone could take seriously a single word said or written by such a man is a source of mystery to me, for he had no principle but avidity, no cause but *Rousseau*. How he escaped the gallows I do not know, for certainly many a thief more 'noble' than he has been hanged. But perhaps I am suffering from pettiness and jealousy of his undeniable genius; even so, it seems to me that no matter how great a man's gifts he cannot be exempted from all laws and customs. Do you not agree?"

"I do agree. I have been among the Indian people of Canada, and I can tell you that they are not the 'noble savages' Rousseau imagined, but a people living by complex, man-made laws and customs, a society as arbitrarily structured and hierarchal as any in Europe. So, at least, was my impression."

After supper Hayden and Robert Hertle retired to the terrace, where Robert smoked, as Lady Hertle would not allow it in her home. The lights of scores of vessels scattered across the dark sound. It was a notably calm night.

"Your ship is in the charge of Mr Barthe, I take it?"

"No, Mr Barthe is ashore with his family. Mr Archer, the third lieutenant, returned to the ship this afternoon and has her in hand in my absence."

"You have hardly mentioned him, Charles. Is he a good officer?"

"He is more than competent, but suffers from what I can only imagine is ambivalence regarding his career. Or perhaps it is merely a lack of passion or energy, I cannot say. I like him perfectly well. His society is pleasant, though he keeps much to himself, and appears to prefer the company of midshipmen to his fellows in the gunroom." Hayden shrugged. "Want of ambition will likely limit his career, or so I would imagine, for he does not lack ability."

"Perhaps serving under Captain Hart has afflicted his passion for the service?"

"It is entirely possible."

"How like you Aunt Bill?"

"She is remarkable. I only hope to be so vital in my eightieth year."

"Yes. I don't know this for a truth, but I suspect that Mrs Hertle and our dear Henrietta will be the heirs of her estate. Not that she possesses great wealth, but even so, this house and a smaller one in London, not inconsiderable monies invested in diverse stocks and land . . . none of it entailed."

"Why would you tell this to me, Robert?" Hayden asked, knowing the answer full well.

"Only by way of saying that Henrietta, in addition to her many obvious charms, will always have a comfortable living."

"A man with my prospects cannot aspire to a match with a woman such as Miss Henrietta, had she not a farthing. Her family would never approve of it."

"Have you met her family?"

"You know I have not."

"Do not be too quick to assume what the Carthews might or might not approve. Mrs Hertle believes that they are guided by the wishes of their daughters in such matters. At least so it was with Henrietta's older sisters, one of whom married a medical student who has not amounted to much, though no one among the Carthews seems to disapprove, for he is such a capital fellow in every other way."

"Well, I am certainly capable of not amounting to much. Does this make me a candidate?"

Robert laughed. "I can't say, but it does seem to me that Miss Henrietta treats you with a certain degree of favour—more so than I have observed with many a young buck who has taken notice of her. And I might say that there have been more than a few."

"That I do not doubt."

Mrs Hertle appeared in the door at that moment and called her husband in to attend Aunt Hertle on some matter. Hayden decided to spend a moment more in the fresh air, judging the strength and direction of the wind, observing the condition of the sky. The open sound was ever a problematic anchorage, and a sharp eye must be kept on the weatherglass and the various changes in atmosphere. He judged the evening relatively calm and likely to stay so.

The scrape of the door drew his attention, but rather than the return of his friend Robert, as he had been expecting, he found Henrietta emerge, arranging a shawl about her shoulders.

"You have been left unattended, Mr Hayden. How thoughtless of us."

"Not at all, Miss Henrietta. Robert was only just now called away, and I have been observing the weather—an obsession of seamen."

"And does it meet with your approval?"

"In every way, even if the night might be a little warmer, though it is not unseasonably cool, by any means."

She came and stood by him, very near to the balustrade, and looked out over the fine view, and up at the river of bright stars. "Will you soon return to sea?" she asked.

"All is uncertain. There is a court-martial to be got through, and then . . . My prospects in His Majesty's Navy are not half so favourable as Robert's."

She straightened her shawl with a sawing motion, then glanced at Hayden, her lovely eyes taking his breath away for an instant. "It is a subject that oppresses you a great deal, I have observed."

"I fear I let it oppress me more than it should. I hope I have not been inflicting my moods upon you?"

She shook her head. "It is your chosen career; how could you not?"

"You are being very kind, but I confess, I should be a great deal happier if my future were more clear."

"Would not we all?" she said with some feeling. "Then duty will keep you in Plymouth for a fortnight?"

"Longer, I should think. The court-martial will not be convened until Captain Hart is entirely recovered, and it is my understanding that the good captain is not healing as he should."

"From what Robert has told us, Captain Hart was ever ready to flog men, innocent or not, and to one poor man did much worse. That he should feel in full measure what he has so readily inflicted upon others is uncommon justice, I think."

Hayden was surprised to hear such emotion in her voice. "Yes, but he shall have his knighthood to console him, apparently."

Henrietta displayed a bitter smile, her full, soft mouth turning down a little. "Though you believe your prospects poor in the service, it is my prediction—and when I choose to make predictions I am seldom wrong—that you shall be given a ship. The Navy will be forced to recognize your talents, Lieutenant. Now see if I am not right."

"I hope with all my heart that you are right, Miss Henrietta, but I did not know it was your talent to predict the future."

She moved a little, side to side, favouring him with a charming half-smile. "It is not, commonly, but from time to time I feel very sure that events will order themselves in a certain manner, and I flatter myself that often I am proved to be in the right."

Hayden repeated that he hoped Henrietta was right, and immediately felt foolish for it. There was a moment of faintly strained silence.

"Perhaps we should join the others," Henrietta said softly, giving Hayden the impression that he had said something she found unpleasant, though he could not think what it could have been.

As he opened the door that she might precede him into the house, she paused in stride and said, "Then we might look for you to call upon us, Lieutenant Hayden?" And then, quickly, "I'm sure Lady Hertle would be very pleased."

"I would like nothing better," he admitted, with a small sense of relief that whatever unpleasantness or misunderstanding had passed between them could be so easily overcome.

Inside, they found Robert overseeing the servants as they exchanged the seascape over the fireplace with a painting of the admiral. It was upon this matter that the newly minted captain had been called to consult.

Lady Hertle gazed up at the portrait of her husband, painted sometime in his fiftieth year, a pleasant-looking gentleman, round-faced and full mouthed. Hayden thought he looked about to laugh or make a jest.

"You see, Elizabeth, it is much better when love creeps up on you unnoticed," Lady Hertle was in the midst of saying. "I knew the admiral for many years, for he would often visit us at our home, and never had the least suspicion that between us lay anything but the fondness you would expect when two young people were so much in one another's society. It was something of a surprise to me when I found myself thinking of him often, in a daydreaming sort of way. I was aware of this 'sea change' in our feelings before the admiral, and was forced to bide my time until he saw it for himself, which happily he did. I must say that men who will engage an enemy in battle without a moment's hesitation are often the most irresolute when it comes to engaging a lady's affections. But finally he spoke, and it still fills my heart with joy to think on it.

"It is a very different thing when you imagine you are in love with someone soon after you have met; then your heart is all aflutter, you can never think what to say and make the most foolish answers to the most innocent enquiries. One lives and dies by every word, and parses every sentence, every look, seeking signs that one's feelings are returned." She waved a hand as though pushing away something unpleasant. "Don't you agree, Lieutenant? Is it not infinitely preferable to discover oneself in love with a young woman whom you have known for some time, rather than a complete stranger whose entire disposition must be created out of hopes and hearsay?"

"I'm sure that is the very best way, Lady Hertle, but one must take love however it finds one, I suspect, not that I am any authority on such matters, of course."

Lady Hertle looked at him in some surprise. "There is a great deal of wisdom in what you say, Lieutenant. Upon my word, you are full of surprises." She turned to the others. "Now, who shall play this evening? My fingers are all swollen and stiff. My dear Elizabeth, will you not play a little for your old Aunt Bill? I have just had the pianoforte tuned."

Elizabeth did play, then she accompanied Henrietta as the latter sang; they then played, at Lady Hertle's insistence, a mistake-filled duet, provoking much hilarity. Finally, Henrietta favoured them with two lovely airs, her rich soprano filling the room. While she played, Hayden thought there was always about her face a look as though she would lose herself in the music—that it would overwhelm her—but that she resisted this fullness of feeling, staying always just within the bounds of what might be deemed acceptable expressions of the music's sentiment.

"You play with your heart, my dear," Lady Hertle said when the songs were done. "Your entire delicate heart."

The evening passed too quickly, to Hayden's mind, and he found himself taking his leave of the company. Mrs Hertle leaned close in a moment when everyone's attention had been taken by a small dog escaping into their company, pursued by a horrified maid, who apologized profusely despite everyone's apparent delight and laughter.

"You did not miss the moral of my aunt's story of her courtship, I hope?" Mrs Hertle asked quietly.

"That one should marry a woman as much like one's sister as possible, but who is no relation at all?" replied Hayden.

"Oh, why must men at all times be so obtuse?" Elizabeth shot at him, and then joined the gathering around the little terrier, who had been swept up into Lady Hertle's arms and was wagging its entire being in excitement.

Having his leave-taking rather overshadowed by a small canine, Hayden went out into the dark street and made his way down to the harbour. Mrs Hertle's last words were not easily disposed of, and he found himself contemplating Lady Hertle's story about her courtship. Was she saying that he should have no aspirations toward her niece Henrietta, because they had known each other only a very short time? She had also opined that men most ready to engage the enemy were often the most reticent to engage a woman's heart—or words to that effect. Certainly she might have been sending a small message that he should not be timid in his pursuit of Henrietta, but if that were so, her other statement seemed designed to work against it. Hayden simply did not have a lady in his life whom he had known for many years, with whom he could suddenly find himself in love and then pursue boldly. He was of the opinion that Mrs Hertle had mistaken the intent of her aunt entirely. There was no message there for anyone, least of all him. Merely an observation of life, one of several she had made during the course of the evening. He determined then to put this matter from his mind.

An hour later he entered the gunroom to find Griffiths seated at the table, the *Times* spread before him, a look of mild indignation upon his studious face.

"Is that the account of our recent cruise, Doctor?" Hayden asked.

"No, it is the account of some other cruise entirely, for I recognize nothing about this story but the name of the ship, and oft-repeated name of the heroic Captain Hart."

"It has not affected you as it did Mr Barthe, I see."

"Our good sailing master was still in an indecent rage when he left the ship. I have never heard such cursing and damning. I even heard him damn the captain's eyes, which I had previously thought the prerogative of Captain Hart alone. But then he had much to say about many another of the captain's body parts. Quite a little anatomical catalogue."

Hayden gestured to the slim newspaper spread upon the polished wood. "It did not surprise you, then, as it did me?"

"Indeed, Mr Hayden, I was taken by surprise for a moment, but then almost immediately felt that my own naïveté alone had allowed this. Anyone more worldly would have realized that Hart would do exactly this." He touched the paper with his fingertips. "I have been to see our former captain this very evening. Or perhaps I should say, to his physician, who led me to believe that Hart was not recovering well. I even thought he made the slightest suggestion that my treatment of the captain was responsible for the tardiness of his healing, though perhaps in this I am mistaken, for when I asked him to state this more clearly he then complimented me on my medical skills—me a mere surgeon—though I dare say I have treated more men who have been flogged than he."

"You did not see the captain, then?"

"No, he was not well enough to receive me, I was told, though I did discover he was quite well enough to meet with a barrister for some length of time this very morning. Terrible what gossips some loblolly boys can be."

"A barrister . . ." Hayden mused. "Certainly he knows that officers are seldom held accountable for losing their ships, except in the cases of the utmost negligence."

"So one would think. But then Mr Archer spoke with his brother, who is a barrister himself, and that gentleman was of the opinion that any officer at a court-martial would do well to have a knowledgeable friend attend him at the court."

"And will Mr Archer's brother be attending, then?"

"So I suppose." He glanced toward the door of Archer's cabin, from which could be heard a soft, even breathing. "Have you witnessed a court-martial, Mr Hayden?"

"I have not."

"I wish I could say the same, but I was called to give evidences at the trial of Mr McBride . . . only to say that the finger that had dropped from the bunt of the sail appeared to have been severed with a knife, and to say also that no man aboard had so recently lost a finger. A small part, though I still feel like a Judas, even so, especially since all of our fears have been borne out and McBride proved innocent."

"Do not take on Hart's sins. It was he who persecuted McBride, and the officers of the court-martial who found him guilty and passed sentence without proper evidence. It was not your doing."

"But I played my part, even so. Perhaps less a Judas and more a Roman soldier. I digress. What I did learn on that day was how brotherly these captains are, for all their posture of disinterest. In McBride's case, the paucity of evidence carried far less weight than Hart's firm assertion that this was the guilty man. Which is a long way of saying they will not find Hart to blame if there is any other upon whose shoulders, perhaps I should say *back*, they can lay this burden." The doctor gazed up from the *Times*, his silvery hair almost aglow in the candle-light.

"There shall be no blame ascribed at all, I'm sure. The resistance to the mutineers was so spirited that all will be held blameless, yourself included, so you may put your mind at rest on that matter. As to who is to blame for the mutiny taking place . . . the mutineers will be held to account for that. No one else. And do not forget, all the officers and loyal crew conducted themselves honourably in retaking the *Themis*."

"Not all, Mr Hayden." Griffiths brushed the paper with the backs of his fingers. "Captain Hart was whimpering in the sick-berth at the time, and ordering you to return him immediately to England. He attempted to steal your command away so that you would not embroil him in a battle to retake the ship he lost. His behaviour was cowardly . . . nay, notorious. If it comes out it will ruin him, and I am not referring to just his career."

Twenty-four

Aboard the *Themis* work proceeded apace, despite the reduced crew—or sometimes, thought Hayden, because of it. The men who remained aboard went about their business with a will, and for those not yet rated able, opportunities were taken to teach them their trade, for it seemed the ship might be in port for some time.

All of the disquiet that had formerly infected the ship was now dissipated, and an easy sense of camaraderie came over the men before the mast. Hayden's orders were obeyed with alacrity, even good cheer, and poor Franks, the hobbled bosun, and his mates were almost at a loss, for they appeared never to have any cause to start a man. In short, the *Themis* became a happy ship for the first time in many years.

The promise of prize money made desertion unlikely, and Hayden began granting brief shore leaves to small numbers of men, who repaid this trust by returning to the ship more or less on time, though rather less sober. The battered frigate began to take on her former lustre as carpenters and riggers plied their trades. Several coats of paint concealed the usual multitude of sins.

Hayden felt that he was suspended upon the surface of time; the weeks of suffering under Hart were past, but great uncertainty lay yet ahead. Between these two terrible seasons, the halcyon spread its charm upon man and sea, and Hayden's spirit took on a strangely resigned contentment, although he suspected the presence in Plymouth of Henrietta Carthew played some part in this.

Hayden took the deck, on one of these golden mornings, and was saluted sharply by crew and officers, several of the latter concealing good-natured smiles. He was wearing his best coat and very clean linen—a sure sign that he went to visit a certain lady—but his contentment was such that he did not mind in the least being the cause of amusement for his fellows.

"The ship is yours until I return, Mr Archer," Hayden said as he went to the rail and his waiting boat. "Do not neglect airing the magazines. There cannot be many more days such as this."

"The magazine scuttles are already open, Mr Hayden. Enjoy your time ashore, sir." Archer did not hide his smile very completely, but then neither did Hayden.

As Hayden's cutter pushed off from the *Themis* (he refused the bosun's insistence that he use the captain's barge), Hayden regarded his ship. Men sat on staging planks hung over the sides, and plied their brushes, a low murmur of amiable conversation, like bees on a bush, emitting from the ship. The cool airs of autumn appeared only at night, most days still unseasonably warm, the rains held at bay.

"She looks very well, Price," Hayden called.

"Thank you, sir." Price twisted around on his staging plank. "If clothes make a cove a gent, then I reckon a coat will make this old lady a . . . well, a frigate, sir."

"I could not have said it better," Hayden observed.

In a few moments he was on the quay, and at the appointed place met Captain and Mrs Hertle in company with Mrs Hertle's cousin, Henrietta Carthew. He was favoured with a smile that never failed to quicken his pulse, and in a moment was walking with Henrietta while the Hertles fell a little behind, stopping to gaze at some object of interest or other.

"Is this not the most exceptional weather?" Henrietta declared. "I can hardly remember an October day so warm."

Hayden agreed that this was so.

"It must be a great boon for your crew and the refitting of your ship. How goes the work, Captain?"

"I am only a lieutenant, as you well know."

"But your captain has quit the ship, I believe you said, and Captain Hertle tells me that in such cases, the acting senior officer is addressed as *Captain*. Is this not so?"

"Yes and no. Were I put in charge of the ship for some reason—a job-captain, as it were—the crew would address me as you say, but as Hart is still officially the captain and only away from the ship, I am nothing more than the first lieutenant."

They had become very contented in each other's company, Hayden fancied. He even began to imagine that there was an understanding growing between them, though often doubts assailed him. But whenever his pessimism would get the better of him, Henrietta would say something to raise his hopes again, almost as though she sensed his thoughts, his moods.

As they walked along the bustling quay, weaving in and out among the costermongers and fishermen, Landry appeared from behind a knot of men and women. He hurried along with his head down, hardly minding where he was going. At the last second he managed to pull up, and as he raised his eyes to make his apologies, he gave a little start of alarm.

"Mr Hayden, sir. I do beg your pardon. I did not see you. Madame, please accept my apologies." He quickly doffed his hat to Henrietta.

Hayden introduced the two. "I am glad to find you under any circumstances, Mr Landry. There is much work yet to be done, and we are waiting on the press to bring up our numbers. But we will speak of it aboard ship."

Landry looked suddenly uncomfortable, or perhaps embarrassed. "By your leave, Mr Hayden, Captain Hart has need of my aid to prepare for the coming court-martial."

"Prepare for the court-martial . . . Whatever do you mean, Mr Landry? Captain Hart will give his account of what occurred and the officers shall all say much the same. The ship's logs and the journals of the various officers will bear witness to his account. What need is there for preparation?"

"I know not, sir. I only know that the captain has told me he will require my services for several days." He shrugged, raising his hands in a helpless gesture.

"He is the captain, Mr Landry," Hayden said, "of course you must do his bidding. How goes his recovery?"

"Slowly, sir, but I believe the worst is past."

Hayden shook his head. "It was a deplorable business, Mr Landry. Well, we should not detain you—a man in so obvious a hurry."

Farewells, and Landry hastened on his way.

"So that is Lieutenant Landry . . ." Henrietta appeared to be deep in thought. "He seemed rather alarmed to see you. As though he had been caught out in some shameful act."

Hayden realized that he had thought the same. "He did look rather dismayed."

"Curious that he is aiding Hart. Did you not say that he defied the captain at the end, and Hart threatened him?"

"So it was, but apparently all is forgiven. Or perhaps Hart has no other upon whom he can call. Landry could hardly refuse him."

"No, I am sure you are right."

The walk continued, though Landry's unlooked-for appearance began to raise questions in Hayden's mind. How long had the man been in Plymouth? Odd that he was not staying aboard the ship, even if just by night.

When they found themselves in a situation that no other might hear, Henrietta had begun speaking to him in French, largely to practice her almost-perfect accent. Their "private language" created a kind of intimacy between them, Hayden imagined, but at the same time he found the experience brought back the confusion and storms of emotion he had experienced on his recent cruise. As he did his best to hide this, Henrietta continued to speak his mother's tongue.

She observed that her cousin bore Captain Hertle's frequent, sometimes prolonged, absences rather stoically.

"Would you think such an arrangement intolerable?" Hayden asked.

"Intolerable? Perhaps. Wearisome, certainly, but then," she said with a quick glance at his face, "it would depend . . . Were I married to a man I loved deeply, I don't know if such a depth of feeling would make the separation unbearable or if such a bond would ease the burden. You are often abroad, Mr Hayden, how bear you this separation from your loved ones?"

"I have no family but my mother in Boston, and we are in each other's company so infrequently I cannot remember what it was like to be often near her. Were I to marry, though, I fear I should miss my wife terribly. I know Robert does so. How I wish this war were over and all of us returned safely home."

"It is the fervent wish of us all, Lieutenant."

She took his offered arm to step over a tread where several stones had become dislodged. Hayden thought she looked for excuses to do this, and a small glow of warmth would spread through him each time.

Hayden left them at Lady Hertle's, though not without paying his respects to the dear lady, and hurried down to find his boat. His coxswain had the cutter riding to a small anchor . . . just far enough from the quay that his men could manage a decidedly bawdy exchange with the waterfront sirens, but not so close that they could be tempted to ruin upon those notorious hearts of stone. Hayden hailed the boat and Childers soon brought her up to the stair, but before Hayden could take up his station in the stern sheets, a letter was placed in his hand.

"Mr Barthe sent this out from the ship, sir," the coxswain explained. "He thought it might require your immediate attention."

Hayden broke the seal, noting it had not come by regular post. Unfolding the single sheet, he found the briefest note directing him to a particular inn. It was signed "Philip Stephens." Hayden bid Childers to lie off again, and hurried back the way he had come.

The First Secretary had rooms overlooking the sound, and Hayden was immediately taken up to meet with him. There was no desk to hide behind this time, no jar containing a severed finger to be produced with a dramatic flourish. Stephens rose to greet him, and the two sat where the light from the open windows fell upon them in elongated squares. The First Secretary was not much given to pleasantries, and from a small stack of papers produced Hayden's last missive to his friend Mr Banks.

Slipping on his spectacles with one hand, Stephens tilted the letter to the sun, as though to remind himself of its contents. Hayden felt his resentment kindle at that moment, and begin to grow. It had been Stephens who had, in full knowledge, put him under Hart's command— an able lieutenant to bear up the weak-kneed captain, as someone among the Lords Commissioners had requested. But Stephens had possessed his own designs; perhaps to intrigue against Hart within the Admiralty, or to expose the well-connected captain to men who apparently were unaware of his true nature. And Hayden had been his instrument in this matter, much to the lieutenant's distaste.

The spectacles were removed, set aside, and the measuring gaze settled on Hayden. "I must say, Mr Hayden, that your own account of your recent cruise differs significantly from the narrative published in *The Times*. Have you seen it?"

"It is a pack of disgraceful lies," Hayden stated unequivocally.

This brought Stephens up short, and he fixed Hayden with a most serious look, but Hayden was in no mood to be intimidated. Stephens had thrust him into an untenable situation aboard the *Themis* and his already precarious career had been brought lower as a result. He wanted no more "favours" from the estimable Mr Stephens.

"You seem to be indignant, Lieutenant," Stephens said, his throaty voice even and emotionless.

"And how could I not be, sir? You put me aboard a ship with a man who must be the most cowardly officer in His Majesty's Navy, a tyrant whose crew had already turned against him, and expected me to rescue him from his own folly. And what did this man do at every turn but undermine my authority and my ability to aid him. From this day forward I will have Hart's mutiny attached to my name, and I was not even aboard ship when it occurred—a ship, I must add, which was recaptured from mutineers against Hart's express wishes!" Hayden fell silent, his mind suddenly in a blur of resentment and rage.

Stephens did not appear to take offence at this outburst, nor did he appear the least contrite. "I hope it will comfort you to know that your account has been related to certain gentlemen of influence, and if I have my way, Josiah Hart will serve in His Majesty's Navy no more."

Hayden threw up his hands. "Certainly it was worth my career to accomplish that," he spat out.

Stephens turned his head and gazed out the window a moment, his thoughts impenetrable to Hayden. His eyes still fixed on the distant view, the First Secretary observed, "The court-martial will begin in four days." He turned back to Hayden and noted the lieutenant's reaction to this news. "You did not know? Having received word that Bourne is soon to return, Hart is suddenly recovered enough to face a court-martial. Much . . . politicking has gone into the selection of captains who will make up the panel. I have done what I could in this regard, but we shall see. Others are perhaps more skilled in these matters than I." He rose and offered his hand. "Good luck to you, Mr Hayden."

Hayden also rose, startled at this abrupt dismissal. Rather reluctantly he took the First Secretary's soft little hand, and in a moment was back on the street—quite stunned. The man had overseen the ruin of his career and did not even offer an apology. At least when first they met Hayden had been offered a commission. From this meeting he took nothing but a handshake.

Robert had warned that he should never have taken the position without some solid promise in return. Perhaps, as always, Robert had known more of the character of Philip Stephens than Hayden had been able to guess from their single meeting.

He cursed under his breath. There it was, clear as clear. The First Secretary had met with him, and nothing whatsoever had come of it. Lieutenant Charles Hayden had no future in His Majesty's Navy.

"But it was me that took the damned ship back," he muttered to himself, gaining an odd look from a passer-by.

In this strange conflict between his two nations, Hayden had chosen England, but England had not chosen him in return.

Not three steps further on he heard his name called and looked up to find Mr Muhlhauser of the Ordnance Board, smiling at him as though they were old shipmates.

Hayden struggled to master his rage and resentment. "Mr Muhlhauser. How good to see you, sir."

Muhlhauser made a stiff leg. "How is your poor head, Mr Hayden? You received quite a blow, indeed; the doctor was most concerned."

"I am no more foolish than previously, so I suppose that is the best one can hope for. And your own wounds?"

Muhlhauser waved an arm that was still in a sling. "All but healed. I should be free of this in a few days."

"I am surprised to find you here. I thought you had returned home." Hayden could not help but remember the failed gun-carriage of Muhlhauser's design.

"I am come for the court-martial, Mr Hayden, in the event that my own evidence is required. Though at this moment I am off to see the First Secretary."

"Stephens?"

"Could it be another?"

"No . . . No, of course not. I should not wish to make you overdue."

The two men parted. Stephens, it appeared, was familiar with a vast portion of the Royal Navy. It pained Hayden's poor, dazed brain to puzzle out what this might mean, so he gave it up, making his way back down to the busy quay and onto the now rather notorious *Themis*.

The gunroom door opened and Archer came in. "Mr Wickham sends his compliments, Mr Hayden, having just returned to the ship."

"And my compliments to Mr Wickham. I shall be glad to have him back. Is he outside?"

"No, sir. He scurried off to visit Aldrich in the sick-berth."

"I should be able to release Aldrich from the sick-berth tomorrow," Griffiths said. "But he is not even to have light duty for at least a week."

"Our ship's company is slowly trickling back, it seems," Barthe observed.

"Yes, I saw Landry today," Hayden informed the others. "Bumped into him, as it were, on the quay. He is aiding Hart in his preparations for the court-martial, apparently."

"We saw him, as well, Mr Hayden. He came aboard ship and fetched a few articles from his cabin. Hardly had a moment to be civil."

They sat about the table, sipping claret, which they drew off from a quarter-keg that stood upon a shelf by the door. Barthe occasionally gazed hungrily at one of the glasses, the play of light through the deep, liquid red, but then he would master himself and glance away, or smile with a kind of bitter embarrassment.

"Perhaps I should write up my day," he said, and rose from the table. "There is such an abundance of work accomplished each day, I can hardly keep up my harbour-log."

The master repaired to his small cabin, but in a moment, his door opened again, a look of bewilderment on the round face. "You have not taken my log to write up some work, have you, Mr Hayden?"

"I should never do such a thing, Mr Barthe. The ship's log is your sacred charge."

"It must be here," the master muttered, and went back into his cabin. The clatter of instruments and books being shifted, a low curse. "Some-one has removed my log from its proper place," he said peevishly. Reappearing, red-faced, the master looked around the gunroom as though expecting to find the book lying there, astray and neglected, on some shelf or table.

A general search commenced, to no avail. The others then began to quiz the master closely: when had he last written in the log? where had he done this? and so on. But Barthe claimed never to have taken the book from the gunroom.

Midshipmen and servants were interrogated. No one had seen the book in question. In the middle of this, Wickham turned up, looking overly pleased to be back aboard ship, Hayden thought.

Griffiths began tallying who, to anyone's knowledge, had cause to enter the gunroom that day, and as names were offered, that of Lieutenant Herald Landry was uttered. A horrible silence fell over the gunroom.

"The court-martial shall require the ship's log," Archer said. "My brother told me that all the officers' journals must be submitted, but the ship's log . . . that is the most vital, for it is the official account of our cruise."

Barthe lowered himself slowly into a chair, his red face draining like a glass. "I am charged with the safe-keeping of the ship's log-book," he said. "None other."

Though it was never mentioned, everyone present knew that the master had once before been convicted of neglecting his duty.

"But clearly you have kept it safe," Griffiths assured him. "It has been removed . . . *stolen*, it seems."

"If the official log is gone," Wickham observed thoughtfully, "then every event might be questioned, the captain and Landry saying one thing, the officers another. The captains of the court-martial will have to decide whom to believe."

"And whom will the captains choose, I wonder?" Griffiths asked.

A very earnest discussion followed, for now that a date had been set, the prospect of the court-martial took on an immediacy it had lacked formerly. Those who had witnessed courts-martial gave lengthy accounts, interrupted by many questions.

"It is the King who will be prosecutor," Barthe said. For reasons he did not like to dwell upon, the master knew more of courts-martial than the rest. "All officers and crew will be tried for the loss of the *Themis*."

"But it was a mutiny," Wickham said, clearly confused. "Are not the mutineers to be blamed?"

"Indeed, Mr Wickham," Hawthorne explained, "they shall attend their own court-martial, and will almost certainly all be hanged. Losing the ship is the single charge against us, for it does not matter by what means a ship is lost—there is a court-martial all the same. Am I not correct, Mr Barthe?"

"Indeed you are. When a ship is lost," Barthe said patiently, "it is sometimes due to an error or negligence on the part of an officer other than the captain—perhaps an error in navigation by the master—so all officers are charged. Of course, it is the captain who will be questioned most closely and is in the most danger."

"Let Hart go to the devil," Hawthorne said, "I am more concerned with the gentlemen of my mess. How do we defend ourselves against these charges? I for one do not want to shoulder the blame, and certainly my part will be called into question, for it is the place of the marines to guard the ship against mutineers."

"You must all write an account of what happened from the moment you became aware of the mutiny," Hayden said. "As accurate as memory can make it. I have no doubt that every one of you acquitted himself with honour. You have nothing to fear."

The lamps burned long into the night in the gunroom, as the officers present framed their answers to any questions they could imagine the court asking.

While these accounts were written, Hayden climbed up to the captain's cabin and sent for young Worth. The boy—he could not have been nineteen—slipped silently in the door a few moments later. The term "plain" applied to the young landsman in almost every possible way. There was about him a look so unremarkable as to pass all notice. Hayden doubted that anyone could tell another what he looked like five minutes after he had left a room. Hair some neutral colour that might deserve the descriptor "brown," features without distinction in either size or shape, height adequate, neither well-made nor ill. He could almost have been invisible so little impression did he leave.

"Worth, be at your ease, you are in no trouble, sir."

The man, whose manner was taut and anxious, did not seem to find this reassuring.

"Do you know, Worth, that some member of the crew has been leaving helpful notes in the pockets of my jacket. This has been secretly done and I do not wish to expose the man who has done it, which means I can never thank him. Very odd, is it not?"

"Perhaps the man does not wish to be thanked, sir," Worth said, his face utterly neutral.

"Which would make him very noble." Hayden fixed his gaze on the man's face for a moment. "It appears that Mr Barthe, through no fault of his own, has got himself into a bit of difficulty. I am seeking a way to extricate him but have realized I require assistance. There is, however, a significant risk to the man who might aid me, so I hesitate to ask . . ."

"What risk, sir?"

"Prison. Perhaps worse."

The boy worried a thread sprouting from a seam in his trousers. "That *is* a risk, sir. Might I ask what a man might do to aid Mr Barthe?"

"The ship's log went missing from Mr Barthe's cabin, which the officers of the court-martial will view as a serious lapse in the performance of his duties. They might also wonder if Mr Barthe has 'lost' this book because the contents reflected badly upon him in some way."

"I swear, Mr Hayden, I don't know where the book is."

"But I do. Or at least I believe I do. Would it be possible to retrieve Mr Barthe's log from a house or some other lodging without appreciable risk to a nimble man with some expertise in such affairs?"

Hardly an eye-blink in reaction. "Oh, I should think it would be, Mr Hayden."

"How many men do you think such an endeavour would require?"

"Three, sir." A slight pause. "I believe I might recommend such men, if I may be so bold."

"I will have the doctor write their names on the sick-and-hurt list. They will be far too ill to attend the court-martial, where I'm sure Mr Landry and Captain Hart will be engaged all of the forenoon at the very least."

Hayden crouched low, inspecting the rudder trunk in the dim light of a lamp held aloft by the carpenter. Pushing the tip of a blade into the wood, he was appalled to find it sliding in with little resistance once the surface had been broken.

"It is amazing to me we have not even seen it weep when the seas built up. I don't know how you noticed it, Mr Chettle, but well done."

"If not for a bit of new paint bubbling up, I should never have suspected for a moment, Mr Hayden. Rotten inside but, for the most part, sound out. We should have had trouble from it in no time, I'll warrant."

"Yes. It will have to be rebuilt." Hayden rose, ducking beneath the tiller. "Sooner rather than later."

"I'll see to it first thing, Mr Hayden."

As Hayden turned away a marine corporal stepped into the circle of light.

"There you are, Mr Hayden," the marine offered. "There is a ship's master to see you, sir. Mr Hawthorne has put him in the captain's cabin to await your pleasure."

"I shall speak with him directly."

A moment later Hayden entered the great cabin to find a man seated by the table, hat in hand, his greatcoat thrown open. Glancing up to the door-sound, he rose, extending a hand, his manner business-like.

"Mr Hayden. How pleased I am to make your acquaintance at last. Ben Tupper, master of the *New England*. I come bearing mail from Mrs Adams, sir, and hearing that you were aboard the *Themis*, I carried it over directly." He proffered a package heavily wrapped and bound in string.

"Why, how very kind of you, Mr Tupper. Very kind, indeed. Will you take a drink with me?"

"It would be my great pleasure, upon some other occasion, sir, but I have an engagement yet, this evening . . ."

"Then it will wait for another time, Mr Tupper. Pray, how fared my mother and Mr Adams, when last you saw?"

"They prosper very well, Mr Hayden. I was at supper to their home but six weeks ago, and Mrs Adams seemed very content and jolly. Mr Adams is also very cheerful, and thriving in his various endeavours. They spoke of you with great fondness, Mr Hayden, and desired I convey these letters to England, though I hardly expected to put them in your hand. I shall weigh in three days' time, Mr Hayden, and would gladly carry your letters with me, if you wish it."

"I shall take the first offered moment to compose my replies and have them carried over to your ship before you sail, Mr Tupper. It is very kind of you."

"Anything for Mr and Mrs Adams, Mr Hayden; they are very dear to me."

Hayden escorted the American master up to the deck and saw him on his way, then hurried back down to his cabin to open his letters. His mother's delicate hand could not reduce her life to black and white, but captured the nuance of her thought, her mercurial emotions. French would give way to English, mid-sentence—once in the middle of a verb—and Spanish and Italian were added for spice. Much concern about her family in France—the little news she had—all well . . . so far. Three letters she had sent, all overflowing with the happiness of her new life in America. (How Aldrich would have approved of that, Hayden thought.) At the same time, her wickedly satirical observations about Americans made Hayden laugh aloud.

In the package he also found a dutiful letter from his step-father, almost without content, and a longer one from Mr Adams' youngest daughter, twelve-year-old Emma, who admired him overly, he well knew.

Answers would have to wait, for there was much to do, and Hayden did not know how to explain his present situation. The truth was he did not understand it himself. He was not charged with the loss of HMS *Themis*, yet had a terrible feeling that on the morrow the full blame for this notorious affair would be his to bear. Perhaps these letters extolling the virtues of life in America meant more than was revealed upon their surface.

The next morning, very early, Hayden received a note from Landry, saying that Captain Hart was sending his barrister, Sir Hubert Chatham, K.C., to the ship to advise the officers on the coming court-martial.

At ten o'clock sharp Sir Hubert came aboard, Hayden meeting him at the rail. He led the man down to the captain's cabin, where he had gathered the officers, young gentlemen, and warrant officers. Introductions were made, through which Sir Hubert stood grave and impatient. Hayden thought he had never met a man so intent upon a single purpose. One had the notion that Sir Hubert never smiled, made a jest, or thought of anything but the business immediately at hand. True to this impression, he began to speak the instant Hayden had completed introductions.

"I have been engaged by your captain, Sir Josiah Hart," he said, inspiring looks of surprise and then consternation all around, "to advise him on the pending court-martial. As you are no doubt aware, you can be advised but not represented by counsel and must speak in your own defence, answering any and all questions put to you by the captains of the panel. The purpose of the court-martial is to enquire into the 'causes and circumstances' of the mutiny. The circumstances are clear enough, and I'm sure all of you are in agreement as much as any men can be who might have witnessed the events from different parts of the ship or in different ways. If, however, your accounts differ significantly, one to the other, the captains who sit in judgement will have no choice but to ask many questions. It is for this reason that you must be certain that you are all in agreement on the salient points: the time and place; who was involved; what was done, by whom and to whom; how you came to be put in the boats. Your accounts need not concern themselves with your subsequent rescue or the events that followed. That is not the business of the court-martial." He paused here, looking quickly around the circle of faces. "Upon one point it is most important that you all agree, for if you do not, questions will ensue that will make many of you most uncomfortable. You must all state that you had no warning whatsoever of the mutiny. There is a very good reason for this. If you had warning, the captains of the court-martial will want to know why measures were not taken to avoid the occurrence of the mutiny. I cannot caution you strongly enough in this regard. I have made this point repeatedly to Sir Josiah: you must all agree that you had no warning of the mutiny, no suspicions of mutinous conduct or language among the crew. To do otherwise will lead to many questions that will aid no one in their future careers in the Navy, and will accomplish nothing, for certainly this mutiny was a surprise to everyone aboard. Am I not correct?"

A moment of awkward silence, and then a few present nodded their heads, some muttered agreement. But a few only gazed darkly at the barrister.

Sir Hubert Chatham did not linger to discuss the case further, but took up his hat and was quickly gone. As the door closed to the captain's cabin, the men seated round the table looked from one to the other.

"Sir Josiah bloody Hart," Barthe spat out to muttered imprecations and much shaking of heads.

"I, for one, am not aware of any hints that our crew were mutinous," Franks stated firmly. "I'm sure you agree, Mr Hawthorne? For if we had any suspicions you might have placed more guards. The arms chest might have been moved to the captain's cabin, or any number of things that we did not do because we were taken by surprise."

Hawthorne nodded, his face dark and unhappy. "As much as I mislike to uphold Hart in even the smallest thing, I fear this barrister is right— we were all set adrift in the same boat and if we do not all pull together we shall go down."

"It will certainly be convenient for Captain Hart if we all agree," Barthe said bitterly. "For he does not want his part in all of this to come out, that is certain."

"I don't know if you comprehended Sir Hubert's entire meaning, Mr Barthe, if I may say so." The doctor fixed the sailing master with a very sober gaze. "If Hart is brought to ruin by this court-martial—and God knows he should be—he will endeavour to bring down all of his officers with him. Mr Archer, Hawthorne, perhaps even Mr Hayden, and certainly he shall not spare you, Mr Barthe. Do not misjudge the vindictiveness of Captain Hart. If you take it upon yourself to expose his failings be aware of what it will mean to you and to your messmates."

"Mr Hayden?" The scrubbed face of Midshipman Hobson appeared in the just-opened door.

The first lieutenant sat at the gunroom table, reading over the accounts of the mutiny written by the crew, or rather, dictated by the foremast hands, most of whom could not write.

Archer's brother, who had arrived from London the previous day, had taken on the defence of the officers, and offered much advice to aid them in writing their accounts. Having been privy to much of this, Hayden had put this valuable information to use in aiding the poor Jacks, most of whom were less able to defend themselves. Aldrich and young Perse had also transcribed numerous accounts.

"They have fired a gun from the admiral's ship, sir."

"I shall be with you momentarily." Hayden gathered up all the papers, arranging them carefully. Perse wrapped them in an oilskin to protect them from wet. Taking up his hat, Hayden went on deck, where he found the other officers of the *Themis*, all in their best uniforms, neckcloths tied just so. A few tried to smile at him, but failed miserably, and their attempts to reassure one another seemed terribly forced. Hayden had not seen them so distressed, even before an action.

They took their places in the boats, which bore them quickly over to the seventy-four-gun ship that would act as their courthouse for the next few days. Despite having not been named in the charges, due to his good fortune of being aboard the prize, Hayden still felt a great deal of apprehension. The entire business was a sordid shame, and he could not help but fear his own fortunes would be brought low by what was about to transpire.

Hart had sent out a note the previous evening, asking that his barge be dispatched for him a quarter of an hour before the court-martial was to begin, and Hayden spotted him now: the stiff, unhappy faces of his oarsmen as they bent silently to work, Hart and Landry seated in the stern-sheets with Sir Hubert Chatham.

"Slack off a little, Mr Childers," Hayden said to the coxswain, who had begged not to be sent for Hart. "Let the captain go aboard before us."

They hung back while Hart went up the side, painfully slowly.

"How has he healed, do you think?" Hayden asked Griffiths, but the doctor shook his head.

"Better than Aldrich, whose health has been ruined, I fear."

A moment later they went up the side of the ship, where all the officers but Hayden and Wickham were placed in the custody of the provost-marshal.

"Good luck," Hayden wished the men, as he and Wickham—not named in the court-martial directly—were spectators only and were separated from the men charged.

A few moments later the rest of the crew—those who had been put off from the *Themis* in the boats—came aboard, for every man would be required to account for his actions during the mutiny. If the officers appeared daunted, the crewmen looked positively despairing, and Hayden went over and offered them what cheer he could, telling them that they had nothing to fear. Many of these men had been wounded or otherwise injured in defence of the ship, and still wore dressings or had visible wounds, a fact that Hayden thought could not be ignored by the court.

The captain's cabin had been cleared of its bulkheads, and three tables, the centre one hardly larger than a desk, set before the stern gallery. A rarefied autumn light streamed in the windows that day, reflections off the water sending brilliant ribbons rippling across the white deckhead. The twelve captains who would make up the judicial panel took their places at the tables, and at the centre, in place of the port admiral, sat

Admiral Frederick Duncan, the senior admiral at that time present. Opposite Admiral Duncan, and facing the windows, stood a desk placed for the judge-advocate. Off to one side, at the sufferance of the court, was a small writing-table where the legal advisors of the accused could easily speak to their clients.

The spectators were to either side in neat rows of chairs, and separated from the court by ropes covered in green baize. The crew of the *Themis* arranged themselves behind the judge-advocate, officers and young gentlemen to the fore, warrant officers behind, and then the crew. They would be allowed to hear each other's testimony, a consideration that would certainly not be extended to the mutineers, who would face their own court-martial in the coming days.

Before the court-martial was called to order, Muhlhauser appeared, and took up a seat beside Hayden, with a whispered greeting. He still had one arm in a conspicuous sling, but otherwise appeared hale.

The captains were first sworn in, and Hayden found himself a little intimidated by the presence of these men, all but one of whom were high up on the captains' list and commanded ships of the line—seventy-fours and larger. They had about them, to a man, a sense of near-majesty, an aura of intimidating, almost frightening, authority. They were well used to giving orders that would see men's lives end, or would put into danger a ship's entire company. They would not hesitate to order an execution if they thought it justified.

The judge-advocate rose and stated the purpose of the court-martial: ". . . to enquire into the causes and circumstances of the seizure of His Majesty's Ship *Themis*, commanded by Captain Sir Josiah Hart, and try the said Captain Hart and such officers and crew as were present for their conduct on that occasion."

The first man called to be examined was Hart and as he took his place, standing to the left of the judge-advocate, the onlookers fell completely silent, everyone leaning forward just a little. Hart appeared pale and aged, Hayden thought, his skin dull and flaccid. He leaned upon a walking stick in apparent pain.

"Can we not have a chair for Sir Josiah?" one of the captains on the panel asked. "The good captain's health is yet fragile."

This was granted without discussion, and Hart lowered his substantial bulk into the seat, though conspicuously mindful not to let his injured person contact the chair back.

"If it pleases the court," he began in a thin voice, "due to my recent mistreatment and trials, I should ask that my written statement be read for me by my advisor, Sir Hubert Chatham."

This too was granted and Sir Hubert stepped forward. He began by thanking the judges for their indulgence, and then in a warm, refined voice read Hart's account, which Hayden guessed had been largely composed by Sir Hubert, for he recognized little of the tone of Captain Hart in the words, and not merely because no eyes were damned throughout the entire document.

"'Mr President, gentlemen, I most recently had the honour of commanding His Majesty's Ship *Themis*, a thirty-two-gun frigate sent by the Lords Commissioners of the Admiralty to harass the enemy upon her Atlantic coast and to assess the strength of the French fleet in as many of her harbours as we could look into. We had begun our cruise on the twenty-third day of September, leaving Plymouth in a south-east gale, and taking shelter in Torbay. Upon the cessation of foul weather we proceeded to the coast of France, where, in the entrance to Brest harbour, we had the good fortune to seize an enemy transport while in the process of assessing the fleet strength.

"'As we proceeded south, on the fifth day of October, we made common purpose with Captain Bourne of the *Tenacious*, a gentleman with whose reputation I am certain Your Lordships are well familiar. My ship then participated in cutting out the French frigate *Dragoon*, anchored beneath the batteries of Belle Île. My first lieutenant was given command of the prize and ordered to sail said ship to Plymouth, by which circumstance he and a number of other men were not aboard the *Themis* at the time of the mutiny. Upon the sixth day of October, at about seven bells of the middle watch, I was wakened by the sound of my cabin door being stealthily opened. Three men, one bearing a lantern, and the other two under arms, entered my cabin and ordered me, upon pain of death, to rouse from my cot and heed their every order. Clad only in my night-shirt, I was allowed first to pull on my breeches, before I was bound and made to lie on the floor of my cabin under guard. At that time a general cry went up and the sound of small arms was heard from diverse places about the ship. Very shortly I could hear, from the gunroom directly below my cabin, a very lively skirmish had been engaged, and the same from overhead on the quarterdeck. My spirits rose at this sound and I tried to reason with the two men guarding me, Dundas and Clark, saying that if they set me free I should see that no charges would be laid against them, but though they looked very concerned they told me only to hold my tongue or they should cut it out.

" 'I heard the last shots fired in the gunroom, and soon after firing ceased upon the deck as well, but it was some minutes before I knew the outcome of these battles. Much shouting and cursing could be heard from about the ship and after a time of silence, I know not how long, a man appeared at my door and ordered me brought from my cabin. I was led up onto the deck, where I found my officers and many of our people had been gathered in the waist, a number of them bleeding and much injured from the recent fight. At first, I was put among my officers, where I received much abuse from the men who had joined in the mutiny. I was cuffed and kicked and struck with the flat of many a cutlass. I was not alone in being so treated, as many a private score was settled at that time, and I am sorry to say that two men who had been loyal to me were killed before my eyes. Before the hour was out, another departed this life, done in by the wounds he had received.

" 'There ensued then a dispute among the mutinous elements of the crew as to what was to be done, some men favouring setting out for foreign parts and others wishing to sail into the harbour of Brest to turn the ship over to the French authorities. As this was argued, a small number of the crew led by William Stuckey took hold of me and seized me up to a grating. Although many even among the mutineers protested this act, the afore-mentioned Stuckey proceeded to inflict a vicious beating upon my person with a cat, saying as he began, "This is on account of

Mr Aldrich." This statement quelled the resistance to Stuckey, and even some of the men who protested my treatment were heard to cry, "Aye, on Mr Aldrich's account." I was afterward cut down from the grating and the doctor was allowed to come to my aid. The said William Stuckey and some others then seized upon acting First Lieutenant Herald Landry and would have flogged him as well, but at that time one of their leaders, Able Seaman Peter Aldrich, came up from below decks and ordered that there should be no more floggings and suggested that myself and the crew loyal to me should be put into boats and set adrift, which was done forthwith. As these boats were without sails and rig, we took to the oars and set out north-west hoping to find a British ship in the vicinity of Ushant, but chanced upon the French prize *Dragoon*, which was being conveyed back to England by my own first lieutenant.

"'As my lords are no doubt aware, with only eighty able-bodied men, we then had the good fortune to overhaul the *Themis* and take her back from the mutineers, returning her to the possession of His Majesty's Navy. This is, sirs, to the best of my knowledge and recollection, what occurred. I submit this account along with several lists: the first, of the men who actively joined in the mutiny; the second, a list of those men who came away with me in the boats; the third is less clear. A good number of men were killed during the mutiny and I have been at pains to separate the loyal men who died in the course of their duty and those who died as mutineers. They are clearly marked. As for those men killed but whose allegiance is unknown, I have placed their names on a separate tally and hope that their parts shall be brought to light in due course. All other members of the crew were away on the prizes or, as I have noted, under the care of the doctor in the sick-berth at the time of mutiny.' "

Sir Hubert made a small bow and returned to his desk.

Wickham touched Hayden's arm. "He has included Aldrich among the mutineers," he whispered, unable to hide his alarm.

"It shall be set straight, I'm sure," Hayden replied, though unsettled himself.

Admiral Duncan waved for a silence, as a little breeze of whispering had followed the barrister's reading.

"Sir Josiah," he began, "I have been informed that the ship's log has been lost. Is this possible?"

"I'm afraid it is, sir. I do not know the circumstances of it, Admiral, for it occurred while I was ashore under the care of a physician, but I'm confident that Mr Barthe, the ship's master, has an explanation. I have, sir, submitted my own journal, which will certainly make up for the loss of the ship's log."

The admiral did not look happy with this answer, nor with the muttering among the *Themis'* people, but then asked if any of the captains wished to put questions to Captain Hart.

"Captain Hart," a clearly displeased captain named McLeod asked, "was such negligence common to the master?"

"I am sorry to say that it was, sir, as Mr Barthe's own naval record will attest."

Hayden felt his back straighten, and he looked over to see Griffiths lay a hand upon the arm of Barthe, who had begun to rise, face glowing crimson, fists clenched. Only Hawthorne and the doctor kept him in his seat, though his response did not go unnoticed by any present.

"Captain Hart," asked Gardner, captain of the seventy-four-gun ship *Goliath*, "were you displeased by the conduct of any man during the course of these unfortunate events?"

"Of the officers who were aboard ship at the time of the mutiny, sir, I have nary a word of reproach. All of the ship's people resisted the mutineers to the best of their abilities. I believe this is proven by the long list of men killed and hurt in the defence of the ship." Hart shifted in his chair, glancing around the cabin guardedly. "Of some, who had the good fortune to quit the ship a few hours before the mutiny," he growled, "I was less pleased."

"What mean you, sir?" the *Defiant's* captain, Bainsbridge, enquired.

Hart did not seem to notice the apprehensive look upon the face of his legal advisor.

"I was absent from the ship for ten weeks before we set out upon our cruise, sir, and was returned only a few days when the mutiny occurred, yet I am on trial for it. Lieutenant Charles Hayden had command of the

Themis for many weeks during my absence and was only off her for a few hours when the mutiny occurred, yet he is held guiltless who is most to blame." As he made this statement, Hart's chin quivered with either anger or the frailty of age. The room fell utterly silent.

"What is it you are suggesting, Sir Josiah?" Bainsbridge asked softly.

Hart did not hesitate to answer, speaking out bitterly: "That the disaffection of the crew began when Lieutenant Hayden, in my absence, took command of the *Themis*—until then there was no sign of it. But during those weeks that I was called away, so material a change in the mood of the crew occurred that, upon my return, I could not comprehend it, which is why the mutiny found me so utterly unprepared."

Muhlhauser and Wickham both looked at Hayden in alarm.

The spineless little tyrant! Hayden thought. He knew full well that he had discord aboard before Stephens put me on that cursed ship. Had not a man been murdered at the hands of one of his fellows?

"We have not convened to try men who were not aboard the ship at the time of the mutiny," Gardner stated firmly, "no matter the good captain's opinion of their service."

There was some protest among the panel of captains, but Admiral Duncan raised a hand. "Captain Gardner is quite right. Let us proceed. Has anyone a question for Sir Josiah?"

Gardner leaned forward. "You have commended your officers for their zeal in defending the ship, but do I understand you witnessed none of this defence yourself, as you were held prisoner in your cabin?"

"That is true, sir, but I am confident the testimony of my officers will bear me out. Allow me to say, in my defence, that if the mutineers had not come at me by stealth I should have joined in the defence of my ship with all my energies."

"Given your illustrious service, sir," Gardner replied dryly, "who could doubt it?"

The meaning of the man's words was not lost on anyone present and there was muffled laughter, which made Hart shift uncomfortably, his face flushing with anger. Hayden remained too enraged even to smile. Perhaps this was one of Philip Stephens' votaries.

Bainsbridge waited for silence and then asked, "So you were taken utterly by surprise, Captain Hart? There was, previous to that night, no occurrence, nothing at all that would have given you cause to believe there was, aboard your ship, a mutinous element?"

"No, sir. Certainly, the crew had become froward and undisciplined in my absence, but even so, every one of my officers was taken wholly by surprise. If there had been any reason to believe mutiny possible I would have ordered more sentries to be placed around the ship, and tipped my officers to be on the lookout, but there was not."

Bainsbridge nodded, apparently satisfied.

"If I may," the judge-advocate interrupted. "I am looking over your lists, Captain Hart, and I make note that you have the name *Aldrich* in the tally of mutineers, yet there is also an Aldrich on the doctor's sick-and-hurt list, and by your own account, the men in the sick-berth did not take part in the mutiny. Had you two men of the same name?"

"There was but one, and he was chief among the mutineers. He was also in the sick-berth at the time of the mutiny."

Gardner, who Hayden was beginning to believe not pleased to be part of these proceedings, pounced on this. "If he was in the sick-berth, Captain Hart, how is it you are so confident of his part in the mutiny?"

"In my account, read by Sir Hubert, I made note that the mutineer William Stuckey said as he began to . . . beat me that he was doing it on 'Aldrich's account.' After this, Aldrich himself appeared on deck and ordered the mutineers to leave off flogging the ship's people, and they obeyed him immediately. Also, sir, the very same Aldrich was flogged but a few days before for mutinous language."

Sir Hubert gave Hart a sharp look and cleared his throat softly.

Gardner raised a single, thick eyebrow. "You flogged a man you have just claimed to be a mutineer, for using mutinous language, and yet you avow that there was no cause for you to suspect your crew were mutinous. Is having a man flogged for using mutinous language not a sign that your crew were talking of mutiny?"

Bainsbridge spoke before Hart could answer. "I think we have established that neither Captain Hart nor his officers had any foreknowledge or reasonable suspicion of mutiny. Men are flogged for mutinous language with distressing regularity, and yet mutinies do not follow. That is undeniable."

"Indeed, that is true," Gardner countered, "but in this case a mutiny *did* follow. It is our task to look into the causes of this mutiny, and flogging a man for mutinous language would seem very pertinent to this point."

"I agree with Captain Gardner," Admiral Duncan said. "Let Captain Hart explain the circumstances surrounding the flogging of this man Aldrich."

Hart cleared his throat and shifted uncomfortably in his chair.

"I should require recourse to my journal for the exact date, my lords, but suffice it to say that it was reported to me that Aldrich, a seaman rated able aboard my ship, was in possession of certain inflammatory pamphlets written by the revolutionary Thomas Paine. I was also informed that he had been reading these pamphlets to the hands, causing discord and much dissatisfaction with their situation. I ordered Aldrich to be flogged as a result."

Gardner looked somewhat confused. "And you learned of this how, Captain?"

"It was reported to me by my second lieutenant, Mr Landry."

"And how came Mr Landry to know of this?"

"Why does it matter how he learned of it?" Bainsbridge complained.

"Captain Bainsbridge," the admiral cautioned. "You may ask your questions in turn, sir."

Hart did not look overly concerned that this line of questioning had been embarked upon, but the same could not be said of his barrister. "I believe Mr Landry learned of it from the first lieutenant, Mr Hayden," Hart answered.

"But Mr Hayden did not report it to you himself?"

"No, he did not."

"Would it not be usual for the first lieutenant to report any matters of concern, such as mutinous language, to the captain himself?"

"It would, sir, but the first lieutenant was remiss, and Mr Landry took it upon himself to report the incident to me."

"Why do you think he was remiss in this instance?"

"I don't believe he comprehended the seriousness of the transgression, sir."

"But you did?"

"It was a breach of the Articles of War, sir."

"Indeed it was. Which pamphlets of Mr Paine's did you seize from Mr Aldrich?"

"None, sir."

"None?"

"That is correct."

"On what evidence did you flog Mr Aldrich?"

"The verbal account of Mr Landry."

"Had Mr Landry heard the pamphlets being read by this man Aldrich?"

"I don't believe so."

"Then I confess I am confused. You had a man flogged, but you did not first assure yourself that there was in fact some evidence that he had contravened the Articles of War. After all, aboard a ship of war there is often antipathy between men of different temperament and I have seen cases where one has accused another of some offence out of spite or malice."

"I asked Aldrich if he had been reading the pamphlets of Thomas Paine to the hands and he admitted that he had."

This stopped even the able Gardner for a moment. "He admitted this freely?"

"Yes, sir."

"Mutineers are not commonly so forthcoming, in my experience, Captain Hart. Be that as it may, certainly you had some reason to suspect unrest among your crew. If you flogged Mr Aldrich for mutinous language, then surely the men to whom he read were guilty of mutinous assembly. Did you flog them?"

Hart was looking both angry and embarrassed by this line of questioning. "I did not," he answered peevishly.

"And why was that?"

"It seemed he had read the pamphlets to most, if not all of the crew, by his own admission."

Several of the captains stifled laughter.

"It would appear, Captain Hart," Gardner said, "that you did indeed have cause to believe elements of your crew were mutinous, yet, despite this knowledge, you did nothing to ensure the safety of your ship."

"I believe much is being made of a single incident," Bainsbridge said forcefully, "an incident so common aboard ship that if we doubled a ship's guard every time mutinous language were heard we should have to carry thrice the number of marines to manage it."

"Has anyone else a question for Captain Hart?" the admiral asked, but there were none.

"You are released for now, Captain Hart, but might be required to answer more questions at a later time. You shall also be given an opportunity to address any evidence given against you, should that be required."

Sir Hubert rose quickly and assisted Hart up from his chair. By the look on Hart's face, Hayden believed this was no act—he was in considerable pain—but he felt no pity for it. The man had just blackened his reputation before the court. His already precarious career was now in serious danger of being sunk altogether.

"Let us speak with each officer in turn," Admiral Duncan directed.

The judge-advocate called, "Lieutenant Herald Landry."

"Should we not speak with the first lieutenant?" Bainsbridge asked. "Captain Hart has said most emphatically that the discontentment of his crew began when the first lieutenant had charge of the ship."

"He had command of the prize at the time of the mutiny, Captain Bainsbridge," the judge-advocate reminded the captain.

"So I understand, but it was he who first learned of Tom Paine's pamphlets. I should like to hear how he discovered this, and why he did not report it to Captain Hart, among other things."

"Aldrich admitted himself that he possessed and read the pamphlets to the crew," one of the captains observed. "We do not need the first lieutenant to verify what has already been admitted."

"Perhaps not, but I for one should like to know what the first lieutenant thought about the state of the ship. Was he suspicious that the
men harboured mutinous designs? He was, after all, on the ship until a
few hours before the mutiny."

"Is the first lieutenant even present?" the admiral asked.

"I am, sir," Hayden answered, feeling his heart begin to beat heavily.

"You are under no obligation here, Lieutenant . . ." Duncan glanced
at a sheet of paper, ". . . Hayden. No charges have been laid against you
and if you would prefer not to speak I will not require it—unless you are
called to give evidence by one of the accused."

"I shall be happy to answer any questions, Admiral Duncan," Hayden
heard himself say. He was not going to stand by meekly and let Hart shift
the blame to him.

Way was made for Hayden and he was, in a moment, let through the
ropes into the centre of the great cabin. He took his place, standing
where Hart had been allowed to sit. There was no doubt in his mind that
not only was Gardner a confederate of Philip Stephens, but he had also
been privy to Hayden's secret account of the voyage. His questions,
though cleverly disguised, seemed too astute to Hayden, otherwise. Hayden also remembered that Stephens had shown little confidence that he
could influence the membership of the panel enough for it to matter.

"Lieutenant Hayden, will you tell how long you had been aboard the
Themis?" Duncan began.

"I came aboard on the twenty-third day of July, sir."

"I realize you have had no time to prepare, or look into your own
journal, but without being too specific as to dates and times, can you tell
us how you came to be aware that Aldrich had been reading pamphlets
to the hands?"

"I was not aware that he had been reading them to the crew, sir, but I
can tell you how I came to be aware that he had read them himself."

"If you please, Mr Hayden."

"One of the midshipmen, Arthur Wickham, came to my cabin in the
gunroom one evening. He carried with him several books that had just
been returned to him by Aldrich." This caused a response in itself.

"Among the books he found two pamphlets, both written by Thomas Paine."

"Do you remember the titles of these pamphlets?"

"*Common Sense*, and *The Rights of Man*."

"Go on."

"Mr Wickham was not sure if possession of these pamphlets contravened any regulations and asked my opinion of the matter. I took possession of the pamphlets and told Mr Wickham that I would speak with Aldrich, aware then that we did not know how the pamphlets came to be among the books. I might bring it to the attention of this court that all of the midshipmen had read the pamphlets, and a number of the other officers had read, if not these particular copies, both *Common Sense* and *The Rights of Man*, as had I. I only mention this to demonstrate that one can read these pamphlets out of general interest, without having mutinous intent.

"I caused Aldrich to be brought before me and showed him the pamphlets, saying that they had been among the books he had returned to Mr Wickham. I believe what I said at the time was that I did not want to know how the pamphlets had come to be among the books or even if they were his, but only if he was party to any mutinous designs upon the ship or her people. He assured me most decisively that he was not. Because Aldrich was the most skilled seaman aboard, esteemed by officers and hands, and I believed him to be perfectly honest, which is borne out by his answer to Captain Hart when asked if he had read the pamphlets, I decided to say nothing more of it. I did not then and do not now believe that Aldrich had any mutinous intentions, nor do I believe that he was in any way part of the mutiny. He came up from the sick-berth because he had learned that the captain was being flogged and it was being said that it was on his account, and he would not have that. Because of the great regard the crew held for him they ceased the floggings when he asked them to. He then fell in a swoon, and was carried back to the sick-berth. It is true that later Bill Stuckey would not allow Aldrich to be taken into the boats, saying something like 'He's one of us,' but this was only his opinion. We do not know what Aldrich would have chosen, because he was never asked. I would venture with great certainty that he would not have stayed among the mutineers."

"These events you are describing were not witnessed by you, Lieutenant?" one of the captains asked.

"I was not present at the time of the mutiny, sir, but relate the events as they were described to me by my fellow officers, all of whom were in agreement on the facts as I have just stated them."

"I come back to your decision not to inform Captain Hart about your conversation with Aldrich," Bainsbridge said. "Captain Hart has said you were remiss. Did you not think it was the captain's place to make his own judgement of Aldrich's culpability, and not yours?"

"Certainly a first lieutenant is given some leeway in what he reports to his captain; after all, one must exercise judgement or otherwise all conversations would have to be reported. I was satisfied that Aldrich's interest in the pamphlets was merely a general curiosity, as it had been with the midshipmen, who read Mr Paine so that they might debate the merits and demerits of his argument. I did not feel any need to report the midshipmen's debating club, either."

"Yes, but certainly the reading of these pamphlets to the crew might have contributed to the discontent, as Captain Hart has suggested."

"That is true, sir, and at the time I warned Aldrich, who conceded that he should be more circumspect in the future, but it was too late to stop the reading of the pamphlets to the crew."

Bainsbridge was not about to let this point go. "Did you ask this man Aldrich if he were aware of crewmen who did harbour mutinous designs, or who talked mutiny openly?"

"I did not, sir."

"And why did you not?"

"I had too much respect for Aldrich to ask him to inform on his fellows, sir. It also seemed to me that no mutineer would be likely to take Aldrich into his confidence. He was the precise opposite of a malcontent—a man who carried out his duties with zeal and great skill. Not the kind of seaman that a mutineer would likely try to recruit."

"But you did not ask him?"

"No, sir."

"It would seem, Mr Hayden, that you were remiss, and very much mistaken," Bainsbridge said forcefully. "You did not report this man Aldrich for mutinous language and a mutiny resulted."

Hayden was taken aback by this assertion. "If I may say so, sir, Aldrich's pamphlets were brought to the attention of the captain, Aldrich was punished, and the mutiny occurred all the same. I would conclude from this that if I had reported the incident to the captain he would have taken the same action with the same result. I might add that the flogging of Aldrich engendered a great deal of resentment among the hands."

Bainsbridge's countenance grew dark. "It does not excuse your lapse in judgement, sir. And if this impertinence is an example of how you habitually addressed your captain it is no wonder that he was dissatisfied with you."

"It was never my intention to appear impertinent, sir, only to defend my actions, which is what we have been brought before the court to do."

Bainsbridge was interrupted before he could say more.

"Mr Hayden," Gardner cut in, "what did the second lieutenant say when you brought up Aldrich and his pamphlets?"

"I did not discuss it with Mr Landry, sir."

"Then how did he learn of it?"

"I do not know, sir, but he did not hear of it from me."

"What I believe we would all like to know," Bainsbridge said, making no attempt to hide his apparent dislike of Hayden, "is how it was that you took command of what Sir Josiah assures us was a perfectly harmonious crew and in a few short weeks turned them into mutineers?"

Hayden drew a long breath that did not have the calming effect he had hoped for. "The disaffection of the *Themis*' crew preceded me by several months, Captain Bainsbridge. A man was murdered on the previous cruise and one of Captain Hart's crew hanged for it. The very day I arrived aboard ship, a foretop-man named Tawney was found beaten near to death. It came out much later that both were involved in the circulation of a petition and had appealed to the men to refuse to sail until the terms of the petition were met. When first I came aboard I found, I regret to say, a great deal of discord and a shocking lack of discipline among the ship's people. To attribute this to me is completely unjust."

This caused a moment of silence among the captains, who had heard nothing of a petition until now. Certainly it had not been mentioned in Hart's journal. But every man in the cabin could guess what the petition demanded. A few members of the panel glanced over to Hart as though seeing him for the first time.

"Do you recall any incidents that would indicate a mutinous tendency among Captain Hart's crew?" McLeod asked Hayden. "Were there floggings of men that, in hindsight, should have indicated to you that there was a problem aboard the ship?"

Hayden recalled the warning of Hart's barrister, but in the face of Hart's accusations, Hayden realized, he had little choice but to defend himself.

"When we sailed from Plymouth the men were very nearly insubordinate; they did not refuse to obey the officers' orders but were very reticent to carry them out."

"And how did Captain Hart manage this?" Gardner enquired very naturally.

"The captain was, at the time, too ill to take the deck. The other officers and I dealt with it by calling the men by name and telling them that if they refused a direct order it would be noted in any future court-martial."

"And were these men among the mutineers, Lieutenant?"

"Oddly, many were not. Many resisted the mutiny—and some, who later led the mutiny, pressed the crew at Plymouth to take their places in weighing anchor, by which I conclude that the mutineers did not want the petition to succeed."

This caused an unsettled silence as people present realized what this implied.

"Certainly you reported this to Captain Hart?"

"I did, sir. He told me that if he had been on the deck the men would have jumped to their places with a will, and that it was only the weeks

that he had been away and the ship under the command of junior officers that had allowed this fractious attitude."

"He blamed it on you?" McLeod asked.

"Apparently, sir."

"That was the only incident of malcontent before the actual mutiny
that you can recall?" Gardner prompted.

"There was another, sir, when we took the transport in the mouth of
Brest Harbour. The gun crews began to argue among themselves and
would not answer to the ship's officers. I was forced to muster the
marines to send the gun crews back to their stations at musket point."

"*You* were forced?" Gardner said. "What of Captain Hart? What did
he order?"

"He was under the doctor's care at the time, sir, and did not take the
deck until we were about to board the transport."

The captains all looked one to the other.

"Was the *Themis* in a state of mutiny, Mr Hayden?" another asked.

"I cannot say, sir. I went away in the boats to board the enemy vessel
and left Mr Landry and the marines to ensure the men remained at their
guns. Afterward, the marine lieutenant, Mr Hawthorne, said that he
could not be certain the whole incident was not merely one group of
men who greatly disliked another, for they argued among themselves,
and there was a good deal of pushing and cursing, I was told."

"And what was the result of this? What did Captain Hart do? Were
the men punished?"

"Men were flogged, sir, but I was not aboard when it happened, as I
was on the prize at the time."

"You have been most fortunate in your absences, Mr Hayden," Bainsbridge commented. "What you are telling us, sir, is that at the time of
both the incidents you have just mentioned, the *Themis* was under your
command."

"No, sir. Captain Hart was in command; I merely performed my
duties as first lieutenant."

"You are making a very fine distinction, I believe. Captain Hart
was incapacitated and you were, in all but title, in command of the

ship." Bainsbridge turned to Duncan. "I have heard all I need to hear from this man."

There was a moment's pause. "If there are no questions at this time," Admiral Duncan then said, "I shall have Mr Hayden stand down . . . ?"

A general shaking of heads.

"Thank you, Mr Hayden; you may resume your place."

The judge-advocate looked up from his papers. "Shall I enter Mr Hayden's name among the officers being tried for the loss of HMS *Themis*, sir?"

The admiral was caught off guard by this question, and for a moment looked bewildered.

"Certainly he should take his place among the men being tried here," Bainsbridge said forcefully. "The man had command of the ship for almost three months before the mutiny took place and was only by the greatest stroke of good fortune not aboard when the crew rose up against their officers. Justice demands he take his share of responsibility for these events."

"It is, I believe, without precedent to try a man who was not aboard a ship when a mutiny took place," Gardner countered, squaring off against Bainsbridge. "And I have no doubt it would be a dangerous precedent to set. Shall we have officers trying to shift the responsibility for events to some poor soul who had command of the ship in the past? It is clear from Lieutenant Hayden's account that there was disaffection aboard the *Themis* before he was given his commission—men murdered and beaten near to death are not signs of harmony, we all must admit."

This set off a heated debate, but Admiral Duncan raised his voice above all others and restored order to the cabin. "I shall take this recommendation—that we include Lieutenant Hayden among the men being tried—under consideration, for as Captain Gardner has rightly stated, such a decision should not be undertaken lightly. However, if, in the course of this court-martial, more evidence comes to light proving Lieutenant Hayden contributed greatly to the discord among the *Themis*' crew, I will be forced to place Mr Hayden among the officers being tried." Duncan nodded to the judge-advocate. "Let us proceed, Mr Sheridan."

Hayden was allowed to resume his place between Wickham and Muhlhauser. There was a brief pause in the proceedings, and Mr Muhlhauser leaned near. "Well said, Mr Hayden," he whispered.

Landry was next called, and the little lieutenant took his place, his account of the mutiny held in a faintly trembling hand.

"Mr President and gentlemen," he began, his voice as quavery as his fingers. "On the evening of October sixth I was asleep in my cabin when midshipman Hobson burst into the gunroom and hollered that the crew was in a state of mutiny. I leapt from my cot and stumbled out to question Hobson when I heard the report of a musket, followed by another. Mr Hawthorne, the lieutenant of marines, woke at the same time, and finding a pistol and cutlass in his cabin, rushed out of the gunroom. The midshipmen all came into the gunroom then, and I sent one of them to rummage all the officers' cabins to look for arms. A pair of pistols were brought from the cabin of Third Lieutenant Archer, and a marine joined us then with his musket. Almost immediately we were beset by mutineers, who began firing muskets at us. We piled all the furniture and bedding before the gunroom door and before the bulkhead, which had been constructed only of thin dealboard. Bashing holes in the bulkhead, we returned fire as long as our powder lasted, at which point the mutineers, who had gathered in numbers, charged and after a skirmish succeeded in forcing their way into the gunroom. We fought with cutlasses and clubs made of furniture legs, but were soon subdued, many of us wounded and two killed—midshipman Albert Williams, and the marine corporal Davidson. We were then much beaten and kicked before being forced onto the deck. Many of the crew had been made to lie on the gangways, where they suffered much at the hands of the mutineers, whose blood was up from the recent fight, and much revenge was taken on us for our resistance and for killing their comrades. An argument ensued between the mutineers as to what was to be done now that they had taken the ship. As this went on, Bill Stuckey and several others seized the captain to a grating and proceeded to flog him without mercy. They had just laid their hands upon my person, and were about to treat me the same, when Able Seaman Peter Aldrich came on deck and ordered them to stop. We were, soon afterward, put into the boats and cast adrift."

Landry raised his eyes from his written account, and gazed up at the captains, his customary look of a dog about to be whipped even more pronounced here.

"Mr Landry," Bainsbridge began, "were you satisfied with the conduct of all the men you had with you in the gunroom? None shirked in their resistance to the mutineers?"

"Quite the opposite, sir. They all fought with great courage and energy. We killed a goodly number of the mutineers and I believe we would have been able to hold the gunroom for some time longer had we not run out of powder. Williams and Hobson were particularly courageous, as was the marine corporal, Davidson."

"Can you tell us who was with you in the gunroom during this fight?"

"Mr Barthe, the sailing master; Davidson, whom I have just mentioned; Dr Griffiths; and the midshipmen Hobson, Madison, and Albert Williams, who was killed. Oh, and Mr Muhlhauser, who was from the Ordnance Board."

"Eight of you in total?"

"Yes, sir."

Gardner did not seem much interested in this line of enquiry and broke in. "You have stated that Able Seaman Aldrich came on deck and ordered the flogging stopped. Can you recall his precise words?"

"Not exactly, sir. I believe he said that they should flog no more of the ship's people, and certainly flog no one on his account."

"But did he *order* them to do it, or did he *desire* them to do it?" Gardner asked.

Landry looked uncomfortable and glanced at Sir Hubert, who sat stony-faced. "I suppose it was somewhere in between, sir."

"Did he implore them to flog no more of the ship's people, then?"

"Yes, sir, I should say that 'implore' is what he did."

"And then he collapsed; is that correct?"

"It is."

"Are you of the opinion that Aldrich was one of the leaders of the mutiny or that he was even involved in the mutiny, and if so, why do you hold such an opinion?"

"I suppose I held this opinion because Bill Stuckey would not allow Aldrich to come away in the boats, when the middies asked for him. Stuckey said that Aldrich was one of them."

"But Aldrich himself was never asked if he wished to come away in the boats?"

"Not to my knowledge, sir."

"Then it is impossible to know how he would have answered, is it not?"

"That is true, sir."

Admiral Duncan, who had remained silent until now, looked up from his clasped hands. "Pray tell us, Mr Landry, what was your part in the defence of the gunroom?"

Landry shifted from one foot to the other. "We had not enough firearms to go around, sir, so I loaded guns for the men who were firing."

"Very commendable. Who fired the guns?"

"Davidson, Williams, and Hobson, to begin, sir, and then Mr Barthe and Dr Griffiths."

"I see. Was this how Mr Williams lost his young life and the marine corporal suffered the same end?"

"It was, sir."

"So firing the weapons would seem to have been the more dangerous task?"

Landry nodded.

"Permit me to ask, Lieutenant Landry, why you, as senior officer, were not at the forefront of this defence? Would this not be the usual place for an officer, rather than, say, a midshipman or the ship's surgeon?"

Landry had the decency to appear embarrassed by this line of questioning. "It was simply how things arranged themselves. I was busy collecting the furniture to make a barricade thick enough that we would not all be killed, and when that was done the guns were already in the hands of others. I then did what I could to aid the men firing. When the mutineers broke into the gunroom I took up my cutlass and fought alongside the others. I believe the men who were in the gunroom will say that I did my duty and did not shirk, sir."

"Permit me to ask, Mr Landry," Bainsbridge began, "if you felt the disaffection among the crew of the *Themis* existed before Mr Hayden came aboard or did the discord that later led to mutiny begin after Lieutenant Hayden took up his position?"

Landry pulled his tiny chin down into his collar, looking neither left nor right. "I should say it began during the weeks that Mr Hayden had command of the ship in Plymouth, sir."

Hayden experienced such a flash of outrage that he broke a sweat. And he'd thought Landry had, finally, made a decision to find his manhood!

"If you please, Mr Landry," Admiral Duncan broke in, "would you speak up so that those of us no longer in the bloom of youth might hear?"

"My apologies, sir. I believe the discontentment began after Mr Hayden took control of the ship at Plymouth."

There ensued much muttering and shifting among the crew of the *Themis*.

"If I may say so, Admiral Duncan," Gardner said peevishly, "Mr Hayden is not on trial here. I believe this is merely a tactic to shift attention from the gentlemen who are actually being court-martialled."

"It remains to be seen if Lieutenant Hayden will be subject to the same charges, Captain Gardner," Duncan countered, to the obvious satisfaction of Bainsbridge and several other captains.

Gardner only glanced up at the deckhead, then back to Landry. "Then let me ask you this, Mr Landry—how do you explain the murder of a member of your crew some weeks before Mr Hayden came aboard, and then the beating of the foretop-man the very day Lieutenant Hayden took up his position?"

"The murder was a personal affair, regrettable, but such things are not unheard of in the service. As to the beating, we do not know who was responsible, sir."

"Mr Hayden has stated that the two unfortunate men were involved in circulating a petition and attempting to convince the crew not to sail. It is Mr Hayden's opinion that the future mutineers perpetrated both these attacks."

"That is Mr Hayden's opinion, sir, but I believe otherwise."

For a moment the panel seemed stymied, but then McLeod pivoted slightly toward the second lieutenant. "Did you believe, Mr Landry," he asked, "that there existed among your crew people with mutinous intent?"

Landry hesitated.

"Answer 'yes' or 'no,' Mr Landry," the admiral ordered.

"No, sir, I did not."

"Even after the troubles with the crew when quitting Plymouth and later at Brest?" Gardner asked quickly.

"Yes, sir, even after those troubles."

"But it was you who then reported that Mr Aldrich had been reading pamphlets that espoused revolutionary ideals to the crew?"

"It was, sir."

"Certainly this concerned you, lest you would not have reported it?"

"It did concern me, sir."

"How did you learn of this, Mr Landry?"

"I don't remember, sir."

"A man was flogged upon your informing on him, Mr Landry; surely you remember how you learned of his transgression?"

"I believe Mr Hayden told me, sir."

"Mr Hayden claimed he did not tell you, sir."

Landry hesitated.

"Mr Landry . . . ?"

"I believe Mr Hayden was mistaken in this, sir."

"Ah. Was Mr Hayden often forgetful of conversations, Mr Landry?"

"I don't believe he was, sir, but only in this case."

"And what became of the pamphlets?"

"I don't know, sir. Mr Hayden claimed to have taken them from Mr Wickham, but they were later found to be missing from Mr Hayden's trunk where he had placed them."

"Perhaps they disappeared to the same place as the master's log?"

"I know nothing of that, sir."

The panel of captains fell unhappily silent. Landry's evidence seemed a mass of contradictions. Hayden found it difficult to read the reaction of the captains on the panel, all of whom were gentlemen well used to keeping their own counsel and guarding their emotions from their crews.

"If there are no more questions at present, I shall allow Mr Landry to step down for the time being?"

The captains all agreed they had nothing more to ask.

"Thank you, Mr Landry," Duncan said. "You may resume your place, though you might yet be recalled to answer questions, and you shall be allowed a chance to speak in your own defence, should that be necessary. Let us hear from Lieutenant Archer."

The young officer took his place, and of the men who had so far spoken, he appeared the most composed despite the fact that he was the youngest. Hayden wondered if Archer's lack of commitment to his chosen career played some part in this. As the other officers had done, Archer read from a written account of the story of the battle on the quarterdeck, which Hayden had heard more than once from Hawthorne, but which saddened him every time.

When he had finished, Archer delivered his account into the hands of the judge-advocate and stood calmly awaiting any questions.

"Pray, Mr Archer, you have made no mention of the numbers of mutineers who besieged you on the quarterdeck."

"It was dark, sir, and difficult to be certain. The first party I saw on the gangway was perhaps a dozen or fourteen men, but there were scuffles going on forward at that time, and some men were climbing aloft who had no business to be doing so; I assume they were mutineers as well. Perhaps twenty or twenty-four men on the deck, all under arms. Most of the watch did little or nothing to resist them, sir. Some might even have joined with the mutineers, so we were greatly outnumbered as we were only fifteen, by my count, three of that number boys."

"How many of these fifteen were killed or wounded, Mr Archer?"

"Mr Bentley of the marines was killed, as were Cooper and Joyce. Two of the three boys were killed—one thrown overboard by a mutineer for no reason that I know, sir. Almost everyone else was wounded in some way, large or small."

"And what part did you play in the defence of the quarterdeck?"

"Bentley was killed almost immediately, sir, and I took up his musket and, with Mr Hawthorne, directed the attack as best we could. I spent all the powder Bentley possessed, and then it was agreed we should surrender, for the ship seemed lost and we were all certainly to be murdered were we to resist any longer."

"Were you then mistreated as the others have told, Mr Archer?"

"Not so much, sir, though the quartermaster's mate, Elliot, was badly ballyragged, sir."

"Mr Archer, would you look over the lists your captain has submitted and tell us if you know of any man there who you believe is improperly accused, or guilty of mutiny who has not been named."

The lists were given to Archer, who read through them slowly. While he remained so engaged there was a small disturbance at the door and a moment later one of the marine guards delivered a wrapped package to Mr Barthe, whose surprise upon opening it could not be hidden.

Bless Worth and his nimble fingers, Hayden thought.

"Well, sir," Archer said after a moment, "I agree with Mr Hayden that Aldrich was not one of the mutineers and that they only desisted from the flogging due to the great esteem felt for Aldrich, not because he was their leader. There are several men here who are named as mutineers whom I cannot confirm or deny, for I saw them neither under arms nor resisting the mutineers. Bates, the cook's mate, was not under arms but was seen to do Stuckey's bidding, though I thought this might have been out of fear, as he was both young and of a timid disposition, though in his defence, he is a small boy. Otherwise this list appears to be correct, sir."

"Mr Archer," Gardner asked, "did the unrest among the crew of the *Themis* predate Mr Hayden taking up his position?"

"I was not aware that there was any material change in the mood of the crew under Mr Hayden, sir."

"But you have not answered my question, Lieutenant. Let me phrase it differently. Precisely when did the unrest begin among the *Themis'* people?"

Archer looked somewhat embarrassed. "I was not aware of any unrest until the night of the mutiny, sir."

Gardner looked both annoyed and astounded. "Mr Archer, a man was murdered and another beaten near to death, and you tell me that you saw no signs of unrest among your crew? What of the incidents at Plymouth and Brest? Did you not think these out of the ordinary, and did they not put you on your guard?"

Archer's next words came from a noticeably dry mouth. "At Plymouth, sir, the men did all go to their stations once Mr Hayden took the matter in hand. And at Brest I believed the matter to be a brawl between two groups of men who did not much care for one another, sir—nothing more. Captain Hart ordered some of the men to be flogged and I thought that would see the end of it."

One of the captains interrupted here. "These men who were flogged, were they later to be found among the mutineers?"

"Some were; some were not."

As there were no more questions for the less-than-forthcoming lieutenant, Archer was dismissed, though it was clear that certain of the captains on the panel were not satisfied with his answers.

Barthe was next called, and came huffing up to take his place, scarlet-faced and, Hayden recognized by his manner, irritable. The former lieutenant, who had stood in this same place once before only to see his career ruined, looked at once apprehensive and resentful. Barthe began by reading his prepared account, a story now familiar to everyone, of the gunroom defence and later bullying on the deck. Barthe, who was liked by the crew, had not been mistreated.

"Mr Barthe, I must begin by asking about the missing ship's log." Duncan looked most displeased as he said this. "This would seem to indicate serious neglect of duty. How do you explain it?"

"The log was stolen from my cabin, sir, but has just been returned to me unharmed." Barthe raised the disputed volume and then delivered it into the hands of the judge-advocate.

Hayden carefully watched the face of Landry as this was announced. It was one of the more satisfying moments of his naval career. The lieutenant slumped in his chair, making weak little motions with his hands and opening his mouth as though to speak or catch his breath. For his part, Hart did not seem to grasp the significance of this moment. But then realization came over the captain—every occasion upon which he refused to engage the enemy would be enumerated in Mr Barthe's log, no matter how circumspect the language. Every incidence of negligence of duty. But perhaps even more shocking to the two officers was the re-alization that someone had known where to find the book and had retrieved it. If this came out in the court-martial there would be no saving them. For a moment Hart could not take his eyes from the of-fending volume, as though he considered dashing forward and snatching it away.

"Mr Barthe," one of the captains asked, "how is it that a log-book—a document of singular importance, as you well know—could go miss-ing? And how is it that we find it returned at this moment?"

"As was reported, sir, the log had been removed from my cabin with out my knowledge or permission. As to its return, I have only had it delivered to me this instant without explanation. I know not from where it came."

This produced a reaction among the captains, none of whom ap-peared impressed with these goings-on.

"This is most irregular, Mr Barthe," Bainsbridge observed.

"And I am deeply sorry for it, sir, but I cannot offer a better ex-planation."

The captains glanced from one to the other.

"Let us hope that such an explanation will come to be known," the admiral said. "For now let us proceed. We return again to the issues re-garding which we have quizzed your fellow officers. Were you in any way suspicious that there was, among the crew of the *Themis*, a muti-nous or disaffected element?"

"I was." Barthe shifted his weight from one foot to the other, his manner more combative.

"If you please, Mr Barthe, would you explain why you believed that."

"When we were anchored in Plymouth Sound in the summer, having returned from a two-month cruise, there were rumours aboard ship that the crew would refuse to sail with Captain Hart and that they would send a petition to the Port Admiral requesting the captain's removal."

This received a strong reaction among both the panel of captains and the onlookers.

"This is a very disputatious allegation, Mr Barthe," Bainsbridge said immediately. "How came you to know of this 'rumour'?"

"It was reported to me by one of the marines, sir—Davidson."

"Was this man not killed in defence of the ship?"

"He was, sir."

"Did he tell you how he had knowledge of this petition, Mr Barthe?" Gardner asked.

"He was friendly with many of the hands, sir, and I had the impression that he was one of the organizers of the petition."

"Did you report this to the first lieutenant?"

"The first lieutenant had quit the service, sir. I spoke of it to Mr Landry and certain officers, but we agreed we would say nothing unless we could learn more."

"So when the captain returned you did not report this, nor did you report it to the First Lieutenant Hayden when he joined the ship?"

Bathe glanced Hayden's way, then drew in a quick breath. "No, sir."

"And why did you not, Mr Barthe?"

"It was only an unsubstantiated rumour. When the captain returned, the crew sailed with only a little grumbling, sir, so it seemed the crisis had passed, and I did not tell Lieutenant Hayden because he was new to the ship and did not then know the crew well enough to deal with such a problem."

"Were you told why the crew would take this drastic step of petitioning the Port Admiral to have Captain Hart removed?"

"Because the crew believed Captain Hart to be a tyrant, sir, and because they also believed he was shy."

"Shy, sir?" Gardner said, looking up at Barthe over a pair of round spectacles. "Captain Hart? Why on earth would they believe that?"

"Admiral Duncan," one of the captains interrupted before Barthe could speak, "are we to allow the character of Captain Sir Josiah Hart to be traduced by the repetition of rumours? Captain Hart's record of service is unblemished, and many a good fighting captain has had crews grumble about his 'tyranny' who only wished to run a crack ship and carry the war to the enemy. I dare say, we have all had the same grumbling upon our own lower decks. It is apparent, though, from the accounts of these officers that they kept much from the captain that would have allowed him to deal with these mutineers before they infected the crew with their radical ideals. Had Mr Barthe and Mr Hayden the common sense to keep their captain properly informed, these unfortunate events would surely have been avoided, preserving many a life. I dare say, Captain Hart has been ill served in this matter."

The ship's bell chimed, and the admiral glanced out the stern gallery window, perhaps surprised by how much of the day had slipped away.

"Let us end for this day," the admiral said, "and return to Mr Barthe tomorrow with clear minds."

The row back to the *Themis*, beneath a sullen and threatening sky, passed in silence, the officers misliking to speak of this matter before the oarsmen. They collected in the gunroom immediately upon reaching the *Themis*, all of them but Mr Barthe partaking of port. The steward and servants were sent off, and an agitated Barthe paced forth and back, three steps, before the rudder-stock.

"Well, it had to be said," he blustered, sensing the mood of his fellows. "The hands were talking mutiny long before we left for our cruise. Now it will all come out. Sir Josiah Hart! Knighted for notorious shyness!"

"Calm yourself, Mr Barthe," Griffiths cautioned. The doctor appeared very concerned, his sombre manner even more subdued than usual. "Although you are to be commended for your honesty, I believe Hart and Landry did a great deal to shift the blame for the mutiny to the shoulders of Mr Hayden and yourself. I am not sure what will happen on the morrow, for surely when two groups are so opposed in their understanding of events, the captains of the panel will be forced to find the truth by instinct. Not the best situation, for I fear it will be natural for them to believe one of their own."

"Certainly the captains can see that *Sir* Josiah Faint-Hart is trying to preserve his now-great reputation?" Hawthorne pronounced with disgust.

"But why should Mr Hayden and Mr Barthe be doing any less?" the doctor countered. "If Admiral Duncan decides to include Mr Hayden among those being tried for the loss of the *Themis*, I have no doubt that things will go badly for you both." He glanced from Barthe to Hayden. "It is clear that Hart has several supporters on the panel, and I dare say that even Admiral Duncan is not beyond the displeasure of Mrs Hart's family."

"I, for one, was thoroughly deceived by Hart's lawyer," Hawthorne noted. "I truly believed that Hart would stand up and claim there was no foreknowledge of the crew's mutinous inclination. Clearly he had conspired with Hart to so throw us off."

"If you had seen the look of dismay on Hart's barrister's face when the good captain began to blame Mr Hayden," Wickham observed, "you would change your thoughts, I think. No, shifting responsibility for the crew's disaffection was entirely Hart's idea, I'm quite sure."

It was Hayden's turn to rise and pace. "Not for a moment did I think, as we rowed to the admiral's ship, that I could be in the least danger." His stomach turned over, and a little sour wine erupted into his mouth, swallowed quickly down.

Griffiths regarded him evenly. "I warned you, Mr Hayden, of the threats Hart made against you while he was under my care. He said he would do for you when we returned to England."

"And I fully expected him to do everything within his powers to ruin my chances for advancement, but never for a moment did I imagine this. Has anyone ever heard of a man not aboard a ship being tried for its loss?"

No one had.

Seeing the look of concern upon the doctor's face as he regarded him, Hayden forced himself to sit, though he did so with difficulty, so great was his agitation.

Hawthorne set his great arms upon the table, leaning forward as though in some pain. "Hart is desperate to preserve his name. I don't think he would be above casting his pet, Landry, to the dogs if he thought it would save him."

"Have you heard about Landry?" Archer asked quietly. "I spoke to a lieutenant on the admiral's ship who told me that Landry is to have a position aboard a flagship. *Landry*, if you can believe it."

A general disgusted shaking of heads and snorting among the men present.

"I was foolish enough to believe Landry had regained his manhood in the end," Hayden said. "Apparently he had his price, as they say every man does."

"Poltroon!" Barthe muttered, resuming his pendulous crossing of the cabin.

"Landry's little verbal broadside inflicted the desired damage." The doctor tapped a thin finger on the table-top. "There was no mistaking the intent of that man—what was his name, the captain missing an ear . . . ?"

"Bainsbridge, Doctor."

"Ah, yes, Bainsbridge. It was he who said that Captain Hart was ill served by his officers who kept from him knowledge regarding the crew's mutinous plans and intent. He also accepted it as undisputed truth when Hart asserted that the discord aboard the *Themis* began while Mr Hayden was in command. Hart shall be acquitted, and you, Mr Barthe and Mr Hayden, will be censured. That is what will occur, I am very sorry to say it, but I cannot see this affair turning out any other way."

Hayden fought the urge to jump up again. "But will Duncan allow them to bring charges against me? Surely, it will open up future courts-martial to all manner of manoeuvring. Why not blame the previous officers for all manner of ills—the state of the ship, the shyness of the crew?"

"I fear, Mr Hayden, that you underestimate the interest of Sir Josiah Hart. Precedents will be set, no matter how ruinous, if it will preserve our brave captain."

"But Mr Barthe and Mr Hayden are not the only ones put in danger by Hart's vindictiveness," Wickham spoke up, his voice filled with concern. "We must, at all costs, be certain that Mr Aldrich is pulled to safety."

"Mr Wickham is right," Griffiths agreed. "Aldrich had not the sense, when questioned by Hart, to deny possession of the pamphlets. He is too honest for his own good. Although I think it can be fairly proved that he did not take part in the mutiny, indeed it was by his influence that Landry escaped a flogging, but even so, his reading of Paine's pamphlets to the crew might be taken as a partial cause of the mutiny, and for this he might be punished."

"But he has already been flogged for this offence," Hawthorne pointed out. "Certainly the court will not feel it necessary to punish him again?"

"So we might hope, but if Hart is to escape unscathed, then others must take his place." Dr Griffiths picked unhappily at one of his fingernails. "It is the way of things."

"I will speak with Aldrich and caution him," Hayden announced, glad to take his mind off his own predicament. "But as Dr Griffiths has said, the man is honest to a fault, and such forthrightness simply will not answer before a court."

Aldrich sat up in a cot in the sick-berth on the after-orlop, reading a book. To Hayden's eye he appeared perfectly hale, though there was always about him now a stiffness of manner, a hint of sorrow—or perhaps shame—about the eyes, which he did much to hide.

As Hayden entered and was greeted by the mate and loblolly boy, Aldrich touched a knuckle to his forehead.

"How went the court-martial, sir?" he asked.

"Not quite as anyone expected, Aldrich." Hayden took a seat upon an offered stool. "How are you feeling?"

"As well as ever, sir. I do not know the reason the doctor has me back in the sick-berth."

"He tells me you have a fever again, which he cannot quite explain, for your wounds appear to have closed nicely."

Aldrich shrugged. Like many a man he was embarrassed by his own illness. "I do not feel fevered, sir."

"Perhaps not, but I will trust the doctor in this matter. We were speaking of the court-martial . . ." Hayden gave him a detailed account of what had occurred that day, watching the seaman's face carefully when he revealed that Hart had named him a leader of the mutineers. Aldrich attempted to hide his distress at this news, but was not terribly successful. Hayden might be in danger of losing his career, but Aldrich could forfeit his life if Hart was successful in placing him among the mutineers. The poor seaman suddenly looked quite ill indeed.

"But I took no part in the mutiny, Mr Hayden, as Mr Ariss here can attest. Nor did I encourage or even speak of mutiny with the other men."

"I know that full well, Aldrich, but Hart's statement to the court was damaging to you all the same, and now we must be very careful to extract you from among the mutineers. Your reading of Mr Paine's pamphlets to the crew will count as a black mark against you, and we must convince the court that you did not do this to inflame the crew's resentments or grievances."

"Certainly that was never my purpose, Mr Hayden. Some of the ship's people asked me if I would read the pamphlets, for they were unable to do so themselves. I was happy to do it, as I believe all knowledge is uplifting, sir, and no one could use this more than the crew of our ship, most of whom, as you know, were brought aboard against their will."

"Mr Aldrich, you must guard what you say. Such language before the court will place you in great danger, I fear. To say you read the pamphlets because you were asked to by others is all well and good. Better, even, if the pamphlets were not yours. But to undertake any manner of criticism of the press or to suggest that seamen should be brought to consider their state unjust in any way would be folly."

"But the condition of the seamen in His Majesty's Navy is very unjust, as you must yourself agree, Mr Hayden. Imagine if it were you taken from your life ashore and forced into a life aboard ship, deprived of the love of your family for years on end. Deprived of the company of the fairer sex, deprived of a multitude of simple pleasures that all but the poorest ashore might know. It is terribly unjust and—"

Hayden held up his hands. "Mr Aldrich! This is a debate that will see you hanged. There has been a mutiny aboard this ship and such talk will be your undoing. You must be prepared to deny any such ideas before the captains of the court-martial. You must say that you read the pamphlets to the crew because you were asked to do so—no more. Keep your opinions of the Navy's injustices to yourself. Deny any part in the mutiny or even any mutinous discussions. You have a very good character among the officers and young gentlemen and we will all speak on your behalf. You did not participate in the mutiny, which can be proven, and you used your influence among the crew to stop the flogging of officers, not to mention saving the *Themis* from being blown to flinders. All this will count on your behalf and should see you free, but if you begin to lecture the officers of the court on radical ideas or even reform of the Navy you will undo all that we might manage to do for you. Do you understand? You are in danger of being hanged as a mutineer, thanks to Hart's malice. You must now make a very careful defence—a single misstep and you will be lost. Is that understood?"

Aldrich nodded. "I do understand, Mr Hayden. It is my weakness to let my enthusiasms overcome my better judgement."

"Perfectly acceptable when you are debating the midshipmen or discussing matters with the doctor, but such talk among the crew, who are less educated than yourself and who might misapprehend your intent, could set the captains of the court against you."

Aldrich nodded again, though Hayden feared the man did not comprehend his danger. Had he learned nothing from his flogging by Hart? Innocence would not protect him.

Hayden left the sick-berth, now doubly worried, for his own situation was equally unclear. Evidently Hart had influence among the panel of captains and they appeared to have conspired to shift the blame to him and to Mr Barthe, who had already been court-martialled once and was therefore a man suspect. The injustice of it offended his every sensibility. Had he not once been amused by Wickham's school-yard sense of justice? And now his own was being revealed. In the court of the Admiralty the courtiers would find some functionary to blame for their failures—and Hayden was just such a lackey. Certainly the First Secretary had treated him as one.

As he reached the berth-deck Perseverance Gilhooly came hurrying along, clearly relieved to have found his master.

"A Lieutenant Janes asked permission to come aboard but a moment ago, sir . . . to see you. He is waiting on the deck, if you please, having declined my invitation to repair below."

"I shall go right along, Perse, thank you."

In a moment Hayden emerged from the companionway into a cool, starry night. There he found Lieutenant Janes—he who had first carried Hayden out to the *Themis* that innocent day in Plymouth. It seemed so very long ago.

"Mr Janes. To what do I owe this signal honour?"

The man turned to greet him, and even in the poor light Hayden could see his manner was most serious.

"I am playing the part of messenger this evening, Mr Hayden. Since last I saw you, I have become third lieutenant aboard *Goliath*—"

"Gardner's ship?" Hayden could not have been more surprised.

"Yes. Captain Gardner has sent me to ask the great favour of you attending him aboard *Goliath*, at your earliest convenience."

"Indeed . . ." Hayden replied, taken wholly by surprise.

Janes leaned forward and quietly added so that no other might hear, "By that I believe he meant, as soon as you could make your way across the small stretch of Plymouth Harbour that lies between our ships. My cutter is at your disposal."

Hayden gave a small bow. "Allow me to change my coat and speak with Mr Archer. Have you any notion of the cause of this summons?"

"I regret, I do not." A polite lie, Hayden suspected.

Not half an hour later Hayden clambered up the side of *Goliath* and was quickly ushered into Gardner's surprisingly richly appointed cabin, where he found not only the *Goliath*'s captain but three others from the panel: McLeod, North, and Spencer. The four officers were seated about a table from which Hayden guessed the remains of a meal had recently been removed. Glasses of unfinished wine and port and cups of coffee were in evidence as were a number of bound books—among them Hayden's own journal. If he had not been certain Gardner was a friend of Philip Stephens he would have felt great anxiety at being called here under such circumstances, but his present emotions were largely of curiosity and surprise.

Instead of the pleasant joviality he expected of officers who had just eaten and drunk their fill, he faced four rather solemn gentlemen, all of them disconcertingly sober. Gardner rose immediately.

"Mr Hayden," he began, "I want to thank you for coming here this night and I do apologize for providing you so little warning. Please, take a chair. You know these gentlemen from earlier this day, but let me introduce you properly."

Hayden made a leg as Gardner introduced his fellow captains, then took the offered seat. There were neither servants nor musicians present, which led Hayden to believe that the captains had been discussing matters of some delicacy—no need to wonder what these might be.

"Mr Hayden, allow me to be perfectly frank with you: it is our hope that you will be willing to aid our understanding of the events that took place so recently aboard the *Themis*. I do want to make it clear that you are under no obligation whatsoever to speak with us on these matters. You have not been charged with any offence; indeed, had you been we could not speak with you outside of the courtroom. Would you be willing to answer some few questions to this end?"

Hayden felt the eyes of these formidable men upon him, and his mouth went dry. "It is difficult, Captain Gardner, to agree in advance, as I am unaware of the exact nature of the questions."

"These enquiries are regarding certain discrepancies between your sailing master's log, the journals of the officers, and Captain Hart's own reporting of events. It is acceptable to me, Mr Hayden, that you choose to answer only those questions which, in good conscience, you feel you can." He looked to the other men present and each nodded agreement. "Can we proceed upon that understanding?"

"Yes, sir."

At a nod from the others, Gardner began. "You have signed Mr Barthe's log often in the last few months, indeed more often than your captain, but even so, Mr Hayden, I must ask you, is this log accurate in its depiction of events?"

"To the best of my knowledge, it is, sir."

The captains all shifted slightly. From outside the stern-gallery windows came a dull murmuring punctuated by the swish of oars—passing boatmen—and then, from deep within the ship, a scratchy fiddle began a sad air.

Gardner continued. "When you took the transport at Brest, Captain Hart was in his cot, ill. Is that correct?"

"Yes, sir, until some little time after we fired the warning gun."

"And did he, in truth, order the boats back to the ship when you were about to board the prize?"

Whose journal contained that? Hayden wondered. He looked from one captain to another. They were asking him to admit that he had disobeyed his captain's direct order.

Sensing the source of his hesitation, Gardner held out an open hand. "Fear not, Mr Hayden. Nothing you say here will be used against you in any way. You have my word."

Hayden drew in a long breath. "Yes, sir. Captain Hart did order the boats back to the *Themis*." He almost added that Captain Bourne had heard these orders most distinctly, but did not want to involve his friend without his permission. Bourne, Hayden recalled, had not included this damning information in his letter to the Admiralty.

"And when you came to Captain Bourne's assistance, after he had engaged the *Dragoon* at Belle Île, this was of your own initiative, not upon the orders of Captain Hart?"

"It was, sir. I believe Captain Bourne and the *Lucy*'s lieutenant will bear that out."

"And finally . . . did Hart order you to pursue the *Themis* after you brought him aboard the *Dragoon*? Subsequent to the mutiny, I mean."

"No, sir. He did not."

"This was entirely your own decision?"

"It was, sir."

"Did Captain Hart advise you in any way? Certainly he must have sent you his encouragement and blessing?"

"I regret to say that no such words were sent to me."

The captains all looked one to the other, unable to hide their growing distress and resentment. No one wanted to speak aloud that Hart had, infamously, ordered the *Dragoon* back to Plymouth and had even tried to wrest control of the prize from Hayden, but clearly they were aware of it, even if they did not want to believe it of a fellow captain.

McLeod then took up the enquiry. "Mr Hayden, soon after you sailed from Torbay it would seem that two unknown vessels were sighted but there ensued disagreement among the officers as to what they were. If one reads between the lines in your sailing master's account, one might be led to believe these were likely transports, not enemy frigates. What was your opinion?"

Hayden met the captain's gaze. "I believed them to be transports, Captain McLeod. Certainly they turned and ran for Le Havre upon perceiving us, which I don't believe frigates would have done so quickly, given their superiority of numbers."

McLeod appeared to be containing a slow-boiling rage. His speech was clipped and very clear. "But you did not give chase to make certain?"

"Captain Hart ordered that we shape our course for Brest."

McLeod shook his head, his eyes, for a moment, closing. "My last question, Mr Hayden," he said, turning his attention back to the lieutenant. "You did indeed inform Captain Hart after the crew all but refused to sail when leaving Plymouth?"

"I did, sir, and he answered as I repeated in the court-martial today."

"He blamed you?"

"More or less, yes."

"Rather more, I think." He turned to Spencer.

Spencer seemed either the most amiable of the gentlemen present or the most skilled at hiding his emotions, for he regarded Hayden very calmly. "The discontent among the crew was manifest when you first came aboard Hart's ship? You have no doubt of it?"

"No doubt whatsoever, sir."

Spencer seemed to have been quickly convinced. "Then you have said all I need to hear."

Gardner looked to the other gentlemen and Hayden could see North hesitating, then the man turned to Hayden. "I would like to know, Mr Hayden, how the master's log went missing and how and where it was found."

For a moment Hayden meant to answer, but then thought better of it. "It was stolen from the master's cabin, but if you don't mind, Captain North, I would rather not answer the rest of that question." There were others involved, and if one of these captains was not what he seemed, Hayden did not want to endanger Worth and his companions.

Gardner interrupted as North began to insist. "We have assured Mr Hayden he could choose not to answer, and we must respect that. I think it is safe to assume that the log was stolen by persons to whom its contents offered the most harm. I don't think we need Mr Hayden to tell us who that would be." He turned to Hayden and smiled. "Thank you, Mr Hayden, you have been most helpful. I think you will agree that it would be best for all concerned if you did not speak of this conversation . . ."

Hayden quickly agreed.

"I will have you returned to your ship."

Hayden rose, bade them farewell, and went to the door, but then, emboldened by frustration, turned back to the gathered captains. "Sir. What is to happen to me tomorrow? Captain Hart has done much to damage me in the eyes of the panel."

"There are twelve captains on the panel, Mr Hayden, and we are but four. Even so, we will do everything that is within our powers to aid you. I wish I could say that we will carry the day, but I cannot make that promise." He patted the master's log. "We have some ammunition, at least."

"It is my impression that Captain Hart has many friends among the members of the panel."

"Perhaps, but I believe there are still some willing to chance the wrath of Mrs Hart's family in a just cause. Or so I hope."

Twenty-five

W hat shall we do with our Mr Aldrich?" Hawthorne lamented. "For a man so learned he is frighteningly obtuse, is he not?"

The *Themis*' officers were spread rather randomly about the captain's barren cabin. They had been discussing what might occur on the morrow, and Hayden had just related his earlier conversation with Aldrich.

"I have seen it many times before," Archer's brother said, "a certain kind of genius married very closely to a ruinous imprudence. No offence meant to Mr Aldrich, but if he cannot limit that great and wandering intellect he shall come to grief, I fear."

A knock was followed by officer of the watch, Lieutenant Archer, thrusting his head in the open door. "Mr Hayden. The provost-marshal is alongside. He has come for one of our people, sir."

"Whom?"

"He will only speak with you, sir."

Hayden, Griffiths, and Hawthorne came to their feet as one, and hastened onto the deck. In the fading light, the provost-marshal stood waiting by the rail.

"May I be of service?" Hayden asked.

The man held out a folded and sealed letter. "From the judge-advocate of the court-martial, sir. Regrettably, Able Seaman Peter Aldrich has been charged with the crimes of mutinous assembly and mutiny under the Articles of War."

Hayden broke the seal and read the document, which, indeed, demanded that Aldrich be placed immediately into the custody of the provost-marshal.

"This cannot be," Griffiths spoke up. "Aldrich is in my care and I will not release him. His health will not bear it."

"Sir, I have the license of the court. He must be given up to me."

"I must agree with Dr Griffiths," Hayden said. "Aldrich has suffered a serious reversal of his health. I will speak to the judge-advocate and the president of the court tomorrow and explain that we cannot release him into anyone's custody until his health is materially restored."

But the provost-marshal would not be so easily put off. "Sir, you put me in a difficult circumstance. I am ordered to place him among the other prisoners charged with mutiny."

Hayden shook his head, feigning a look of great concern and seriousness. "And I should happily comply, would Aldrich's health allow it. I shall take all responsibility for the court's displeasure, sir. I give you my word."

The man wavered a moment, then nodded, made a little bow, and retreated over the rail down into the waiting boat. When the boat began to immerse into the gloom, Hayden said quietly, "And I wondered, Doctor, why you had returned Aldrich to the sick-berth."

"I feared these very circumstances. There is a great deal to be lost by appearances, as we all know. If he is among the mutineers he must extricate himself, but if he stands among us, and we can convince the officers of the court that he deserves to be with us, then they must prove him guilty."

"I don't know if it will make any difference, but we shall do everything within our power."

Twenty-six

"I t is judged by the court that there is enough evidence to justify these very serious charges that have been laid." Admiral Duncan folded his hands together and placed them on the table. "Peter Aldrich will have the opportunity to defend himself, as will every man so charged. If you can ensure his detention, Mr Hayden, we will leave him in the care of your surgeon for the time being."

"He is far too ill to make any attempt to escape, sir, but we shall keep him under guard until he is recovered enough to be placed with the other prisoners."

"That will satisfy, Mr Hayden," Duncan replied.

"While we are deciding who shall be charged," Bainsbridge broke in, "let us return to the matter of Mr Hayden, who stands before us. I believe we now have heard enough evidence to conclude that the disaffection of the crew began while the lieutenant had command of the *Themis* in the absence of Captain Hart. In truth, I believe it is clear that Mr Hayden and his lax methods were the cause of it."

Several members of the panel nodded their heads in agreement and more than one said, "Hear."

"Perhaps we have been attending different courts-martial," Captain North countered quickly. "I, for one, have not heard near enough 'evidence' to make me wish to take the unprecedented step of including in this court-martial Mr Hayden or any other man who was not on the ship at the time of the mutiny. Quite the contrary."

Several members of the panel began to argue this at once, but Duncan raised his voice over all and brought silence to the cabin. The people watching all leaned a little forward, and Hayden observed Wickham glance his way. He forced his hands to unclench.

"It is clear we are divided on this matter," Bainsbridge offered into the silence. "I propose we put it to a vote."

"This is not a parliament, Captain Bainsbridge," Duncan responded angrily, "or so I might remind you. We do not vote on matters of jurisprudence. I have decided not to include any men who were not aboard the *Themis* at the time of the mutiny and that is my final word on the matter. You may return to your place, Mr Hayden."

Bainsbridge did not seem the least intimidated by the anger of Admiral Duncan. "Well, I am not satisfied. Mr Hayden is escaping a situation for which he was chiefly responsible. Justice is not being served."

Duncan clearly took offence at this last remark, and drew himself up, face rigid.

Hayden proceeded to his seat, well aware that the dispute over his fate had not been decided.

Gardner spoke at that moment, his voice reasonable and calm. "I believe Captain Bainsbridge is correct in one thing: we have not looked sufficiently into the question of who bears responsibility for this mutiny. It is clear that the unhappy event could not have been quite the surprise Captain Hart first suggested. I would like to revisit the incident at Brest . . . when the transport was taken. Let us call upon Captain Hart once again, for I have read the account in the master's log—in truth, I have read all the officers' journals—and have many questions. I realize that Captain Hart was in his cot at the time and only emerged onto the deck after Mr Hayden had gone away in the boats to take the transport, but certainly Captain Hart perceived trouble among the members of the crew—marines with levelled muskets were keeping the men at the guns, after all. And yet he has claimed there were no signs of unrest among his crew. And what of the refusal to sail at Plymouth and this petition mentioned by the master? I understand the captain was once again in his cot, but surely he must have much to add to our knowledge of these events."

"Yes," a man behind Hayden whispered to his companion, "strip the blackguard of his borrowed feathers."

Bainsbridge began a quick kneading of the spot over his heart. "I believe these matters have been dealt with most thoroughly, Captain Gardner."

Hayden saw Hart's barrister glance at his client as though to say, *Did I not warn you?* Hart looked discomfited, but also a little confused. It occurred to Hayden that Hart did not quite perceive what went on. That his own perversity in bringing up Aldrich and the pamphlets and then trying to shift the blame to Hayden had begun all the difficult questions that followed. And now Gardner threatened to reveal all of his shyness and negligence of duty before the court.

Captain Gardner leaned forward and levelled his gaze at Bainsbridge. "If we are going to talk of including officers who were not even aboard the *Themis* at the time of the mutiny, I say we should be doubly rigorous in our quizzing of those most likely to have answers: the officers and crew who *were* aboard at the time of the mutiny. The accounts of the master and of the officers suggest much fertile ground for such an enquiry."

Bainsbridge was so taken aback by this that for a moment he could not speak. Surely he comprehended Gardner's repeated insinuation that there was damaging evidence against his friend Hart in the various logs and journals.

"Perhaps the admiral is correct in this," Bainsbridge answered quietly, "and I am being obdurate in the matter of Mr Hayden. But I strongly oppose going back over events that have already been deliberated. I object to it most emphatically." He nodded in deferral to Duncan, but his eye was on Gardner, who sat back in his chair and interlocked his fingers on the table before him. Hayden thought the man might smile, but he did not.

Simpson, the youngest captain on the panel, waved a hand in dismissal. "You both search in the wrong place to find the guilty. It is the men who attempted to deliver one of our frigates to the French who must bear all blame. I am only interested to know if Captain Hart and his crew did everything within their powers to resist these traitors, and it is clear from the evidence given by the gentlemen who have spoken thus far that their defence of the ship was more than spirited—it was exemplary. That is what we are here to discover. Let us move on."

"Yes," Duncan pronounced, "let us proceed. Who is next to be heard?"

And proceed they did. Hardly a question was asked this day but what did each man do to resist the mutineers, and if they could not resist, why? Even Gardner had no questions about the causes, mutinous language, or assembly. He did not pursue Mr Barthe's assertion that the crew had been ready to refuse to sail with Hart and to petition the Admiralty for his removal. The warrant officers and midshipmen were very quickly heard, and then the crew even more perfunctorily. The great cabin was cleared so that the captains might consider their judgement in private, and Hayden went up onto the deck with a few of the *Themis'* officers, where they stood speaking quietly.

"What in hell's name has just occurred?" Barthe asked quietly. "I had not finished having my say. What of the matters we spoke of but one day past? Have they forgotten?"

"Not forgotten, merely chosen to ignore," Archer's brother said, earning a look of disgust from the ship's master, who then turned away. "Some arrangement has been reached during the hours of darkness, but whom it will favour is beyond my powers to predict."

Hayden's stomach had been worrying him all morning; now it began to churn terribly at this news. He went to the rail and stared off across the listless bay. Gardner had not sounded overly confident that he could sway the panel, though Hayden owed him thanks for silencing Bainsbridge and protecting him from being charged. It was still possible that he would be censured by the court. They could hold him responsible but not find him guilty—which would have much the same effect on his career and on the way he would be perceived in the eye of the public.

All his attempts to force Hart to carry war to the enemy had resulted in this?

For two hours the crew of the *Themis* paced the deck—a windless watch, the day metallic—leaden sky, mercuric sea. The gulls did not fly but bobbed slowly upon the harbour slick, mute, and mournful. The tension in the faces of the men, in their carriage, was not easily hidden. There was surprisingly little conversation, and that whispered.

"Do you think it will be much longer?" was asked several times within Hayden's hearing—each time by a different man.

The middies gathered together by the rail and talked quietly among themselves, solicitous of one another, their mouths all squared by anxiety. Hart and Landry stayed apart and were approached by no one—shunned. Several intense, whispered conversations ensued with their barrister, but no one took any notice. For all the brotherliness of captains, Hayden thought that Hart looked quite anxious—which well he should. If the truth ever came out about him he would never recover.

Perhaps an hour into this fretful watch Dr Griffiths stopped Hayden's deliberate progress across the deck.

"Was it just my misperception, Mr Hayden, or did it appear that Gardner and Bainsbridge reached an accommodation—no mention of mutinous assembly or petitions or incidents at Plymouth, and in exchange Bainsbridge left off insisting that you be included in the court-martial?"

Hayden could not speak of his meeting with Captain Gardner and other members of the panel. "I believe that was no misperception."

"Good to have Gardner on your side. He seems formidable."

"Those gentlemen are all formidable, and Hart has more friends on the panel than I."

The doctor stood closer than normally he would, speaking very low. "The longer they debate the less sure am I of the outcome. I thought that all was decided before we began today. I can't imagine what it is they argue now."

"A baronetcy for Hart? Post rank for Landry? Infamy for all the rest?"

Griffiths tried to smile. "It is too true to make jest of, I fear. I understand they require a surgeon of the hulks—my next commission."

Hawthorne joined them. "Did I hear laughter? Muted, but laughter all the same?"

"We are discussing our likely futures," Hayden replied.

"Ah. Now, that is a subject for drollery. Do you think it possible to pay passage to Canada and buy a sizeable plot of land for ten pounds thruppence?"

"Why travel so far, Mr Hawthorne?" Griffiths enquired. "Why not simply purchase a manor house here in England and ride to the hounds and spend the rest of your days at sport? Certainly you could do all that for ten pounds and have thruppence left to guard against misfortune."

"You, Doctor, should know that any respectable manor house would cost at least three times that sum. No, it is the cold winters of Canada for me."

"You have not a thing to smile about." Barthe stopped in his orbit of the deck, his usually florid face pallid and doughy in the flat light. "I have been in this exact position before—waiting upon the pleasure of the court—and I will tell you, no joy will come of it. Hart shall prance away with a light step and the court will bring down its harshest judgement upon those least able to defend themselves." He gazed at his companions a moment, an odd look coming over his face. "But perhaps you should laugh while you may. There will be no mirth when all is done."

The officers and crew of the *Themis* went warily down into the great cabin and stood, hats in hand, their manner funereal, only the deck offering up an occasional complaint as the men shifted about upon the planks. Among the captains of the panel Hayden saw no smiles. Indeed, they appeared almost to a man out of sorts or displeased, as though what had transpired satisfied no one. The lieutenant felt his mouth go dry, fists forming into tight balls.

The admiral stood, taking up a sheet of paper that lay before him. "It is the decision of this court-martial that Captain Sir Josiah Hart and his officers and loyal crew did vigorously defend their ship against the mutiny of the sixth of October but were overwhelmed by superior numbers and surprise. Captain Sir Josiah Hart, his officers, and crew are therefore honourably acquitted."

There was, for a brief second, silence, and Hayden waited for Duncan to go on, to speak his name, announce the utter ruin of his career. But the admiral instead turned to one of the captains and began speaking quietly. The court-martial was over.

Hayden did not know whether to be relieved or enraged. He slumped in his chair a moment as congratulations were being offered all around. Someone pumped his hand. And then another. Over the babble, Muhlhauser shouted something that did not register. At least one frightened crewman hid his face and wept.

The crowd in the cabin all began to file out, following the jubilant crew of the *Themis*, some of whom began to caper before they reached the door. Hayden stood and waited for the people next him to move. Griffiths caught his eye and smiled, obviously relieved, though certainly the surgeon had never been in the least danger.

Hayden wondered if he should speak with Gardner, but then seeing the crush around the captains of the panel thought better of it. He did notice, as he shuffled out with the crowd, Hart approach Duncan and the other members of the panel. These gentlemen stood in small groups by their tables, speaking among themselves and to a few friends. As Hart came up to the admiral, Duncan turned his back on the man and began speaking to North in such a way as to brook no intrusion. For a moment Hart stood, a blush of crimson overspreading his face. He then turned his attention to Spencer, who cut him just as sharply. Bainsbridge and a few others came to Hart's rescue then, leading him quickly away.

Hayden noticed Wickham observing this same spectacle.

"And to think I once believed him quite the greatest man of my acquaintance," Wickham said, unable to hide a certain sadness of tone.

So fall the heroes of our youth, Hayden thought, but said nothing.

He seemed to float in a kind of daze up onto the deck and down into the waiting boat.

As soon as they had travelled beyond earshot of the flagship, Barthe's rage exploded. "Was that not the most perfect example of Admiralty justice?" the master wondered bitterly. "The mutineers shall hang, and the man who drove them to it receives a knighthood. Fucking Navy!"

Hayden sat down at the table in the captain's cabin and wrote letters for several of the accused mutineers. In each he said that they had been, prior to the mutiny, men of upstanding character and diligence. He knew that the letters would have no effect whatsoever—the men would all be hanged—but he wrote them attentively anyway, perhaps for no other purpose than to give the men hope for a few days or to assuage his own conscience. He wondered now, in retrospect, if he could not have done something to avert the mutiny. It was a question upon which he went back and forth almost by the hour. Certainly, Stuckey and his friends had been very cunning to exploit the natural anger that resulted from Hart flogging Aldrich, and the captain's shyness at Belle Île—just when the men were gaining a measure of self-respect. No one could deny that Hart had done much to undermine his first lieutenant and had refused to listen to his warnings. But despite all that, Hayden wondered if he could not have done something more—gathered all the officers to repeat his warnings about the state of the crew, attempted to convince the captain again. He wondered if his wounded pride had led him to let the situation fester, thinking, "I have done my duty, now let Hart reap what he has sown." And now many a man would hang, whose major offence was no longer being able to bear the tyranny and shyness of Captain Sir Josiah Hart.

A knock was followed by the doctor, whom he invited in.

"How fare you this evening, Mr Hayden?" Griffiths said, slurring his syllables noticeably.

"I am writing letters attesting to the good character of several of the mutineers. A rather futile business, but I feel I must do it."

"Good for you, but do not waste too much effort in grief for them. We all suffered under Hart's persecution and yet we did not choose to join the mutiny. For many it was the decision of the moment, perhaps, and their resentment betrayed their better judgement, which though it quickly returned, came too late. Even so, they so chose and we did not. Do not waste your energies in pity for them."

"But I do." Hayden leaned forward and spoke so very softly. "After all, did we not once conspire to give Hart his physic at an opportune moment so that we might take a prize? Was that not our own little mutiny?"

"I have no idea of what you speak, Mr Hayden. Indeed, I fear you are drunk. Captain Hart suffered from migraine and stones. I gave him physic when such was required. Here, let me fill your glass." He reached for the decanter, almost knocking it over.

"Have you not had enough, Doctor?" Hayden wondered.

Griffiths sat back in his seat and closed his eyes. "Not nearly enough. I can still feel. I am not yet numb, to which state I aspire. Did you note how adeptly I said that? . . . *To which state I aspire.*" The doctor fell silent. For a moment Hayden thought he had passed out.

"Do you know," Griffiths said softly, "of all Hart's crimes, and they are manifold, the hanging of McBride is the one that seems to me most vile."

"You should not blame yourself, Doctor; you only gave evidence that the finger did not belong to any man who remained on ship."

Griffiths waved a hand drunkenly. "Forget my part. I shall be damned for it or not. Hart had a man hanged for a crime he did not commit. Certainly McBride was an obdurate and quarrelsome individual, but he did not deserve death for it." A pause. "*I* am quarrelsome on occasion."

"I have never witnessed it, Doctor."

"Hart should have been made a Companion of the Order of Blackguard Knights."

Hayden laughed. "An O.B.K."

In the silence that followed, Hayden was sure he heard a voice call out that a captain had come alongside. The sounds of feet thumping down the companionway stair. A sharp rap at his door.

"Captain Gardner asking for permission to come aboard, sir."

"Gardner? At this hour?" Hayden rose quickly. "Help the doctor to his cabin, will you, Mr Jennings. I believe he has a touch of the sea-sickness."

"In port, sir?"

"I believe it was claret."

Hayden hastened up the ladders, where he found Gardner climbing unceremoniously onto the darkened deck.

"Captain Gardner, my most profound apologies. Not even a bosun to pipe you aboard, sir—"

"It was my purpose to draw no attention to myself, Mr Hayden. It is I who should apologize for appearing unannounced. May I speak with you in private?"

"Certainly, sir. By all means."

They repaired to Hart's cabin, where Hayden poured his guest some wine.

Gardner glanced around the barren compartment. "Hart has taken his belongings ashore?"

"Yes."

Gardner nodded approvingly. "I do not think he will go to sea again."

"With his knighthood and now great reputation can a pennant be far off? Admiral Sir Josiah Hart." Hayden felt his bitterness and anger rise up like bile. His eye fell upon his guest. "He has been saved by the court-martial, after all."

Gardner turned his intelligent gaze upon Hayden. "It was not Hart I wished to save, Mr Hayden, but you. Oh, in a perfect world, matters would have arranged themselves differently, and Captain Hart would have been exposed to the world for what he is . . ." Gardner paused. "But the world is less than perfect and arrangements have to be made. Hart was held accountable for none of his failures, but in return you escaped censure. And I must tell you that without the support of

Admiral Duncan, Hart's friends would have seen you blamed in Hart's place."

"I apologize, Captain Gardner. I spoke without thinking, an unfortunate habit of mine."

"We all must speak our minds now and then. But it should comfort you to know that Hart is done in the service. Even his supporters in the Admiralty must realize that now; his acquittal and knighthood are his compensation. It was a devil's bargain, perhaps, but something good came of it—your future in the service."

"I owe you and your friends a great—"

"You owe me nothing, Mr Hayden," Gardner interrupted. "Both my good friends Mr Bourne and Mr Stephens—who is soon to receive a knighthood himself, much deserved in his case—have given you such an excellent character that I felt obliged to do everything in my power to extricate you from your unfortunate situation. In this I had help, for I could never have done it alone." A grin, lopsided and conspiratorial, appeared on the man's face.

The grin disappeared. A sad shaking of the head. "It is almost a crime that Hart should receive credit for your deeds, but I think the truth shall soon be in circulation." For a moment Gardner was silent, as though he had lost his train of thought. "There is another matter upon which we must speak, Mr Hayden. A matter worthy of your greatest attention. It was my distinct impression that this seaman, Peter Aldrich, was dear to all of the officers—with the notable exception of your gallant captain." He paused but did not allow Hayden time to respond. "The man is in very grave danger, Mr Hayden. He was flogged for mutinous language, and though the court will not punish him again for this offence, he is certainly guilty of mutinous assembly, or will be seen to be so—"

"But his reading of the pamphlets was done in complete innocence—because he believed knowledge to be uplifting. He would have just as happily read the crew the doctor's medical books."

Gardner raised thick, angular hands, stark palms out. "I do not doubt you for a moment, Mr Hayden, but the captains of the court do not know your Aldrich. It will be seen that he read seditious texts to the crew, who then mutinied while he was in the sick-berth, too ill to join them. It is true that he did stop the floggings, but even if the man is not seen as part of the mutiny, he will be perceived as contributing to the unrest that led to it. He may not hang, but he will almost certainly be flogged around the fleet—a hundred lashes if the court is lenient, three hundred if it is not."

"He will not survive it," Hayden said, feeling the blood drain from his face. "Three dozen lashes were almost his end."

After he broke his fast, Hayden paid a visit to Robert Hertle aboard his new frigate, christened *Fairway* by the Lords Commissioners.

"I suppose *Roadstead* was already taken," Hayden observed, as his eye ran the length of the expanse of new-planked deck, almost virginal in its purity.

"At least it is not a name of the *Indomitable* school. *Indefatigable* et cetera."

"*Impregnable* . . . ?" Hayden suggested. "No women allowed."

"*Indefensible*," Hertle countered, "for sea-lawyers."

"*Irresolute?*"

"We all know whose ship that would be."

They both laughed.

"I am so relieved that you were not dragged into the court-martial, Charles."

"Hart and the others were all honourably acquitted."

"Acquitted, perhaps."

Hayden glanced up at the men working aloft, shading his eyes against the sun. "When do you sail?"

"On the morning tide."

"Mrs Hertle will be very sad to see you go."

"She won't watch my ship leave—a superstition. Mrs Hertle and Henrietta went up to London yesterday."

Hayden was rather taken aback. "They left . . . ?"

"Yes." Hertle glanced at him, and then down at the spotless deck. "You should have spoken, Charles. *I* think you should have spoken. I know . . . you are dissatisfied with your prospects . . . but now Henrietta believes you are uncertain of your attachment. And I have begun to wonder myself."

"I am not the least unsure. You cannot know, Robert, what an unrelenting cause for worry is a narrow income. Henrietta is used to a life of comfort, of going up to London whenever the whim strikes, of wearing the latest fashions—of *buying* the latest fashions. A lieutenant's eight pounds eight a month will not keep her in such style, and her father has numerous daughters. He cannot possibly offer them all a living."

"Have you forgotten already Lady Hertle and her two fine homes?"

"It is not my practice to think of a woman in terms of her fortune."

"You *are* uncertain of your own attachment. Certainly you must be, for these are the slimmest excuses. Henrietta Carthew shall never be poor, and do not think other men are insensible to this."

"And would she follow a failed naval officer to America? Will she forsake England and her remarkable family for the uncertainties of Boston or New York?"

Robert crossed his arms and regarded his friend. "If your attachment were profound you would not be asking such questions. You would not even be terribly concerned about having your suit rebuffed. I know of what I speak. When love is like a madness you care very little for how dignified you appear or about where or how you might live. It is better that you said nothing, Charles." He pushed away from the rail where he had been leaning. "Come, let us have the rest of our tour."

Over a dinner in the captain's cabin, Hayden related recent events, the court-martial, Hart's knighthood, the unheralded visit from Gardner. He chronicled these proceedings with little zeal or even interest, feeling the sting of Henrietta's rather abrupt removal to London and wondering all the while if he had made a terrible error. Perhaps he *was* unsure of his own attachment . . .

Hertle remained silent, pensive, while his friend spoke. When Hayden finished, his manner did not change, as though he placed everything said upon a scale and watched, now, as the balance rocked one way then the other.

"I believe it is good news that both Philip Stephens and Captain Gardner—who will soon have his flag—have gone to some effort to shield you from the taint that your fellow officers will never quite be rid of . . . Hart's mutiny."

"Stephens made me no promises, which distressed you in the past."

"Yes, but he has done much to preserve your reputation, so that you might find employment in the future, I would venture."

"Perhaps he has some other captain who needs a nursemaid."

"Stephens knows how diligently you prosecuted the war against the French on your recent cruise. Others must know it, as well, despite the *Times* account. Let us hope that something will come of it. But I will tell you, stealing back the master's log probably had more effect than you realize. Until then Hart probably thought he could lie and bluster his way through the court-martial, but after that some arrangement had to be reached." Hertle sat back from the table. "So, what is your opinion of my ship?"

"She is everything a man could hope for, though I dare say her crew will take some working up, as I have seldom seen a more unlikely collection of landsmen and bleaters."

Hertle laughed. "They shall take some labour. I will have someone read Tom Paine to them each evening to improve their minds. That should answer."

But this jest did not sit well with Hayden, whose smile disappeared.

"I am very concerned about Aldrich, Robert. If he does not hang, Gardner believes he will be flogged about the fleet, which will kill him just as dead as a noose."

"The man was very foolish to have read such pamphlets to a disaffected crew. It might have been done in innocence, but so have many a black deed. The courts do not much care for a man's good intentions if another's death has resulted. Aldrich showed very little common sense, if I may use the term."

"Aboard our ship, common sense was on everyone's lips but in no one's character."

After attending to some business ashore, Hayden returned to the *Themis* just as the sun set into a shoal of coal-dust cloud. Down into the bowels of the ship he went, seeking the doctor, whom he found in the sick-berth, decidedly pale if not ashen.

"Good evening to you, Doctor."

"And you, sir," Griffiths said, his face turning suddenly rosy—embarrassed, no doubt, by his antics of the previous night.

"Might I have a word with you?"

"You may."

Hayden noticed Aldrich, who sat up in his cot, reading by the light of a lamp. "How fare you, Mr Aldrich?"

"In the pink, sir, though the doctor does not agree."

"I would heed Dr Griffiths, Mr Aldrich. He is a higher power in this place."

Hayden led the doctor quickly up to the empty great cabin. A servant came scurrying in to light the candles.

"Sorry, sir," the man said. "Wasn't sure if you'd be using the captain's cabin this evening."

Hayden waited until the man had gone and then closed the skylight overhead. He beckoned Griffiths to the stern gallery, and they both took seats on the sill-bench.

"What is so secret that we must cloister ourselves away to speak?" the doctor asked, looking both ill and somewhat alarmed.

"I had a visit from Captain Gardner this evening last."

"Gardner? Of the court-martial?"

"The very one. He is of the opinion that Aldrich will be flogged around the fleet for his contribution to the mutiny—that is, if he escapes hanging."

Griffiths did not argue, but his sallow look turned very dark, mouth forming a thin, harsh line.

"I do not think Gardner will be proven wrong in this," Hayden whispered.

"Yes, absolutely. Damn . . ." Griffiths glanced up at Hayden. "I don't think Aldrich's constitution will take it. Is there any hope for the King's mercy?"

"I think it unlikely, but even if that were not so, it is a thin rope to cling to."

"Yes. I agree. Is it just my present lowered state or do I sense that you have not told me this without purpose?"

"Are you willing to risk your career, if not infamy?"

"For Mr Aldrich? My career, is yours. Infamy? You had better tell me what is in your mind . . ."

"There is an American ship in the sound, the *New England*; she belongs to a Mr Adams of Boston, who by chance happens to be my mother's new husband. I have spoken to the master. He will take Aldrich secretly aboard and convey him to Boston, upon the first fair tide . . . if we can find a way to get Aldrich to the ship."

Griffiths' manner grew even more grave, and he rose and paced slowly across the cabin.

"I would not bring you into this, Doctor, but I don't think I can manage it without your help. I will row him to the *New England* in the jolly-boat, but I must get him out of the sick-berth and into the boat."

Griffiths stopped and turned to Hayden, his sickly look pushed aside by one of determination. "Leave that to me. Four bells of the middle-watch."

"One of us must speak with him. There can be no argument. To stay here is to die. There will be no justice. He must be made to understand."

The doctor reached a thin arm up to a beam, leaning his small weight against it. "I will see it done—do not be concerned, Mr Hayden—but we will have to get him past Hawthorne's marines . . ."

Hayden himself stood, rubbing his hands together. "I have not worked that out quite yet. I might call them away for a few moments on some pretext while you get him to the boat . . . ?"

"I think it better to ask Mr Hawthorne for his help."

Hayden stopped, shaking his head. "I was loath to involve yourself, Doctor. Let no others share the risk."

The doctor gestured down toward the gunroom. "Hawthorne is as attached to Aldrich as any, and he is angry enough at the injustice that has been done—bloody Hart being knighted! He will see the marines out of the way for a few critical moments, I am sure." The doctor was silent a moment. "I suspect Aldrich hasn't a shilling to his name . . ."

"I will give him what I can, but I own that will be very little."

"Yes, I can do the same, and it will likely be less. We daren't ask anyone else."

Hayden raised his hands. "I shall give the master a letter to my mother requesting that she offer Mr Aldrich what aid she can."

This did not seem to impress the doctor. "Better not to have such things in writing. If Aldrich is apprehended we shall claim he escaped. Hawthorne is always bragging about his success at cards, perhaps he has some small sum he might lend . . ."

"Shall I speak with him?"

The doctor shook his head. "I will do it. It was my suggestion. But you may count on his aid, I am sure. Four bells. I shall meet you in the cockpit."

The doctor went out and Hayden sat staring at the deck for some moments. Perse appeared a moment later, following a knock, respectful in its volume.

"The midshipmen are awaiting you, sir. Supper, if you remember?"

"Ah. Perse, my thanks. I am much distracted this day."

Hayden quickly readied himself and went down to the midshipmen's berth, where a table had been laid, the young gentlemen in their best uniforms, clean linen, faces scrubbed to a seraphic shine.

The middies were in high spirits after their honourable acquittal, and many a toast was offered: to the justice of the court, to Mr Archer's brother, to Mr Archer for having a brother, to each and every captain of the court, to the admiral . . . Hayden had difficulty playing his part in the proceedings and he noticed that, alone among the young gentlemen,

Wickham remained quite sober. Several times the lieutenant caught the nobleman watching him, an odd, quizzical look upon his young face.

The evening did pass, finally, the middies all more or less happily drunk; Hobson and Stock became somewhat quarrelsome toward the end. Taking himself through the doors into the gunroom, Hayden found Hawthorne and the doctor seated at the table with Mr Barthe. In manner, the three men appeared terribly grim.

"Three men too serious," Archer declared as he stumbled through the door, then leaned upon the table with an exaggerated casualness. He was in the same state of inebriation as the middies, and was taken aback when no one smiled at his wit. "Is something amiss?"

"No," Griffiths answered, trying to smile, "all is right with the world. But I fear your tomorrow, Mr Archer, will much resemble my today." Griffiths rose from his chair. "Good night to you, gentlemen. Until tomorrow . . ." He then nodded to Hayden, a slight tilt of the head toward Hawthorne.

Hayden retired to his cot, and the darkness of his cabin, but he did not go easily to sleep. He lay listening to the night sounds, the movement of the guards, the chiming of the ship's bell, and the calling of *All's well*. The wind backed to the north-east, and rain spattered down on Plymouth Sound. Hawthorne's infamous snoring droned—as regular as a clock's pendulum. Hayden imagined he could hear the doctor shifting restively in his cot—awake for the same reason as he.

Four bells of the middle-watch took him by stealth—he had fallen asleep perhaps an hour before. Rising quickly, Hayden pulled on his clothes as silently as darkness would allow, and slipped out of his cabin. Hawthorne appeared at almost the same moment, and the two went out the door, and quickly down the stairs. The middies were all too drunkenly sleeping to notice their passing.

At the foot of the ladder the doctor awaited them with a lantern, a sheepish-looking Aldrich at his side. Hayden put a finger to his lips and led them back up the ladder to the berth-deck. Up again to the empty gun-deck, no sentry there to take note of them. Pausing, Hayden put his head out the companionway. The rain had ceased sometime earlier, but the wind still blew uneasily, and the stars were not to be seen.

Hawthorne put a hand on Hayden's shoulder and pressed past him onto the deck. He waved a lantern at someone forward, and then motioned for the others to follow. A cold wind whipped Hayden's unbound hair about his face. The jolly-boat had been streamed aft without a boat-keeper that night. Hayden and Aldrich quickly drew it alongside.

"What is the matter here?" came a voice out of the dark.

Hawthorne spun about and raised his lantern to reveal Wickham, buttoning his coat against the night.

Griffiths stepped forward, placing himself between the midshipman and Aldrich, as though he would hide the seaman's identity. "It would be better if you went back to your cot, Mr Wickham, and forgot what you saw here this night."

"It would be better still if I came to your aid," Wickham said. "You are no oarsman, Doctor, and would be better aboard, where you might be called to see to a patient. Let me go with Mr Hayden and Mr Hawthorne. We three are old boat-mates, after all."

"Do you understand what goes on here?" Hayden asked the boy.

"I believe I do, sir."

"Then better you take no part in it."

"Mr Aldrich is as dear to me as any of you, I dare say—"

"We have not time to argue," Griffiths hissed. "Let Mr Wickham go in my place, for he is not wrong about my skills as a boatman."

The four men went quickly down into the jolly-boat, pushing off into the darkness, the chill wind immediately taking hold of their little ship so that she paid off to leeward.

"Take the tiller, Mr Hayden," Hawthorne said, relieving the lieutenant of an oar. "You know where it is we go."

And so Hayden sat in the stern-sheets and acted as coxswain while the other three manned the oars. He guided them among the great, silent ships, giving each a large berth to avoid any boats rowing sentry. They did not want to be challenged that night.

In a short time they had crossed the sound to where the American merchantman swung to her anchor. Hayden brought them quietly alongside.

"Mr Hayden? Is that you, sir?" came a voice from above.

"It is, Mr Tupper. Shall I send our package up?"

"If you please."

Hayden leaned forward and grasped Aldrich by the hand. A purse was pushed into the seaman's fingers.

"I cannot accept this!" Aldrich objected.

"You may pay it all back. Mr Tupper will give you the address of my mother and you may return the monies to her." Hayden released the man's hand. "Whatever your inclination, Mr Aldrich, never go to sea again. Stay to the land, for the British will ever be on the lookout for you. Do you understand?"

"I do, and thank you, sir. Perhaps one day you will visit me in America, and I shall have a house and a family of my own."

"That is my fondest hope, Mr Aldrich. Now up you go."

Aldrich took the others by the hand in turn, showering them with thanks before he went up the ship's side to disappear over the rail.

"Good night to you, Mr Hayden," Tupper whispered from above.

"And you, Mr Tupper. I am in your debt."

"Not in the least. I am so indebted to Mr and Mrs Adams for their innumerable kindnesses that your obligation is already cancelled. Good luck to you."

They rowed blindly back to the *Themis*, finding her by a flash of lightning—the only such glare that night. A portentous crash of thunder rolled across the bay, echoing among the low hills.

"Apparently the Almighty is not pleased with our most recent act of rebellion," Hawthorne whispered. He bent to his oar like a seasoned hand now.

"I take it as a sign of His approbation," Wickham answered. "How could it not be? Saving an innocent man from flogging, if not death. No, we shall not be damned for that. We shall be taken up into Heaven when our time comes—blind, perhaps, but blessed all the same."

"Blind to our own follies, at least," Hayden said. "Here is the ship, at last."

Twenty-seven

Aldrich's disappearance cost Hayden censure from the president of the court-martial, but Hayden apologized profusely, and bore it with well-concealed joy. Despite a reward being offered, Able Seaman Peter Aldrich was not to be found in or around Plymouth. There was much speculation that he had been swept out to sea as he attempted to swim ashore and had been drowned.

A new captain was appointed to the *Themis*, and as it was his intention to bring his own officers and midshipmen with him, all of the *Themis'* officers and young gentlemen found themselves ashore and going their separate ways. The dashing Hawthorne, never without an invitation, posted off to Bath to visit with friends, and no doubt many young ladies. Barthe went home to Kent. Griffiths to Portsmouth. After taking his leave of Lady Hertle, Hayden posted up to London in company with Lord Arthur Wickham. The boy's sunny disposition made what would have been a dismal retreat almost bearable. Wickham was not overly troubled about finding another ship, but Hayden could not allow himself to feel the same. He might soon be following in the wake of Aldrich.

Hayden also felt they were escaping the court-martial of the mutineers, which was to begin in a few days' time—neither Wickham nor himself would be called to give evidence as they had not been present. He was very glad that he would not be aboard for the hangings which would surely follow.

"Will you come by my father's house?" Wickham asked. "I'm sure Lord and Lady Westmoor would be delighted to receive you."

"Is Lord Westmoor in the habit of receiving lieutenants who have been dismissed their ships?"

"He is in the habit of receiving my friends."

"How kind of you to think of me so," Hayden said. "I will certainly come by if it is at all possible. I dare say, I shall not be given a new commission any time soon, so I will almost certainly be at my leisure."

"Is that what concerns you so, Mr Hayden? Gaining another commission?"

"Oh, that and the realization that I have been rather foolish in regard to a certain young lady."

"Ah, I heard you had a visit from a lovely woman one day. It was all the talk of the middies' berth for a few days."

"I did not know they were so indiscreet."

"Oh no, sir. There was no disrespect meant to either Miss Henrietta or yourself. The middies all said that the lady in question was seen to treat you with a great deal of favour. They thought you most fortunate, sir."

Hayden sat back in the coach seat, unable to hide his distress. "I will tell you, Lord Arthur, if ever you set your sights on a woman, do not vacillate. Better to be refused than to have a woman slip away, thinking you do not care for her. No, never hesitate."

Wickham looked at him oddly, as though he wondered if Hayden practised upon him. "You would never be hesitant with a lady, Mr Hayden. I have seen you go right at a French frigate in a little brig-sloop without an instant of indecision."

Hayden had to smile, at his own folly as much as Wickham's words. "Apparently a woman is far more daunting than a frigate, Mr Wickham. A single verbal broadside, the tiniest hint of resistance, and I am thrown upon my beam ends. It is said that a fire-eater on the quarterdeck can be the shiest man in the ballroom."

"Well, Mr Hayden, I am far too young and inexperienced in these matters to venture an opinion . . . yet, if you let a prize slip away, you must contrive another plan and chase her again. That is how we do it at sea, and I think such a strategy will answer equally on land."

"Do you? Well, it could hardly prove less successful than my actions so far."

Their conversation covered much ground on their journey to London. Freed of the ship, Wickham proved to have a surprising breadth of interests for one so young. It came out, in addition, that his family possessed a large library in which Lord Arthur had been encouraged to roam from an early age. Hayden could not help feeling envious as the young middy spoke of volume upon volume that he had first encountered on the shelves of his father's library. Books were not inexpensive things, and to possess more than a few he thought a great luxury.

"I should rather have Lord Westmoor's fine library than a coach and four," Hayden admitted to the young man.

"It is much better that a house have a good library than a fine ballroom, I think," said Wickham. "Though one could not condemn a house that claimed both."

"No. One could not."

The journey to London, atop a swaying mail coach, was a tiring business and Hayden was glad when it was over, and the crowded streets of the great city checked their headlong rush. He took his leave of Wickham at the posting inn, and arranged for his trunk to be delivered to his familiar lodgings. Setting out at a brisk walk, he was soon in the environs of Robert Hertle's home. It had been his intention to leave his card with the footman, hoping Mrs Hertle would send him a note at his inn, but found instead that Mrs Hertle was not at home, or, indeed, in London.

"I should not tell this to anyone else, Lieutenant Hayden," the footman said, "but Mrs Hertle is visiting Miss Henrietta's family . . . in the country."

"How pleasant for them. If I may, John, I shall leave Mrs Hertle a brief note . . ."

Hayden repaired to his lodgings in not-the-best-of-inns. For a time he paced the small chamber, considering what he would do now that the Navy had seen fit to strand him ashore once again. He had written to a prize agent upon his arrival in Plymouth and it seemed now that a brief visit to them would be in order—first thing in the morning. He could make a call upon Philip Stephens to beg a commission, but then Stephens certainly was aware of his present situation—and likely not much troubled by it.

"Perhaps I should have taken ship with Mr Aldrich," Hayden muttered.

That night he ate dinner in his rooms, after making a careful count of his available funds. Even the small sum he had given to Aldrich had pushed him perilously close to insolvency. If the ship had not been paid off, according him some monies, his straits would be dire. Because he had previously resided at this inn, the owner would likely extend his credit for some weeks, but he would need the prize money from his recent cruise very shortly.

After dinner he took a tour of the dim streets, walking through the theatre district and then back to his inn, where sleep did not find him. The complete absence of any motion coupled with the sounds of the city put him out of sorts, and he lay awake, feeling surprisingly alone.

A sunrise turn about the streets thronged with tradesmen's carts, and then a rude meal from a street vendor, did not lift his humour. He returned to his rooms in a rather foul mood, to find a note from Wickham's father, the Earl of Westmoor, inviting him to dine in two weeks' time, and very considerately explaining that the great man would not be in London until that date. This notice from a man of significance raised his mood more than he would have supposed, and Hayden set off for his prize agent's with a better outlook, and a small bounce in his step. The city did not look so dingy, the people less ill-favoured.

His visit to the prize agent was not quite so cheering. The transport and its cargo had been valued below his hopes, and there was yet no word on whether the *Dragoon* would be bought into the service. Monies from the transport would be allocated, but he could not expect to see them for some weeks.

Upon departing his agent's he happened upon an acquaintance who was presently first lieutenant aboard a seventy-four-gun ship. They greeted one another with pleasure, and stood for a moment in the street speaking of their recent duties, mutual friends, and exchanging other gossip of the service. There was, finally, a lull in this flow of conversation and Hayden expected the man to excuse himself for an appointment with the very prize agent he had just left, but instead the other lieutenant lowered his voice and leaned nearer.

"I am not sure if it is my place to repeat this, Hayden, but I was to the country house of friends but two nights past and who should come to dinner but Sir Josiah and Lady Hart . . ." He took a long breath. "Sir Josiah spent some time speaking of you in the most severe terms, disparaging your character and accomplishments in the most denigrating language. Before I might come to your defence, which I fully intended to do, that service was rendered by another—Lord Westmoor, much to everyone's surprise, for Lord and Lady Westmoor have long been friends with Sir Josiah and Lady Hart. His Lordship spoke of you in the most salutary terms, saying, 'My son gave me a remarkably favourable report of Lieutenant Hayden's character and detailed accounts of taking a transport in the entrance to Brest Harbour, as well as cutting out a frigate beneath the guns at Belle Île. Hayden was in command of the brig that went to Bourne's aid, I understand, for my son was also aboard this ship and observed all that happened first-hand. A most enterprising young officer.' As you might imagine, this was terribly humiliating to Hart and will perhaps teach him to be more circumspect in the future. I tell you this only that you might know Hart is endeavouring to blacken your character among gentlemen of influence."

"Kind of you to tell me," Hayden answered, feeling the heat of anger flush into his face. "I cannot say that it surprises me, but it is distressing all the same. For no reason that I know, the man hates me like no other."

"But it must lift your spirits to know that you have a man such as Lord Westmoor in your camp. I am sure it shall quickly pass among the families of London that His Lordship made a very severe rebuttal to Hart's claims, not to mention refusing to speak to the man the rest of the evening."

"I don't think Hart will be so easily put off from maligning me. He has little self-control in such matters."

They parted there, Hayden barely aware of what went on in the street around him as he made his way back to his lodgings. He could not imagine that Hart, who had all the glory of their recent cruise, a knighthood, and a place in society, should be reduced to attacking him at dinner parties. But then, perhaps Hart was afraid that Hayden went about telling people the true story of their cruise and so was trying to blacken *his* character to discredit *him*.

A week, then ten days went by in some isolation, Hayden hoping each day to receive a note from Mrs Hertle informing him that she had returned to town with her cousin Henrietta and was once again ensconced in their lovely home, but no such letter came. The daily disappointment of his hopes had the effect of reducing his expectations a little each morning, until he would no longer allow himself to hope for such a letter at all.

On the tenth day after his arrival in London, a letter did arrive, and though he had convinced himself it would be a letter from Wickham or some other shipmate, it was not. Nor was it a letter from either Mrs Hertle or Henrietta. Instead, it proved, upon opening, to be a missive from the First Secretary of the Admiralty, requesting he meet with him at the Admiralty building.

Far too impatient to send a polite answer and await an exchange of letters arranging a time for such meeting, Hayden hurried directly to Whitehall and sent up a note to Mr Stephens requesting a date for their proposed meeting. To his surprise (but answering his secret hope), the First Secretary caused Hayden to be brought to him that instant.

There again he found Stephens sitting behind the now-familiar writing-table, spectacles carefully polished. Polite inquiries of the briefest nature, while Stephens shuffled through a neat stack of papers.

"Ah!" he pronounced. "Here it is." But if this signified anything of import, it was not the First Secretary's intent to reveal it immediately.

"In the ebb and flow of men's fortunes, it appears, Mr Hayden, that you have had a change of tide. Despite the efforts of certain persons, the Lords Commissioners have taken notice of your recent enterprises. I don't know quite how this occurred, but they have seen fit to raise you to the rank of master and commander."

Stephens smiled happily at Hayden's surprise.

"May I be the first to offer my compliments upon this happy occurrence."

Hayden was so overwhelmed that all he managed was a stammered reply, hardly equal to the occasion.

"I have your commission here. But that is not the end of good news, or so I hope you will judge it. You have a ship," he said, his eyes darting down to a piece of paper before him. "The *Kent*—a ship-sloop of ancient vintage, I fear."

"I know that ship," Hayden replied. "Many's the time I have shared a harbour with her. A pretty little thing with a raised quarterdeck and forecastle. A deck of six-pounders, and swivels on the quarterdeck."

"Carronades, now, I understand. An experiment by the Admiralty. More successful than the last you participated in, I hope. Poor Muhlhauser, he had such hopes for his new gun-carriage." A second of wool-gathering. "Your ship is en route to Plymouth as we speak, and should make that harbour tomorrow or the day next." Stephens rose and extended a hand. "I wish you great success in her, Mr Hayden."

Hayden took the offered hand. "I don't know how to thank you, sir . . ."

"In deeds, Mr Hayden, but I am certain the First Lord's confidence has not been misplaced." Stephens reached toward another small hillock of paper. "Lest I forget . . . Certainly you should have these, I think."

A little bundle tied up in string was dropped into Hayden's hand, and it took him a second to realize what it was: his collected letters to Mr Banks.

"Thank you, sir," Hayden said, some little feeling creeping into his voice.

"I'm not in the habit of apologizing, Mr Hayden . . ."

That unwavering, disinterested gaze fell upon him and Hayden mumbled something he hoped was polite.

He was on the street in a moment and almost run down by a hackney coach the next, such was his distraction. He almost sprinted the distance to his inn. A quick note to Mrs Hertle, sharing the news, and asking that she remember him to both Robert and Henrietta. A second to Wickham's father, regretting that he must quit London by the morning mail coach. A missive to his prize agents, alerting them to his new stature, followed by a letter of gratitude to Philip Stephens, and, finally, a letter bearing the good news to his mother, which would not be read for some weeks.

The carriage ride to Plymouth was oddly solitary, as the others stationed outside with him were all strangers one to the other and little given to speech. He missed Wickham's voluble presence, and in this forced reflection traversed an emotional landscape almost as varied as the terrain through which the mail coach passed. He was, for a time, elated at his good fortune. Master and commander at last! And then he felt a sudden deflation, realizing that others of similar length of service had command of post ships, and this chariness caused a certain disgust with himself, his ingratitude to the world revealing his overweening pride.

He would then turn from this to the subject of Henrietta. For a time he would believe that she cared for him still and that their understanding must surpass any small hesitation upon his part. Surely she would realize that they had, in truth, spent little time together—too little for either of them to enter into a plan to marry. Her common sense and reason, he told himself, were too great to mistake his intentions. Half an hour later, however, he was sunk in misery at his own folly, convinced that she felt he had rebuffed her when she had given him every opportunity to speak. He imagined her now the object of some gentleman of large property and even greater understanding. It occurred to him that he would be very unlikely to meet a woman more suited to his temperament. He would then enumerate her many qualities, a considerable list, only to increase his misery tenfold.

Thus passed the thirty-six hours of his journey to Plymouth.

Upon his arrival, he learned that his new command had not yet reached port, and he took a room overlooking the sound, still too excited to feel much disappointment. He sent a note to Lady Hertle, and received in return an invitation to visit.

At four o'clock he knocked on her door and was shown up to the drawing room, where he found Lady Hertle swathed in a thick shawl and huddled near to the hearth. She greeted him with great affection, and called for coffee.

"I hope you will pardon me, Mr Hayden, I have been beset by an autumnal cold and am only now on the mend. Henrietta has caught it from me and is abed with it yet."

"Miss Henrietta . . . is here?"

"She set out for Plymouth some few days ago upon learning I was ill, dear girl." She shook her head gently. "As if I had not had a cold before. I am not so old and fragile that a sniffle will put me in my grave. She attended me dutifully, and now her good deed has been repaid by contracting the same illness that she so ably nursed me through. Poor child." From a table, Lady Hertle retrieved a carefully folded letter. "Henrietta asked me give you this, Mr Hayden, when she learned you were coming to visit." Lady Hertle rose stiffly. "You might read it, if you like. I must excuse myself a moment."

Hayden was left alone, and had just broken the seal on Henrietta's letter, when he heard footsteps. Looking up, he was met by the sight of a pale, unhappy-looking Henrietta Carthew, eyes red and puffy, the fingers of her right hand kneading a handkerchief.

"Miss Henrietta," Hayden said, rising from his chair. "I am so terribly sorry to find you ailing."

"A trifle, Mr Hayden. Hardly worthy of notice." Her eyes travelled to the letter he held. "You have read my letter?"

Seeing in her what he thought could be only extreme distress, a sudden dread came over him. "I have but broken the seal."

She came quickly forward, extending a hand, which trembled ever so slightly. "May I ask the great favour of returning my letter, unread, Mr Hayden? I fear I wrote it in a distressed state of mind, and it is a foolish letter, describing perceptions that were fleeting and perhaps groundless."

Hayden offered up the letter immediately, which she all but snatched from his hand. She then sat down quickly and covered her face with delicate hands, the letter still caught in her fingers and rustling faintly.

"I have caused you distress, I fear." Hayden sat down on the same sofa, half-turned toward her.

She shook her head, and then whispered. "It is just this wretched cold. It has deprived me of sleep and frayed my nerves." She dabbed her eyes with a hanky, and forced herself to sit up. "I'm recovered," she lied, and tried to smile.

Hayden glanced at the door, expecting Lady Hertle to return at any time.

There was a moment of indecision, his breath suddenly absent. Then he recognized his hesitation and resolved to overcome it at last. "Not knowing the content of your letter, I trust to your good nature to stop me if what I say is rendered senseless by what you have written."

But Henrietta raised her hand, gazing into his eyes as she did so, an anxious, questioning look upon her face. "I suspect you have received as much 'advice' from Robert, and perhaps others as well, as I have from dear Elizabeth and my other cousins. All well-meaning, I am sure, but we must find our own way through this. That is what I have realized."

Hayden sat back a little, nodding his head. "Yes, Robert told me that I must doubt my attachment as I did not speak when last you were in Plymouth, but I do not doubt it. I have not spoken becau—"

"Because you are not ready," she said, placing a hand upon his chest and then quickly drawing it away. "Our acquaintance has been brief and I do not want you to speak until you are certain. I do not care what Elizabeth and Robert think. What do they know of our hearts?"

"Yes. Yes, exactly so. Then my hesitation has not injured you?"

"I was told it should. For a time I even half-believed it, but no, I think you were right. I should like to know you better, as well. Just because two people are good and kind does not mean they will make a success of life together. It is a great decision and we may make it in our own time."

"I cannot tell you how relieved I am to hear you say this. When you fled Plymouth, I believed . . ." but Hayden was not sure what he meant to say and fell silent.

Henrietta reached out shyly and touched his hand. "You need say no more. We are of one mind in this. Are we not?"

"Entirely of one mind."

She smiled, and for an instant her small illness was banished. And then . . . she sneezed. "Is this not romantic? Just like a novel? The heroine shivering with fever, eyes puffy, her voice reduced to a vulgar croak?"

With mock delicacy, she applied a hanky to her nose, and then laughed. Again she touched his hand. "I am content to be patient, as long as I know I have not lost your attentions altogether."

"I am as fascinated by you as ever, and that is saying a great deal." Hayden raised her hand to his lips.

"Lieutenant Hayden! You take great liberties."

"But I am lieutenant no longer. I have been made master and commander, given a ship, and upon my quarterdeck I shall be called 'Captain.'"

She smiled again. "Captain Hayden," she pronounced, as though appraising the sound of it. "Did I not predict this happy event?"

Hayden had forgotten. "Indeed, you did. And what do you predict today, I wonder?"

"I shall not press my luck in this. The gods might feel I have overstepped myself as oracle. No, I predict nothing. I will be patient and see what comes. To learn that my friends were wrong, as I knew in my heart they were, is enough."

They were silent a moment, sitting near to one another on the sofa. "But I do not wish to contemplate too much on the future," Henrietta said thoughtfully. "Even when it turns out happily it is seldom what one expects."

"That is true."

"You see? We *are* of one mind."

Hayden could not help but smile, he felt so thoroughly content, joy coursing through him like a great sea. "Now let us discover if we are of one heart."

"Yes," she murmured, "let us discover that."

HISTORY AND FICTION

The War of the French Revolution and the Napoleonic Wars have been fodder for novelists from the outset, and novels set in the British Navy of that era have long been a species of their own. If anyone can lay claim to having invented the type, it would likely be Frederick Marryat (whose books appeared between 1829 and 1847). His novels were immensely popular and surprisingly highly regarded; he counted Dickens among his fans. Marryat actually served in the Royal Navy during the period, so we must assume he got the details right, although with the caveat that "realism" as a literary movement was still many years in the future.

To set off into these same waters is to invite comparison, if not accusations of imitation. It can't be helped. Reviews of the early Patrick O'Brian novels compared them to C. S. Forester's Horatio Hornblower books and generally found Jack Aubrey came off second.

People always want to know, when reading a historical novel, what part is fact and what part is fiction. If the novel, as has been said, is about *truth* rather than *fact*, I think the question should be asked, "What part is fact and what part truth?"

As to the facts, in writing *Under Enemy Colors*, I made every attempt to get the history right, to be accurate regarding the details, and to recreate the atmosphere to the best of my ability. In this I have been much aided by having spent most of my life by the water (I grew up in a house on a beach) and having sailed for thirty-five years. I am not, however, a trained historian. I am a novelist and I'm sure I have made some mistakes. My apologies to the experts among you.

Almost all the main characters are fictional, with the exception of the First Secretary of the Navy, Philip Stephens (later Sir Philip). Various historical personages are referred to but do not appear (Admiral Howe and Tom Paine, for instance). None of the fictional characters are based on specific historical figures, though I must say that Captain Bourne was influenced by the many great frigate captains of the era, Henry Blackwood being my personal favorite. All of the events could have happened, and in some cases similar events did happen. The characters in this book were so numerous that I reduced the size of the gunroom mess to essential members, which meant as important a figure as the purser was never seen. If I have taken some liberties with historical detail, it is in the court-martial, where accuracy has been slightly compromised for dramatic reasons. In every other way, I have tried to make the book as authentic as available resources would allow.

The *Themis* is a fictional ship and conforms to no class of frigate, though she would have been similar to the *Pallas* class. In fact, her existence in 1793 is slightly problematic, as the first eighteen-pounder thirty-twos (to the best of my knowledge) were not commissioned until 1794. I thought Captain Hart would have a thirty-two-gun frigate, because he had too much influence to be sent into a twelve-pounder twenty-eight, but his detractors would have prevented him from being given a larger thirty-six- or thirty-eight-gun frigate. The thirty-two seemed to suit him perfectly, and I wanted a battery of eighteen-pound guns so that she could feasibly take on the larger French frigates. Thus the *Themis* was slightly ahead of her time.

One of the things that always astonishes me when I'm watching a film that involves a sailing ship is how the captain orders a course change and the helmsman simply spins the wheel and off they go in a new direction. As anyone who sails knows, virtually every time you change course you trim your sails. Unless you are sailing in the trades or the westerlies, winds have a frustrating habit of varying, often in both direction and strength (in truth, they can do this in belts of "constant" winds too). I remember a day when a friend and I set out to sail back to our home-harbor—an easy day's sail. We began the morning wearing bathing suits and sunglasses, with a lovely fair wind from the northwest. Sixteen hours later, in a howling southeast gale, we tied up at the dock wearing, beneath our foul-weather gear, every piece of clothing we had aboard. In between we'd had wind from all points of the compass. We'd been becalmed, drenched in a deluge, and chilled to the bone. We changed our headsail so often that I lost count and reefed and shook reefs out of the main over and over. Imagine how much sail-handling that would have meant aboard a square-rigged ship? You might have noticed, in this book, that, unless following a change of wind, every time the course was altered, sails were trimmed and yards shifted.

So much for the facts. As to the truth, well, everything that is not fact is my attempt to reach the truth.

For devotees of Laurence Sterne, yes, it's true, Griffiths' rant against the lack of originality in books is taken almost word for word from Sterne's *The Life and Opinions of Tristram Shandy*, but in Griffiths' defense, the brilliantly comic Sterne stole it from Burton's *Anatomy of Melancholy*. Sterne's book, and his theft from Burton, would have been well known to readers of that time, though apparently none of Griffiths' supper companions caught the reference.

Anyone interested in reading more about the British Navy in this era is in luck, as a little industry has sprung up publishing books to fill that need. I highly recommend Brian Lavery's *Nelson's Navy*, John Harland's *Seamanship in the Age of Sail*, and the nautical dictionary titled *The Sailor's Word-book*, for starters. If these three books do not satisfy your hunger, not to worry, there is a veritable feast of titles out there waiting for you.

Will there be another novel following the career of Charles Saunders Hayden? One is in the works. And yes, Mr. Barthe should reappear, as well as Wickham, Griffiths, Hawthorne, and various others from the cruise of the *Themis*. Look for Mr. Hayden's new vessel to heave into view sometime in 2009.

Oh, and by the way, the scientific name for the Sardinian warbler is *Sylvia melanocephala*. *Scorbutus cani*, the name given by Hayden in the novel, translates roughly as "scurvy dog." Hayden, apparently, thought himself a wit.

S.T.R.
British Columbia
February 2007

ACKNOWLEDGMENTS

This book, two years in the writing and many more in planning, would never have come into being without the help of many people. I'd like to thank my friends John and Francine, who put their many years and thousands of miles of sailing experience at my disposal and read the manuscript with great care. Many thanks to John Harland for his painstaking reading of the manuscript and for putting his encyclopedic knowledge at my disposal; any mistakes, however, are mine. For the French translations I have to thank author Margo McLoughlin and author and translator Guillaume Le Pennec (who so ably translated several of my previous books into French). My agent, Howard Morhaim, read numerous drafts and, as always, gave me the benefit of his insight. I thank my editors in New York and London, Dan Conaway and Alex Clarke, for their fantastic enthusiasm and constant support. Last, but first in my heart, I thank my wife, Karen, for her support and for all of her intelligent feedback on this book from inception through to final copy. I couldn't have done it without you, darling.